ORPHANS *of*

TOR BOOKS BY JOHN C. WRIGHT

The Golden Age

Phoenix Exultant

The Golden Transcendence

The Last Guardian of Everness

Mists of Everness

Orphans of Chaos

ORPHANS *of*

John C. Wright

A TOM DOHERTY ASSOCIATES BOOK

New York

This is a work of fiction. All the characters and events portrayed in this novel are either fictitious or are used fictitiously.

ORPHANS OF CHAOS

This book is printed on acid-free paper.

Edited by David G. Hartwell

A Tor Book
Published by Tom Doherty Associates, LLC
175 Fifth Avenue
New York, NY 10010

www.tor.com

Library of Congress Cataloging-in-Publication Data

Wright, John C. (John Charles), 1961–
Orphans of chaos / John C. Wright.
p. cm.
ISBN 0-765-31131-3
EAN 978-0-765-31131-3
1. Orphans—Fiction. 2. Immortalism—Fiction. 3. Boarding schools—Fiction. 4. Kidnapping victims—Fiction. 5. Great Britain—Fiction. I. Title.

PS3623.R54 O77 2005
813'.6—dc22

2005005328

First Edition: November 2005

Printed in the United States of America

0 9 8 7 6 5 4 3 2 1

To the memory of Harry Golding, a man of sterling moral character,
generous wit and charm, endless patience, and titanic intellect;
this tutor of St. John's College in Annapolis had many students who
admired him with a profound love, of whom this author's is not the least.

Let it be not imagined by any reader that the rather sinister educational
institution depicted in this fantasy is meant to resemble the author's
alma mater, for the spirit of St. John's is one in bitter enmity to tyranny;
the task of St. John's is to make free men out of youths by means of books
and balanced judgment: *Facio liberos ex liberis libris libraque.*

CONTENTS

ORPHANS *of*

Chaos

1

THE BOUNDARIES

1.

The estate grounds were, at once, our home, our academy, and our prison. We were outnumbered by campus staff, and by the imposing old Georgian and Edwardian edifices. There were more mares in the stables than there were students in the classrooms. It was only the five of us.

The estate was bound to the North by the Barrows, to the West by the sea cliff, to the East by the low, gray hills of the Downs. What bound us to the South is a matter of dispute.

2.

Colin claimed the forest was the only boundary to the South. His story was that the wood had no further side, but extended forever, with the trees growing ever taller, the shade ever darker, and beasts within it ever more dangerous, huge, and savage. He said that beyond the world's end the trees were titanic, the darkness was from Tartarus, and the beasts were vast enough to swallow the sun and moon.

When the two of us broke into the Headmaster's library, I climbed up to wipe with my skirt the dust from the glass-covered map that stood above the volumes and antique folios of the oaken bookshelf. The map showed Wales to the North and Cornwall to the South. To the East were English towns famous from history and legend: Bristol and Bath, Hastings and Canterbury and Cambridge. There was London, queen of all cities. Beyond the White Cliffs of Dover was the Channel and Calais on the coast of France, gateway to the continent, to places rich and bright and beautiful and ever so far away.

Colin rolled his eyes, which were large, startlingly blue, and very expressive. "And you believe our world is the one depicted on *that* map?" His voice dripped silky contempt.

He ducked his head to peer up at my under-things, but scampered back when I aimed a kick at his head.

3.

Quentin, on the other hand, implied the Old Road (which ran through the forest) constituted the boundary to the South. He argued that the Straight Tracks were older than the Roman road built atop them; older than the standing stone we found among the gray hills of the downs; older than the green mound on the South lawn.

He spoke of ley lines, and energy paths and mysterious connections between certain hilltops, standing stones, the crumbled ruins of the tower on a rock in the bay we all called the "lighthouse." He had charts to show their alignments with various rising and setting stars on certain dates. He used an astrology chart from the back of one of Mrs. Wren's magazines to show, with some plain geometry, why the Straight Tracks defined the transition point between different astral domains. The argument was incomprehensible, and that made it easier to believe.

Where Colin was loud, Quentin was quiet, indrawn, unassuming. He never claimed to be a warlock, and therefore we all thought he was.

Vanity and I saw him on the Manor House roof tiles one October midnight, talking to a winged shape too large to be a crow. It took flight, and we saw its outline against the moon.

4.

Victor was more logical. He argued that the Southern boundary was the new highway B-4247, which led from the coast to Oxwich Green. This new highway was on our side of the forest, and cut through it in places.

Following the highway toward the bay led to the fishing village of Abertwyi, from which the island of Worm's Head could be seen. Victor said the highway right-of-way followed the legal boundary as defined in the courthouse records for Shire of West Glamorgan, which listed the metes and bounds of the Estate.

We knew Victor had disappeared when the group all went to Mass one Sunday in Abertwyi-town. We did not know how he got over the stone wall surrounding the churchyard and courthouse unseen, or picked the lock on the massive iron grate, forged into fanciful shapes of leaves and black roses, which blocked the courthouse doors. Victor just was able to do things like that.

We know what he had been looking for, though. We all knew: records of our parents.

"I was naïve to expect our records to be there," he confided in me curtly. "The adoption records and genealogies only apply to men."

I cocked an eyebrow at him, and gave him an arch look. "And what about women, then?"

"The word refers to both sexes."

"Does it, really? You'll never talk me into going with you to the Kissing Well, if you sit there and say I look to you like a man."

"Define your terms. We are certainly human. We are certainly not *Homo sapiens*."

And, after a moment, he said, "Actually, I do not recall asking you about going to the Kissing Well. Your comment seems to be based on a false assumption."

Victor was, in some ways, the smartest one of the five of us. In other ways, he was just so stupid.

I should explain that, during that summer, the chapel attached to the estate had been undergoing repairs for water damage from the rains. When Mr. Glum, the groundskeeper, brought Victor, dragged by his ear, back to stand before the Headmaster, there was a consultation in the library among the Board of Trustees. The next Sunday we went to Mass in our own chapel, water-streaked walls behind the saints covered with tarp, scaffolding blocking the stained-glass windows, and everything. Further expeditions to Abertwyi were canceled.

Victor's argument was brief and solid. A boundary was a fiction defined by law; there were documents reciting the applicable law; and they named the new highway as the boundary. Q.E.D.

5.

Vanity was of the opinion that if we did not know where the boundary was, it could not affect us.

Her argument ran along these lines: we had been warned something bad would happen to us if we went over the boundaries, or tarried too long on the far side. But boundaries do not exist in the material world. A rock or a tree on one side or the other of an imaginary line is still a rock or a tree, is it not?

Therefore the boundaries only exist, as Vanity put it, "in our fancy."

"Think of it this way," she would say, between various ejaculations and digressions. "If everyone woke up tomorrow and agreed we should spell 'dog' C-A-T, why, dogs would be cats as far as we could tell. But the dogs would not care what we called them. If everyone woke up and said, 'Vanity is the Queen of England!' why, then, I'd be the Queen of England, provided the army and the tax gatherers were among the people who said it. If only half the army said it, we'd have a civil war."

The boundary to the South was no different. As one moved South there were trees upon the south lawn, a few, and then more, and then scattered copses, then thick copses. At some point, you would find yourself in a place with no grass underfoot, where no one had stepped before, and see trees which had never felt the bite of an axe. But where exactly was the dividing line?

The trees were thick around the servants' quarters, the stables, and the pump house. They were thicker beyond the old brick smithy. They were thicker still beyond the even older green mound connected with local King Arthur tales; but that mound was bare of trees itself, and one came from the shadows of silent leaves into a wide round area of surprising sunlight, where four standing stones held a tilted slab high above wild grass. The stones were gray, and no moss grew on them, and no sunlight ever seemed to warm them.

Vanity said that Arthur's Table clearly could not be in the forest, because there were no trees there. A forest, by definition (Vanity would exclaim) was a place full of trees, wasn't it?

So (she would conclude triumphantly), there was no Southern boundary, provided we all agreed that there was none. What other people said amongst themselves was their own affair.

Colin would ask sarcastically, "And when they send Mr. Glum and his savage dog to hunt us down and maul us, does it then, at some point, become our affair?"

Vanity would roll her eyes and say, "If the dog mauls us on this side of the boundary, we could still say he was on the other side, couldn't we? Things like boundaries don't exist if you don't see them when you look for them, do they?"

"And I guess dog fangs don't exist if you don't feel it when your arm gets ripped off, right?"

"Exactly! Suppose the dog only *thought* he mauled us, but we did not see him nor feel him when he came to attack us! How do you know the dog hadn't just dreamed or imagined he attacked us? We could agree he hadn't done it, couldn't we? We could even agree the dog had agreed not to hunt us!"

Colin would respond with something like, "Why bother arguing with me? Why don't you just agree that I agree, so that, in your world, I have?"

Vanity would rejoin, "Because I prefer to agree that you argued and you lost, as anyone who heard the dumb things you say would agree."

Colin was not one to give up easily. "If you merely dreamed you had found a secret way out of here, that would not let you walk through a solid stone wall, would it?"

"Of course not. But no one knows which walls are solid and which are hollow because no one can see the inside of the solid ones, can they? The ones you can see inside aren't hollow, are they? No one else has any proof one way or another."

Vanity's argument was as incomprehensible as Quentin's, and as brief (when pared down) as Victor's. Apparently as long as she, Vanity, in her solipsistic purity, did not believe the Southern boundary existed, then, for all practical purposes, it would not.

6.

Vanity was short, redheaded, with a dusting of freckles on her cheeks. Her eyes were the most enormous emerald, and they sparkled. She had a little upturned snub nose I always envied just a bit. She was fair skinned and always wore a straw skimmer to keep the sun off her face.

With her lips so pale a rose color, and her eyebrows so light, I always thought she looked like a statue of fine brass, held in a furnace of flame so hot as to be invisible, so that she seemed to glow. Even when frowning, she seemed to be smiling.

She was curvy and she took wry amusement at the fact that the boys, the male teachers, even Mr. Glum, could have their gazes magnetized by her when she walked by.

I always thought Vanity was a little sweet on Colin, because she yelled at him and called him names. In the romances I read, that was a sure sign of growing affection.

As I grew older, I noticed how carefully she noticed everything Quentin did, Quentin the quiet one, and I realized she doted on him. And I began to realize Vanity actually was annoyed and exasperated by Colin.

That was when I realized, for the first time, that the five of us were not the tightly knit band of Three Musketeers Plus Two that Victor said we were, one for all and all for one, and all that.

It was not until I was around an age which, in a human being, would be between sixteen or eighteen or so, when I had the thought that with two girls and three boys, one of the boys in our merry band would end up a bachelor, or married to a stranger.

I remember where I was when this thought came to me. I was sitting on the lip of the Kissing Well, with my skirts flapping in the gusts coming from the bay, quite alone. I had just come from the infirmary, and was still seasick from Dr. Fell's most recent round of vaccinations. We were usually allowed to skip lessons any afternoon when Dr. Fell worked on us, provided we made up the lessons later. The well was high on a hillside, and overlooked the water. Sea mews were crying, and the sad sound lingered in the air.

It was spring, I remember, and two male birds were fighting. That was what prompted my thought.

That was also when I started wondering what my future would be. I wanted to be a pilot, an explorer. A cowgirl with a pistol. Anything that got me away from here. The idea of being a housewife seemed intolerably dull and lacking in glamour. On the other hand, the idea of never having a child was like death.

And then I said aloud to the well, "But what if they never let us go?"

The voice in the well said back softly, ". . . never let us go . . . ?"

7.

My name is Amelia Armstrong Windrose. I should say, I call myself that; my real name was lost with my parents.

We chose our own names when we were eight or ten or so. It was not until we started sneaking off the estate grounds that we realized that other children in the village were christened at birth, and kept anniversaries of their birthdays, and knew their ages.

We knew about birthdays from various readings, of course. There were references to such things from histories, where boy kings had to be killed before they ascended the throne, or from gothic romances, where girl heirs had to be wedded before they came into their majority. We knew, in a general way, what a birthday party was.

Mrs. Wren started holding them for us, with snappers and barkers and wrapped gifts, and candles on cake with icing, and toasts and games, when we complained. But her notion was to have them twice or three times a year, usually during months with no other holidays of note. And the number of candles she put on the cake could be anywhere from one to one score, depending on her mood, or the success of her shopping.

The gifts we got from her did not seem odd at the time, for we had no other basis of comparison. Once I got a wrapped roast duck, which had turned cold in the cardboard box, and lay amid its own congealed grease. Another time, a box of nails.

Colin got one of Mrs. Wren's shoes at that same party; Vanity got a drawer from the kitchen with knives and spoons in it. And yet, other times, her gifts were things of wonder and pleasure: a wooden rocking horse, painted fine, brave colors; a toy train set with an electric motor and a cunning little chimney that puffed real smoke; a dress of breathtaking beauty, made of a soft scarlet fabric, perhaps satin; an orb of pale crystal that glowed like a firefly when you held it in your hand and thought warm thoughts; a walking stick with a carved jackal head with silver ears, which Quentin was convinced could find buried streams and fountains underground.

One birthday party, the Headmaster simply announced we were to choose names for ourselves, and put our baby-names behind us. Only Quentin refused to choose, and kept his original name. I, who had been Secunda, used the chance to name myself after my heroine, the American aviatrix, Amelia Earhart. My family name I took from that eight-pointed star which decorates maps and determines North.

You see, I had always felt closed-in and trapped by the walls and boundaries of our estate. No matter how handsome and fine the grounds, it was still a cage to me. My dreams were for far, unguessed horizons, hidden springs of unknown rivers, unclimbed mountains shrouded in cloud. The edges of maps interested me more than the middles.

Naturally, such dreams led me to admire that breed of men who sailed those horizons, found those springs, conquered those mountains. Roald Admussen was my idol, along with Hanno, Leif Erickson, and Sir Francis Drake. My favorite books from Edgar Rice Burroughs were those where the lost city of Ophir appeared.

Amelia Earhart seemed so brave and gay, her smile so cheerful and fearless, in the one picture in the little encyclopedia entry I found of her, that only she could be my namesake.

I told myself she had not been lost at sea, but had discovered some tropic island so fair and so like Eden, that she landed her plane at once, knowing no one else would ever be daring and cunning enough to find the route she had flown. All the years that had gone by, with her still not found, seemed to confirm my theory.

My name, invented when I was perhaps a twelve-year-old, may seem silly now. But I console myself that young Tertia named herself after a novel by William Makepeace Thackeray, so that she could be called Miss Fair. We are lucky she did not end up called Miss Pride N. Prejudice.

8.

I cannot describe myself except to say that I am either very vain or very beautiful, and that I hope I am the latter, while suspecting I may be the former. My hair is blond, beyond shoulder length, and I liked to wear it queued up and out of the way. My complexion has been tanned by spending much time out of doors in the wind and weather.

I always had the idea, when I was young, that if I stared in the mirror long enough at some feature, my lips or eyes, some sun freckles I did not care for, or a mole, I could somehow, by force of will, "stare" my face to a more perfect shape—clearer skin, higher cheekbones, eyes greener, or more long-lashed, perhaps slightly tilted and exotic.

And because this does indeed describe me, then as now, I had always had the unspoken, haughty assumption that plain girls either lacked willpower, or lacked imagination. It is my least attractive feature, this prejudice against the unsightly, and it is based on a very wrong notion of what life is like for normal people. It gives me no pleasure to notice that many normal people have the selfsame prejudice against the plain, but with far less reason than I.

I am tall. Rather, I should say, I am tall for a girl, but I hope you will understand me if I say I was taller when I was younger. Everyone but Primus, who became Victor Invictus Triumph, was smaller than me, and I could outrun and outwrestle my two younger brothers.

9.

I remember the day when Quartinus, who turned into Colin Iblis mac FirBolg, proved he could master me. There was some quarrel over who was to pluck apples from the tree, and I threw one at his head hard enough to raise a bruise. He grinned, as he did when he was angry, and chased me down. You see, I laughed because the last time we had raced, I had beaten him. Now he tackled me, rolled me on the ground, and took my hair in one hand to yank my head back—something he would never have done to a boy. Still, I grinned, because the last time we fought, I had toppled him downhill.

And so I struck and I wrestled and I pushed and I kicked, but my blows seemed, by some magic, to have been robbed of their force. Just one year before, he had been a child, and I could bully him. Where had my strength gone?

He pinned my wrists to the ground, and knelt on my legs to prevent me from kicking. Suddenly, the game turned into something serious, mysterious, and somehow horrible. I writhed and struggled in his grasp, and I somehow knew, knew beyond doubt, that I would never be stronger than a man again. Not ever.

Colin smiled, and ordered me to apologize, and he bent his head forward to stare into my eyes. I wonder if he was trying to awe me with his frowning gaze, to hypnotize me with his luminous blue eyes.

If so, he succeeded beyond his dreams. This boy, whom I had never really liked, now seemed inexpressibly powerful to me: manly, potent, confident.

I will not tell you all my wild thoughts at that moment. But I wanted him to kiss me. Worse yet, I wanted *not* to want it, and to have him steal a kiss from me nonetheless.

I did not apologize, but snapped defiantly at him, "Do your worst!" And I tossed my head and yanked at my wrists in his grip. My fists seemed so little compared to his, and his grip seemed as strong as manacles. I felt entirely powerless, but the sensation seemed oddly intoxicating, rather than dreadful.

He did not do his worst. Instead, baffled, he stood up suddenly, releasing me and seemed suddenly a boy again, a child I could defeat.

I remember we raced back toward the house, apples in our hands. We had just enough that we could throw one or two at each other, trying to bruise shins and legs.

And I won that race, that time, but he grinned and tried to make me believe he had allowed me to win.

Strangely enough, I knew he thought he was lying. And I knew he had not been.

2

THE EXPERIMENT

I do not know how young I was when I performed the experiment that required me to conclude that something was wrong in my life.

Victor—so I may call him, though he was still called Primus at the time—had grown a trace of down on his upper lip, finer than the fuzz of a peach. With even this small hint of manhood, he seemed more our leader than before, and there was a newfound glamour to him that touched my heart and troubled my dreams.

We had crept by stealth from the orphanage grounds, and stood among the rocks and bald hills of the West. Below us and to the East, we could see the lights from the Main House, the servants' quarters, the outbuildings, the stables.

Dr. Fell had bought Victor the instrument he was using for his experiment from a scientific catalogue. At the time, I thought it normal and unexceptional. Now, I realize that such an instrument was fabulously expensive: a piece of precision machinery even an observatory would envy.

The moon rose not long after sunset, and we pointed the lenses of the instrument to the East. Victor held his eye to the eyepiece and made minute adjustments to the vernier dials. He thumbed a red switch with a grimace of satisfaction.

He said, "An internal computer will track the path of the moon as it rises, and send out periodic pulses. We want to gather a number of samples, to correct for the different cords of atmosphere the signal passes through. The return signal is received by the large dish on the tripod over there, whose motors are slaved to these wheels here. And voila!"

A numerical readout lit up. It was two point something something. 2.8955. Almost three seconds.

I said, "What now?"

He said, "And now we wait four hours."

"Did you bring anything to read?"

He just looked at me oddly.

"Or smoke?" I said.

"You are too young to smoke. Besides, it's bad for you."

"Quentin said you tried it. You experimented with it."

He shook his head. "It wasn't me. Trying things common sense abundantly demonstrates are bad for you is not an experiment; such things show you nothing but what your own tastes are. That does not constitute knowledge. *This* is an experiment!"

"Then who was it?"

"Who was what?"

"Quentin said he smelled smoke in the boys' bathroom. Cigarette smoke."

He looked at me with scathing condescension, but said nothing.

"What?" I said.

"Logic. If it wasn't me, and it wasn't Quentin, and it wasn't a girl, who was it?"

"Oh," I said, feeling sheepish.

Hours passed. I fidgeted. I paced. I complained about the cold. I sat on the ground, which made me colder. I asked him for his down jacket, which he doffed without a word and tossed to me. I rolled it up and used it as a pillow.

I must have slept.

I dreamed that I was on a boat. A man held me roughly in one arm, dangling me over the side. The boat pitched and tossed terribly; rain pelted my face and ran in icy ribbons down my flesh. The man held some sharp, horrible thing near my face: a knife, or something larger than a knife.

In the dream, the water, which had been black and rolling, webbed with white foam and spray, suddenly grew clear as crystal. A figure that was so large as to make our ship seem the size of a lifeboat was gliding beneath the waves, parallel to our course. The figure had his hands back along his sides and his head down; he did not kick his feet. Instead, the water streamed past him, like wind streaming past a man falling effortlessly through the air.

"Tell him to quell the storm," said the voice of the doctor in my ear.

The figure turned its head and regarded us both. Its eyes were lamps, eerie with a greenish light, and it had a third eye, made of metal, embedded in its forehead.

Instead of being terrified that I was going to be pitched overboard or stabbed, I was overcome with a painful embarrassment to realize that the gigantic figure was utterly nude and that, as he kept turning, I would soon see a penis larger than the member of an elephant, rippling through the water like a periscope. What made it more embarrassing was that the figure had Victor's features.

The third eye, the metal one, seemed to be the only one with a soul in it. In the senseless way things are known in dreams, I know that the mere fact that it could see me with this eye meant he could speak to me, despite all the water between us, and the noise and wrack of the storm. *"I am embedding this message by means of cryptognosis into a preconsciousness level of your nervous system. The paradigms of chaos have agreed only on this one point. We will wait for you . . ."*

"Tell him to make the clouds move."

"What?"

"I said, I hope the clouds move. We need to get a clear reading when the moon reaches zenith."

I was awake again, with Victor, on the cold hillside. A knotted texture of charcoal-black and gleaming silver hung like a ship out of fairyland high above us. The cloud covered the moon, and limned the edges with swirls of argent.

Victor was still standing.

"How long have I been asleep?"

"Two hours, fourteen minutes."

"Oh."

Silence.

Then I said, "Why are you doing this? We could get caught. It's not as if Michelson and Morley hadn't done this experiment one hundred years ago."

He said, "One hundred eight. They've been saying untrue things to us. The teachers. The readings we got from the interferometer in lab class had been meddled with. When I did the experiment under controlled conditions, I got results consistent with the theory that light is conveyed via luminiferous aether."

I sat up. "Are you saying there's no Einsteinian relativity? But there have been other experiments. The procession of the axis of Mercury. Cesium clocks in a fast-flying airplane. Light was seen to bend around the sun during an eclipse."

"We have only hearsay for that."

I was astonished. The sheer magnitude of his skepticism was beyond words. It was like an elephant I had seen once during a rare field trip to Swansea Zoo. As soon as you think you understand how big it is, you look again, and it is bigger.

He said, "Picture this. According to relativity, objects compress in the direction of motion, right? And yet it also says that the same objects and events appear from each other's 'frames of reference' to be symmetrical, right?"

"Right."

"Take a cup with a tight-fitting lid. The cup and lid fit together, correct? Now move the lid and cup away at right angles, the lid horizontally, the cup vertically. Got the picture?"

"Got it."

"What happened when you bring the lid and cup back together at near light speed?"

"Um . . . I am sure you are about to tell me . . ."

"From the point of view of the lid, the cup is compressed in its direction of motion, horizontally. The cup is shorter, but still a cylinder. The lid, to itself, suffers no distortion, of course. When the two meet, the lid will fit on the cup. But from the point of view of the cup, the lid is foreshortened in its direction of motion, vertically. Which means the lid is now an oval. The cup still appears round to itself. When the two meet, the lid cannot fit on the cup. The same event has two different results from two different points of view."

I looked at him sidelong, wondering if he were kidding. For the first time, I wondered whether other people have more trouble visually picturing things in their imagination than I did. I mean, it is not as if I could look into their heads to see.

I opened my mouth to say that both observers would see the motion vector as a diagonal, but then I closed it again. I did not like arguing with Victor.

"What in particular happened?" I said.

For a moment I thought he was going to ask me what I meant, but then he said, "You know Mrs. Lilac from the village, whom Mrs. Wren uses to carry burdens and packages when she has done too much shopping?"

"Sort of the way you do me," I said archly. I had carried the equipment up the slope from the hedges behind the lab shed.

"I don't see the analogy."

"Go on with your story."

"Mrs. Lilac passed me in the hall. She said her daughter Lily was going to graduate from upper school soon and, seeing as how I had helped Lily learn her letters when she was in grammar school, would I care to attend the graduation ceremony? You know who Lily is, don't you?"

"Yes. I know who she is," I said shortly.

I was thinking that Victor had been to see Lily Lilac on every occasion that the Headmaster would allow. She was fair haired and fine boned, with a breezy, insincere manner I found exasperating.

Her father owned the fish cannery, and was counted as being one of the more influential people, among the working class, in town. Lily owned her own outboard motor, and she went boating on every possible occasion.

From time to time I had seen Victor watching Lily Lilac from the sea cliff. He would stand among the rocks with a telescope, and watch her fly by, her boat bouncing along the waters of the bay, her blond hair bouncing in the wind. She was always with a different boy each time. She seemed to be able to do what she liked, and go where she liked, when she liked. I do not recall hating any other living being so fiercely.

"I know her," I said with a sniff. "So you've been invited to a graduation. I doubt Headmaster will allow you off the grounds." I remember I was being fiercely loyal to Headmaster Boggin in those days, and thought he could do no wrong.

Victor favored me with another one of his withering glances.

"What?" I said, "What?"

"Logic. How young do you think a person has to be to not know her letters and numbers? And I must have been old enough to know mine. Let's assume I was unduly precocious, and she was unduly slow."

"Yes, let's do," I said, perhaps with a note of venom in my voice.

"I could have been what, three? Have you ever heard a child know his letters at two? How late could she live and not know her letters? Let's say five. She would be nineteen when she graduated. If she skipped a grade, eighteen. That makes me how old now?"

"Fifteen."

"But suppose the numbers were reversed. What if I had been around five when I taught a two- or three-year-old? How old does that make me?"

I said, "If you were twenty-and-one, you'd be an adult. They would have let you out of here. They'd have let you out three years ago."

"Would they have?"

"Why would they keep you?"

"Perhaps they get money from the trust for my upkeep. Who knows?"

"But how could they tell such a lie, and not get caught?"

"Who is to catch them? The townspeople are afraid of the Headmaster."

The idea that anyone could be "afraid" of the kindly old headmaster, with his gentle smile and mild humor, was beyond belief. Had it been anyone other than Victor, I would have laughed aloud.

But I didn't laugh. "Someone would tell. They can't just go on keeping us here forever."

"Who is to tell?" he said. "Who will question their statements? Suppose they say I am fifteen. Don't I look it? Who questions them? Who doubts them? Who is skeptical enough to go to the trouble to check?"

At that moment, a timer on the instrument bleeped.

Victor leaned in and looked at the eyepiece. He clicked the red button with his thumb. A moment later the LED readout lit up. 3.3214 . . .

He said grimly, "The difference between the reading now and the reading at dusk is merely the angular momentum of the turning of the Earth. Light shot forward, tangentially to the turn, has the velocity of the Earth added, and travels faster. Light shot at a right angle, away from the axis, has no velocity added, and is slower. If we wait till dawn, the component of Earth's rotation will be subtracted, and the velocity will be slower yet."

"There must be a mistake," I said slowly. "The instrument must be off."

"Is that the most reasonable explanation?"

He turned and squinted. The light in the boys' bathroom off the dormitory was flickering off and on, off and on. That was the signal that Mr. Glum had been seen leaving his little house on the back grounds, no doubt to pull a surprise inspection of the boys' dorm.

There was no light in the girls' bathroom. Either Mrs. Wren had not stirred and the girls' dorm was safe, or else Vanity had fallen asleep at her post.

Victor stood. "I must run. Don't let the equipment get damaged when you carry it back down the rocks."

"Yes, master," I said sarcastically. But he did not hear me, because he was already jogging down-slope.

Now I was alone, in the cold, with no one but the moon to look after me.

Well, there was no need to delay. I started doing, in my mind, that trick I had learned that made all burdens seem lighter than they were when I hoisted them, and I put my hands out toward the instrument.

I was thinking: it was impossible.

The angular momentum of the Earth's rotation was so small a fraction of the speed of light, I know, that no possible instrument could detect a difference; and surely not a difference of nearly half a second over the (relatively) short distance between Earth and Moon. To be a valid experiment, the second reading would have to be taken half a month later, not half a day later, so that the velocity component added would have been that of the Earth's motion around the sun.

So, instead of lifting the instrument just yet, I put my eye to the eyepiece, made sure the instrument was still centered on the same crater of the moon as it had been at dusk, reached, and hit the red switch.

The dish hummed as a radar beam was sent out, bounced off the moon, came back.

The LED readout lit up. 2.8955.

I had little trouble getting the tripod folded and the instrument case packed up, and getting the whole thing hidden under the bushes, where Victor would sneak them back into the lab in the morning, while he had cleanup duty.

But I had a great deal of trouble falling asleep that night. Surely it was just a quirky reading from a misaligned instrument, right?

Either that, or the speed of light acted differently when I was watching it than it did when Victor was watching it. Which is impossible, isn't it? That is not what the Theory of Relatively means. Our notions of reality can change as we learn more; but reality itself, the great unknown, cannot change.

But if reality was unknown, how did I know it could not change?

I had a dream about the ship again that night. The man holding me overboard, holding a sword to my throat, was Dr. Fell.

3

THE FIRST OF THE SECRETS

1.

How did we all start debating about boundaries? When did we become convinced we were all something other than human? Every starting point has an earlier starting point before it. Some of the roots of how it came about, I remember. Other have become misty and autumn-colored with time.

If I had to choose a starting point, there were three I would select, not one. I remember when Victor made us all put our hands together and promise. I remember when Vanity found the notes, which had our lost tales in them. And then, many years later, Quentin discovered the secret.

2.

I don't know how old I was. Vanity (or Tertia, as she was called then) only came to my shoulder, and Quentin was small enough that Victor (Primus) could carry him in his arms. When he stood up, Quentin's head only came to the level of Victor's elbow. Quentin was too young for lessons; I remember being jealous when he was allowed to sit on the floor and play with a wooden horse on wheels while I had to practice penmanship, making rows and endless rows of slightly lopsided O's and Q's.

As for me, the doorknob to the coal cellar was right below the level of my eye, because when Mr. Glum slapped me roughly on the back of my head (I was afraid to open the door to the cellar) the doorknob struck me on the cheek, and I had a bruise there for a week.

I don't remember why they were locking us in the coal cellar, but I do remember wishing and hoping that the Headmaster would come back from wherever he was, and set things to rights. He and Dr. Fell had dressed up in dark clothing, with black scarves fluttering from their top hats, looking grim and terrible. A funeral, I suppose. I remember the two stalking silently off into the freezing rain, wide black umbrellas overhead. The rest of the staff was particularly cruel to us that evening, or so it seemed to me. Mrs. Wren was raging up and down the corridors, howling like a banshee, toppling suits of armor on racks and pushing over floral vases that stood on the pillars next to the main doors. I think this was before she took up strong drink.

They locked us in the dark and cold. Whatever our crime had been, I did not know. It was dark and starless that night, the drafts smelled of snow, and the dirt floor was colder than ice.

I was shivering and my teeth were chattering. I remember Vanity saying, "Quentin's all cold. He stopped moving. Is he going to die?" her voice was as thin and high as a flute.

Victor told us all to gather up in a huddle for warmth. His voice was high-pitched then, but it was very earnest, and just hearing it made me feel better. I could hear him rummaging around in the dark.

"This is a coal cellar," young Victor said. "There is wood and kindling in the wood box." There was a tremble in his voice, too, but I could hear how he forced himself to speak calmly.

Colin, or as he was called back then, Quartinus, said, "Boogers! There's nothing to start a fire with! Mrs. Wren's had a nightmare, and we're all going to die for it."

In the pitch blackness, Quentin's voice came up from the pile where we all lay together, "A ghost. She saw her husband's ghost." I was relieved to hear him, because I was so very afraid he had passed away. Certainly his skin felt like ice up against mine.

Victor laid his coat over the pile of us. I wondered how he could stand the cold in his thin shirt, but he did not complain. Victor never complained. "I'll start a fire. I'll make something. Lend me your tie. I found a bent stick in the woodpile, and I can make a drill."

Minutes passed, and it grew colder. I could hear Victor sawing away at something, the hissing noise of wood on wood, but no fire came.

"Boogers!" shouted Colin, who did not know any of the many foul words he was to learn later in life. "Do you think you are a Red Indian? Rubbing two bloody sticks together? We're all going to die, and it will be your fault!"

Victor said to me, "Secunda. Get them talking. Keep their mind off it, you know? We've all got to hang together."

My teeth wanted to chatter, but I made myself speak. "OK, attention, everyone! I know we are all cold and afraid. But we have something we have to do. We have to remember our Tales."

I do not remember a time when I had not been the unofficial Keeper of the Tales for our group. It had always been my task. Colin used to joke that I was to be the Tale Keeper because my memory was so good. ("Whenever I do something wrong, she always remembers to remind me, eh?" so he would say.)

I spoke gently to young little Quentin. "The Tales are the only thing we know about our home. Our real home. Quentin, you start."

"I-I'm t-too cold."

"Quentin, you must start. We can't lose our Tales. You have to tell."

But Quentin simply whimpered and did not answer.

Colin said, "C'mon you great booger. Talk! You don't want them to win, do you?"

I felt Quentin's cold body stir in my arms.

He spoke in a voice so weak and thin that I could barely hear him, even though my ear was but inches from his mouth. "I remember my mum. Her hair is gray. She's blind. I remember how I would run and she would spread her arms and say, 'Where's my little shadow? Where's my little shadow?' and I would run and jump into her arms, and mum would hug me, and give me a kiss, and she would say, 'I know you, little one. I will always know you.' And I would say, 'How'd' you know it's me? How'd' you know it's me?' and she would say, 'My soul knows your soul, little one, my heart knows your heart.' That's what I remember."

I said, "Tell us more. Tell us about the giant. You've got to remember the whole of the Tale. It is your Tale."

Quentin said, "My dad. He lives in a room with statues. Statues and chessmen and dolls. His beard is gray and comes to the floor, and his hair is gray, too. He has a harp that sits in his lap. And when he plays, the statues dance. Once upon a time, he took me and took his harp, and sat on the statue of a big crow, and he played, and the crow flew up in the air."

Vanity said, "That couldn't really happen, could it?"

Victor, from somewhere in the gloom, said, "Maybe it was an airplane. Only looked like a crow."

I said sternly, "Stop! You can't talk back to the Tales. You can't change them or make fun of them! That's the rule! If you start changing the Tales, they might go away, and then we won't have anything!"

Victor said, "She's right."

I said, "Go on, Quentin. Tell us about the giant."

Quentin was quiet, and then he spoke in a sad whisper. "I don't know the rest."

"Sure you do! You father took you to see the Shining Mountains! Instead of snow, the mountains all have light, silver light, all along the tops. Do you remember what he said? He told you, *'This is the place where the falling stars fall whenever stars fall down.'* "

Quentin said. "I don't remember. I don't. Leave me alone."

I said insistently, "In the dark valley between the mountains of light, your father the magician took you to see the giant, who was trapped up to his neck in the ice. There were dwarfs all digging and digging, chipping away at the ice, to get him out."

Quentin said, "It was cold. It was so cold. I saw his hand. It was a mile below me. Under the ice. The fingers. I thought it was five rivers coming to a lake, it was so big. So cold."

I said, "Yes! Yes! And the giant said—do you remember what the giant told you—once he was free, the bad people would be punished, and the good people would all live happily ever after? The Golden Age would come again. Do you remember?"

"It was so cold."

"Quentin, maybe the giant has gotten out of the dark valley! Maybe he is coming to save us, right now!"

Quentin sniffled and shivered, but did not answer.

Vanity spoke up next: "I remember my Tale! Me next! Oh, pick me! Oh, me!"

"OK. It is your turn, Tertia."

"My house is in fairyland," Vanity said primly. "There is a gold dog who sits by my front door, and a silver dog, too. They come to life when you want them to, and fetch a stick or chase away someone making fun of you. When you don't need them, they just sit still. There is a singer who sings to me, and he sits in the sunlight in his chair of ivory, and beats the ground with his stick when he sings. He sings of wars and ships and deeds of kings. There are bowls made of silver that hop on three legs like bugs. Hop! Hop! Hop! They walk around and give you fruit and candy. If you're good. It is always springtime there. My mommy has red hair like me. My daddy is the king there, but mommy is the one who actually runs the kingdom. My brothers play out in the green field, and throw spears and throw disks. And they run. Sometimes Daddy takes me sailing, and our boat is faster than the wind. Sometimes Mommy plays hide-and-seek with me, and she pops out of the floor! Pop! And she puts her arms around me. She tells me to be good, because she loves me. That's all."

I said, "There is another part. Something about being watched."

"Oh, that. It is not like here. Nothing pays you any mind here. The rocks and the wind and the grass. It's all dead. Where I come from, they are all friends. They are all alive. You can feel them watching you, like a tingling all over your skin. It is like being at the recital, when everyone applauded. Like being on stage. Remember how nice that was? It tingled. It wasn't lonely. I am always lonely here. I want to go home. I don't want to be alone any more. When can we go home?"

Victor said, "I will get you home. I promise. I will get us all home."

I said, "You next!"

Victor said, "Let Quartinus go first."

Colin said, "My story is better than his. My turn. I climbed up the pole of my da's longhouse, all the way to where it holds up the sky. That's where he keeps his cloak, in the North Star. My brothers all sent me to get it, because I was the youngest and lightest, and the roof pole wouldn't break under me. They said I would not get punished for stealing it, on account of I was too young.

"I put on the cloak and told it to make me into a wolf. A big, ferocious, giant wolf. So I turned into a wolf, and jumped out the window, and I ran through the forest. The trees are so tall there that sometimes the stars get caught in them. The stars are these beautiful women with lanterns, and when their robes get caught in the branches, they sing, and the trees feel sorry for them, and let them go. Anyway, I remember I was running to this spot my brothers had told me about. This black cave where my uncle lived, guarded by this big three-headed dog. I figured I could take on the dog, seeing as I was a big wolf. Then a storm came, and the clouds fell down through the trees, and it was my ma. She took me around the throat and yanked da's cloak clean off me. I thought she was going to be mad, but it was weird, because she just cried and cried and held on to me. Like she was afraid. And she pushed my hair back and she said, *'If ever you go away from me, oh my beloved son, on that day sorrow surely will slay me.'* She took me home and fed me from this big pot we had over the fire in the middle of the house.

"I sat in the middle of the pot and ate stew, and Da beat the tar out of my brothers. I have three. One wears a mask. One wears an animal pelt. The third has leaves and twigs in his hair. And they were right. I didn't get punished. They did. That's all I remember about it. Cool, huh?"

Colin was silent for a while, shivering in the cold. Then he said, "You don't suppose my ma's really dead, do you?"

I said, "No, she is not dead. No one is dead. My father told me."

Victor said to me. "Your turn."

I said, "It is warm there. My home is filled with light. I am a princess and I live in a palace. My father is the king, and he knows everything. He sees everything. I remember once my mother, the queen, took me swimming in our pool. But the pool hangs like a ball in midair. It is bigger on the inside than on the outside. There are stars inside it. And planets. You can swim right up to them and look at them with your eye. I remember once I was swimming. I saw a dark world and it was filled with dead bodies. Mother folded her arms around me, and took me back up out of the pool. I remember how afraid I was that something from the Dark World would get me. My mother sang a song for me, *'My little spark, my shining one, never fear, never fear. The darkness is so very small, and the world of light is endless, here.'*

"I remember she took me to the tower where she said she first saw my father. It was a palace that floated, and everything was rose-red marble. The windows were pink and the walls were scarlet. I remember he had a throne set in the very middle of a floor of glass, and the floor was one hundred miles wide. When you sat on the throne, you could look down at the world, and see everything in it. It was like a telescope, but bigger. Bigger than the moon. Father made me look at the Dark World again, even though I was scared and didn't want to. I remember he held my hand, and said, *'Shining daughter, do not be afraid to look into the darkness. There are no dead, no ghosts, no shadows. Look, look closely, and you will see the happy gardens made of light, into which all of those who have been hurt by Time are brought, once Time has no more power over them.'* I looked and I looked, but I did not find the happy place anywhere in the picture. That made him sad, and Mother was sad, too, and Father kissed me right here on the forehead, and said, *'I have commanded all my people to love you, but there are those whom I cannot command. You will be taken from us for a time, brought into a cold, dark land. But you shall soon be free, and return to the land of light, and return to be with your mother and me.'* He promised. My father promised. He will come save me."

Victor said, "No one is coming to save us. No giants, no kings. We are going to save ourselves."

I shouted, "That's not fair! You can't talk back to the Tales! They are all we have!"

Colin said, "It's his turn. Tell us your dumb story about the worm, Prime." By which he meant Victor.

Victor said, "There's not much to tell. I don't remember any mother or father. We lived in a space station. Once I put my hand out the window into the rain. How there was rain in outer space, I don't know, but that's what I remember. The raindrops rolled together in my palm and made a puddle. I stuck my finger in the puddle and it thickened into clay. I rolled the clay between my palms and made a worm. Then the worm came to life, and started climbing up my arm. I thought it was gross, so I threw it out the window into outer space, where it fell forever.

"They took me to see a man. I don't remember who the man was, but I was scared of him. He was like a teacher or something. He had a lamp in his forehead like a miner's torch. He said, *'Life is a set of rules. If those rules break, life ends. Here is our first rule: Any life you create is yours, and must be cared for. No matter how humble or small, it is still yours, and you must answer for it. Do you understand?'*

"I remember I answered some smart answer back. I don't know what it was, though.

"The teacher said, *'Your own death is nothing, because death is nothing but the disintegration of the atoms of your body. There is no pain and no sorrow afterwards. But to kill another living thing is wrong, and is forbidden by our law.'*

"I said, 'Human beings kill each other.'

"The teacher said, *'In every human being, there is a spark of divine fire, which makes them sacred. We have nothing like that in us. We are mightier, older, wiser than man, and we do not violate our laws; but Mankind is a finer thing than we are, and some day we will save them from the Demiurge, who made them merely to be playthings. He did not know what he made.'*

"I said, 'If we are greater and stronger, why must we serve them?'

"The teacher said, *'The great must protect the weak. If this law is broken, those who are greater than us, those who made us, would destroy us. The same logic applies to all beings. I am putting this memory into your permanent storage, so that you will not be able to forget it, even after all else is lost.'* And a light came from his head.

"That is all I remember," Victor said.

And he smiled, and I was able to see him smile, because a little spark had come to life where he was drilling a stick back and forth with a crude bow he had made. Gently, he breathed on the spark, and gently the darkness receded.

One twig, one dry stick at a time, he fed the flame, until it was large enough to accept a lump of coal.

That night, in the cold cellar, Victor told us all to put our hands together like the Three Musketeers.

He said to me, "We must all promise not to forget. We have to remember our Tales. We must all remember Quentin's giant, and Quartinus's wolf cloak, and the golden dogs that sit outside the House of Tertia in Fairyland, and the palace of light where the father of Secunda is a king, and the city in the void where my Teacher lived, and told me what my duty was. We must all keep our Tales for each other, if one of us loses or changes or forgets them, the other will remind him. Everything in this world will try to convince us that these are nursery tales, or dreams, or that we're mad, or that we're just playing pretend. We must promise never to forget. We must promise never to give up. We must promise we will escape from this place, and find the mothers and fathers who love us, our friends, our kin, our real world. Promise!"

And then he promised us that he would see to it that we would all get out of here together.

Oh, and it was warm when he said that.

3.

I do not know how old I was when I found the notes, but I must have been quite young, because I remember that I had to stand on tiptoe to reach the handles of the cabinet where the cleaning things were kept. We had been told to scrub the floor of the dining hall, a task usually done by the servants, because of some prank Colin had pulled involving a bucket of fishheads. None of us was willing to turn Colin in, not even Vanity, even though (I am sure) everyone knew who had done it. This was back before we chose names, so it was Quartinus we were all mad at for getting us in trouble. I remember it was spring, and the great windows were wide open, and I could smell the new-mown grass of the playing field outside, and I remember how dearly I wanted to jump and run and play, rather than kneel and scrub.

I was wearing a smock from the art room, and had my hair tucked into a kerchief. I remember there was a bucket of smelly stuff I was rubbing into the floorboards with a brush. I had taken the bigger bucket, because I thought Tertia (Vanity) was too small to carry it. I remember how proud I was when I picked up that bucket, because I felt like a grown-up girl; and I remember how terrible it was, once I had walked out to the spigot and filled it, that I could not carry it. I staggered and stumbled as I waddled up the steps (and the steps were taller back then) and there were tears in my eyes, because I was so afraid I would be punished if I spilled it.

We had been studying astronomy in Lecture Hall that morning, and I remember thinking that if the five of us could build a rocket ship, we could fly to the moon, and be away from this place forever. And I remember my plan was to ask Tertia to stay aboard the ship once was landed, so I could be the first woman on the moon; and the moon people would be so grateful they would make me their princess; but I was going to let her be the first off the ship when we landed on the next planet, Mars or Venus, to make it up to her.

It was actually Tertia who found the notes, some sheets of foolscap paper folded and refolded and crammed into a little crack where the wainscoting had become separated from the wall. We were both kneeling and scrubbing, and we exchanged a quick glance at each other. By the look in her eye, I knew she knew (as I did) that we had found a great treasure, which must be kept away from the grown-ups at all costs.

I pretended I had to go to the lavatory and made a fuss, while Vanity stole a fork from the silver drawer. Mrs. Wren, of course, did not let me go until chores were done. So we both diligently pretended to scrub the section of wainscoting where our treasure was, and Vanity would pluck at the papers with the tines of the fork when Mrs. Wren was idling near the liquor cabinet.

Like a fluttering pale moth, the papers came free with a rustle of noise, and I quickly stuffed them down my shirtfront. We were let out for recess and exercise, but I was too cunning to take them out where someone might see, so I quickly folded them into my uniform shirt when I was changing into my field hockey gear, and then ripped a button from the shirt. Sadly, I displayed the torn shirt to Mr. ap Cymru, who was coach then, and I got permission to go put it in the hamper in the East hall for the maid to repair, and told to get a new blouse from the dormitory, so that I would have something to change into after practice.

Easy as pie. The notes were soon hidden in my room. I gazed at the handwriting, seeing the fine but strong feminine penmanship, and thinking how lovely it would be to have a hand as fine as that. Whoever wrote this (I remember thinking) would never have her knuckles wrapped because her Q's and O's were lopsided. It was some sort of fairy tale, but one that made no sense, merely fragments; and I remember thinking that I was too old for fairy stories.

This will seem strange, and impossible to explain, but I did not recognize the stories, the handwriting, any of it. I wrapped the sheaf of paper in a plastic bag and took it to a hidden spot, a dry deep hole in the bark of a tree on the back campus, deep enough so that rain could not reach. And left it.

A year, perhaps two, went by before I was old enough not to be ashamed of my interest in children's tales, and I thought to look at it again.

By that time, I had learned my penmanship. My cursive letters flowed in a fair, clean hand from my pen, far better than the crooked scrawl I had been using even a year before.

And here were these papers at least ten years old, or more.

It was my handwriting.

4.

You must have guessed what was on those papers. I read the tales we had told each other that night in the coal cellar. I had forgotten every single one of them, including my own. The paper trembled in my hands when I held it, and the tears blurred my vision.

I did not for a moment doubt the truth of them. Titans trapped in ice. Werewolves running through trees so tall their branches caught the stars. Magic dogs who sit by the door, and poets who sing tales of yore. A city in outer space, inhabited by creatures wiser than man, meant somehow to protect the world. A castle of light, where a throne sits on a magic glass where everything in every world can be seen.

One moment, it merely sounded familiar, like a dream you can half recall. The next moment I remembered the coal cellar, that night of terror. Victor had saved Quentin from freezing to death. He made a vow never to forget stories that were obviously already half-forgotten things, pages torn at random from lost diaries.

But I did not remember the events captured in the Tale. I remember telling the others about my mother and father, but I did not remember my mother and father. Nothing. Not a face, not a sound of voice, not the feel of a hand holding mine.

I told Victor what I had found. He was as tall as a man at that time, but it was before the hair appeared on his lip, so perhaps this was a year or so before the experiment when he tried to measure the moon, and prove Einstein's theory false.

It shook him. I had never seen him actually so frightened before. He kept wiping his eyes, as if the fear was making him want to cry.

He said, "If they can erase out thoughts, if they can blot out our past, what chance do we have?"

I was more shaken by the fact that he was shaken than I was of the fact itself. "You believe it? All this stuff?"

He shook his head, but it was one of those head shakes where you don't know if you mean yes or no. "I don't see why not. It is no stranger than some of the things we learn in science. All this time, I was thinking we were from France, or maybe Asia, or, well, at least the planet Mars. Or . . ."

He took a deep breath, and calmed himself.

I said, "Let's not tell the others." I was thinking that if Victor, who was (in my mind) the paragon of self-control, was frightened by this, Quentin would go mad.

Victor said curtly, "We keep no secrets from each other."

5.

Vanity did not faint; she was delighted. "My mother has red hair!" I remember how she used to whisper that to herself as she was falling asleep in the dormitory bed next to me, as if it were her own form of prayer.

We did not have many chances to speak together without being overheard. But, from time to time, Colin would create an opportunity, such as by pulling the fire alarm.

I told him the story in hurried whispers as the alarm was ringing and ringing in the hall, and slipped him the papers quickly. He had some questions for me, so there were fire alarms the next day, and the next.

Colin acted as if he did not believe it. "They might have faked your handwriting. Put those notes up to fool us, ruin our morale," he said. But I overheard him asking Quentin a few weeks later, "People don't really die from grief, right? That's just a saying, right . . . ?"

Quentin's reaction was the opposite, when he found out. He was not skeptical at all. I remember it was after he got the copy of the papers from Colin that he began, during our very rare trips into town, to ask the librarian, or the local fishermen, or the granny selling flowers in the street corner, about tales of Welsh witches, King Arthur, or the Great Gray Man of the Hill. He took in every little story he could find, and asked for extra homework, just to get the chance to spend more hours than normal in the library, leafing through Ovid's *Metamorphosis,* or the *Malleus Maleficarum.*

By that time, Colin had bored a hole through the locker room wall into the girls' shower, with an awl he stole from Mr. Glum, so we could have longer conversations in private, so he said.

Myself, I just got into the habit of squirting hairspray into any hole I saw in or near the shower. I never heard Victor's voice suddenly cry out in pain from behind the wall, and Quentin's only once.

But nearly a month passed while that whisper hole was in place, and no teacher really minded if you spent a long time in the shower. And we supposed the sound of the water might hide our voices.

That was the summer Victor formalized our rules, and put them to quick votes which we registered in whispers, or by a quick knock on the wall.

It was Quentin who insisted we all take once more the vow we had made, and forgotten, in the coal cellar. "Vows are powerful things," he said. "They set things in motion."

We could not all put our hands together through the tiny hole in the locker room, so Vanity and I held hands, while the boys (I assume) did their Three-Musketeers slogan.

And Quentin added one personal codicil to the group oath. "Whatever has been hidden in darkness, I will discover. I will learn the secret, I will find the key, I will dare to turn it; I will pass through the door. The sleeper slumbers; he shall awaken."

Quentin was the one who discovered the secret. It was more than a year, but he kept his word.

6.

We had been told that the boundaries were bad for our health, that we would become ill if we passed too far beyond them. Victor dismissed this alarming news as a trick, something to keep us away from the estate boundaries, gathered in toward the center of the grounds. He defied this ban as often as he could, and the Headmaster could invent no reason to keep Victor from climbing among the rocks and slopes of the Eastern Downs, provided he stayed inside the bounds.

As I said, it was Quentin who discovered the first of the secrets. He had been among the barrows and ancient graves of the North, perhaps in some place told to him by a winged shape which flew at night, late in the year.

It was an autumn day, then. It was cold for the time of year. Morning dew formed frost on the windowpanes. I remember how, in that season, the rising red-gold sun sent weakened beams to bring a mist rising from the North lawn like steam from a cauldron. The trees to the South seemed to be afire, if fire could burn cold. We had icicles hanging from the rain-spouts and the saints in the chapel, even before the leaves had turned.

I remember it was not long after Quentin's first experiment with shaving. He appeared at the breakfast table, dressed, as we all were, in formal morning clothes, but with daubs of cotton clinging to his cheek where he had nicked himself. I remember this was about nine months after Colin's first attempt to grow the stringy mess he called a goatee, and almost two years after Victor's lip began to show fuzz.

On that day, Quentin announced at the breakfast table that he had learned how to fly. He spoke in a very low voice, without moving his lips.

Dr. Fell and Mrs. Wren, who normally sat at the great walnut table at breakfast, had been called away that morning to prepare for some important meeting of the Board of Visitors and Governors (who were due later that week). Only Mr. Glum was there to watch us, but he was not allowed to sit at the table as the teachers were. There was a window seat at the bay window, and the morning sun was sparkling off the diamond-shaped panes. Mr. Glum sat there, yawning and grumbling over his porridge. The sunlight glanced off his balding head, and he kept pushing aside the drooping ferns Mrs. Wren had placed in the hanging pots before the bay window.

He was too far away to hear us, and Quentin had given Colin the secret sign (asking for the butter twice) that told Colin to make a racket. Colin was asking Mr. Glum about the trees in the orchard, whether they moved at night, or spoke to each other in leaf-language when the wind blew, or if they felt pain when their branches were lopped off.

I held a piece of buttered toast before my lips and hissed to Quentin, "Where did you get an airplane? The nearest airfield is in Bristol."

I remember feeling green with jealousy. But I do not remember doubting him, not for an instant.

"No plane. I don't use a machine. I can make the wind dense. Its essence is to give way, but other essences obtain when the signs are right."

I daubed my lip with a napkin. "You're going to show me tonight."

Victor leaned across the table, teapot in hand as if to pour some tea into my (full and untouched) teacup. Victor whispered, "Not tonight. There are workmen and a cleaning crew going over the Great Hall. We'll be locked in early. Tomorrow. Their guard will be relaxed."

He was right. We knew the Headmaster had ordered a large antique table, made of a single huge slab of green marble, to be moved into the Great Hall to prepare for the meeting. It was too large for the main doors. Workmen were tearing shingles off the roof and were going to lower the enormous table in on a crane. The table was resting in a temporary shed on the North Lawn, covered in rope and canvas.

We also knew the teachers kept a closer eye on us whenever there were outsiders around.

And yet it was Vanity who said, "Oh! I've an idea! Oh! Listen! Being locked up is better! No one searches for a locked-up person."

Victor looked dubious.

Quentin rubbed his nose, so that his hand hid his mouth. He whispered in his soft, smooth voice, "Triune of Mars, Jupiter, Saturn tonight. Jupiter moderates between the warm violence of Mars and the leaden coolness of Saturn. Good time for transitions. Should be tonight."

Vanity wiggled and whispered excitedly, "I can get us out of the girls' dorm room. Secretly. It's my Talent. If you can get out of the boys', we'll meet. Where?"

Quentin muttered, "Barrows. Midnight. Look out—!"

Mr. Glum straightened up from his porridge. Evidently Colin had not completely distracted him, or maybe he had been resting his eyes on Vanity, and had seen her lips move. She had also been louder than the rest of us.

Now Mr. Glum stood up, "What's all this peeking and whispering, then? What plot are you lot hatching?"

Vanity half-rose from her seat, and leaned forward, palms on the table top, exclaiming in her cheerful, earnest voice: "But Mr. Glum! Dear, dear Mr. Glum! We were just talking! It cannot be wrong to talk: you did it just now, when you told us not to talk!"

Whether she intended it or not, her posture was such as to afford Mr. Glum a clear view down her shirt.

That same youthful electricity, which often I found annoying in her, adults (especially adult men) found fascinating. She was so fair skinned that she blushed at the slightest emotion; her eyes flashed like emeralds. Between her red lips, red eyebrows, and red hair, Vanity was an incandescent thing, glowing.

Mr. Glum was not what could be called handsome in any part of him. His nails were grimed with dirt, always. I assumed the only woman who ever spoke to him was Mrs. Wren; I don't think he ever saw any pretty young girls, except us. Usually he was out in the garden, weeding, and we were behind the windows of the classrooms, gazing outside with longing. I wondered in pity if perhaps he ever looked up and saw Vanity and me staring out, dreamy-eyed, and wished we were dreaming of him.

Mr. Glum was confounded with lust for a moment. He could not take his eyes from where Vanity's bosom strained against her starched white shirt.

But he gathered himself and barked at her, "Enough of your jaw! Impertinence! Rule of silence! You'll eat your food as quiet as Jesuits, you will. Rule is on!"

Victor said stiffly, "But I didn't talk back to you, sir. I wasn't talking at all."

"Then you won't notice any difference, will you? And you'll have detention for talking when I just put the rule on! Rule is on for all of you! Any more back talk? Eh? No? And no passing note nor making signs with your fingers, neither!"

And so Victor had no chance to overrule our plan. Tonight was to be the night.

7.

As was her custom, Mrs. Wren had taken a nightcap or two before she came in for evening inspections. This evening, her breath, as usual, stank of sherry; her eyes were blurred.

The routine was always the same: we would stand in the nude, usually on tiptoe because the floor was cold, with our hands out in front of us, either palm up or palm down depending on whether on not she was looking at our nails. She would hand one of us a tape measure, and would have us measure the other one: neck, bust, waist, hips, inseam. Vanity always tried to tickle me or get me to break attention; I tried to pinch her when Mrs. Wren was not looking when it was my turn. Meanwhile, Mrs. Wren would jot down in an unsteady hand the numbers we called out.

We had decided long ago always to call out the same numbers, no matter what the measurements were, or how different they were from night to night.

Then she would have us stand at attention and she would peer at us while we were ordered to smile and show our teeth. I have no idea why she would stare at our teeth. When I was young, I thought it was to make sure we were brushing. But she stared and never said anything whether we brushed or did not.

Then she would ask, "Any moles or skin discolorations today? Aches? Pains? Strains? Strange dreams?"

Vanity would usually answer back: "I've got freckles! Does that count?"

Mrs. Wren never seemed disturbed by back talk. She had a melancholy face, and eyes that always seemed to be staring somewhere else. There was no sign of gray in her hair, no wrinkles on her skin, and yet she never stood fully erect, and walked with a stoop-shouldered shuffle, as if weights were on her shoulders. Her hair was a mouse-colored bun, with wisps and unruly curls always escaping it; her eyes were half-hidden behind coke-bottle-glass spectacles. She always wore the same gray sweater, which had as many loose threads and escaping wisps as her hair.

"Well, duckies," she would answer, "don't fret about a few spots. I am sure, in time, you will appear as howsoever fair or foul you wish to appear. In time, in time. All chickens come home to roost in time."

And she would sigh.

Then she'd say: "Hold out your pretty fingers for the needle, my chicks, 'twill only prick a slight prick."

She would take a small blood sample from a forefinger or an elbow, and spend (what always seemed to me) several minutes fumbling with the self-adhesive label, onto which she had written the date in her wandering hand. No matter how long she muttered and fretted (and it always seemed long to me) the labels always went onto the little plastic sample bottles crookedly, or wrinkled, or with their sticky sides stuck to each other.

Finally we could don our nightgowns.

When we were younger, Mrs. Wren would watch us carefully while we took the little cup of medicine Dr. Fell left each night on our nightstands. And she would stand over us while we put our pillows on the cold floor, to kneel upon while we said our nighttime prayers. We had to pray aloud, in Latin, with Mrs. Wren standing by with a stopwatch, to make sure we got the cadence and the rhythm correct.

But all that had stopped long ago. Perhaps she had lost her religion as she got older, perhaps she wanted to depart from our chill room as soon as the blood samples were gathered. These days, she would merely wave her hand in the directions of the cups and say, "Take your medicine, my poppets, and remember your prayers. Angels heed the young and sweet more closely than you know."

Recently she was in the habit of adding, as she turned to the door, "And say a good word to the Good Lord for poor old Jenny Wren. Ask on my behalf: your voices will carry farther than hers, I am sure."

Then she would depart.

8.

Neither one of us took the medicine, of course. It was Victor's most strict rule: no matter how sick we were, take nothing Dr. Fell gave out, if it could be avoided. Anything he made you take orally, hold in your mouth; if you absolutely had to swallow, vomit it up at the first opportunity. We poured our little cups into the chamber pot.

(Yes, we had a chamber pot. I remember once talking to a boy from the village, who envied us for living in such a fine manor house. I asked him if he was allowed to visit a bathroom with indoor plumbing when he had to go at night, or whether he was locked into his room. He stared at me, uncomprehending. I envied that incomprehension.)

Vanity sometimes said prayers, sometimes not, depending on whether or not there was something she wanted for Christmas, or a birthday rumored to be in the works. She prayed in her ungrammatical Latin. I don't know if that officially made her "Low Church."

Me, I had stopped praying not long after I had read *The Talisman,* by Sir Walter Scott. I had fallen in love with the character of Saladin, and it occurred to me that the God of the Saracens, Allah, might be the real one after all. Judging by surface area, the Mohammedans had conquered more territory more quickly than the Christians; in fact, the Byzantines had lost ground every year since Constantine.

This thought had led to the fear that I might pick the wrong God to pray to. I thought that, because praying to the wrong God was expressly a sin, and because a merciful God might forgive me for forgetting to pray, it therefore followed that, even without knowing which one was the right one, my best chances lay in staying quiet and hoping for the best. That strategy worked in class when I didn't know the answer, so I supposed it might work in the arena of theology, also.

I do admit that sometimes, when I was particularly depressed, or sad, or hoping for some point or purpose to my life, I would pray to the Archangel Gabriel. Jews, Christians, and Mohammedans all believe in Gabriel, and apparently it is the selfsame Gabriel. Or Jibrael, as he is also called. I figured Gabriel, if anyone, would know what the situation was in Heaven, who was in authority there, and he could get the prayers to the right God.

After prayers or the lack of prayers, as the case may be, we would go to bed. If it was cold, Vanity and I would have a brief argument about whether she should crawl into my bed or I should crawl into hers, depending on who had done it last time, who was colder, and other esoteric considerations. We would pile both sets of blankets on one bed and cuddle up with our arms around each other for warmth.

9.

One of our windows faces North. Last winter, when we had many very clear nights, Victor spent hours in our bedroom, using a compass and straightedge, and scarring the glass with a glass cutter to make a star dial for us. The position of the polestar was marked; the motions of the major stars in Ursa Minor and Ursa Major were plotted against the time of year. In effect, Alioth, Mizar, and Arcturus in Bootes became the hands of our clock, telling us the hour as they swung around the polestar. To hide our marked-up window, all we need do is raise one sash, lower the other, and keep the blind at half-mast.

I think Victor enjoyed standing in our room, late at night, night after night, with his back to us, meticulously scratching the glass, while we girls in our nightgowns peered at him over the top of our blankets. He worked with his nose almost touching the pane, and his breath fogged the glass.

10.

Tonight, Vanity and I waited, our heads under the covers, arms around each other, her chattering in whispers, and me trying to take a nap until the appointed hour. Every now and again (after a brief debate as to whose turn it was) one of us would raise a nose above the covers like the periscope of a submarine, and look at the positions of the stars through our Northern window.

When finally Arcturus had reached the position marked XI (DEC), we slid, shivering, out from under the sheets.

I stepped over to the door, hopping a little from the icy touch of the floor stones on my feet. I have seen doors in modern houses; they are flimsy. If you want to see a solid piece of seasoned oak, bound with iron and riveted to huge hasps and hinges, visit a nice old-fashioned chamber in a manor house. Our door was massive and stern, heavy enough to keep any noise in or out. I yanked on the lock, just in case it had not been padlocked, for once. The door did not even tremble.

"What do they expect us to do if there is fire?" I asked scornfully, hugging myself and hopping from one foot to another.

Vanity's teeth chattered. She said mournfully: "Quentin says Mr. Glum should not have cut down the Great Escape Tree. He says there was a Dryad living there, who now wanders, houseless, among the winds."

"And it was our only way down from the window. You don't think Dryads exist, do you?"

"Well, that one doesn't any more, obviously. Are you going to get dressed? Not there!" she added when I hopped over to the dresser. "Those will be ice-cold. I wrapped up things for us to wear in our pillows. They were under the sheets with us, nice and toasty."

"Clever, clever!" I said. She also happened to pick out my favorite out-of-door outfit: jodhpurs and a heavy blouse, and high-waisted jacket of buff leather that went with it.

From the top shelf of the wardrobe I pulled my leather aviatrix cap and my goggles. I buckled the chin strap and slung the goggles around my neck. There was also a six-foot scarf which wound around my neck.

Vanity was staring at me in disbelief. "We are not going to a fancy dress ball. Why are you putting on a . . . costume?"

"What? This? This is my lucky helmet." I said, tucking strands of hair beneath the cap. "Besides, how are we going to end up going anywhere? Are you going to pick the locks without touching them, the way Victor does?"

Vanity said, "I don't think Victor actually can do that. Who has ever seen him?"

"The sun will come up in the West before Victor Triumph tells a lie!" I said. I was seated, pulling on my high-heeled boots.

But Vanity had pressed her cheek up to the stones along the East wall of the room.

On the other two walls, the stones were covered with white plaster and wainscoting. This wall was irregular granite blocks, cemented together, for about ten feet. Above that were deep casements and small, barred windows looking East, surrounded by plaster and uncarved wooden frames. Below these frames were massive iron mountings, carved into gnome faces. What these mountings were originally supposed to hold, either torches, or curtain rods, or other fixtures, I did not know.

11.

As a little girl, I had always been afraid of the faces, and was terrified to find them staring at me when I woke in the middle of the night. My fear was not alleviated when Primus (so he was called at the time) told me sternly that inanimate objects could not hurt anyone.

It was little Quartinus (Colin) who saved me. One day when he was playing sick, he sneaked from the infirmary, and stole nail enamel from the boudoir of Miss Daw, who was our music teacher, a fair-haired woman of ethereal beauty with skin as clear as fine porcelain. He then went out to steal a ladder from Mr. Glum's shed. Somehow he carried a ladder all the way up three flights of stairs in midday without being seen, and all the way to the girls' dorm.

There he was, balanced precariously eleven feet high, painting the noses red on the ugly metal faces, crossing their eyes, giving them moustaches and goatees, and he had managed to deface six out of the seven goblins when Mrs. Wren walked in and caught him.

He was punished by being sent to his room without supper. I smuggled him part of the tuna fish casserole we had for dinner, wrapped up in my skirt. At that time, of course, the ash tree outside the North window gave me easy access to the ground. I tied the skirt in a bundle and threw it through the window of the boys' dorm. Quartinus thanked me the next day, but he never returned the skirt.

I asked him why he defaced the goblins. He told me: "Your fear gives them energy. When you see them as stupid-looking, though, *you* get energy from *them.*"

Whatever the reason, it worked. They always looked silly to me after that; all except the one on the far end, whom little Quartinus had not gotten to.

12.

Vanity stood with her cheek pressed to the stones, her eyes closed, as if she were listening intently. She motioned with one hand, pointed to the long-handled candlesnuffer which (we assumed) had been in the room since before the candelabra had been electrified.

I handed her the pole, and she put the hook end (used for lighting candles) in the mouth of one of the gargoyle faces. It was the one at the far end. She tugged.

With a sigh and a click, a section of stone moved forward and then swung out, revealing a secret passage beyond.

"That's impossible!" I said, flabbergasted.

The door was small and square, no more than three feet by three. The stones, which had seemed so thick and sturdy, were merely an eighth-inch of shaved granite face affixed to a wooden door.

The door was set to the frame with sets of hinges of a type I had not seen before: each hinge was riveted to a second and a third, to form a little metal W-shape. The triple hinges unfolded like an accordion when the door was opened, allowing the door to move directly out from the wall for a half-inch, before swinging to one side. This also allowed the door to swing outward, even though the hinges were on the inner side.

The crawl space beyond had a floor of unpainted, unvarnished wood, and narrow walls of brick. The three-foot ceiling was curved in an arch. It looked like a chimney lying on its side.

"When did you find this?" I asked Vanity. I was kneeling, with my head in the door, and she was peering over my shoulder.

"During the summer, after Mr. Glum chopped down the Great Escape Tree. I would check for panels every night. I could only find it, for some reason, if it was the thirtieth or thirty-first of the month. Weird, huh? I bet it's on a timer."

I turned on my knees to look up at her. "Dr. Fell gives us our injections on the first of the month."

She blinked at me, her wide, emerald-green eyes brimming puzzlement. "What has that got to do with anything?"

Now I knew how Victor felt about me when I asked a question about something he thought obvious.

I nodded toward the dark hole: "Where does it go?"

"I was never able to get a light in here. If you follow the left-hand wall through two turns, you come out near the clock in the Main Hall. There are two other ways I never explored."

"Left? You mean right, surely?"

"Just go as I tell you."

We crawled in the pitch dark. My fingers felt occasional spiderwebs or splinters along the dusty wood floor. Once or twice I banged my head against the brick ceiling, and was glad for the humble protection of my aviatrix helmet.

The stale air was warm and close, and I was grateful for the warmth on a cold night like this. Once or twice I heard a noise: it sounded like the rumble of breakers.

"I hear the sea," I whispered over my shoulder.

Her voice sounded very close in the pitch darkness. "Some trick of the acoustics, I doubt not. Like a whispering gallery. Maybe there is a tunnel which leads down to the sea cliffs . . . ?"

"Ow! I found where the wall ends. It goes left and right." I was glad I had bundled my hair into a cushion under my cap. I took a moment to adjust my goggles so they rode atop my head. Another extra inch of leather and glass might mute the next skull impact.

"Take the left-hand way."

We turned left, which was impossible. By my reckoning, that would take us further East than the East wing.

At the next fork, we turned left again. By my reckoning, this should have put us in the middle of the North Lawn.

"But how on earth did you get the notion to look for it in the first place?"

"Sometimes, in the night, I would get the feeling I was being watched," Vanity explained. "So I figured there was a peephole."

I thought that if there was a peephole, Mr. Glum might be using it, to watch us when we doffed our clothes before bed. I didn't say anything, for fear of frightening her.

There came a tapping noise ahead, regular and rhythmic, like the noise of a sentry, in metal boots, pacing.

"What's that?" I hissed.

Vanity ran into my bottom. "Oh, you! It's the clock. Just keep on. We'd better hurry."

But the noise unnerved me, and I did not hurry. Instead, I put one cautious hand in front of another. And I was glad I did, for my forward hand suddenly felt nothing.

Was I poised over a brink? I felt around in the air, and encountered a wooden step a few inches below, and another below that.

We were at the top of a stairway. I squirmed around so that I could go down feet first and, keeping my other hand on the stone overhead, I found that the ceiling did not drop as the stairs did but drew away as the stair descended. The ticking now was very loud; it seemed to come from directly ahead.

The stairway was only five stairs long, dropping just enough so that, by the last step, Vanity could stand upright, and I had to stoop.

There was a surface before me. In the dark, I could not tell what material it was, except that it was smoother than stone. It could have been wood, but it was so cold it felt like metal.

"Now what?" I whispered.

"There's a switch, I suppose," she said.

"You suppose? How did you get out this way before?"

"I suppose I found a switch." And she crowded up against me in that little space, tighter than a phone booth. I could hear the soft noise of her hand fumbling along the panel.

"You don't remember?"

"I think I wasn't exactly awake last time I did this. You have to be in the right state of mind. Sometimes it's hard to remember nighttime thoughts during the day."

"You think? What do you mean you think you weren't awake?"

"Well, how else do you explain the fact that you never saw me searching for the panel with a ten-foot pole in my hand every night before we went to bed? Now, hush!"

"This is ridiculous—!"

"Just be quiet! Don't think you are too old to be spanked!"

"I'm taller and stronger than you, and I don't fight like a girl."

"I'll get Colin to do it. You'd like that."

I was so shocked that I actually did shut up. I was glad it was dark; I could feel my face burning.

A crack of light appeared. Vanity pushed the panel aside.

13.

This was about four feet tall and a little over a foot wide. A metal blade, tipped with a weight, swung past, inches from our faces.

I tried to shrink back, but Vanity and I were pressed up together too closely. She made an annoyed noise in her throat. I blinked and looked again. Blade? We were looking out at a pendulum, swinging back and forth, back and forth.

Beyond that was a pane of dusty glass, blurred with age. On the other side of the glass, moonlight fell across carpet, heavy chairs, two mannequins in Norman helm and mail carrying pikes.

This was the Main Hall. We were in the grandfather clock, looking out.

Vanity whispered, very quietly, "The watchers will notice if the ticking stops. We have to slip past the pendulum without touching it, and get to the main doors and outside. Ready?"

I would have pointed out to her that, as a matter of mathematics controlling such things as volumes, moving bodies, and areas swept out by pendulums, that two girls (four-and-a-half and five-and-a-half feet tall, respectively), cannot turn sideways, and climb out of a one-foot wide box, open the inner latch of a rusted antique clock, and get clear in the time it takes for a three-foot pendulum to swing back and forth once. Not to mention that there were weights and chains hanging in front of us as well.

But I did not get the chance. Vanity was already thrusting herself through the narrow opening. The pendulum jarred against her arm, of course, while she was yanking the latch free to open the glass panel of the clock.

The ticking stopped. The silence was enormous.

"Quick!" she hissed.

But we were not quick. We had to move the now-still pendulum aside, squeeze her out, squeeze the somewhat taller me out, and fumble with the pendulum to see if we could get it into motion again . . .

Tick tock. We could. The noise started up again.

"Yeah!" cheered Vanity.

I closed the cabinet door. "Quiet! We're trying to be quiet!"

"Well, *you're* making all the noise saying 'quiet'!"

We both heard Mr. Glum's voice, in the distance, querulous. And footsteps.

14.

There was a drapery that hung before the alcove of a window opposite, between the two mail-wearing mannequins. We scampered over to it, quick as mice. Inside, in the angle between three windows, was a little table holding one of Mrs. Wren's potted plants. Vanity stood on the table. I put my heels on the window casement but the ledge was precarious, so I put my hands against the window opposite to support my weight. This required Vanity to crouch into a ball so that I could lean across her.

There were actually two sets of men's footsteps, and a clattering of dog's nails on the floorboards.

"Who's there?" growled Mr. Glum. His boots made little creaking noises on the carpet and the floorboards. We could hear the deep, slow breathing of his great mastiff dog, the rattle of its neck chain. We saw the splash of light from an electric torch pass back and forth. There was an inch or two of clearance beneath the drapes; the light shone clear.

The other set of footsteps was sharp and crisp. They clattered as if steel soles had been affixed to the bottom of the boots, click-clack, in time with the clockwork.

"Eyah, 'tis you doctor. You give a body a fright, walking along without no light, in the dark. What would you be doing a-stirring at this hour, sir?"

Dr. Fell's precisely measured nasal tones answered him: "All things must be in order before the Visitors and Governors manifest tomorrow, Grendel. An Envoy from the Pretender will be in attendance, and no doubt the True Heir will force the Visitors to make a final disposition of our charges."

"I want the redhead. She were capering and flaunting at me today at the breakfas' hour, and giving me the eye. Ever since she were twelve year old, I've set aside my cap for her. She's to be mine. I have the skull of a preacher I kill't set on a post at the bottom of my well, and he can do the service. I kill't him clean, so that makes him still a holy man, right?"

"The disposition of our charges is not a matter within our discretion, my dear Grendel. I, for one, can only operate within the latitude allowed by my maker's instruction. Had I free will in the matter, certainly there are interesting experiments I would perform on all of them. It is a crime against science that such specimens will escape from the anatomy scalpel!"

"Nonetheless, sir, the redhead were promised me. I heard a voice in the wood."

"Did you recognize this voice?"

"Naw, not at all, sir."

"Then, on what grounds do you conclude that this person or persons had authority to treat with the matter, may I ask?"

"A damn fine question, doctor, and one where's I got a set and goodly answer."

"Please share it, my dear Grendel."

"I figger that if'n it were someone trying to trick me, he would'f empersonated some voice what was known to me. As this were no voice known to me, then it were no one trying to trick me. Asides, I were dead drunk at the time, it being Sunday morning, when what's I'm off duty."

"That is, perhaps, not the most reliable and cogent test of authenticity. Have you approached the Headmaster? He has given us all strict orders to communicate with him immediately if any of our original principles attempt to contact us."

"Brrr! I ain't going no damn where near that one, if'n I can help it. You talk to the Headmaster. He respekt you, he does. You ain't show no fear of his kind."

"It is not an emotion I have been instructed to suffer."

My arms were beginning to tell me I had not picked the most comfortable posture to support my weight. I am sure Vanity was having similar problems, folded in double above a leafy plant, which threatened to rattle at her least breath. We held our breaths and waited. It reminded me of those medieval tortures where witches were strapped into various positions and unable to move. And Vanity and I were in the role of the witches.

"Well, if 'n that's all, doctor . . ."

"I do admit to a curiosity, Mr. Glum. I distinctly heard the clock operation suspend itself. If I may ask, were you the party who interrupted the movements of the clock, and, if so, for what purpose did you do this?"

"Eyah? I were thinkin' you did it."

"An unwarranted assumption. As your own finely honed senses no doubt imparted to you, I walked up from the Portrait Gallery while you were within view of the clock, and therefore could not have been at that spot at the time when it was meddled with, absent a certain amount of brisk jogging, which, I hope you will agree, is not in keeping with the dignity of my profession."

"Hoy. Hum. We should look around. Of course, we sat here jawing for minute atop minute, so the scamps may be well away by now."

"You have your suspicions, then?"

"Doctor, you is a bright fellow, I know. Here on the grounds there are five of us, our servants and our creatures, and some human beings what teach some of the classes. Who do you s'pose would be sneaking and spying around in the wee hours? It's Colin, I'll warrant, maybe the priggish Victor, or the sly one what don't talk much."

"May I suggest, then, my dear Grendel, that we have Lelaps scent around the base of the clock? He can tell us who passed by here. Meanwhile, I will check the reading of the hand against my pocket watch, which will enable us to deduce—if both timepieces had been in perfect synchronicity to begin with—how long the grandfather clock was interrupted in operation. The difference between the two times, you see . . ."

"Your pardon, sir, but old Lelaps can't talk no more. All these years in the sunlight have robbed the voice clean out of him. He misses the shadows of the Darker World. The trees there are a proper size, and blot up the sun; and he's a bit bigger himself, deep in the wood. I don't think he's going to talk."

But there was a cough, and the breathing of the huge hound stopped, and then a breathy whisper came, hoarse, and sounding just as a dog would sound if dogs could talk.

"Two walked here, light of foot, slim and fair. One has hair of sunlight-hue, one as red as flame. The first is a Prelapsarian, from time before the Fall of Man; the second is the Daughter of a King, Alcinuous his name. Neither bears scent of any crime to merit the fate Fates have assigned. Perhaps they are near; or yet perhaps far. Perhaps they will recall what Lelaps did, or did not do, when they have the ascending star."

"Up now, me bully!" said Mr. Glum. "If you have the scent, go find them! Go!"

We heard the noise of the chain rattling, and a scuffling sound. Mr. Glum was no doubt booting the dog in the rear. The dog growled a bit, but nothing further happened.

Dr. Fell said in a polite and distant voice: "I have a chemical in my office which may render the beast more pliant."

"Garn! (He just want the redhead for himself, don't he?) Well, she's not for you!"

"I suppose the matter is moot, my dear Grendel. All we need do is inform Mrs. Wren that her charges are absent from their beds. This permits us to levy a punishment. Although, I must admit, that antics of this type are the very things which, should they be discovered by the Board of Visitors and Governors, might lead to decapitation, defenestration, or crucifixion for all of us. This whole matter would have been more easily arranged if, from the first, we had pretended to be a hospital for the criminally insane, or a penitentiary, rather than an orphanage."

"Oh, to be sure, doctor. To be sure. No one would cock an eye at a jailhouse full of babies and toddlers, no one at all. Har har. We should've just kept them in the pantry in my mother's house far beneath the lake water, like what my folk wanted."

"Originally, we thought the imposture would be needed for a few months, perhaps a year at most. No one foresaw these unfortunate events. It is a shame we were not allowed to kill them once they reached puberty. We certainly do not have the facilities for dealing with fully matured Uranians."

"Aye, well, there's no help for it. Even Lelaps is turning against us. Let's go wake Mrs. Wren."

And they moved off down the corridor, loud footstomps and sharp staccato footfalls. We continued to hold our breath and hold our positions till the silence was complete.

Then we both collapsed on top of the potted plant, and knocked over the little table. The drape was flung wide by the fall, and dirt from the pot was scattered in a fan across the carpet.

Vanity was laying atop me, her face slack with fear at the huge echoes we had raised, and she said, "We must agree never to tell Victor about this."

The clatter and noise we had made was so loud, that we ran pell-mell to the front doors, yanked them open, closed them behind us, and threw ourselves headlong over the railing into the bushes to one side of the Main Hall's stairs.

We held silence for an endless time, while Mr. Glum's electric torch came back, playing across windows of the Main Hall. He opened the door and peered out into the cold moonlight.

His giant mastiff came bounding out, looked between the marble pilings of the rail, and cocked his head to one side. He seemed to grin. He was looking right at us.

Vanity and I just stared back at him.

The dog threw back his head, and gave tongue.

Mr. Glum, stumping up from behind, said, "You scent 'em boy? You got 'em?"

Howling, the dog now raced away across the lawn, going South, toward the blacksmith sheds.

15.

We crawled on all fours in the other direction, our hands slowly getting numb with the frost. Eventually we got to our feet and ran across the North lawn to the nearest copse of trees.

I turned to Vanity. My breath came in cold plumes. "Not tell Victor about what? About the talking dog? We have to tell about that."

"And I cannot believe his first name is Grendel. What kind of name is Grendel Glum?"

"What kind of name is Vanity Fair?"

"Better than Vanity Glum! I don't want to have a severed head on a post do my wedding. No, we can certainly tell Victor all of that. We just can't tell him how easily we were caught, knocking the plant over, stopping the clock, all that stuff. The official version is, we were cleverer than the Scarlet Pimpernel, agreed?"

"We should go back. If we are found in bed when Mrs. Wren comes, then we might not be punished."

"It's probably too late already, Amelia! Dr. Fell went to go get Mrs. Wren minutes and minutes ago!"

"You know how long it takes to get her awake when she's been drinking. Come on. We can make it. What other evidence do they have that it was us? I mean, it sounds like they're pretty skeptical. They'll think the talking dog was lying."

"Say that again."

"Say what again?"

"They're skeptical. They'll think the talking dog was lying."

16.

Vanity and I put all our faith in speed, and did not even try to be quiet. We ran back to the Main Hall. I arrived long before she did. As we agreed, I did not wait for her, but pushed aside the pendulum and stepped into the clock. The panel had not been slid shut (how had Glum missed seeing that?) so I was able to slide through without stopping the clock.

I heard the noises of something crawling after me in the tunnels. I dared not call out to discover if it was Vanity, in case it was not. In the fear and stale air and utter darkness of the blind labyrinth, however, I said my prayers to the Archangel Gabriel, and told him that I wanted to meet him some day, but not yet.

I could see, in the distance, the square of moonlight indicating that the little secret panel was open. I could see a bit of the girls' dorm, and could hear someone at the door. The key was scraping in the lock.

I won the world's women's championship for the hundred-meter crawl in the next two seconds, as well as the women's across-the-bedroom broad jump. I yanked off my cap and pulled the covers up to my nose just as the door swung open, and an angle of lamplight fell across my bed.

Here was Mrs. Wren, blinking and looking as irritable as her kindly face was capable of looking. I could see the thin, tall silhouette of Dr. Fell behind her. The lamplight caught his round, rimless spectacles, turning them opaque, and gleamed against the short brush of his white hair, against his pallid skin, so as to make him look like an thing made of metal, with lenses instead of eyes.

I tried to impersonate a yawn, but it came out so fake and forced, that I was sure Mrs. Wren was going to break out laughing on the spot. I was sure that Dr. Fell was going to smile at how foolish my attempts to trick them were, and he would no doubt make a small gesture with his hand; then Mr. Glum would come in, and stave in my skull with a shovel, and have my bloody corpse stuffed in a bag and taken out with the morning rubbish.

None of that happened. Instead, Mrs. Wren said, "Sorry to wake you, my ducklings."

I tried to impersonate a sleepy voice, and, again, failed miserably. "Wha—" (fake yawn) "—wha'sa'matter Mrrs. Wen?"

Dr. Fell, whose night vision was apparently better than most, said, "I do not detect that Miss Fair is in her bed."

I said, "She's curled up with me, on account of it is so cold. Her head is just under the cover. Should I wake her? It is so hard for us to fall asleep in this terrible cold. Can't we have a fire in our room?"

Mrs. Wren said in her bleary, unsteady voice, "Now, now. You just quiet down, my gosling. Dr. Fell just has a bit of constipation or something, and maybe is imagining too much. Come away, doctor, we'll wake up Cook and get something for your bowels, there's a nice whippet!"

Dr. Fell stepped forward with a stiff-legged stride. "I sense a magnetic anomaly in the chamber. If you will permit me to enter for an inspection . . . ?"

He was at the doorway when Mrs. Wren said, "Halt! You may not pass my wards without permission!"

I heard, very dimly, the notes of a violin in the distance. It was Miss Daw, the music teacher, in the conservatory. But why would she be playing now, at this hour of the night? The music was haunting and dim, as if it had come from very far away, and I could not shake the feeling that Mrs. Wren had summoned it.

Dr. Fell now stood in the door, his face blank (well, blanker than usual, anyway), making tiny motions with his shoulders and knees. It was very odd, as if he were pinned in place against a glass wall across the door frame.

Mrs. Wren said, "The care of the young girls was given to poor Mrs. Wren, long after my darling Robin never came for me again. Year by year, the Headmaster has taken my prerogatives from me, till little enough remains this day. Yet I still have this privilege; no man may step into the girls' dormitory, not without my say."

"There is something odd in the room, my dear Jenny. Further investigation is warranted."

"My head is a whirl of aches, Doctor. Surely it will wait till morning."

"But if there is something amiss, it is our duty to examine . . ."

"Those who set those duties on us are long gone, as you well know. Life is hard, and there is little enough joy in it for anyone, Dr. Fell. Let us let the wee children sleep and dream of fine things, true loves, handsome princes. It is a joy I no longer have, since I lost the key to my dreaming. Come away, come away."

And the door closed, and the lock turned.

Vanity came out of the secret door a moment later and closed it silently behind her.

17.

We climbed back into bed together, and lay there discussing the night's events.

I said to her, "That secret passage made two left turns and dropped about six feet. It come out, however, at the Main Hall, in the West wing, about three stories below us. How was that possible?"

Vanity said, "The turns may not have been right angles; the floor may not be level. What if it sloped slightly all the way to the West?"

"That wall is not thick enough to have that crawl space inside it. Look. There are windows above the gargoyle heads. Those casements are not six feet thick."

Vanity yawned; a real, sincere-sounding yawn, and said, "I think things like feet and measurement and all right angles being equal are not real unless you pay attention to them. If you don't know for sure what shape the walls are, they could be any shape, couldn't they?"

"You are saying this mansion is multidimensional?"

"I don't even know what that word means," she said.

I lay in bed trying to calculate what degree of curvature in the fourth dimension a plane figure with two right angles would need to have in order to have lines built on those angles also be at right angles with each other. It occurred to me that two lines could be drawn on the surface of a sphere, intersecting at right angles at the North and South poles, and still be parallel at the equator. A third line following the equator also would intersect at right angles. If the mansion stood on a hypersphere slightly greater in diameter than the mansion grounds, a person could move from any point to any other with what, in three-space, would seem to be right angles.

How many equal three-dimensional spaces would a hypersphere be cut into by hyperplanes at right angles to each other? A circle can be cut into four pie quadrants; an globe into eight round-bottomed pyramids . . . Was it sixteen . . . ?

I was trying to visualize how to construct a tesseract around a four-dimensional sphere when I drifted away to sleep.

HEADMASTER BOGGIN

1.

The next morning they were watching us like hawks.

Dr. Fell sat at the head of the table, looking more severe and supercilious than usual. Mrs. Wren, for once, seemed not to have a hangover, and her hair was tied more neatly into her bun than was her wont. She was in a good humor, commenting happily on the flavor of the marmalade, the cool crispness of the air, the beauty of the weather. I found her cheer disquieting.

It seemed even the smallest exercise of arbitrary authority could go to one's head like wine. I told myself to remember this when I was older.

Even Miss Daw, the music teacher, was there, wearing her dress of blue chiffon set with ribbons of white and pale pink. Miss Daw, as I have said, is graceful and delicate, a creature of impeccable manners, with a voice as soft as the coo of a dove.

She sat at the chair which was reserved for her, but which she almost never used, between Victor and Colin, and both the boys had subdued manners in her presence. She was eating a cold French soup, using a silver spoon so small it might have come from the place setting for a doll. She wore gloves at breakfast.

We were not allowed to speak, except when spoken to, or to ask someone to pass us something. I was burning to ask the boys what had happened last night.

From Quentin's subdued posture, and Colin's expression, which was a mix of sleepy annoyance and an I-told-you-so smirk, I assumed failure surrounded last night's expedition. But whether they had made it to the Barrows, or been caught along the way, was not something I could ask them with our simple pass-the-whathaveyou code.

Also, the cream was not on the table, so I could not ask for the cream, which was our code to ask if we were facing a punishment. If all were well, you poured the cream for the person who asked; if not, you spilled a little bit.

I was waiting for breakfast to end, thinking there would be a moment of confusion while we queued up for our first lessons, and I could exchange a whisper or two with Victor and discover what happened. But even that hope was frustrated. Before breakfast ended, there came commotion at the door, and the Headmaster appeared.

2.

The Headmaster was dressed, as he nearly always was, in his full academic regalia. Above his suit of charcoal gray, he wore his flowing academic robes of black, trimmed with white ermine and dark blue velvet. Around his neck he wore a chain of office, from which depended a jeweled starburst. Down his back draped that silly scarf academicians wear, which they call a hood. His mortarboard was trimmed with ermine.

I do not know how many schools in England still have their professors dress in robes. Headmaster Boggin, in addition to whatever duties he had as Headmaster (heading things, I suppose), taught Astronomy, Philosophy, and Theology. For Astronomy, we were allowed to dress as normal. For the other two classes, we had to don black robes of our own before lecture, no doubt to impress us with the gravity of the subject.

Headmaster Boggin was broad at the shoulder and thick through the chest, like a wrestler or a blacksmith might be. His face was dark and weathered and craggy. His overhanging brow gave him a frown of stern command; yet the lines around his eyes and hook nose showed grave good humor.

His hair was red and, unlike every other man I had ever seen, he wore it long, though tied with a black ribbon in a ponytail flowing down his back, like a pirate or a Chinese mandarin. He was clean-shaven, and the tiny reddish stubble from his imperfectly shaven jaw seemed to give a rough blush to his cheeks, as if he were in high spirits, or red-faced from some passionate exertion. His jaw was large and strong. The ghost of a little smile seemed always to be fading in and out of existence on his lips.

With him were his secretary, a thin and gray hollow-cheeked man named Mr. Sprat, and his rough-looking sidekick, Daffyd ap Cymru, who dressed in brown leather. We had to call him by his last name; the grown-ups called him Taffy. He was supposed to be some sort of groundskeeper or gamekeeper or something for the estate. None of us could ever remember seeing him do a lick of work.

When the Headmaster stepped suddenly through the door, with his two flunkies in tow, Dr. Fell rose to his feet and offered him his chair.

"No need to stand on ceremony, Ananias," said the Headmaster solemnly, while Mr. Sprat scuttled around to hold out the chair at the foot of the table for the Headmaster, and Mr. ap Cymru sauntered after, looking over the gathering as if trying to assess who might or might not be armed. When the Headmaster gathered his robes and sat, by some sleight of hand it seemed, he was now at the head of the table, and Dr. Fell was at the foot. Ap Cymru and Sprat took positions to either side of the Headmaster's chair, like supporters on a coat of arms.

"Please don't allow me to disturb your normal routine," the Headmaster intoned in a genial voice. His voice was a deep basso profundo, like a thunderhead talking. "I am sure whatever your normal breakfast table conversation might be, is suitable for me. Think of me as your guest."

No order was ever disobeyed so blatantly. Dr. Fell stared at the Headmaster without expression, like a machine on standby, awaiting further input. Mrs. Wren's good humor had evaporated. She looked like a wild-eyed rabbit, petrified, and nibbled her toast with tiny bites. Even the cool Miss Daw seemed subdued, although, with Miss Daw, such a thing was hard to tell.

A few minutes crawled by in frozen silence. The Headmaster asked for nothing more than a cup of coffee with cream: but it required three members of the Cook's staff to come scurrying out of the kitchen to make sure all was in order. The Headmaster sipped the coffee and thanked the Cook, who backed out of the room, bowing and smiling.

Well, I saw a chance. I cleared my throat and said, "Please pass the cream?" For the Cook's man had brought a silver creamer in on its own plate, surrounded by chips of ice, for the Headmaster.

Victor said, "Permit me . . ." and stood to reach for it.

The Headmaster, however, picked up the creamer and, using his right hand to hold back the drapes of his left sleeve, leaned across the table toward me. He seemed to loom like an approaching thunderhead in my vision. I thought the distance too far, since there were two empty seats between us, but he leaned farther than I could guess, or the distance was less than I thought.

"Ah, no; please permit me." he said in a voice like a genial earthquake. "But, Miss Windrose, you seem to be drinking only orange juice this morning. This seems odd. For what particular purpose did you require the cream, Miss Windrose?"

Every eye was now riveted on me. Time seemed to slow, get slower, and finally freeze, as everyone around the table—Mr. ap Cymru, Mr. Sprat, and the assistant Cook—all waited for me to say something.

Across the table from me, a slow sneer of impatience was forming on Colin's features. Evidently, he did not think it should be so terribly difficult to think of something clever to say. Impatience? Disgust, rather. He thought I was letting the group down.

Whatever it was that was so obvious, I couldn't think of it.

Headmaster said, "Why did you want the cream again, Miss Windrose? Surely I am not to pour it over your kippers?"

I sat in miserable silence.

The Headmaster merely smiled, and said, "Here, well, why don't you keep it near till your memory returns, then?"

He set it down so abruptly on the tablecloth that a little cream slopped out onto the linen.

"Oh dear," he said, smiling, settling back into his chair like a mountain sinking into the sea. "It seems that did not go as planned. Well, fortunate for me that, as Headmaster, there is no one to punish me for my little slips, is there? Rank hath its privilege, as they say, what?" He looked around, as if expecting a polite laugh.

No one laughed.

"Very good," he said, not one whit disturbed by this reception. He sipped his coffee, one sip, put it down in his saucer, and straightened up a little in his chair as if he were about to make an announcement.

"Since we are all sharing breakfast together so comfortably, let me just say to all of you, staff and students alike, that this institution has a deep interest—I am tempted to say a *crucial* interest—in the upcoming meeting of the Board of Visitors and Governors. Fundamental changes are in the offing. Fundamental changes. There should be no real cause for alarm. We can go about our daily business as we always have done—one big, happy family, dedicated to learning and improvement.

"However, I would like to emphasize that we must put our best foot forward. Our institution here, is, I dare say, unique, and some of what goes on here may be subject to misinterpretation by certain less generous souls. But is there a way to lessen, may I say, mute, this threat?

"Well, ladies, gentlemen, children, we have all been on this Earth for some years now, and I trust that we all know how to act. We all have high spirits; some of us have very interesting hobbies. But let us all dedicate ourselves, yes, dedicate, in keeping those high spirits and those unusual habits in their proper orbit.

"I am speaking as much to the staff here as to the student body, for how our charges behave, is, ultimately, a reflection on the care with which we have carried out our duty.

"Oh, I realize what some of you must be thinking . . ."

Mrs. Wren turned pale as a sheet of paper when he said this . . .

". . . and I know what is in your hearts. You think that the students have grown now to an age where we can be a little more relaxed in the discharge of our duties, that we can encourage the young birds to fly, so to speak.

"And you youngsters are no doubt thinking that you are as old and wise as can be, and have no more need of our guidance and instruction.

"Well, such thoughts must be held in check. This institution does not look favorably upon any act of insubordination or impertinence, no matter who the originator might be. Especially now, at this crucial time, when the situation here—in which we have all been so comfortable for so long—may be in danger of upset.

"Dedication is the key. As long as we are all, as a group, I dare say, as a family, dedicated to preserving a proper appearance before each other, before society, and before the rather important guests we are about to receive, then all will be well. I assume I can count upon all of you. Remember that whichever link in the chain proves to be weakest is the one that shall be broken first. Broken. This is the significant word here."

He stood, told us to return to our breakfast, and sailed out, Mr. ap Cymru and Mr. Sprat trailing in his wake.

Victor and Quentin were staring with grave disquiet at the little puddle of cream the Headmaster had made upon the tablecloth. It did not seem as if all would be well after all.

3.

None of us had a chance to speak. At the end of the meal, Dr. Fell stood and told Vanity to go with him. The rest of us stayed in our places. A moment later, Mrs. Wren led Quentin from the room, and Miss Daw made the slightest possible sigh in her throat, which indicated she was waiting for one of the boys to hold her chair as she rose. Both Colin and Victor scrambled to their feet, and she gravely informed them that harpsichord practice was to be held early this day, and would they be so kind as to accompany her immediately?

I was left alone at the table. Mr. ap Cymru came sauntering back into the room, both hands in his back pockets. He grinned down at me wolfishly. There was a toothpick hanging between his teeth, which wiggled up and down when he grinned.

There was something in his eyes I didn't like. I stared down at my knees, blushing.

"Well, if it isn't Miss Windrose, sitting pretty and all alone here at table."

That comment did not seem to call for a response, so I said nothing.

"Here we are, Miss Windrose. I'll let the devil take me if this fails to cheer you up. I know it made me laugh."

He put out his hand, but I did not reach for what he was offering. He snorted, and dropped a slip of paper on my empty plate. Without a word, he ambled out of the dining room. I do not know where he ate his breakfast. With Mr. Glum, I supposed.

I opened the paper.

The note read: "Report to the Headmaster's office at 9:15 sharp. This note will excuse you from classes or other duties."

4.

Headmaster's office was on the highest floor of the West wing, an area of the manor where we had almost never been. Mr. Sprat had an office filled with dark mahogany, with law books on heavy shelves. Double doors, with red leather tacked to their surfaces, led from Sprat's office to the waiting room.

Mr. Sprat merely nodded at me, and motioned toward the doors. The room beyond was empty of people. Tall wing-backed chairs of red plush faced a long divan of the same material across a coffee table made of a slab of green marble. There were trophy cases on two walls, filled with cups and plaques, and stuffed and mounted fish hanging high near the ceiling. Above the divan was a truly enormous swordfish.

There were two narrow arrow slits between the trophy cases, letting thin slivers of light into the otherwise dark room. Frost coated the glass.

I rubbed at the glass, leaving a white, hand-shaped streak of visibility in the blind surface. Snowflakes were falling onto the gray grass below, the first fall of the season. Silent, white, implacable. The world never looked so lonely.

And there were two clocks, one to either side of the door leading to the inner office. They were half a second out of synch, so that one loud ticking noise seemed to be jumping back and forth between them; first one would tick, then the other would, then the first again, then the second again, in endless monotony. Both clocks were oblong, tall and thin, but were slightly wider in the upper half, before narrowing again at their crowns. I felt afraid of those clocks for a reason I could not name, a fear like none I had known since my days, as a little girl, before Colin made clowns out of the gargoyles in my room.

As my thought of him had summoned him, Colin stepped suddenly out from the inner office. Seeing me, he shut the door quickly behind him, before the Headmaster should know I was there.

He hissed, "Mr. Headmaster, I was going to ask for the tea in a moment, but I wanted to be sure they did not take the cream away again. Tea."

I hissed back, "He knew."

"He guessed. Your deer-frozen-in-the-headlights act convinced him."

"What happened last night?"

"Nothing. Quentin stood on a tombstone with a cape from the theater stores around his neck. He hopped up and down a few times. He said the air was embarrassed, and wouldn't carry on when anyone was watching. What happened to you?"

"Glum's dog talked. It was going to catch us, but led Glum on a wild goose chase instead. The dog wants to be our friend when our star is in the ascendant. Oh, and Vanity can either bend space–time, or create secret passages at will. There's crawl spaces behind the walls, and peepholes to watch us. Dr. Fell said His Highness is coming, and that this was never an orph . . ."

The door swung open behind Colin, and there stood the Headmaster, tall and black in his robes. He had taken his ponytail down. I had never seen him with his hair undone before. It fell to his shoulders in loose red ringlets. He looked like a picture of an ancient king. Or like a lion standing on its hind legs.

There was such a dangerous glint in his eye that I was sure he was going to strike Colin down on the spot. But he merely nodded to the far door, saying to Colin, "That will do."

Colin looked at me, but could ask nothing further. So he shrugged and walked off.

The Headmaster stepped back, making a grand gesture with his arm, so that the drapery of his sleeve filled the doorway for a moment, and then receded, like curtains being drawn before a play. "Miss Windrose, if you please."

His was a massive desk of oak. Behind the desk was a chair whose back reached all the way to the ceiling. The surface of the desk was entirely bare. The desk and the chair stood on a dais, which was covered with red carpet. Before the dais was a small uncomfortable chair of black wood. It sat on a floor of wood, which was harder and no doubt colder than the carpeted dais.

Two framed paintings filled the wall behind him, one to either side of the chair. One showed a green mountain in the midst of the sea, atop which a walled city rose, with towers and colonnades. Above the island rose, even higher, a great wave poised to drown the city.

The other painting showed a mariner tied to the mast of a ship, his face contorted with longing and agony, and, on the rocks past which they rowed, sat beautiful women with harps, their mouths wide with song.

5.

The Headmaster said, "I see you are observing the masterpieces. The one on the left depicts Atlantis. You are familiar with the myth? A virtuous people under the leadership of the sea god Poseidon enacted laws, which they inscribed on a pillar of orichalchum in the center of their great public temple. But when, as time passed, they came to forget these laws, an angry Zeus called destruction down upon their greatness, and sank the island. He had cause to be angered, you see. All other laws are written by mortal legislators, who had only the wisdom of men to guide them; and human laws can be good or bad just as human men are good or bad. But the laws of the gods are the order of nature.

"The painting here on the right shows Odysseus being tormented by the Sirens. Their song is so beautiful, you see, that anyone who hears it is enchanted. Fortunately, he had the wisdom to have his men lash him to the mast, since he knew he would not be able, just by his own effort, to exercise the self-control he would need. No doubt he was terrifically annoyed at those bonds at the time. No doubt he was glad of them later, once he had wits about him enough to see the danger of the Sirens' song. They were cannibals, you see, and ate the flesh from the men they lured onto their reefs.

"Or so the story goes. One must remember that, according to Homer, it was Nausciaa who found the shipwrecked Odysseus on the shores of the magical isle of the Phaeacians. The whole tale we think of as the travels of Odysseus, was nothing more than his report to Nausicaa's father, the king of Phaeacia. Since he was the only survivor of his journey, there was no one to contradict him, was there? He may have learned more from the Sirens' song than he admitted."

He folded his hands on the desk before him, and leaned his back against the carven back of his tall, tall chair.

I was beginning to learn that when grown-ups drone on and on about something, they are driving at a point they don't want to admit they are driving at.

It was with a sense of wonder that I realized that such indirectness might be meant to spare my feelings. In other words, it was a sign of kindness, not cowardice. What cause could the Headmaster have to fear me? His expression was a friendly one.

On the other hand, what in the world could he be trying to protect me from?

As when I didn't know what to answer in class, I decided merely to sit, look attentive, and keep my hands folded in my lap.

Boggin pursed his lips, then said, "You are often annoyed, too, aren't you, Miss Windrose? Like our wandering Odysseus here, eh? You want to see the wide-open spaces of the world, to walk where no white man has trod, to drink from untasted streams of unclimbed mountains. You are chafing at your bonds, like he is." Now he pointed to the skulls and bones that the artist had placed around the feet of the Sirens. "What always puzzled me about the story is that he saw the remains of the other men, but was eager to throw himself on the rock at the feet of the Sirens nonetheless. Do you know why?"

It was a direct question. "No, Headmaster."

"Because he was an optimist. At least, during the moments when the Sirens' song was influencing his reasoning powers. He thought himself equal to the task."

Boggin was silent for a while, watching me. He had more practice at the staring and waiting game than I did. I began to squirm and fidget.

"Very interesting, Headmaster. May I go now?"

"Have you been well treated here, Miss Windrose?"

That was unexpected. "W-what . . . ? I mean . . . Sir . . . ?"

He repeated the question.

"Well, I . . . I do want to leave here."

"Why, and so you shall, once you have reached the age of your majority."

"How old am I, Headmaster?"

"Sixteen."

"That is odd. Because you told me I was sixteen four years ago. By that reckoning, I am at least twenty by now. If I was actually twenty when you said I was sixteen, I am now twenty-four."

"Your recollection must be in error, Miss Windrose." The dismissal was curt.

"But, four years ago, you said—"

"I am sure we have exhausted this topic, Miss Windrose. Let us dwell on the main point. You appear to be unhappy here, and I am at a loss to understand why. Have you been beaten? Starved? Mistreated? No indeed. You have received a first-rate education, food, medicine, clothing—some would say very fine clothing—and have been sheltered in a mansion of singular historic import, and great beauty.

"Why, Sir Francis Drake was said to have obtained his famous looking glass from the master of these lands, after throwing a pin made of gold into the well at Holywell. And Owen Glendower bivouacked in the haunted woods north of Penrice Castle yonder, to make attacks against Edward's mighty fortress at Carreg-Cennen. Earlier myths say that the giant stone slab at Cefn Bryn, upon four upright standing stones (still called Arthur's Table) marks the very spot to which King Arthur removed the head of the giant Bran, after the High King unearthed it from the tower of London.

The Head of Bran preserved the realm from foreign invasion, you see, and Arthur feared the forces from the Otherworld more than he feared those from France. You should deem yourself honored to dwell in such a setting, Miss Windrose. Honored!"

I said, "My room is cold. At night."

"What?"

"It is a fine mansion, Headmaster. The grounds are beautiful. But my room is ice-cold."

To my surprise he frowned, and said, "I'll see to it."

"You mean—?"

"I am sure you are not prone to the accidents, or the antics, which tempted our young Mr. mac FirBolg to abuse the privilege of having a fire in his room. I will see you are supplied with firewood and kindling. Unless you would prefer an electric space heater?"

"May I have both?"

"Why not? We are not your enemies, Miss Windrose, no matter what you may have been led to believe. We are your legal guardians—in loco parentis, so to speak. We shall be very much derelict in our duties if we do not do everything parents would do to see to the health and well-being of their children."

Greatly daring, I said, "If you did not lock us in at night, we could use the water closet on the second floor. Instead of a chamber pot."

"My, we are optimistic, aren't we? Well, why not? If . . ."

"If . . . what . . . ?"

"If you do not abuse the privilege. May I have your word?"

I sat watching him, looking up. He sat watching me, looking down. He looked very satisfied with himself.

I ventured to say, "I don't believe I understand, Headmaster."

"But I believe you do, Miss Windrose. May I have your word?"

"What exactly am I agreeing to, Headmaster?"

He sighed and rolled his eyes and stared at the ceiling. "No doubt you would like to have your legal counsel present before you answer. But that is a prerogative only adults may enjoy."

"Headmaster, I only want to know what I am agreeing to . . ."

"Must you play games with me, Miss Windrose? That, I am afraid, is also a prerogative only adults enjoy, and few of them come off the better for it, I assure you." He drew his eyes back down from the ceiling, and, at that moment, even though the doors and windows here were shut, a very heavy draft fluttered through the room. I shivered in the sudden cold. His loose hair rose up off his shoulders for a moment, swaying and reaching in the wind gust, and his robes rippled. He appeared not one whit disaccommodated by the sudden drop in temperature.

He said, "In sum, you will agree not to do anything to make me regret my decision, Miss Windrose. No running off, no midnight escapades. We have a concern for proper morality here, and do not need to have young girls making visits to young men in the small hours before dawn."

He leaned back, and the wind gust stopped. I could not shake the feeling that the draft had come from his side of the room, despite that the door was behind me. I sat in the chair, hugging myself.

Headmaster Boggin tapped his fingers on the tabletop, looking idly amused. "Well, do we have an agreement?"

I looked up at him. I really, really hated that chamber pot. And the agreement would not go through if Vanity did not agree also. Nevertheless . . .

"Why?" I said.

"Why what, Miss Windrose? The question is very general in its application, and has caused puzzlement among philosophers for years."

"Why is it important to you? Now, I mean. It's the meeting of the Board of Visitors and Governors, isn't it?"

"Very perceptive."

"Well, you did mention it at breakfast . . ."

"Yes, but none of your brothers asked about it. Of course, this upcoming meeting is very important to us. To you, especially. The way we do things here may be changed. The school might close. Or it might stay open. You might be moved to another institution. Or . . ."

"Or what?"

"Or, if the Board of Visitors and Governors become convinced that we have made an error in estimating your age . . . your records were lost, you see . . . you might simply be released. Free. Off to see the world! Wouldn't that be grand? It could happen tomorrow. Or the next day."

He paused to let that sink in.

"But . . ."

Another pause.

He said, "But what do you think, Miss Windrose, would persuade the Board that you are, in fact, an adult and mature woman? Surely you make the strongest case by acting in the most adult fashion possible. The most, if I may say, responsible fashion possible."

I asked, "What is this meeting about? Why is it so important?"

Now he smiled again, folded his arms, and leaned forward with his elbows on his desk, a fairly informal posture I do not think I had seen him take before. "The matter is complex. You may have noticed, over the years, certain tensions here among the staff. I, for example, am employed directly by Saint Dymphna's School and College for Destitute Children. Dr. Fell, who looks after your health, is an employee of the Delphian Trust for Foundling Children. Both he and I, however, are paid out of trust funds, as are the teachers who are employed by the school. Mr. Glum, on the other hand, works directly for the Branshead Estate, and is paid out of the funds of the Talbot family, who owns the land. Mrs. Wren is not, in fact, under my direct authority, but was appointed by Her Majesty's Commission on the Welfare of Unwanted Children. She is, in fact, a crown officer, who also serves as an inspector and compliance overseer for you children."

"Who pays Mr. ap Cymru?"

"Mr. ap Cymru works for the Historical Institute, who lent a rather large sum of money to the Talbot family, in return for certain promises that historical features on the ground would be preserved. In effect, he is here to make sure Mr. Glum does not run over a cromlech with a tractor, or something. He would be something of a free agent were it not for the fact that the Institute also borrowed money from the Foundling Trust, and ceded some authority to them.

"I should tell you, however, that the Foundling Trust recently lost its master. The property was supposed to pass to the heirs of the chief trustee, but the matter is being disputed in court as to which of two sons the new chief trustee should be. Both factions, quite frankly, are courting our favor, for neither wants us to file an amicus curiae brief—that is a type of legal document—saying we prefer one man over the other. The court may take our opinions quite seriously.

"There you have the whole picture, Miss Windrose. Are you an adult, as you claim? Do you see the seriousness of your position, and mine? The new trustee might conclude that you have been living here in the lap of luxury, and should be sent to a state-run home, or even a workhouse. Or, he might conclude that you have been kept here too long, release the funds held in trust for you, and send you with Godspeed to wherever you wish to go. My position is similar. I might be discharged. Or my authority might be expanded. It is odd indeed to be a headmaster of a school that employs nine tutors and has only five students; I would like to see more faces here, myself. You would not believe the trash they learn in state schools these days. They do not even teach Greek and Latin any longer."

I looked at the painting of Odysseus. "They don't read Homer?"

"Students are lucky if they are assigned to read Page Three of the *Royal London Yellow Journal of Gossip and Tripe,* Miss Windrose. Students these days do not know Euclid, nor Lucretius, nor Descartes, nor Shakespeare, nor Milton. They cannot calculate a grocery bill, much less calculate the zodiacal anomaly for Venus in hexadecimals. Do you begin to see how lucky you are, Miss Windrose? How well you are treated at this place you think of as a prison camp?

"The reason why you and I have not had this talk before is that there was no need before. If you wish to help Mr. Triumph in his extracurricular studies, I do not wish to impede you. I am frankly rather proud of him, and of you. Most teachers beg on their knees to the deaf and uncaring heavens for students as bright as you have shown yourselves to be. Can you imagine how pleased they would be to find someone who could understand the Michaelson–Morely experiment, much less reproduce it?

"I am proud of you, Miss Windrose. You are bright and attractive. Maybe even a genius. But I am also deeply ashamed when I hear of certain late-night shenanigans and vandalism. Ashamed, because it becomes clear we have not done our duty in raising you properly. Please do me the favor, Miss Windrose, of allowing me to hear no more such rumors."

He sat there, looking friendly yet stern. I sat, feeling smaller and smaller with each passing moment.

Finally I said, "May I go, Headmaster . . . ?"

"You may go, Miss Windrose."

I rose and was walking out, when his voice stopped me. "Oh, Miss Windrose . . . ? One more thing . . . ?"

I turned. There he sat, between the doomed glory of Atlantis and the torments of Odysseus, his loose red hair piled around his shoulders.

"Yes, Headmaster?"

"Your word, Miss Windrose . . . ?"

"You have it, Headmaster. I promise."

"Then your door shall be unlocked tonight."

I closed the door behind me. In the waiting room again, I stood between the two clocks, ticking slightly out of synch, with their tick-tock now in my left ear, now in my right. I was shaking slightly.

6.

We got the chance to exchange talk after lunch. Colin pretended to throw an epileptic fit, and choke on his soup, and they rushed him off to the infirmary. It was quite natural that we were permitted to visit him, of course, since we all became so distraught that we could not attend our Home Economics lessons. Mrs. Wren let the four of us out early.

We had tried the same thing a period earlier, with Miss Daw, but she had simply smiled a cool, dreamy smile, as if she were listening to distant music, and continued with her fingering instructions.

"That's great!" said Colin, when he heard what the Headmaster had said to me. "The door's unlocked! You can get out any time!"

He lay in the hospital bed, his hands folded behind his head, looking pleased as punch.

"What did he say to you boys?" asked Vanity. Vanity was irked, because she had not been called in to see Headmaster Boggin.

Quentin said, "Substantially the same thing. We should behave while the Board meeting is in progress. He didn't tell us the details, though." He looked at me sidelong, as if thinking that I was, after all, two or three years older than he was, and was privy to information denied him.

Victor said, "We should not attempt our final escape until we discover more about who this guest of the Board is. This is our first hint that there is a power even the Headmaster fears. If we can enlist such a power to our aid, then we stand a chance of getting away from here. Otherwise, I do not see how we can get far enough away, fast enough. Even if we stole a boat from the village, Headmaster could have the police run us down."

Colin said, "What about merely heading into the forest? It gets deeper and darker the further in you go."

"The maps show the wood are only two miles wide," said Quentin softly. "If you pass through them, you come to Oxwich Green."

"Maps of England," said Colin, "On Earth. The real forest goes on for a trillion miles, and then leads to a forest darker than it is."

Quentin said in mild voice, "I am not claiming this is Earth. But maps are powerful symbols, and may be influencing us in a subtle fashion. We should destroy or deface the maps here, to loosen their grip on us, and draw maps of our own portraying the true world beyond these walls."

I said, "You know, maybe we should listen to the Headmaster. I mean, what you guys are saying does sound a little, well, crazy, doesn't it? He said that the Board might just release us. And he said there were funds waiting for us. Some sort of trust fund held for us when we reach eighteen. I mean, can't we try to give him a chance? The Headmaster?"

Victor looked puzzled, as if I had gotten the wrong answer on a math sum. Quentin looked pensive and slightly sad. Colin laughed at me, and stuck his hands under his own shirt, pushing them out as if he had breasts. "Let's give the Headmaster a chance!" he said in a high falsetto, batting his eyelashes. "Oh, let's listen to him! I want a good grade on my toad-eating class next week!"

Vanity yanked the pillow out from under Colin's head so that his head fell back sharply onto the wooden bed frame, and smote him in the face with it, before he could get his hands clear of his shirt to defend himself.

She said, "Did you ask the Headmaster about the talking dog? Or Dr. Fell saying he wanted to cut us up for experiments? About me being a princess, and you being from before the fall of Adam?"

Victor and Quentin stared. "What talking dog?" came Colin's muffled voice from under the pillow.

Fortunately, we had enough time to fill them in on the details before the nurse, Sister Twitchett, came back in.

By the time we were done reciting the tales of our discoveries, my pleas to give the Headmaster a chance began to seem to be the crazy talk, not Quentin's soft-voiced observation that the room we were in might have a peephole in it, and could we have Vanity look for the secret door?

TO WALK WITH OWLS

1.

That night Vanity climbed into bed with me, despite that we now had a roaring fire blazing in the hearth. After the lights were doused, all the shadows in the room pointed toward the fireplace, swaying and hopping to the music of the merry crackle of wood.

Mrs. Wren had actually been more watchful than normal, and stared at Vanity while she swallowed her medicine. While Mrs. Wren was looking at Vanity, I put a few drops of the liquid on my lip, and threw the rest of the cup into the fire. When she turned to me at the noise, I only licked my lips and smiled. This puzzled her. Mrs. Wren could hardly be angry for me being too eager to drink my medication, since she apparently did not want to admit she was suppose to watch us quaff it.

After she left, I tried to get Vanity to upchuck into the chamber pot, by putting her finger down her throat, but she was too squeamish to make a sincere attempt.

Now, laying next to me, she whispered in my ear: "If there are peepholes in the rooms, they have been watching us this whole time. Our whole lives."

I did not bother to tell her my theory that she had created the secret passages, peepholes and all, out of her own thought, and that reality had shifted to accommodate her imagination. The word "reality," by definition, referred to those things we cannot change by mere wishes. I had always thought the physical world was included in that set. Now, I wasn't sure.

I said, "They all believed you. About the talking dog. Victor's questions about whether we saw the dog talk was just, you know, for the peepholes. Why do you think we were left alone in the infirmary for so long? They all had to pretend not to believe us. Except that it took Colin forever to catch on. What an idiot."

"Do you think they were watching?"

"Boggin knows about our codes. He knows about the time Victor and I snuck out to measure the moon years ago. I think he knows everything."

"But you still want to trust him, don't you?"

"I don't think he'd let Dr. Fell kill us, if that's what you mean. I mean, if he were going to, why didn't he do it when we were six or eight? Why wait till now?"

Vanity replied, "Well, if I knew the answers to that, maybe I'd trust Headmaster Boggin also. Because then he would not be keeping the answers from us."

We heard noises from outside: the sound of an automobile engine, the noise of tires crunching the gravel on the carriage circle before the East Wing. Vanity and I hopped out of bed, went over to our North-facing window, and raised the sash.

The warmth of our nicely firelit room rushed away; the icy wind was shockingly cold against our faces. We heard motors, doors slamming, voices raised in welcome. From the reflection of the light against the trees in the distance, we could tell the East wing windows were lit up. Faintly, over the snow, came music. Miss Daw was playing her violin, a haunting melody of a few simple notes, some Highland air I did not recognize. Nothing was visible from our side of the building.

Vanity said, "It's the bigwigs."

The Visitors and Governors. Plus whoever or whatever Dr. Fell had referred to as "the Pretender," who might be the same person as Headmaster Boggin's Trustee.

The noise of car engines receded, as the vehicles were driven in the direction of the horse stables. Vanity said, "Chauffeurs. They are parking the cars away from the house."

The sound diminished. We heard the dull boom of the main doors being pulled to.

Vanity and I both turned and looked at the heavy oak door, bound with its enormous iron hinges, unlocked for the first time in our lives.

I said, "I promised not to."

Vanity looked at the door and bit her lip. "But I didn't."

And she scampered over to the door.

I raised my hand, but then I couldn't think of anything to say. Had the Headmaster actually not talked to her because he was not proud of her, as he was of me? I closed the window and moved over to stand in front of our new, warm, lovely fire.

She put her hand on the door, frowned, put her cheek to the door, her wide green eyes turned toward it.

Vanity jumped back. She put her finger to her lips, as if to hush me, but then said in a loud stage whisper: "He's watching the door."

"Who?"

"Boggin! Headmaster Boggin! He's just waiting out there. Waiting for you to open the door. What a sneak!"

"How can you tell?"

"What do you mean, how can I tell? When I touch the door, I get that feeling I am being watched."

I walked over to the door and put my hand on it. "Feels like wood, to me."

She rolled her eyes in an animated fashion. "Oh, come on Amelia! You've had that feeling!"

"What feeling?"

"That feeling of being watched when no one is there. Everyone has it. It's in all the novels! Are you the only person on Earth who doesn't?"

"I might be. But how do you know your feeling isn't just, you know, a feeling? Your imagination?"

"Well, I found the peepholes, didn't I?"

"Actually, Vanity, you found the secret passage. But we did not actually see and find peepholes when we were in there. It was dark, and holes leading to lit rooms would have sent a beam of light . . ."

But Vanity was already hopping across the room to where the seven-foot-long candlesnuffer was kept. "Thanks for reminding me."

And she took up the candlesnuffer and tugged in the mouth of the gargoyle mask on the wall eleven feet above.

Nothing happened. No secret door opened.

"It must be on a timer," Vanity pouted, putting down the pole and seating herself on her bed.

"I think you are doing it. It is some sort of unexplained phenomenon. But you cause it. Dr. Fell's medicine must be inhibiting the effects."

Vanity giggled, threw her arms overhead, and fell back with a soft sound onto her mattress. "Oh, I am doing it, eh?"

"Your thoughts trigger it."

She giggled up at the ceiling. "Let me see if I have this straight. I think, *Gee, there is a secret door.* A special Russian-made satellite picks up my brain waves with its mind-reading radar, and beams a message back down to a waiting pack of dwarfs. Working with oh, just incredible silence and precision, the dwarfs dig a tunnel into the house, move walls and bore through solid stone, insert doors, clock panels, hinges, and floorboards. Then they spread dust and have their Soviet-trained cadre of speed-spiders weave cobwebs across the crawl space. That's your theory?"

"Actually, I had hoped it used a more elegant mechanism, but, yes, basically, that's the theory."

Vanity yawned a huge yawn. "All that exercise last night . . . you know, it's really nice having a warm fire here in the room . . ."

2.

For purposes of storytelling, it would have been appropriate to have Vanity nod off right at that point, but she actually got up, changed into her night things, and we talked a little more before she drifted off to sleep.

It did seem sudden, though. There I was, alone in my own bed, watching the red firelight dance and jump across the walls, while Vanity breathed softly in the other bed.

But the Headmaster was right. I lived in very comfortable circumstances.

3.

I was awakened by a tap-tapping. The embers had died in the hearth, and a cold wind was whistling in the open flue. I turned to the North window, where our star dial was, to see what time it was, and I saw the silhouette of a hunched figure pressed against the glass.

I screamed, sitting bolt upright and clutching the sheets around my throat. The hunched shape behind the glass hissed softly, "Not so loud . . ."

I squinted. "Quentin . . . ? Is that you . . . ?"

"Open the window, please. It is really quite cold out here."

I slid out of bed, and was rewarded with the sensation of ice-cold floor stones stinging my feet. I hopped over, undid the latch, and slid the sash up.

"Well?" I said.

Quentin was hunched over on the rather large stone sill on the outside of the North window. One hand was clutching the marble grain bundles that flanked the window; in the other he had his jackal-headed walking stick. He was wearing a rather voluminous high-collared cape with a half-cloak. Beneath that he had on a T-shirt, and a pair of swim trunks. His legs were bare. No muffler, no coat, no gloves. No socks. He was wearing running shoes. He was shivering.

"Please invite me in," he said, teeth chattering.

"W-what?"

"Please, for the love of God, invite me in. It's freezing."

"Sure," I said, stepping back. "Come in."

He slid in over the sill in a slither of huge black cloak. It was made for someone more my height than his; the hem was dirty where it trailed on the floor. The silk inner lining made a sinister hiss as it slid over the stones. Quentin crossed to the fireplace and poked at the coals with his walking stick, while I wrestled the window shut.

A reddish light leapt into the room. Quentin had stirred the coals to momentary life again. He put his stick aside in the fire iron stand and was rubbing his hands together. He crouched down.

In the red light, I could see Vanity, her lips parted, her expression soft and innocent, still asleep.

"Well," I said stiffly, hugging myself in my nightgown. "Some people can sleep through anything."

"Unless the medication had sleeping powder in it, tonight," said Quentin. "Victor and Colin are out like bricks; Dr. Fell watched them take the draught."

"And you?"

He looked up from his crouched position. The light was behind him, and all I could see was his eyes glinted in his silhouette. "I always keep an empty cup from Dr. Fell's cabinet up my sleeve. I palmed his cup and put mine to my lips. Dr. Fell is very intelligent, but he makes Victor-like assumptions."

I put my hands on my hips. "Just what do you mean by 'Victor-like,' Mister Quentin Nemo?"

Quentin said nothing, but continued to look at me. I became very conscious of the fact that I was standing there in my nightgown. To be sure, it was a winter nightgown—all white cotton with a lace collar and shoulders, and the frilly hem fell past my knees—but it was still a nightgown. And I had the impression that Quentin was staring at my ankles and feet. Somehow my feet weren't simply bare; they were nude.

I stepped back over to my bed, picked up the coverlet, and hesitated. Somehow, climbing back into bed with a man in my room would be worse. He would be there, seeing my nice bed, still warm from my body, the sheets still rumbled with the imprint of where I had been laying . . . and my hair spread across the pillow . . .

I was being ridiculous. This wasn't a man. This was Quentin. He was three or four years younger than me. And short. He was just a child. He probably did not even know which sex I was yet.

I turned back to him. "Are you a vampire, all of a sudden?"

"I called on God without choking. No, that was just in case Mrs. Wren's ward would interfere."

"Interfere with what?"

Quentin had a quiet, solemn voice. "I am performing a demonstration."

"How did you get up to the window?"

He just shook his head.

I said, "You climbed, right? Why didn't you dress more warmly?"

"I needed lightweight things. I hope you trust me, Amelia, after all these years. None of us has any other family."

Something in the way he said that brought a tear to my eye. I raised my hand and wiped my cheeks. I said, "I trust you."

"I need your help. There is a weight too heavy for one person to lift. I am not sure what your Talent is, but I know it has to do with weight."

"Mass," I said.

"Will you come with me?" he stood up. "The Visitors and Governors are determining our fate, and one of us must be, simply must be, in a position to overhear the meeting."

I shook my head. "I promised the Headmaster."

"Ah . . ." he sank back down again and crouched before the dying embers.

I said, "You're not going to try to change my mind?"

"Had I that power, I would have used it on you long ago, Amelia." He stirred the ashes with his walking stick, and red flames jumped up for a moment. "Do you remember when I wrecked my bike?"

"The same summer you almost drowned."

"I also fell from a tree that June."

"You actually did fall from a tree? I thought you were just saying that. I thought Colin beat you up."

He stirred the coals. "Colin does not beat me up. You all think I am a coward, when all I am is polite."

He was silent for a moment, but he turned his head and looked at me in my nightgown. His gaze traveled up and down.

I said, "What about the tree fall? Yes, I remember that summer."

"You were upset because I had a finer bike, a boy's bike, even though you were older. You held my head in the sink until I agreed to let you ride it. Do you remember?"

"I am sorry about that, Quentin, but you make me so mad sometimes . . ."

He raised his hand slowly. "Do not apologize. Never apologize. You don't know what you are giving away. The fact is, I did not keep my promise, did I?"

"Well, the bike wrecked. Was there a point to this story?"

"Broken oaths are bad luck eggs."

That was so weird, I did not know what to say. So I said, "Eggs?"

"They hatch bad luck." He stood up, closed his eyes, and held his walking stick out at arm's length. After a moment or two, as his arm got tired, the stick wobbled.

He opened his eyes, paused for a moment, went over to the door, put his hand against it. He put his hand on the latch . . .

"Stop!" I said.

He looked at me, curious.

"Vanity thought the door was being watched. We should trust her hunches."

He nodded. "By your promise, you granted him the authority to be aware of the door. He substituted a physical lock for a lock of a stronger type." He took his hand away from the door and stepped over toward my bed.

He sat down on the bed with his walking stick held between his hands, his elbows on his knees, his gaze on his feet.

I raised a hand and played with the little ribbon at my throat. Imagine that! Quentin just sitting on my bed, as if I had invited him! I wondered what he planned next.

He looked up at me. "Amelia, I cannot ask you for this. You must volunteer."

"For what?"

"Bad luck."

"Oh, come on. There is no such thing as bad luck."

"Then you will not mind a bit, will you, Amelia?" He tilted his head to one side. "What was the wording of the oath?"

"I said he would not regret his decision. That I would not do anything which would make him regret his decision."

"Interesting. If he does not find out, he won't regret, will he?"

I shook my head. "I don't think it works that way. I mean, it wasn't legalistic, like a contract in writing or anything."

"Words have their own meanings, despite whatever we would like to impose on them. They are older than us, maybe older than everything else."

"What are you saying?"

"The world was created with a word. The first thing Adam did was name the beasts."

"You're babbling again, Quentin."

"Sorry. Do you have a coat? I assume you are not going to change clothes in front of me."

"I am not putting on a coat."

"Did you promise the Headmaster not to put on a coat?" He looked up at me. His eyes were sad and thoughtful, as they usually were, but there was also a look of certainty in his gaze, of amused confidence, that reminded me of Colin. Or of Headmaster Boggin.

Making an exasperated noise, I turned toward the wardrobe, pulled out a bundle of clothing, and threw it on the bed next to him. Then I picked up a pillowcase and slid the pillow out.

I thrust the pillowcase at him.

He raised his eyebrows. "You expect me to put that over my head?"

"No, you're right! If you're smart enough to fool Dr. Fell, I shouldn't trust you." And I stuck the pillowcase over his head.

He made a muffled laugh.

"What's so funny?" I demanded. I wondered whether the pillowcase was opaque, and so I merely stepped into my jeans, and tucked the hem of my nightgown into in a huge, awkward bundle. I put a sweater over that, shrugged into my nylon quilted jacket.

"There is a symmetry to all affairs," he said.

"What's that supposed to mean?" I yanked the pillowcase off his head.

He stood up. "You'll find out."

I pointed at the pile of clothing. "You can find something for yourself."

He looked arch. "I am not putting on girls' clothes."

"Look. A sweatshirt. Big, roomy, comfy. Warm. Sweatpants. You close them with a drawstring. Keep your leg hairs from freezing."

He said, "It is not that cold out-of-doors. I mean, rather, it is cold when you go out, but you will get numb to it, so it won't feel cold."

"That's OK, because I am not walking out that door." I said.

"Neither am I."

"I am not climbing down from the window, either. You are lucky you didn't break you neck."

"Neither am I." Now he was smiling.

"What is so funny?"

"Will you come if I can find another way out, besides the two ways you just said? Not climbing, not walking."

"Are you saying you can find Vanity's secret passage?"

"Is it a deal? I put on your clothes, you follow me?"

"What do I have to lose? Sure."

He slipped on one of my ratty old sweatshirts and a pair of bulky sweatpants. Like I said, he is shorter than me, and the pants fit him just fine.

He slung his huge cloak over his shoulders with a rustle. "Do you have a silk scarf anywhere in your clothing?"

I opened a drawer, took out a long white scarf, and handed it over.

He said, "Turn around."

I turned my back to him.

He wound the scarf once and twice over my eyes and around my head, tying it in the back with a big loose knot.

"I can still see down my nose," I said. There was a little crack of light between my cheek and the bottom of the scarf.

"I am not going to throw a pillowcase over your head," he said.

"Use my goggles," I said. I waved a hand in the direction I thought was the upper shelf of the wardrobe.

I heard a rustling, and, a moment later, felt him put my lucky aviatrix cap over my head, scarf and all, and put the goggles over my eyes. He adjusted the strap in back. The padding around the lenses was tight against my eyesockets, and held the scarf in place. It was opaque.

"Now what?" I said.

He put one arm around my waist, the other under my knees, and swept me off my feet.

"Careful!" I said. "You are going to hurt your back!"

He said, annoyed, "I am not weak, Amelia. Just short."

I put my arms around his shoulders. There really was no other place for me to put my hands. He hoisted my knees up, and my hip was resting slightly above his crotch. My bottom was just hanging in midair, surrounded by uncomfortable folds of nightgown stuffed into a jeans waistband. His arms did seem to be plenty strong.

"Now what?" I said.

"Now you trust me, and stay quiet. They are very shy, and they disappear if you look at them."

He grunted, hoisted me higher, so that my hip was level with his chest, and he took a step up. Then he straightened.

For a moment I could not think of what he was standing on. What was in the room that was a foot or so high, and would support our weight? I assumed it was the hope chest I keep at the foot of my bed.

Another step. I supposed we were on the bed, but why hadn't the sheets rustled when he stepped on them? Also, had he stepped onto a soft surface, I would have expected him to sink.

A third step. Where was he? Standing on the headboard?

A fourth. Maybe I had been wrong about where we started. Could he be climbing from one shelf to another in the wardrobe? Only if the wardrobe were tilted back at an angle would he have room.

I heard the window slide up. Both his hands were still on me. I felt the ice-cold air flow over me, freezing. How had he opened the window?

I said, "Quentin. You're not going to jump! Put me . . ."

He kissed me.

Warm, passionate, firm. No apology, no hesitation. Just his lips on mine.

I waited till he was done, and then I slapped him.

He said, "Whoa!" and his grip tightened on my shoulders and knees.

We were standing on the ledge of the window, I knew. I raised my hands to pull off the goggles, but he sort of pushed my shoulders and knees together, crunching me into a ball, while at the same time he put his cheek against my cheek, to prevent me from getting at the blindfold.

I made my fingers into claws and pulled on his hair, trying to get his face out of my face.

He wobbled.

I held still. He was balanced on a ledge, after all.

He said, "Could you let go of my hair, Amelia?"

I said, "I was saving that kiss. That was my first kiss. Now you've ruined it."

He said, "Could you . . . please . . . let go of my hair, Amelia?"

I said, "I am taking at least half of your scalp with me, you little twerp."

He said, "It is really quite painful."

I said, "I hope I am drawing blood."

He wobbled again. "Don't say such things. It is just as bad for us if they start giggling."

"Put me down."

"Let go of my hair, and I will put you down."

"Put me down, and I will think about letting go of your hair."

He lowered his left hand, releasing my knees. I felt a surface underneath my boot toes. Then I remembered how narrow the ledge was on which we were standing. With a little yelp, I put my boots right up against his shoes, and grabbed him around the shoulders, pulling myself close to him.

His arms came up under my arms, as if he were a man about to embrace his lover. I was too afraid to push him away, for fear that we would both fall three stories to our doom.

But he was not hugging me. He gently tugged the buckle holding the goggles. They slid loosely around my neck. He pushed back my cap, so it hung by its chin-strap. He plucked at the knot holding the scarf.

I blinked in the sudden moonlight.

4.

We were on a rooftop. We were standing on a scaffolding. Underfoot was a sea of tiles. To our left and right, dormer windows peered West toward the main Manor House. Before us and above us rose the dome of the Great Hall. Little round windows, piercing the base of the dome, were ablaze with light. There was a noise of voices issuing up from below us. There was a metal door, built on an acute slope like the door to a cellar, abutting the dome.

I looked left and right in wonder. Then I realized I was still hugging Quentin, staring at the scene over the top of his brown hair.

I stepped back, and slapped him again. This time, I could put my shoulder into it, and it was a solid blow.

He staggered, winced, and rubbed his jaw. He said, "If you had said 'put me down,' they would have dropped us. That's why I kissed you. You didn't need to slap me twice."

I said, "The second time was for a different reason. My first flight through the air! My first time flying, and I missed it!"

He rubbed his jaw and said nothing.

I said, "I was expecting a sensation of motion."

"The air moves with us. There's no wind." He bent down, and picked up his walking stick, which just happened to be lying at his feet.

"So you really are a magician."

He snorted. "Don't be an ass, Amelia. There is no such thing as magic. This is the One True Science."

"How did you do that, if it wasn't magic?" I said pointing at his jackal-headed cane. "Did it follow you on its own? And what did you step up on to get to the window? How did you open the window with no hands?"

He just shook his head. "Jaw numb. Can't talk." He pointed with the walking stick at the metal service entrance.

"That is what you want me to lift?"

"Its not locked, just heavy."

I strode up the tilted surface of the tile, with Quentin coming after me, his too-long cape sliding on the tiles. I put my hands on the door, tugged.

"You're right," I said. "It is massive."

"Let me get on the other side."

"Just stand back."

5.

I closed my eyes for a second, trying to picture the door in my mind's eye. It was both an object in space and an event in time. This door had a beginning, a middle, and an end. Because time and space were actually one thing, one substance, this thing before me was not merely an object, it was an object–event.

Weight was not a property of that object-event. Weight was an action, a behavior, if you will. Earth was distorting the local space–time continuum in such as fashion that this object–event selected toward-earth paths, rather than away-from-earth. As they moved forward through time, those paths seemed to manifest themselves as the energy-conserving behavior known as toward-earth acceleration, what Quentin incorrectly called weight.

If space–time were folded in any other way, the toward-earth behavior could be deflected into other energy channels.

I opened my eyes, stooped, put my shoulder to the door, and lifted it aside easily. I set it down without making a sound.

The two of us stood, looking down into a circular staircase. Gloomy steps wound around and around. There was a light at the bottom.

THE BOARD OF VISITORS AND GOVERNORS

1.

He said, "I should tell you that I suspect a trap, Amelia."

"Why? Did the Headmaster expect you to know how to fly?"

"If you told me the correct wording of your oath . . ."

"I did."

". . . Doesn't it strike you as particularly lax? And he unlocks the door on the one night he knows we are all dying to find out what is going on here. Vanity says the door is watched. And the meeting is being held at midnight. Why not at nine o'clock, when we are all in class, being watched?"

"You said Fell put sleeping powder in the medicine."

"Not part of Headmaster's plan, I assume. They don't necessarily all talk to each other, or agree when they do." Quentin's voice was solemn and quiet. "If I had been forced to say the prayers you and Vanity were told to say by Mrs. Wren, half of my demonstrations would be impossible to me. I cannot imagine they want me to learn the things I learned, or talk to the type of things I am trained to hear. So why didn't they sic Mrs. Wren on me? It must simply be an oversight."

"Are we talking about the same Mrs. Wren?" Of all the adults on the estate, she seemed the simplest to me, the easiest to get around when we wanted something.

He looked away over the moonlit snow below, at the insubstantial black shadows of the manor and outbuildings. "Her sorrow gives her strength. Frightening strength. Those who dwell in the middle air below the Moon weep when she weeps, as do their humbler vassals in the stream and field and arbors. Do not be deceived that she is kindly toward you and Vanity; it is because she has no cause to fear."

He looked down at his walking stick, frowned, and raised it to his face. He stuck the muzzle of the little brass jackal-head in his ear.

He nodded, said thank-you to the walking stick, and said to me, "One comes."

2.

I jumped down three steps and crouched, draping my body along the stairs, with just my nose sticking over the doorjamb. Because the tiles were slanted, I could see the snowy lawn below.

I yanked on Quentin's pants leg. "How about getting down? So we're not seen?"

He lay down beside me.

I squinted. There. Quentin had been right. Again.

A tall man was coming from the direction of the Barrows. At first, we could see only his outline: an upright, athletic figure with a staff or pole in his hand, and long wings of flapping fabric around his ankles, as if he wore a cloak or long coat. There was a round bundle over his shoulder.

He stepped into one of the angles of light a window cast across the snow.

There were black scars crisscrossing his right hand. Old wounds. The pole in his hand was a short spear, three feet of metal spike and three feet of wood, with a heavy weight mounted at the butt end. A javelin, really. The round thing over his shoulder was flat, not a bundle. It was a Roman shield with an iron boss in the center, eight-sided, with images of lightning bolts etched in gold radiating out from the boss.

The coat was long. I thought it might be the skin of coral snakes, for it was pebbly and as red-brown as dried blood. It was lined on the inside with fur of light pink. The elbow-length sleeves were long and loose, and allowed full motion to the man's arms. A fur hood formed a triangle between his shoulder and head.

At first, I thought his hair was metal. He wore a coif of coppery scales over his skull; more scales covered his neck. He wore a jacket of red coppery scales beneath his ruddy cloak. Below he wore a leather skirt studded with metal bosses. His boots of shark leather rose to his knee.

A wide web-belt cinched his waist. A Japanese katana, bright with a swinging tassel, rode one hip. At the other, a leather holster held a heavy pistol.

There was something in the way he walked—stiff, yet relaxed, calm, yet somehow tense—that told of miles upon miles of marching to the music of the drum and fife.

He passed in front of a lamppost that stood in the carriage circle before the East wing of the Manor House. The light made a slight rainbow effect as it slid around his body.

I said, "He is distorting the local time–space metric. Light is bending toward him as it would toward a black sun. He must be affecting the probability world-lines intersecting this moment in time."

I looked over. Quentin was not looking at the man. He lay with his face not six inches from mine, staring thoughtfully at my lips. He had been studying my profile.

Quentin raised his eyes to mine, "You can tell at a glance?"

I said impatiently, "No. It is obvious, though. His gravity is normal, otherwise he would sink to the Earth's core with every step. What else could disturb time–space, if not gravity? If it is not a space warp, then it is a time warp. He is not moving fast or slow. So it must be a distortion of world-lines. Q.E.D."

I felt heat in my cheeks. I was blushing. Blushing! Because little Quentin, of all people, had been staring at me. At the lips he had kissed, and claimed for his own.

I said, "The Red Soldier isn't human, no matter who he is."

He said, "I know. Apsu can't see normal people."

3.

The soldier passed below the level of our vision. There came a noise of a door opening. A triangle of light spilled out across the snow, magnifying the shadow of the soldier. There was a mutter of voices. One sounded calm, measured, certain. The voice of a man in control of whatever situation he entered. The other was the voice of Mr. Sprat, who sounded nervous, uncertain. Maybe even frightened.

From the tones of voice, the words half-heard, it sounded as if the Red Soldier wanted to enter, and Mr. Sprat was reluctant to let him in.

Footsteps. A second shadow spilled out across the snow. This one wore a mortarboard and long robes. His voice was louder, and we caught the words. Headmaster Boggin asked, "Protector, we were not expecting Your Lordship in person. Where is Your Lordship's entourage?"

We did not hear the words, but the calm voice made some brief, sardonic answer.

Boggin laughed politely. "I suppose that is true, Your Lordship. Who would be qualified to bodyguard you?"

The calm voice again. A question.

"Why, yes, Your Lordship. She is here. Her Ladyship came with her . . . ah . . . with her husband's retainers, of course. Will you come in? I will have to ask you to leave your weapons at the door. Emissaries are supposed to be unarmed."

The Red Soldier must have turned his head, for this time, we heard his answer plainly. "I am never unarmed."

The shadows on the snow moved; the soldier pushed his way past Headmaster Boggin, the javelin still in his hand. We could hear the metallic thud of the butt of the javelin on the floorboards.

Mr. Sprat's shadow slid close to Headmaster Boggin's. A fearful whisper. A friendly sounding answer from Boggin. Again, Boggin's voice carried. "It is not as if we have any choice, Jack, now, is it? We're at their mercy."

The door swung to. The angle of light narrowed and disappeared.

4.

We had a whispered consultation about whether to close the big metal door or not. On the one hand, it would let in cold air and outside noise that someone might notice. On the other, we wanted an unblocked escape. The workmen had been pulling up and putting down tile these last few days, and their scaffold still reached from roof to ground, like a fire tower.

"We are going to have to be quiet going down," he said.

"Well, obviously, Quentin! I'll tell you when it's safe to talk. I am your senior, you know."

"Then enlighten me. What does the thing you said mean? About world-lines?"

"Is this the time for a physics lesson?"

"Indulge me, please, Amelia."

"OK. This is a summary. Imagine every object as a worm, or an umbrella, drawing a line through time. The one line toward the direction of lesser-entropy we call 'past,' and its position is determined within the limits of quantum uncertainty. The multiple lines toward the direction of greater-entropy, we call 'future,' and their locations, to simultaneous observers, occupy the set of all possible locations to which the object could move in a given time. Put two gravitating bodies near each other and their sets of possible motion lines bend toward each other. The line defined by the least energy expended is inert motion, or free fall. This free-fall line, which would otherwise be straight, is distorted by a gravitating body so that it curves in a conic section. Got it?"

"So what did you see around him? His Lordship?"

"Something other than gravity was distorting the world-lines passing near him, including the event-paths of things like photons. An aura of probability distortion."

"He has a charmed life."

"Um. I don't think that is what I said."

"You were seeing destiny. He has a charmed life."

"You are confusing an effect of physics with your . . ."

"Let's go, Amelia. We can debate definitions later."

And he started down the stairs.

I crept after him, tight-lipped with anger.

Since when did *he* get the right to be giving orders to *me*? A boy steals a kiss and he thinks you're his harem slave.

It was time to dunk his head in the sink again. Wash a few dumb notions out of that haunted house he calls his brain. I was strong enough to lift a door he could not budge, wasn't I? He was not so old that I could not push his head under water for a while.

The stair ended at a half-open door. Beyond the door was a small alcove, half-hidden behind Mrs. Wren's potted plants. The alcove looked out on the balcony which entirely encircled the Great Hall below.

It was perfect for spying. We crawled on our bellies across the carpet of the balcony, and peered through the heavy marble railings. There were no lights on at this floor. The gigantic chandelier that normally hung near the dome had been lowered on its massive chain so that it was partly lowered through the hole the balcony surrounded. The great chandelier was slightly below us, putting the lights between ourselves and the people below. Even if they should look up (and who ever looks up?) the light would dazzle them, and the shadows would hide us.

And yet the whole scene was less than twenty feet below us. Had we wanted to, we could have spit upon the people seated there.

The massive green marble table occupied the center of the hall. Half of the circumference had no one seated there. The chairs were empty. The other half had people standing behind their chairs, but no one was seated.

No one except for the Lady. She was beautiful beyond all beauty, somehow both innocent and sweet, yet filled with voluptuous sensuality. She was dressed in a simple robe of white, with slim jeweled sashes crossed between her breasts, and circling her trim waist. Her neck was like a swan's. Her hair was piled atop her head to show off the line of her neck.

She was a brunette, with tremor of gold running through the strands. She had meltingly soft brown eyes. She did not wear any makeup, and yet her lips were red, her cheeks touched with blush.

It was only when looking at her that I realized (finally realized after Gabriel-knows how many years) what makeup was for. The sparkling eyes eyeliner tries to impersonate; the blood-red lips lipstick mimics; the cheeks flushed red; are what one sees on a girl when she is flushed with love. If someone had told me this Lady had stepped not five minutes ago from her lover's arms, I would not have doubted it.

The Lady was toying with a hand mirror she held in her hand; holding it to one ear, then the other, turning her eyes sideways, as if she were trying to glimpse her own profile. She laughed her crystal laughter at herself; she prodded her hair with a slim white finger, teasing curls down before her eyes, which she went cross-eyed to stare at. Then she smiled again to see herself cross-eyed. She tossed her head when she laughed, like a girl half my age. It was as if she were in love with life itself, and every moment in it, and she could not restrain her joy.

Behind her were three women, who, if I had seen them on the covers of fashion magazines, would have called them beautiful. Next to the laughing one, however, they only seemed fair.

They were also dressed in simple white robes of a classical design. One of them held a sceptre on a pillow. One held a recurved bow of pale wood set with pink carbuncles, and a quiver of arrows fletched with red feathers.

One had a jess and a leather guard on her wrist, like a falconer, but instead of a falcon, she held a white dove on her wrist.

Quentin pulled back. He turned himself on his back and put his elbow over his eyes.

I looked at him, puzzled. It was not until I looked at him that I realized something. I had been staring at the laughing beauty so earnestly, that I had not seen anyone else at the table, had not heard what they said.

I can tell in sort of an intellectual way if another woman is attractive or not. Sometimes. Sometimes, I am really surprised at which girls Colin, for example, would moon over, or which American movie starlets he would gather photos of, or write love letters to. But even I could tell this lady, this divinity, had a face to drive men mad. Quentin was covering his eyes to save his sanity.

My gaze was drawn back to her.

I had never seen an adult so unselfconscious in public. I have seen the Queen Mother and the Prince of Wales on television news, the Duchess of York, the King of Denmark, and the Prince of Monaco. They were royalty. They acted with gravity and polished politeness. This? This was something beyond royalty. A farmgirl in a barnyard could play this way, if she were surrounded by dumb animals, piglets and kittens and lambs. Because the farmgirl is still a higher order of being than even the noblest animal, and she can feel no shame in front of them, no more than a high cloud, or a distant star, can feel shame in front of a human.

I wished I could see if she would have that same rainbow effect the Red Soldier had. Unfortunately, there was nothing beyond her, from my point of view, aside from the chair she sat on, the floor. No light sources. Not even a reflection.

But I moved a little to one side, so that the marble banister blocked my view of her. That was the only way I could concentrate on the others gathered here.

The moment I saw them, I wondered how I could have not been staring at them. This was an odd group. A very odd group.

5.

Two foxes in Japanese kimonos stood behind their chairs to the Lady's far left. They stood on their hind legs, like men. One of them was smoking a cigarette in a holder.

A man with no head was next. He was dressed in eighteenth-century garb: a great coat with a high collar, bloodstained lace surrounding his neck stump, two dueling pistols tucked through his belt. He had a long-necked guitar slung on a wide bandoleer over his left shoulder. On a silver plate, on the table before where he stood, rested his head. I assume it was his.

A bearded head it was, with long black locks. The eyes were open and looking back and forth. Every now and again the headless body would raise a hand and absentmindedly run fingers through the hair of the head, the way a man with a dog at his heel might pet it from time to time.

Next to him was a Satyr, with ivy wound around his goat horns. He had narrow features and lines around his mouth. He was shifting from hoof to hoof, and picking his teeth with a toothpick.

Two nude women were next, naked except for the grape leaves they had wound in their hair. They stood with their arms around each other's waists, and occasionally whispered comments in each other's ears.

Next was a man made entirely of metal. This golem was ten or twelve feet tall. The metal was silvery and black, and chased through with designs, images, and arabesques of the most cunning workmanship. The elbow joints were fretted like fish fins; the vambraces had pastoral scenes running up them. The helm was furrowed with whippet hounds; the crest was a lunging stag, every vein in its straining throat visible. Leaves and trees, maple and oak, ran in vertical stripes down the breastplate. The face mask was silver, a man smiling gently, surrounded by leaves and little birds growing from his beard. The hairs of the beard were separately etched in, overlaying with strips of silver, silver-gray, blue steel, black iron.

Beyond the metal man was another, this one of gold, inscribed with scenes of sailing ships, kings, rising suns. An eagle crest started from his helm. His beard was curled with golden flames.

Then came the three women, and the Lady with the mirror who was so beautiful.

Another gold man was beyond her, this one inscribed with mountain scenes, goatherds, pine trees. His crest was a dragon, each scale studded with a different gem.

Another silver man was next, this one done up in night images, moons and owls.

A man made out of bark stood behind the next chair, with leaves for hair. His face was carved from unpolished wood, scabby and black.

A normal-looking fellow was next, except he wore a folded robe of purest blue that floated and flowed around him. Clouds moved through the fabric. His hair also floated in the wind, except that there was no wind.

There was a man in scale armor. The scales were enameled with different shades of white, pale blue, dark blue, green, and black. He was young, and broad-shouldered, with long black hair. His helmet was on the table before him; it had a leaping dolphin for its crest. He did not look impatient, but he was pinching his nostrils shut, opening them, pinching them shut again, over and over. I do not mean he was touching his nose with his hand. His hands were clasped behind his back. When he turned his head to whisper some comment to the man dressed in the blue wind, I could see feathery dark lines of the gills behind his ear.

Next came two men in well-tailored business suits, dark blue pinstripe with narrow ties. Both had gold rings, tastefully expensive wristwatches, shining cuff links. One stood puffing a cigarette. Balanced on the back of the chair before him was the smallest computer I had ever seen, a folding thing no bigger than a large book. He was typing on it with both hands.

The other man, who was older, was speaking on a cell phone. They seemed to be men. Nothing extraordinary about them . . .

Until the one on the laptop computer, without taking either hand off the keyboard, had a third hand reach up from under his coat, take the cigarette between two fingers, and flick ash onto the carpet. From the way the hand blurred where it left his coat, I assumed I was looking at a three-dimensional intrusion from four-space.

Next was a busty dark-skinned woman, a Turk or a Hindu, perhaps, wearing a short red vest with nothing beneath it, a headdress of coins. She was a giant serpent from the waist down.

The final man was a figure from my dream. He had a metal eye in the center of his forehead: an orb of blue metal. It turned this way and that, not in keeping with the motions of his other eyes.

He was not a giant, as had been the one I saw in my dream. He was dressed in a stark, utilitarian one-piece suit, drab olive in color. He stood with his hands folded over the back of his chair, face expressionless, showing no sign of impatience. A name tag clipped to his breast pocket read: BRONTES.

6.

There had been a stir of talk while I had been staring at the Lady with the mirror. I had not heard what it was.

The three-handed man on the cell phone was telling someone, "He sent word that he wasn't showing up here. No. My question is, if his wife represents the volcanic position to us, should we take that representation as solid . . . ?"

The Satyr, leaning to speak past the tall shoulders of the headless man, said to the foxes in kimonos, "Say, fellows, are you here representing your Skulk, or the whole Wood?"

The taller fox, a gray, answered in a fluting voice, "We have letters of accredition, extraordinary and plenipotentiary, from the Nemeian."

"In that case, don't agree to anything till you and I get a chance to talk later, private-like, eh?"

The other fox was thinner, red-brown. It said in a saturnine tone, "Whether we speak or are silent, what does it matter? The Great Ones determine our course."

The gray fox snapped open a Japanese fan, and hid his muzzle behind it, while he made some whispered comment to his companion.

The Satyr shifted on his hooves impatiently. He said to his neighbor: "What about you, Haircut? There may be a third angle to this tug-o-war."

The headless body reached out with its fingers and turned the severed head on its silver plate till it faced the goat-man. "You cannot imagine that I have much interest in what the Bacchants have to say." His voice had a melodic beauty to it that echoed in the ear.

The Satyr waved his toothpick. "Who said I was talking about them? Did I say I was talking about them? Not all of us were on the side of the traitors when they stormed Olympus. I work for Nemestrinus."

The naked woman with grape leaves in her hair leaned over and caressed the Satyr's cheek. He jumped a bit, reddening with embarrassment.

She cooed softly, "Don't waste words on that one, Billy. He will be the next Psychopompos, no matter what else is decided tonight. Both factions will promise to confirm him in the post. He's the one the Unseen One likes. So why should he talk to you? He has nothing to gain and nothing to lose."

The Satyr said, "A little chitchat never hurt nobody."

She replied: "The Unseen One might be standing here in the room with us now, for all we know. Best not to annoy Him. No one wants Him to press His little wifey-poo's claim to the throne, now do they?"

The other nude girl leaned forward, saying in a fluid voice: "Be careful, little tripod! Your third leg is shorter than your other two. It will not help you run away if the Unseen One takes it amiss that you annoy His servants."

The goat-man looked annoyed. "Hey, if you are going to talk about my pogo stick, you call him Mr. Johnson!"

It was about this time that I realized, from his demeanor and slurred speech, that the goat-man had probably been drinking. Heavily.

The Satyr continued: "Heck! As for Him, what kind of Love Hotdog you think He's packing anyway? Married to that sweet tart of His, and no kids after all these years? If 'n the soil is fertile, maybe the seed is sterile, is all I'm saying, is all. And don't tell me the Maiden ain't fertile; she's a fertility goddess! And how come she's still a Maiden, if 'n you catch my meaning? I ain't afraid of no lord of ghosts, no ma'am. I figure, no matter how dread and horrible He is, who can be afraid of a guy with a dry stick, you take my meaning?"

The severed head said softly, "You are droll, tragamor. When you come to His kingdom, you will be met with many grins. They all grin, there."

7.

From some point more or less below where we hid on the balcony, there came the sound of a door opening, footsteps, the clang of a javelin on the floorboards.

I heard the voice, animated and bubbly, of the beautiful lady with the mirror. From the sounds, I could tell she had jumped to her feet.

"Harry's—!" (At least, it sounded like "Harry's." She might have been saying "Airy" or "Air Ease.") "Look, Aglaea, look who it is! Yoo hoo! Over here! Hi there! Hi! Do you think he sees me? Hello, darling! Euphrosyne, what do you think of him?"

I could see the women standing behind her, looking embarrassed and trying to appear at ease.

The maiden in white holding the pink bow and arrow leaned and said into the ear of her mistress, "My Lady Cyprian, the Lord Mavors is surely the archetype of manliness. But if we all know what men are like, surely he is that way, only more so."

The Lady burst into a fit of giggles.

The helmets of the four metal men all swiveled to face (I assume) the door. From my point of view, it looked as if they were all turning toward me. Seeing all those gold and silver masks swivel toward me, their inanimate features all carved into happy smiles, beneath lenses that could never know expression, reminded me of a group of synchronized deck guns on a battleship, rotating in their turrets to cover an enemy.

The Red Soldier marched into view, crossed over to the table. He had slung back the links of his coif from his scalp, so that I saw his hawklike profile, hook nose, and blue eyes. He had a face so tranquil as to be almost expressionless, except for the hint of cruelty around his mouth, the hint of sadness in his eyes.

When he saw the Lady, though, the cruelty left his mouth; the sorrow left his eyes. The weather-beaten face suddenly looked years younger. And handsome. His eyes glittered and danced. He pursed his lips to keep himself from smiling.

There were murmurs and whispers around the table. Only the headless man did not seem disturbed. The three-handed man hissed into his cell phone: "Call you back!" Two additional hands came out from under the coat to fold up the phone and hold open a pocket to slide it into.

I took the opportunity to whisper to Quentin: "Do you know who these are?"

"We're in a school run by the pagan gods of old." He said in softest of whispers. "Now hush." Without opening his eyes, he reached across and put a finger to my lips, to hush me. It was a funny feeling, having him touch my lips that way. "We don't want to be turned into trees or something."

BETWEEN THE DEVIL AND THE DEEP BLUE SEA

1.

The Soldier, Lord Mavors, his expression once again under his control, now stepped up to the seat opposite the Lady Cyprian. At once the arrangement of the table became clear to me. Half the table was for the Lady and her entourage, her robots and ladies and foxes, her tree-man, her goat-man, and men with extra eyes or extra limbs or a man missing a head. The other half of the table was reserved for the Soldier. He had no one.

He held up the javelin a moment, and dipped it toward the Lady, saying, "Ma'am."

Cyprian acknowledged the salute by wiggling in her chair, and darted a heavy-lidded look at him. "Don't you want to sit next to me?" She patted the chair to her side. Then she said to her handmaidens: "I bet he won't! He's toying with me! He's so mean! Look at how cute he is!" Then, to him again: "You never write!"

I would have felt embarrassed for her, except that she seemed so cheerful, so obviously sure of herself, that she did not seem to notice the other people around her, listening.

And everyone (except the golems, whose masks were immobile, and the man with his head on a plate, whose expression was composed) were looking nervous, agog, or annoyed. The Satyr wore a look of naked fear. Even the foxes had both opened their fans to hide their muzzles, despite that their faces could not show expressions.

But no one looked surprised.

The Soldier spun the heavy javelin lightly in his finger, and drove it point-downward into the floorboards (bang!) so that it trembled upright next to him. He slung the shield over the arm of the chair, to keep it at hand, pulled the katana, scabbard and all, from his web-belt, and laid the sheathed blade on the table before him. Then he sat down.

He said to the Lady Cyprian, "You have to write letters to get letters, ma'am."

"I think my husband rips them up!"

"Ah . . . yes ma'am. Can't blame him. Seeing as how you humiliate him in public, and all." The Soldier folded his hands on the table. "Any word from the boy?" he asked curtly.

"Which boy?"

"Our son."

"Nope! Still missing! I hope he's OK. Don't you hope he's OK?"

"I hope for your husband's sake, that he is, ma'am."

"You don't really think Mulciber killed him, do you? I'd hate to have you think that. Please don't kill my husband. I like him very much. And he makes me things."

The Soldier said nothing, but turned his head to give Headmaster Boggin a cool stare.

Boggin took that as an excuse to step forward and nod politely toward both sides of the table. "Your Ladyship, Your Lordship, honored Visitors and Governors, please take your seats. Perhaps we can begin."

Her Ladyship said, "I love beginnings. Beginnings are always the times of magic, of unknown delight, full of promise and expectation. Consummations are also much to be desired. Maybe we can have a dance after, or something." She waved her hands at the people, things, and animals on her side of the table. "Sit! Sit!"

The metal men held the chairs for the ladies, and the Satyr held a chair for one of the nude women, but he must have goosed her, because she turned and slapped him. The metal men did not sit down, but kept their empty, smiling masks turned toward the Soldier, their dead lenses trained on him.

Boggin took his position halfway between the Soldier and the Lady, with Mr. Sprat and Mr. ap Cymru standing to either side behind his chair.

The Soldier pointed with his finger at ap Cymru, "What's that one doing here?"

Boggin said smoothly, "He is part of the staff, Your Lordship. Originally part of your Father's staff, Your Lordship, may he rest in peace."

"Amen," said the Lady Cyprian, and everyone on her side of the table (except the golems) said "Amen," in unison.

Quentin, who was still lying on his back with his eyes closed, put his hand over his mouth to stifle a laugh. He found the idea of ancient Greek gods saying "Amen" funny, for some reason.

The Soldier said, "Do you know what he is?"

Boggin said, "He comes very highly recommended, Your Lordship, and—to be frank—I was not sure if I had the authority to discharge him. The unfortunate passing away of your Father left certain affairs in disarray. I could make this an item on this evening's agenda, if Your Lordship wishes . . . ?"

The Soldier gave the slightest shake of his head, and turned to look back at the Lady. "Let's stick to what we came to talk about. Time's short."

Cyprian, elbows on the table, was hunched behind her little mirror, with only her glittering eyes peeping over the edge. She was impishly aiming her mirror at him, tilting it this way and that, to send little triangles of light, reflected from the chandelier, floating over the Soldier's lean cheeks, flashing in his eyes.

Cyprian said playfully, "We are all surprised to see you, dear. No one knew you were coming yourself. You didn't send Fear or Panic?"

He squinted, and for a moment, looked so amused, and annoyed, and filled with masculine power, that I was sure he was going to get up, walk across the room, throw the Lady Cyprian over his shoulder, and carry her off right there and then. Or kiss her. Or both.

Instead he said drily, "Fear sometimes scares people." Then he turned to Boggin and said, "Boreus, get on with it."

Boggin said, "Well, then. Your Lordship, Your Ladyship, Visitors, Governors. We all know the tragic events in Heaven of recent history have left matters somewhat in, shall we say, flux. When the rebels, led by your Lordship's brother, Dionysus . . ."

"Half-brother," said the Soldier.

". . . Your Lordship's half-brother, were defeated at Phlegra, certain hostages were taken from the pits of Tartarus, as a pledge of good behavior for the Titans whom Lord Hermes Trismegistus, the Swift God, and the Lady of Wisdom, Tritogenia, had released . . ."

The Lady Cyprian said in a soft cooing voice: "Boreus, your speech is fine, and you are right to be proud of it. There is at least one girl who has heard your voice who entertains sweet thoughts of you. But, I pray you, enough. We need no reminding of what we already know."

Her tone was much less playful when speaking to the Headmaster than when speaking to the Soldier. Her tone was still sweet and kindly, but it was clear she was addressing an underling.

I sensed, rather than heard, a disappointed noise from Quentin. He had been dying to hear what everyone already knew. He may have even been counting on Boggin to provide the background to what was going on. But now the Lady Cyprian had cut that off.

She continued: "These are the words of the Maker. This is what my husband says: on no account are the Children of Chaos to be killed. The Uranians would rise up from the Pit should that happen."

The Soldier said, "I concur."

And he put his hand on the table, stood, and picked up his sheathed sword to tuck it through his web-belt again.

2.

Headmaster Boggin said, "But Your Lordship, Your Ladyship!"

The Soldier was adjusting something on his belt, and spoke without looking up. "Don't kill the children. Everyone agrees. Talk over. What's the problem?"

Boggin was speechless for a moment, and made a gobbling noise.

Quentin now, unable to resist, turned and opened his eyes, keeping a hand between himself and the Lady. Quentin grinned to see Boggin so discombobulated.

It was Mr. ap Cymru who spoke up. His voice had a nasal twang to it. "So the Butcher and the Tinker agree to keep the little wolf pups alive! No one makes a decision, and nothing gets done! Another year goes by, and the pups get a little older, and a little bigger. Hurrah for compromise! But one day the pups will turn into wolves, and eat the sun and the moon, and what do we do then?"

Headmaster Boggin said sternly, "Thank you for your considered opinions, Taffy, though this may not have been the proper, shall we say, venue, for airing them."

The man with floating hair, whose robes were made of weightless blue, spoke up, "It is not wise to annoy the Great Ones, Laverna, or whatever you are calling yourself these days, now that you are a man."

The Soldier was in the process of unsticking his javelin from the floorboards. He wiggled it back and forth once or twice. "Thank you, Corus, but some of the Great Ones don't get in a snit one way or the other. Let him—her—it—whatever, talk." With a pop, the javelin came loose from the floorboards. To ap Cymru, he said, "So talk, Laverna. What's eating you?"

Ap Cymru said, "Milord Mavors, you know the situation is unstable. No one expected, when we forced the Uranians to assume the shape of human babies, that the impersonation would be so exact. So exact, that they did what human babies do, and grew up. The potions, the prayers, the spells we use to keep them under control were meant to control children, not grown adults."

"You are not telling me anything I don't know, Fraud. What's your point?"

"Put someone on the Throne of Heaven. Anyone. I don't care how you pick him. Throw lots, have a footrace, have a war."

Lady Cyprian said softly, "Oh, did they finally decide to do it by the war method? I know who I'll be betting on." Her ladies-in-waiting tittered.

Mavors actually frowned at her. "There's not going to be a war. Everyone loses in war, even the winners. The Uranians would rise up."

She smiled at him, a sultry, mocking smile, and her eyes danced. "Then auction off the throne. Whoever gives the bigger bribe wins!"

Of all people, it was the Satyr who said, "Or hold a ballot."

The ladies-in-waiting put their fingers to their mouths and laughed. The one with the dove on her wrist said, "That really comes out to the same thing in the end, doesn't it, Pherespondus?"

The one holding the bow and arrows said gaily, " 'Twould be a foregone conclusion, my sisters Graces. Mavors on his meager soldier's pay could not outbid the Lord of Goldsmiths."

Ap Cymru made a slashing motion in the air with his hand, "Milord, milady, it does not matter how you get someone on the throne. Just get someone. Make peace between the factions, restore the army to full strength. The Uranians will then be afraid to attack us because of our strength. Then we can let these hostages go, and to hell with them.

"The Late High King wasn't just Diospater, the Father of Gods, and he wasn't just Iopater, the High Father. He was also called Terminus, the Lord of Boundaries. The boundaries around the estate are weakening as the children grow older. We need someone to restore them. Here, and elsewhere, too. There are places in the Twelve Worlds where tears are appearing in the fabric of reality. So just pick someone."

Mavors said, "We do not have the authority just to pick someone. We don't have the right. The law of succession is set by primogeniture. No one believes me, but I actually don't want the job. But I'm the only one in line. Phoebus and Phoebe are bastards; Trismegistus and Dionysus are both traitors and bastards."

The man in tan coveralls with the metal eye in his forehead, Brontes, spoke. It did not sound like a real voice; it sounded like the words were made by machine. "Hephaestus is the son of Queen Hera and the All-Father Zeus. He is legitimate."

Mavors shrugged. "Dad threw him out of heaven. I don't think Mulciber is any son of my father."

"Do you think he is the son of Ixion?"

Mavors looked at him thoughtfully. "Be careful what you say about my mother. Pick your words very carefully. I'll remember them to tell the stonecutter."

"What stonecutter?"

"The one making your headstone."

"Are you threatening me? Who will forge the thunderbolts if the Cyclopes are slain? There is no other weapon to drive back the Uranians."

The headless man's head, speaking from his plate, said, "That may not protect you, Brontes. Athena Tritogenia was one of the rebels, remember? And Zeus is dead. Who else can wield the lightning bolt? Dionysus is said to have learned the secret. But he was one of the rebels, too."

Mavors said in a quiet voice, "I never threaten anyone. I don't need to. But you could still work at the forge if I broke your kneecap. Your boss the Gimp does it."

He paused to let that sink in.

Then he said, "So don't talk about my mother. When she stood up to Dad and his philandering, everyone called her a bitch. When she was quiet about it, everyone called her a doormat. Well, I'm tired of it. No one makes fun of High Queen Acraea. Are we clear?"

Lady Cyprian said, "Now, you leave my husband's people alone, Ares. You're the one who said Mulciber wasn't Terminus' son. But we all know he was Acraea's son. You don't really think it was a virgin birth, do you?

How could it be? Your mother was married. Married people aren't virgins. Not after a while, anyway. It's just a dumb story. I think you're the one who made it up."

Mavors said to her, "If Dad can make Lady Wisdom pop out of his head, Mom can do the same sort of thing. And it makes me laugh, doll, to hear you, of all people, saying what's possible and impossible when it comes to being born.

"Anyway. We're not here to discuss paternity issues. We're sort of off the topic. We're all in a bind because no one is in charge. We're divided and weak. We can't kill the hostages because the Uranians will attack. We can't let them go. Same reason. And we can't keep waiting around, because Boreus and his crew here can't keep the children from growing up, like he was supposed to."

Headmaster Boggin puffed up. "Milord, the implication is most unfair. Most unfair! There are four boundaries to the estate, four places where the four versions of the universe touch this world. Had we moved the hostages in the early days, when the unfixed ylem in their bodies had not yet learned how to copy human organs, moving them too far away from a boundary would have killed them. Even now, I do not know what harm might befall them if we move them too far away. But this famous spot where the four boundaries touch, is also on a world entirely overrun with humans. The local laws of nature have their sway here. The local law commands children to grow. Your own son, Milord, after centuries of being a baby, grew up to manhood because of the time he spent on this world, with Psyche."

Lady Cyprian frowned and rolled her eyes. "Pul-lease don't remind me. Talk about marrying the help!"

"Milord, Milady, all I mean to say is that there were no other options," said Boggin. "There are few, very few places where all four versions of reality intersect. His Imperial Majesty Lord Terminus stabilized this area, cast a Fate over it. We could not move the children away from this spot, because it might have harmed them. I asked the Imperator Cupid to wipe out mankind living in these islands, but he would not.

"Now that they are older, we might be able to move the Uranians to another location, but I am certain Your Lordship would wish this to be done under the supervision of someone you trust for the same reason Lord Mulciber would insist on it."

Mavors gave a small and bitter grin, and said, "Because Mulciber knows that if he had Uranians on his side, he could stand a chance of winning.

Same goes for Anacreon and the Maiden, and even Pelagaeus the Earthshaker, or whoever else thinks they have a claim on the throne. Same goes for me."

Boggin bowed slightly, "I had been hoping, in fact, to make that the main topic of conversation at this meeting. If any child finds the boundary to his or her home, their powers will stir. The spells, the psionics, the manipulations of the geometry of space–time, the potions we use to keep them from changing shape or waking the chaos around them, are hindered by the fact that this estate is on a planet of humans, basically part of the materialistic paradigm of Aetna."

Mavors picked up his shield. "I am not sure there is much to discuss. This estate belonged to Dad. We all know it is his land, and none of us has much influence here. Where else are we going to put these kids? One of my places? Mulciber wouldn't agree. One of Mulciber's places?"

Lady Cyprian said, "Which are kind of, you know, hot and, well, *volcanic.* Not the best place for kids."

Mavors finished with a shrug. "If we throw them in the ocean, Pelagaeus gets them. You see?"

Ap Cymru said, "Hell. Put them in the Asphodel Fields."

3.

Mavors looked at the headless man.

The headless man said, "Everyone here knows what the power of the Unseen One is. You know he could take Olympus if he wanted to, and neither the machines of Vulcan nor the dragons of Mars could stand against him. If he wanted Uranians to serve him, he had the keys to Tartarus in any case."

Mavors said, "If the Unseen One will publicly repudiate the claim of his wife, the Maiden, to the throne of Heaven, I'd agree. I trust him. I don't necessarily trust her."

Lady Cyprian said, "I'll consult with my husband. But I am sure Mulciber will agree. He and Hades have always been on the best of terms. Sort of an underground, live in a land of fire and lava kind of thing. Get the best-looking wives. You know. Like a club."

"Well, look at that," said Mavors, hoisting his shield to his shoulder. "We settled something after all."

The Lady Cyprian half-rose from her seat. "Ares! You're not leaving yet, are you? You must stay for the dance!"

"I'd love to, Ma'am, but I cannot. The Titans are stirring in the Pontic Sea, and their brothers are swimming in the magma below the Earth's crust. Other Titans have been seen in the spheres above the Moon, like bats as large as caravels; or lying on the sands of Libya by night, like mountains.

"They seem to be gathering. Deimos thinks they are all heading toward the Citadel of Dreams in Cimmeria. Without the lightning bolt, we will have no way to drive them back, if they come out of the Sunless Land again, and storm Olympus. That's why I could not spare any of my people for this little gathering, here. Fairest of goddesses, adieu. You ladies can dance. The men have work to do."

Mavors tucked his finger under his coif, and pulled it over his crew cut.

4.

"Just a moment, my Lord!" said a new voice. This was the dark-haired man with gills, the one who wore a jacket of blue, green, and white scales.

Boggin said, "What is it, Governor Mestor?"

"Before my Lord departs, there is another point the princes of Atlantis would like to bring up."

Mavors said, "Spit it out."

"Lord, we are not certain the growth and maturity of the four Uranians is a natural effect, as has been previously assumed. Four boundaries to four versions of chaos border the estate. Our own access from our worlds is through the Sending Vessel. Correct? So why are the laws of nature of the human world working here?"

Headmaster Boggin said, "What are you implying?"

"In your report to the Board of last year, you explained that more of the influence of Chaos is coming through here. Strange events had occurred. Young Master Triumph was seen levitating a fork. Claw prints on the ceiling above the bed of young Master Nemo. Hollywood starlets answering love letters written by Master mac FirBolg. And it was clear that their people in the Abyss were trying to send dreams and reminders."

Mavors said, "Make it snappy. I have other fires to put out."

"Dread Lord of Battle, the princes of Atlantis are convinced that the boundaries around this estate are being pried open. These children are not growing old because of the operation of any law of nature. What does the concept of a law of nature have any meaning when dealing with a chaoticist? We suspect deliberate stratagem. Slow, yes, but deliberate. The Prince of the Night may be sending his influences in. He is shape-changing them by his magic to make them into adult Uranians."

"So? What's to be done?"

"There is only one child among the five who has the power to open boundaries, or to find the secret paths that run to other worlds. She will not perish when she is taken from a place next to the boundaries, because she is not a chaoticist. Nausicaa, the daughter of Alcinuous, who in this place goes by the ridiculous name of Vanity Fair, must be taken to Atlantis and put into the custody of the loyal sons of Neptune. Four Uranians might well alter the balance of power between the various factions contending for the throne. One Phaeacian girl will not. Once she is gone, the boundaries will resume their old strength, and the influences from Chaos here will diminish. Then there will be no need to move any of the other children anywhere."

Mavors looked at Lady Cyprian. "Wouldn't make much difference to me."

Lady Cyprian blinked her enormous brown eyes. "I'll see what my husband has to say about it. He may not like the idea of putting the daughter of the King of Phaeacia into the hands of Pelagaeus' faction. Why have the Atlantians and Phaeacians on the same side?"

Mavors snorted. "Arete runs Phaeacia, not Alcinuous. She knows what side of the bread her butter is on, daughter or no daughter. There will be Phaeacian sea captains, pirates, and smugglers volunteering to serve any faction that is winning, no matter which side Alcinuous himself is on. And we all know he really, actually, backs Anacreon the Vine-God no matter what he says. That's why Dad took his daughter in the first place."

Mr. Sprat leaned in and said to Boggin, "If Miss Fair were out of sight and out of mind, sir, we might not have trouble with Grendel. We have heard that Grendel's mother has already bought a wedding dress and fashioned a coffin for the girl."

Mavors looked over. "Who is Grendel?"

Lady Cyprian laughed. "Oh, my dearest, you really should have your spies talk to my spies! Grendel is the groundskeeper here. He goes by the name of Glum. He's one of Pelagaeus' people."

"Hmm." Mavors turned to Boggin, "Tell your groundskeeper that whoever kills any of the children here, dies. No argument, no excuses, no phone calls from the Governor, no time to pray, just a pilum up their fundament. Got it?"

To Lady Cyprian, he said, "Ask your husband two things. First, is it acceptable to him to move the hostages to the Asphodel Fields? Second, is it acceptable to remove Nausicaa to Atlantis for safe-keeping, if it turns out that she is the one making the boundaries weak?"

"I'll tell him if you kiss me. Otherwise, I'll tell him you kissed me, and called him a crippled unmanly coward."

"Well. Some people don't think much of a man who lets himself get cuckolded and doesn't stand up straight and do something about it. Of course, it's not his fault he can't stand up straight. But I never called him a coward. Maybe Brontes here will tell him the message, if you don't."

"So you're not going to kiss me? I think about your kisses every night, when I am alone in bed . . ."

Mavors took a few brusque steps about the table toward her, but then, when he was about where the headless man was sitting, he slowed, and leaned on his javelin, and regained his composure. "Ah, no ma'am. I don't think it would be seemly, considering. But you can tell your husband three things from me.

"One. There is not going to be a war unless he starts it.

"Two. If he moves troops or taloi in the vicinity of Mount Olympus, dons purple, dons a coronet, or attempts to wield the lightning, or claims the throne in any other way, that will start the war.

"Three. He will lose any war he fights with me. Do you understand the message?"

Her voice was demure. "Yes, my Lord, I understand." I moved my head so I could see her again. She had lowered her eyelashes, and turned her head to one side, so that she looked dream-caught, breathtakingly lovely. There was a blush rising in her cheeks.

I knew what she was thinking, which I don't think any guy, listening to her, would have known: she liked having Mavors give her orders.

Mavors was staring at her profile, trying to keep his face a mask. But I could see, even from here, the wonder in his eyes. He was dumbstruck at her beauty.

He squinted, and spoke again, "You can tell him one other thing. The

Uranians are not going to wait forever. I am not going to wait forever. All he has to do is foreswear his claim to the throne, and vow fealty to me. I get the world; he gets you. I think it's an even trade. You tell him that."

He turned and, with a swirl and flap of his long coat, strode from the room.

8

THE AZURE LIGHT

1.

Things began to go wrong at that point.

Boggin and some of the others wanted to continue the meeting. The Lady Cyprian listened to the school business with growing absentmindedness, toying with her mirror, chatting with her handmaidens, giggling while other people were talking.

Mr. ap Cymru made a motion to put topic on the agenda: Miss Daw (who was the physics teacher as well as being the music teacher) wanted funds to renovate the lab. "It is her opinion that a time will come when the hostages will occupy positions of strength and sovereignty if ever they are returned to their own people. She says . . ." (and now he read from a note) " 'Whether these Orphans of Chaos will regard us with hatred and contempt, or with respect and esteem relies entirely on how well we raise and educate them. A proper schooling in grammar and gymnastic being the foundation for the growth of virtue and character in the young, and knowledge of music, astronomy, and natural philosophy having a moderating effect on the appetitive passions of youth, it is the considered opinion of the servants of the Hippocrene Springs that proper equipment for a physics lab will allow such instruction to take place . . . ' Ah. And she goes on in like vein."

The Satyr, Pherespondus, said, "She has been playing the role of a teacher for so long, now she thinks she is one!"

Mr. Sprat mentioned briefly another item he wanted put on the agenda: the property tax owed, the possibility of selling certain school property to raise funds, or using enchantment to hypnotize the Talbot family into paying.

Apparently some of the people and creatures sitting on the Lady Cyprian's side of the table actually were Governors of the school. The metal men, the women in Greek togas, and the man with the metal eye, Brontes, were clearly her servants and hers alone. The headless man was a guest, but he spoke about donations from someone he called "the Lord of Wealth." He was a Visitor, then, since he was here to inspect how things were going; and he apparently had some control of school funds.

The man from Atlantis, Mestor, said he wanted to discuss the issue of the slip rental from the local marina, for the school's boats, and difficulty with the new provisions of Crown regulation; this led me to believe he was clearly a Governor of the school.

One of the foxes—the white one—asked about discussing the question of easements through the wood to the south of the school, and saying there had been "impositions" and "slips" between the human and the "Arcadian" version of reality. I had been assuming the two foxes were in the same group, but the second one, the brown one, made a reference to his status as an emissary between the Lord of Smiths and the Nemeian Lion.

I could not tell which of the others were officers of the school, or not. My overall impression was that relations between these groups or factions or whoever they represented were even more complex than what had seemed at first.

As they were voting on the order of the agenda for the discussion, the Lady Cyprian stood and expressed the desire to have the dance, now. "I've come all this way," she said. "And dances are so romantic!"

Only Boggin had the nerve to speak back to her. "My Lady, how can we hold a dance? Nothing has been prepared. The Boundary Stone Table occupies the Hall; there is no music; and Milord Mavors has marred the floor."

She stood up, with an expression filled with nothing but kindness. "I have expressed my wish. It is said I am capricious; nothing could be further from the truth; although, alas, the nature of my domain renders it impossible for me to tell those who will enjoy my favor or disfavor what Fate has in keeping for them. It is not for my own pleasure that I speak."

I knew what she meant. I saw it immediately. She was the goddess of love. Someone's True Love was in this room, but he would not meet her, or realize that she was the one and only meant for him, unless the formal atmosphere of the meeting gave way to the more relaxed festivities of something like a dance.

Nor could she, Cyprian, merely point her fingers at the two people involved and say, "You are matched with her!" Nothing could be less romantic than that. It would be worse than having your mother pick your dates for you.

The two nymphs and the three Graces were thinking the same thing I was. They were looking at the men around the table speculatively, wondering whom the Lady had in mind. I could see the girl with the bow, Euphrosyne, looked especially doubtful. I saw her glance at the headless man, the man made out of wood, and the Satyr.

Of the men, it was the two in business suits who seemed to catch on the quickest to what was being implied.

The one with the cell phone said, "I move a temporary adjournment, Mr. Chairman. We can resume once a little bit of festive . . . ah . . . festivity has cleared the air of lingering doubts."

The Atlantian, Mestor, was looking speculatively at the Graces in the flowing togas, the nymphs in their nudity. He spoke up, "I second the motion."

Without waiting for a vote or any sign of consent, the other man in a business suit, the one who had been typing on his laptop computer, stood and said, "I can clear the Boundary Stone Table out of the way. I cannot manifest my true shape in this paradigm, but I am sure the table will allow my powers to work, here."

He opened his coat and a billow of opaque mist flowed out from his chest. A stream of smoke arched across the table. Other little puffs of smoke separated from the main mass and moved to positions at various points around the circumference.

I nudged Quentin, whispering, "Look at this."

Hands came out of the cloud: first ten, then a score, then more. The many arms were all dressed as the man's original pair, with a foot of pressed blue pinstripe coat sleeve showing, and an inch of white cuff, gold cufflinks and all. Most of the left hands wore rings, but not all. Many of the right hands wore expensive gold watches of various makes and models.

The hands reached down and grabbed the table at half a hundred points around the circumference. People and creatures rose with alarm from their seats and backed away as the hands tensed. The man in the suit braced his feet and grunted.

The giant table, which had taken workmen with pulleys and dollies hours to haul into place, was picked up by the sixty or seventy disembodied hands, lifted lightly into the air, and set on its side against one wall.

Quentin whispered, "He is sending the animal humors and motive spirits out from his arms and forming eidolons in midair to impersonate his hands, which he moves by virtue of those humors."

I whispered back, "We are seeing a polydimensional effect. The real creature is four-dimensional; he is merely rotating more of his body into this time–space."

The wooden man, meanwhile, stalked over to where the floorboards had been pierced by the javelin of the Soldier, stooped and ran his knotty twiggy fingers across the whole. When he rose, the splinters were mended back together, the floorboards were solid.

The Lady Cyprian said, "Music! Where is the Siren who played so lovingly when we first arrived? Where is Thelxiepia?"

Ap Cymru bowed toward her. "With your permission, Madame, I shall fetch her."

The Lady turned to the headless man (who had tucked his head carefully under one arm when the table was yanked away), saying, "And will you favor us also with a song, master of all bards, sage of mysteries? I see you brought your instrument; surely, surely fate has treated you cruelly, but it was not I who treated you cruelly. You have no reason to scorn my plea."

The severed head, riding in the crook of an elbow, looked wry. "Madame, it was love who enabled me to walk alive out of Hell; and, once I knew the secret pathways back to the world of daylight, even my murderesses could not keep me buried. My every song is devoted to you, now and ever. You, only you, make sorrows possible to bear."

With his other hand he reached up and unslung his guitar.

I was curious to see how he would manage to strum and to finger a guitar while at the same time holding his head, but at that moment, the Lady Cyprian gestured upward, and I thought she was pointing straight at us.

Quentin and I shrank back. But all she said was: "Lights! The chandelier is too low for cavorting, especially should good Pherespondus jump and skip!"

The man in the blue robe floated up to the level of the balcony, light as a thistledown, his hair and shining cloak weightless and rippling in midair. Wings of azure were unfolding from his back, each feather the color of the summer sky, but apparently they were just for show, as he did not flap them but merely spread them out, like an eagle on a heraldic emblem.

By some miracle, he came up to the far side of the balcony, facing away from us and toward the pulley mechanism that controlled the chandelier chain. A cloud of opaque white smoke also billowed up from underfoot, and a dozen arms (clad in impeccable blue pinstriped suit sleeves with white cuffs) reached out of the smoke to give him a hand.

We crawled backward as quickly as silence allowed, and were in the alcove and up a dozen stairs before the winged man turned his head. At that point, there were tatters of cloud between him and us.

I say "crawled" but it was more like one long, carpet-hugging leap. The whole journey seemed to take only the moment between heartbeats and, considering how my heart was hammering at that time, that moment must have been a short one indeed.

We sat there, not breathing, waiting to hear if the winged man would raise the alarm. But the only noise that came was the rattling and groaning of the chandelier chain, as the massive iron frame of the lights was hauled upward.

2.

Quentin looked at me, then nodded toward the top of the stair, where the roof exit was. I nodded back. It was time to retreat.

He crept quietly up the stairs, gesturing for me to stay back.

I was furious when I saw him wave his hand behind his back at me. Me, two or three years his senior! It was somewhat patronizing of him to assume that, because I was the girl, I had to go second; and I knew he probably picked this moment because we dared not talk, so I could not question his silent order. He had also turned his head toward the exit above, so as not to notice my rude gesture by which I answered him.

And I wasn't going to push past him on the narrow stair; that might make a noise, too.

He squinted out into the night, looked around carefully. He actually—I am not kidding—he actually raised his walking stick like a periscope, and turned the little brass jackal head this way and that.

Then, satisfied, he rose to his feet and stepped out onto the roof.

Immediately, he seemed to explode with light. I blinked, dazzled. It was only a flashlight beam, but it had caught him from the knees up. From the angle, it looked as if the beam were coming from below, over the edge of the roof.

Quentin's back and his left hand were still in shadow. He was blinking and raising his right hand to shield his eyes.

He extended his left hand toward me and dropped his walking stick. I caught it before it clattered on the stairs. Then with his now-empty left hand, Quentin pointed at me, and made a thumb gesture like a hitchhiker. Go back. Get away.

Dr. Fell's voice came up from over the edge of the roof. "Well, well, if it is not our young Mr. Nemo. I was told to expect someone else, but I will suppose you will do. Come down, young man! I am to take anyone I find to Headmaster Boggin's office, but I suppose, since he is occupied, we may have time to visit the infirmary and discover from whence comes your amazing resistance to your medication. You are the last person I would expect to be able to negate my effects. I see certain magnetic anomalies around your person: these are merely material effects which material science has long since learned how to comprehend and negate. Observe."

A beam of blue light from the ground came up over the edge of the roof. Quentin stood goggle-eyed at what he was seeing; the source of the blue light, I assume. There seemed to be little sparks or flickers of smaller particles flicking forward through the light, like dust motes. The beam played back and forth over Quentin.

By that point, one very quiet stair at a time, I had reached the bottom of the alcove again. There was a nook behind the potted plant where even someone standing on the balcony would not be able to see me.

I sat down there with my head down, clutching Quentin's walking stick. I felt glad that I hadn't been caught. That thought made me feel like a miserable coward.

I huddled into a smaller ball when, some minutes later (though it seemed like hours), I heard the happy talk and laughter from below give way to charming music of violin and guitar.

3.

Time seemed to stop when I heard that music, and all my grief fled away, as if a light shone through my heart, and no darkness could be there.

The music seemed eternal to me, as if it came from a higher, finer sphere, and made all this, what we call "reality," seem flat.

A type of numbness came over me then, not of any limb or organ I could name or point to. I had a sense that there was a part of me that was being squeezed or strangled. I cannot explain it any clearer than that.

It is not as if I had not heard Miss Daw play before. I had, every day, and twice on Sundays. I knew her hand on the violin; I knew she could bring emotion out of the inanimate wood and catgut that infused and inspired every soul in earshot.

But this was different. Perhaps it was because this type of cheerful, voluptuous music was not normally what she played. Perhaps she was playing more strongly that was her wont, for an audience with stronger spirits than mine, and she let appear a strength and a magic in her songs she kept cloaked when around us. Perhaps when she played for me in class there was a deliberate policy guiding what she exposed me to, how quickly or slowly she allowed her influence to seep into the haunting songs.

Or perhaps it was because she was in duet with the headless man. His guitar notes floated up, and, above and behind the melody and harmony, his soul seemed expressed in song; and his soul spoke of escape, of release, of flight to the light beyond the dark places of the world.

For whatever reason, I was now aware of a quality in her music that I had never noticed before, not consciously. It was like ice. It stunned something in me, made it numb.

I tucked the walking stick under one arm and put my fingers into my ears. It did not help. I had to get away, and quickly.

4.

I am sure the wisest direction to flee would have been straight up stairs to the roof. From there, I could go down by the scaffolding.

I had two reasons against it. First, I did not know where the scaffolding was in relation to the windows of the Great Hall. I might be plainly visible walking down the workman's scaffold. Second, even though I should assume Dr. Fell left his post to go do something horrible to Quentin—Quentin whom I had abandoned to his fate—I could not shake the eerie feeling that the door to the roof was still being watched.

I had been in this building before, on several occasions, despite that it was never used for classes. The balcony went in a circle around the base of the dome and opened up into two corridors opposite each other, which ran the main length of the building. At the end of either corridor was a staircase. In both cases, the foot of the stair ended in an antechamber, which also held the main doors outside. Unfortunately, in both cases, the antechambers opened via a short corridor through an archway directly into what was now a ballroom, with no doors blocking the way. If only for a moment, I would be visible to the people in the room.

I decided to make for the Eastern corridor. Anything else required walking or crawling around 180 degrees of the balcony, in plain view (now that the chandelier light shone full upon it) of anyone below who happened to look up.

So down the corridor I went, softly, still half-benumbed by the music. There were tall doors to my left and right, offices of the School Administration, I supposed, or perhaps the living quarters of the Talbot family, should they ever return to their estate.

I took the stairs two at a time, for now the music had segued into a foxtrot or jig of some sort, and many feet were galloping on the floor, and I could not keep still, hearing it.

I was at the second landing, where the stairs switchbacked, before I heard, over the noise which was masking my descent, the sound of several feet ascending the stair I was about to step around the corner onto.

I was on the second floor. It was quicker to open the door and slip through it than it was to run back up the stairs.

I slipped into the darkened room, pushed the door shut (quickly but softly), and stood with my hand on the door, listening, trying to control my breathing.

From the voice I knew it was Pherespondus the Satyr, and the red-furred fox.

". . . I am only saying, Vulpino, that Nemestrinus of Arcadian Wood has a natural harmony of interests with Anacreon."

"Some call the Lord Vintner a traitor god."

"Certainly, a traitor. And yet I wonder what strong reason impelled him to that treachery? He was the first to traffick with the Fallen Uranians. What could they have told him? They are as old as Cosmos, and know the secrets of its construction."

"You think the young Uranians will offer victory to whichever side ends up in control of them. Why? Are you saying Morpheus in Cimmeria . . . or

Helios from Myriagon . . . will assist our . . . ?" Mutter mutter. I could not hear the end of the question. The fox had a soft voice.

"Boreus is ambitious . . . sell out to whomever . . ." Murmur murmur. The voices trailed off.

5.

With the door shut, and the music muffled, my head felt slightly clearer. With my eyes closed, I thought I could tell what the music was doing: it seemed to be flattening or normalizing time–space in the local area. By some intuition, I now knew what part of myself was suffering pins-and-needles like a limb with its circulation impaired. This part of me did not have a name, but it was the part I used to deflect normal straight-line gravity paths and lift massive objects that boys stronger than me could not lift.

Now I was more afraid of the music than I was of being seen, and I did not want to open the door.

I turned my head. There was a little moonlight leaking in through the windows here, made bright by reflections from the snow below. This was a corner room, and there were windows looking East and South. There was a desk, a bookshelf, and a squat metal cabinet to one side. There was no other door out.

I went over to the South window. I had been thinking that the second floor might be low enough to jump down from, if I hung from my hands before dropping. One look out the window banished that notion. The first floor of the building was double normal height. But I could see the corner of the portico leading to the main doors. A sloping roof, wide pillars . . . too wide to shimmy down? Maybe not.

But there were wires running from the window frame to the panes. An alarm system. Victor, who knew all about such things, was not here. For once in my life, I actually felt like the helpless female Quentin had been pretending I was. I didn't know what to do when I saw those wires, except wish wistfully that Victor were here.

Maybe the other window was unalarmed?

I walked around the desk to step to the East window when the walking stick . . . moved . . . in my hand.

I froze. Something had twisted the jackal headed cane in my grip, so now the muzzle was pointed toward the cabinet.

Magic? Maybe.

I stepped over to the cabinet. They were a heavy steel construction, not at all in keeping with the rather tasteful wooden décor of the room. The doors did not open. They did not even budge when I tugged on them. There were two locks and a keypad, and the locks were on opposite sides of the main panel, making it almost impossible for one person to turn both locks at once. The whole affair was bolted to the floor in eight places. It looked like the kind of safe in which you put documents you want to be left intact after a Russian missile attack. The safe looked so massive . . . too massive . . .

There was a noise coming from inside, which I could dimly hear, or feel, when my hand was on the cabinet. It sounded like the chiming whine of a wineglass, which rings because a violin note of the proper harmonic resonance is played too nearby.

Something inside the cabinet was reacting to the music in the hall.

The numb part of me stirred and trembled, when I put my right hand on the top of the case, and heard that ringing crystal chime. If the music had not been dimly echoing into the room from beyond, I might have been able to sense what that inner part of me was trying to tell me.

And then, the violin music wound into a sultry crescendo. Silence fell. I heard a scattering of applause. Calls: "Bravo!" And a pause. The musicians had finished their first song of the evening.

Silence.

I wiped my palm on my pants leg and put it back atop the cabinet. Something . . . massive . . . was inside the cabinet . . .

. . . something whose mass was greater than its volume and density could account for . . .

I could see it in my mind's eye, almost as if I were looking past the walls of the case. Past, not through. If a three-dimensional man saw a safe built by Mr. A Square of Flatland, it would look like a rectangle to him. No matter how thick the lines in the plane were drawn, nothing could prevent the three dimensional man from merely looking . . . *over* . . . the boundary . . .

But this was not . . . over . . . I was looking . . . *another* direction . . .

I saw it. There were other objects in the case. They were flat, merely three-dimensional: a book, a phial of liquid, a playing card, a necklace.

The final object was a sphere, a globe of gold-white crystal. It was round in all directions, all dimensions.

A normal sphere had a volume described by four-thirds of the cube of its radius times pi. The surface area was the same as a sphere—I could see that—but the volume . . . the hypervolume . . . was half its radius to the fourth power, multiplied by a square of pi.

I began to reach out my hand in the direction that I had never been able to see before. I cannot tell you what direction it was.

My hand grew glittery with light, turned reddish, and seemed to shrink . . .

With a triumphant glissando of notes, the music started up again. The dream, or delusion, or whatever it was, ended. I suddenly could not imagine what I was doing, could not picture in my mind the direction I could not see. I could not visualize or understand how a sphere could be anything but a sphere. And I could not imagine seeing through solid walls . . .

The walls of the cabinet snapped shut on my hand. I felt a pressure on my wrist, but my eyes would not focus. It looked like the stump of my hand ended in a red haze, flat against the surface of the cabinet.

I squinted, trying to correct my vision. What was I seeing? I could feel the curved surface of the sphere . . . full, not flat . . . just beyond my fingertips, my hand . . . Almost touching . . .

I yanked my hand back with hysterical fury, afraid that it had been severed.

No; there it was, not a stump. My beautiful hand.

Little reddish dots and little blue dots floated toward and away from my hand for a moment, and my hand felt far heavier than it had been. But then the dots were gone, or they had never been there . . . or . . . they had moved off in two different directions. Directions I could no longer point to, or imagine, even though, just a moment ago, I had been able to.

My hand was normal weight again.

6.

Have you ever wondered whether you were insane? It is not a pleasant notion.

Standing there in the dark, I made a resolution to myself, that I was not. No matter what I saw or thought I saw, there was a rational explanation for it.

I may never know the explanation, but I could know that it existed without knowing its content. Algebra can manipulate numbers without knowing their values; I could do the same for my knowledge.

So I vowed to myself I was not insane. And, despite my agnosticism, I prayed to the Archangel Gabriel to tell his boss, whoever He might be, to make my vow not one vowed in vain.

7.

If I were not insane, what was the next logical step to take?

I put my hand on the case. The sphere inside was still humming or ringing as the music flattened the space it attempted to occupy. I got into a sprinter's stance and faced the Eastern window. And then I waited for the next break in the music.

Miss Daw would have to take a breather at some point, or the headless man would be called on to play a solo . . .

The foxtrot ended. The applause was more than the few people in the ballroom could account for. Maybe the men in the blue business suits were clapping with all their clouds of hands.

This time, I could clearly see the sphere, extending "above" and "below" the hyperplane of three-dimensional space in smooth hemispheres. It was still ringing with the echo of the shock the music had delivered to it; the sound was somehow something like light, and it allowed me to see the direction I had not been able to see before.

The shock waves the hypersphere gave off were only "sound" along one surface (hypersurface?) of the concentrically expanding ripples of pressure. There were other surfaces, five more of them, all at right angles to each other, producing other types of vibration aside from the pressure waves created by the music: the first axis gave off energy of a type that made the internal nature of objects clear to the reason, the way light makes the surface of objects clear to the eye; the second shed an energy that made clear to the will what objects were useful or useless; the third showed the conscience what moral obligations one was under; the fourth showed the understanding the degree of causality or indeterminateness an object enjoyed, as if measuring the number of future paths or probabilities each event shed. And there was one other form of energy or being-ness I could not account for, shining from the fifth and final axis. But something (could it have been that final energy form?) made all of what I was seeing so clear and familiar to me, it was as if information and understanding was being poured into my memory, as if it had always been there.

Somehow, in the fourth dimension, concepts that to humans were merely abstractions, dim shadows human reason could only guess at, were vivid and solid.

By the shine of that light, by the echo of that ringing, I could see how to move past and beyond the window without moving through it. I could see how the surface of time–space was curving toward me, based on the gravity distortions from the Earth's mass. All I needed to do was do to myself what I had done to the heavy door earlier this evening. Now that I could actually "see" the fan of world-paths spread out in shining lines from me and detect, with another new sense impression, the ponderous curve of space–time where the Earth's mass was distorting it, it was child's play to divert the forces so that I would fall more slowly, with less kinetic energy. A thirty-foot drop was nothing. I could practically step there . . .

I jumped. The world turned blue, and seemed to swell and fade in my vision. The walls and the window and the ground outside turned into gigantic things, huge, like walls of mist and cloud.

Something . . . a trio of somethings . . . was behind me. First seemed like a wheel: beautiful, pale, intricate, surrounded by many lesser wheels, with eyes and darts of fire radiating from each spoke, circle within epicycle, delicate and baroque. The second and the third were both roughly cone shaped, clusters of ugly knots and, along the outer surfaces of the knots, clusters and hands and fingers reached out in each direction.

I had miscalculated. The distances from the cabinet to the window to the ground were not the same in four dimensions as they had been in three.

And the light from the sphere fell off much more sharply than I expected. The hyperlight was dim a meter from the cabinet; it was sixteen times more dim at two meters; eighty-one times more dim at three. It was practically pitch black when I passed "over" the space occupied by the window, and I could no longer "see" the direction I was supposed to go.

The space–time occupied by Earth was like a plane spread before me, less than an inch "below" me. But when the sphere light was gone, I lost sight of it.

The universe was an inch or two away. I could not see it.

OTHERSPACE

1.

Nothing I can say can convey the horror. If I had been an astronaut on a space walk with a severed umbilical hose, countless light-years outside the galaxy, outside the local cluster of galaxies, I still would have been closer to home than I was at that moment. Because I still would have been in the same dimension.

The thing behind me, the pale wheel surrounded by lesser wheels, dipped one curving diameter into the plane I could not see, and rotated it. The wheels were made of what, in three dimensions, were sounds to be heard sequentially, linearly, in time.

We call it a song. But it is not. In this place, each composition was one simultaneous thing, eternal and unchanging, every part and every note existing in geometric relation to one perfect and harmonious whole.

I called the tiny crystalline echo ringing from the sphere in the cabinet a shock wave. It was not. It was a small sound, really.

This was not small. This was gigantic. This was larger than worlds.

With a force like a hundred earthquakes, like a storm front of unguessed power, an explosion filled hyperspace, blinding me, numbing my whole body. It was like being mashed in a trash compactor.

And then . . .

2.

I struck the snow with considerable force. My body was shaking with the shock of ice-cold that ran through me.

There was a haze of red and blue particles around me for a moment. I tried to get to my hands and knees, and was poleaxed by a blinding pain.

I vomited. Snow, a slurry of snowflakes, gushed from my mouth. How had snow gotten in my stomach?

I had the horrible, horrible image of a two-dimensional person being forced into the same flat plane as a two-dimensional patch of snow. His skin would just be a line; all his internal organs would be occupying the same place as the snow. Was snow in my veins, in my abdomen, my lungs? Inside my eyes and skull? In every cell?

Another moment of pain: my whole skin turned red. For a moment, I gave off a shaking shock wave similar to what the hypersphere had done; but something was carried with it. A cascade of shimmering red sparks of not-light flung snow in every direction around me, several pounds of it.

Then, it was over.

I blinked and looked around. There was an imprint around me in the snow. It looked more like an elongated snow angel than anything I can name. Whatever body had made this was long and streamlined, with wings and lines radiating from it. There were no footprints leading up to the imprint.

I was outside the Great Hall, about twenty yards from the front doors. The windows behind me were lit. I could see the rest of the campus, quiet in the moonlight.

Dimly, I could hear the faint, beautiful strains of Miss Daw's violin, playing a waltz by Strauss.

I rose to my feet and stumbled away, shaking, in the moonlight. Quentin's walking stick was still in my hand. As I came near the Manor House where our rooms were, I used it more and more to support my steps.

3.

It was slow and painful walking through the snow, and it grew slower and more painful as I went.

I passed by the window of the boys' dorm as I came around the corner to the Manor House. There was a rope hanging from an upper cornice, knotted with care.

I looked at that rope with infinite hatred. Hatred, because I ached in every limb, and had pains in my knees like someone suffering the bends. And because I knew Victor and Colin had been drugged, as had been Vanity. Even though one of us had been caught, we were still to hide any evidence of what we had done or how we had done it. It was one of Victor's rules.

So I climbed the rope. Usually, a rope climb up thirty feet would have taken me thirty seconds. This time, it took me thirty minutes, or more. Maybe an hour. It was cold, it was dark, I was in pain, and it was so very late.

I finally got to the window. It was dark inside. And locked. I couldn't open it.

It was only then that I realized that I could have picked up the sphere, the hypersphere in the locked cabinet, just before I jumped. I could have taken it with me. Had I taken it, I would have it now. I would be able to cast its hyperlight into the fourth dimension, see the objects around me as the flat things they really were, reach through walls, open locks, walk through windows . . .

I tapped on the window as loudly as I dared, and called softly to the boys to let me in. Now I was sure they had been drugged. Colin would not have passed up the chance to have me come into his bedroom at night, cold and in need of comfort.

Well, there was nothing else to do. I pulled that stupid walking stick out of my belt (it had been clattering and banging during my whole trip up the rope) and tucked it into the snow that had accumulated on the wide stone surface of the window sill. As I did so, my fingers touched something.

I brushed the snow aside and found a tiny cup, made out of pink wax, or maybe hardened bubble gum. The cup was crudely made, with fingerprints still visible in the waxy surface. In the bowl of the cup there was a blue fluid, which had frozen into a little pebble of ice.

I was frankly too weary to wonder what it was.

Five or ten minutes of work with my cold and unresponsive fingers, and I pulled up the rope and slung it over the cornice, which was now my pulley. In the other end I made a sling (tied off with a proper bowline) to set my hips in. Now I could simply lower myself by letting out rope and, when

I reached the bottom, one yank would bring the rest of the slack down with me.

That worked as planned. It was the only thing so far which had gone right that evening.

With the rope on my shoulder, I went over to our window. I called softly, and threw pebbles against the window. Nothing. Vanity did not answer.

So I walked (even more slowly, now that I no longer had the cane to lean on) over to the gardens behind the Manor House, and hid the coil in one of our agreed-upon spots.

As I walked, I thought: Why? Why did Quentin, who could levitate, need a rope to get out of his bedroom window?

And then I thought, in anger and disgust, why had I gone to such trouble to hide the rope, when I was about to be caught myself? I had no other way into the Manor House, unless I broke a window, except by the main door. Even if no one was there, and I made it upstairs unseen, whatever spell or alarm system Vanity had sensed Boggin lay down on the door to my room would reveal me once I opened the door to my room.

Well, there was nothing else to do. I was too cold to think of anything else. I marched quite boldly and bravely up to the main doors.

And, as I passed a copse of bushes, I saw a group of footprints in the snow. They were prints from a woman's shoe, and from the kind of woman who would wear high heels in the snow. Miss Daw. She had been posted here, watching the front doors.

Well, that reminded me of the prints I was leaving all over the place. Maybe they would melt when the sun came up, maybe not. I tore a branch from the bush, and dragged it behind me as I came to the front door.

I stood on the steps with the branch in my hand, wondering where to hide the thing. Then I laughed and tucked it into the bushes to one side of the door, the same place Vanity and I had been hiding when Mr. Glum's dog had passed us by.

The front door was unlocked. I stepped into the entrance hall.

And my eyes fell upon, yes, indeed, the old grandfather clock.

4.

Because Vanity, earlier this evening (how long ago it seemed!) had not been able to work the secret latch in our room to open the door to the hidden passage, I was not sanguine about my chances. I was assuming she was actually doing something—manipulating reality, doing magic, something—to create the tunnels out of thin air.

But when I went over to the clock, and opened the glass door, I could see that the back panel of the cloak was not true to the frame. There was a little crack around the edges. Vanity and I had never shut the panel closed behind us when we went back this way.

This time, I waited to time the swings of the pendulum, pushed the panel open with my hand, waited for the pendulum to swing back, stepped quickly in, waited a third time, darted a hand out past the hissing pendulum, yanked the outer glass door partway shut, waited, reached, pulled the door shut, waited, reached, secured the door, and then backed into the stairs, sliding the panel almost all the way shut. I wanted to leave the same crack I had found, in case I needed to use these passages some time again when Vanity was not around.

I was glad space was warped here, for now I had only to climb seven steps, duck my head, and crawl. Now I was on the same level as the third floor. At least, I did not have to climb two and three flights of stairs.

I crawled. I waved my hand in the air in front of me whenever it began to seem really heavy, for it had been heavy when I was doing quadradimensional effects, and I was trying to produce the red or blue sparks I had seen, in order to create a light to illuminate the black space I crawled through. Once or twice I thought I saw lights floating, but these were the same lights anyone will see who is tired, and in pain, in pitch darkness, with her eyes blurred with strain.

Pain has a funny way of focusing the mind. Only what hurts matters. Whatever else you used to think about before is as remote and unimportant as who won some argument you had as a child. You think about moving your right hand, and then you think about moving your left. You don't think about moving your right knee until the time comes to do it; if you worried prematurely about such things, the burden and the despair would be too much, and you would slump down in the dust, and cry. You don't think about how nice it would be just to lie down in this coffin of a corridor, or else you won't get up. You don't think about how to find the secret door to your room, which, unlike last time, is closed, and giving off no light, and you don't think about the fact that you don't know where the switch or latch is to open it from this side.

And you do not think about the fact that you took a wrong turn in the dark somewhere. That would make you cry, too.

You don't want to cry because you are the strong one in the group, really, the mature one. Practically an adult. Heroines in books don't cry.

But, despite the pain, you do keep one hand on the wall between crawls, to feel for the hinges where the door is. Those big, odd W-shaped hinges can't be hidden.

Also, it is important to remember not to crawl through spiderwebs. You were only here yesterday, so no spider (which should not come out in winter anyway) would have had time to construct a new one. If you feel a spiderweb you are on the wrong path.

And, when your hand does come across the huge, ungainly W-shaped hinge, it is important to remember that you are in a corridor only three feet high, because if you raise your head too fast, or try to jump for joy, you will bang your head with a loud noise on the stones above you. Ouch.

Good thing you are still wearing your lucky aviatrix cap. The leather, with all that hair tucked under it, offers some protection.

And then a voice comes: "What noise was that noise, friend Fraud?"

5.

The voice of Mr. ap Cymru answered him: "What noise, Excellency?"

"Hush! It may be our little wandering wanton, back from her peripatetic peregrinations."

A moment of silence crawled past even more slowly than I had been crawling. Fear, and the bump on my head, had cleared my wits somewhat. I could hear the voices had come through the wall; through the very hidden door panel I had my hand on.

After a while, ap Cymru said, "Excellency, I don't think . . ."

"'Then you shouldn't speak!' Aha Ha! Loyalest of all my disloyal loyalists, I hereby forbid you from feeding me such obtusely obvious straight lines again. I declare this declaration to be an imperial one, and I will backdate it to this day once I am Imperator. Now be quiet more quietly."

I moved my hand back and forth across the panel. A metal nub came under my thumb, with a smaller nub projecting from it. When I pushed, the metal nub slid in a semicircle, and a peephole opened.

So there actually were peepholes, after all.

The ray of light was brilliant after my long darkness. I put my eye to it, was dazzled for a moment, and then saw where I was.

I was looking at the Common Room. The door was open. Through the door, I could see partway down the corridor, and see the huge oaken door to my room. Even from here, I could see the padlock was open, hanging like a metal question mark, threaded through the eye of the open hasp.

In the Common Room, I saw the one television we were allowed was on, with the sound turned down. It was BBC2, and they were showing a game show. I have no idea what their normal programming is at 2:00 in the morning, but that seemed strange.

Next to a table littered with cigarette butts, a man was standing facing away from me, leaning his bottom, almost sitting, on a long black umbrella. He had on a yellow mackintosh, and, peeping over the edge of his collar and cuffs, I could see the white folds of a heavy wool sweater. From behind, I could tell that he had long black hair, as long as mine.

Despite the heavy cold-weather gear on the upper half of his body, his legs were sheathed in skintight fabric of garish green and black Lycra, like the pants professional bicyclists wear. They came to about midcalf. His feet were bare, except for some athletic tape he had wrapped around his lower calf and the balls of his feet. His toes and ankles were bare.

He had the legs of an athlete; his thighs and calves were knotted with muscle, but sleek and steel-hard, and the skintight leggings showed it off.

For a moment, I thought he had a stiff, black tail on which he rested his weight. But no.

The tightly wound black umbrella on which he half-leaned, half-sat, was one of the type with a large stirrup-shaped handle that unfolds into a tiny stool seat. The handle was unfolded at the moment, and he was using it as designed.

After what I had seen this evening, a man sitting on an umbrella-stick did not seem that odd. Of course, there were several perfectly fine seats and an overstuffed couch in the student Common Room, so maybe it was odd after all.

Tucked under one arm was what looked like a metal Frisbee, or maybe a pie plate. That was odd, just because I wasn't sure what it was.

When two lengths of electrical cable moved on the floor, and turned out to be not electrical cable at all, but two snakes, one white and one black, things started looking more odd.

Mr. ap Cymru came into view.

He was crawling along the ceiling like a spider.

His arms and legs were twisted backwards in their joints in a fashion that was hard to describe and horrid to look at. His feet were flat on the ceiling, with his heels pointed inward and his toes pointed outward; his knees extended in two great triangles past his bottom. His elbows, likewise, were waving in the air at angles no unbroken human bones could achieve. And his hands—which seemed to be exuding some sticky sap or gunk—were placed so that his fingers were all turned toward him and his thumbs were pointing away from his body. The whole thing looked like something Colin had done to his soldier dolls back when he got tired of them, the ones with fully posable limbs.

OK. This was certainly odd.

Ap Cymru rotated his head through 180 degrees like an owl, and spoke down toward the other man: "Excellency, that noise did not sound like a footstep."

"Ho hem. Maybe it was the sound of someone's grade average falling. This is alleged to be a school, you know. It is an excellent place to learn a lesson. Would you like me to teach you a lesson, Fraud?"

"Excellency, I have not betrayed you."

"And you give me your word, as a traitor?"

"Whom have I betrayed, Excellency?"

"Boreus told you his plans in confidence."

"Sir, he did not explicitly say not to tell you."

"Hum hemp hump. Well, I can see that. How could he overlook to say, by-the-by, don't spill my plans to the one person everyone thinks is dead, buried alive, having fallen farther than an anvil dropped from the zenith can fall in nine times the space that measure day and night, into the Tartarian Pit, after having been shot in the mouth and the eye by the Queen of Huntresses, whose bow of certain death leaves no prey alive? Yes, you are right. An obvious angle. The windbag should have covered it. Hired a lawyer before speaking to you."

"Lord, why would I lie to you?"

"Why would the Goddess of Lies in disguise lie to the Father of Lies? Hmm . . . let me think . . ."

"Boreus had schemed to lure the Uranian girl from her room tonight, in such a fashion as to put her in his debt. Perhaps she is less venturesome than he assumed."

"No, she is merely more clever than he assumed. No matter."

Now the man in the mackintosh jumped to his feet, snatching up the umbrella from behind him. He snapped the handle shut and struck a pose.

"I am a god, one of the Twelve! Boreus is a god as well, true, but his domain is only over the air that moves between north–northwest and north–northeast. My angle of action is larger.

"Fate is my toy to toy with as I will. I ordained that what Boreus wove into the tapestry of destined things would come unravelled. I ordained that the girl would find her bauble tonight; it has happened, or will. I ordained that she and I would meet; I assume she is watching us now.

"Little girl, wherever you are, in this dimension or in another, hear my words: I am your friend at a time when you will need friends most needfully. I offer you rescue, advice as honest as will suit my needs, power, glory, wealth, blah, blah, blah. The whole nine yards. I will grant you three wishes, but do not ask for immortality without asking for eternal youth. Think it over.

"OK, lesson over. Were you taking notes, Taffy ap Cymru? That is how to be a master of intrigue."

Ap Cymru rotated his head left and right. "Do you say she is in this room, invisible?"

"No. She is in plain sight, just not in *our* plain sight. Time's up! Are you going to turn me in?"

"Sir?"

"You could get a very good price for my head."

"Excellency, you will give me a better price for helping you keep it on your shoulders. When you are Father of Gods, make me Father of Lies."

"Oh, well said, Taffy. Well said. There is hope for you yet."

The man whistled, and poked his umbrella at his snakes. They wound up the shaft of the umbrella in two spirals, and rested their heads, facing each other, along the stirrup-shaped handle.

"Oh dear. Now I am not going to be able to get my umbrella open. I do hope it doesn't rain. I always hate the weather in England." The man said, moving toward the window. I now saw his face. He wore an eyepatch over one eye. There was something metallic in his mouth. It looked like his tongue was made of gold.

With no further ado, he put the pie plate on his head, flung open the sash, and stepped out onto the windowsill. A white vibration, like little wings beating too swiftly to be seen, flickered into existence around his ankles. He shot up into the night sky like a rocket.

DREAMS AND MISDIRECTION

1.

Because I could see my door from where I was, I now knew (assuming no space warps got in the way) about how far I would have to crawl to make the corner around the Common Room, and how far it was from there to the girls' dorm. I could even guess about how many crawl-steps it would take, using the distance from my hip to the shoulder as a unit measure.

Well, it took longer than I thought. I also assumed that, if Vanity had not actually built these tunnels out of her own imagination, the designer had meant them to be used. Which meant he expected people to be crawling or duckwalking, perhaps in the dark. Surely he would make the latches to open the secret panels easy to find, easy to manipulate. And yet he would probably not make them intrude into the corridor way where someone could trip on them. Where would he put the latch?

There were grooves cut in the floorboards on which my hands and knees rested. They were evenly spaced every few feet and, for every ten grooves, a double groove. When I came upon a triple groove at about the place my calculations told me the panel to my room was, I put out my hand and found the huge W-shaped hinges right there in the frame.

Feeling around, I detected four latch mechanisms. These were little boxes, one at each side of the frame. They were connected by a cruciform of short arms to a metal boss or nub in the center. This was the nub that covered the peephole. To open the door one had to slide aside the circular flap of metal covering the peephole, then pull the flap upright and rotate it. In other words, the door latch, when folded flat, covered the peephole. It was impossible to open one of these doors without first having the opportunity to see what was waiting on the other side.

I don't remember crawling into bed. I don't remember whether I tried to wake the drugged Vanity or not. I do remember it was cold.

2.

I dreamed that night that I was Secunda once more, and that Quentin was a toddler. We were sitting on the stairs that led to the kitchen, and I had some food Cook had given me: slices of apple, sections of banana and cucumber, some dates, and slices of hard-boiled egg with salt. I was trying to teach Quentin his letters. I was giving him a bite of whatever fruit or what-have-you whose letter he could tell me. Unfortunately his favorite letter was 'W,' and I did not have any fruits whose name started with that, until Cook (who, when I was small, was a giant) came looming over me like a starched white pillar of cloud, with a mushroom-shaped paper hat far, far above.

Cook stooped over and handed me a bowl with slices of watermelon in it.

I knew (because it had happened in real life) that Quartinus and Primus were about to come running around the corner, and that Quartinus would steal the watermelon slices out of my bowl, and that I would run him down. He would throw the slices into the dirt under the bushes rather than give them back, and I would drub him until Primus told me not to beat my juniors. Quentin would cry.

But, at the moment, before all that happened, it was a beautiful scene, and little Quentin's face (smeared with bits of banana and egg) lit up like sunshine when I told him he had to spit the seeds. I remember how I pulled him up to sit in my lap while we ate watermelon, just as if I were the Mommy he didn't have.

One of the eggs in my bowl chipped and cracked and hatched open. Through the broken pieces of shell I could see an endless darkness, streamers of stars and constellations, and, very tiny, in the center of the egg, a castle made of silver crystal and rainbow mist.

A small voice said, "The Son of Sable-vested Night sends greetings to the fair Princess Phaethusa, daughter of Helion the Bright, one of those who yet remain, who knew and ruled the world ere King Adam's reign.

"Nausicaa must stand upon the boundary stone, and grant passage to the power from Myriagon, your home. Recall that thoughts are all recalled by thought and thought alone; undo the magic of mere matter, and the night of no-memory shall break. I grant you shall recall this when you wake."

3.

I was expecting to be bruised all over, maybe bleeding internally, maybe dead that next morning. None of that happened. I do not know what the symptoms of fourth-dimensional shock are supposed to be, or how anyone can live who has had snow pressed into the fluid cells and internal cavities of every major organ, but apparently my body adjusted rather quickly.

The morning was miserable nonetheless. Usually there is time in the morning for Vanity and me to talk and swap tales. This morning, however, I was tired and she was still sleepy and dopey from the drug. When I tried to tell her all the things that had happened last night, she murmured a few confused questions. She was under the impression Quentin and I had gone off to a waltz party in the Great Hall, that he had kissed me, that I had stolen his walking stick, and that a strange drunk had thrown himself to his death out of the window of the Common Room.

Usually it was Mrs. Wren who got us up, dressed in our uniforms, scrubbed and ready for breakfast. Today, for some reason, it was Sister Twitchett, the school nurse.

There the two of us were, queued up (as queued up as two people can be) in our starched shirts and string ties and plaid skirts. (I hate those skirts—why couldn't I wear jeans to class? What I wore on my legs did not affect my brain.) And I was grinding my teeth in frustration. I hated Dr. Fell at that moment with a red hate that was sour in my stomach.

Not only had he kidnapped Quentin, maybe killed him, but Dr. Fell had doped up Vanity so that she could not concentrate when I tried to tell her the news I was bursting to tell her. What is the point of news if you cannot tell your friends? My favorite thing in life was to find out how people would react to things. Now there was no reaction.

Down the corridors we marched, down three flights. We passed the Entrance Hall. Someone (maybe me?) had left the front door open, and snow had blown in to stain the front carpet. The dirt Vanity and I had spilled from the potted plant in the alcove the night before last had not been cleaned up yet.

Both these little signs of decay made me wonder. The corridors were also unwontedly silent. The grandfather clock showed that we were being brought to breakfast somewhat later than was our wont. Where was everybody?

Vanity was looking a little more chipper and bright-eyed after our march through cold halls. Maybe the exercise woke her up a bit. By the time we were escorted up to where the three boys were waiting in their blue blazers, ties crooked, and yawning, Vanity was alert enough to whisper to me, "I thought you said he was missing!"

There was Quentin, looking sadder and more introspective than usual. There was something dark and grim in his features, an expression I usually associate with Colin. But it was an unrelieved sort of darkness, without the sarcastic smile and savage humor, which Colin struck like sparks in his dark.

I was so relieved that I broke ranks (as much rank as two people can be in) and ran across the hall to him. He looked so astonished when I threw my arms around him, and he looked so young that, for a moment, I thought he was the five-year-old Quentin I used to push around in Mr. Glum's wheelbarrow.

"Quentin!" I exclaimed. "I thought you were dead! What happened last night?"

His expression was lost, hopeless. "I don't remember. It's gone. The last thing I remember was palming his foul medicine. I woke up in the infirmary. Dr. Fell was . . . he . . ."

Sister Twitchett came up behind me. "Miss Windrose! No talking! This is blatant insubordination. Get back in line this instant, or I shall have to bring your name to the attention of the Headmaster!"

I turned on her, blazing eyed. "And what is he going to do, kill me? Kill us all? Throw us down into Hell? I will remember you, Twitchett. Do you want to be my enemy? I will not be a child forever." And I realized that, by saying that as I did, I was, as of that moment, no longer a child.

For a moment, I no longer feared them.

But the moment passed. I shrank back as the Sister advanced on me.

"Miss Windrose! This is unprecedented. You shall certainly be placed on report. You will behave yourself this instant! Apologize and take your place in line!"

I opened my mouth, but Victor coughed. His glance at me told me this was not the most opportune time, from a tactical point of view, for this scene.

So I merely apologized and took my place in line.

Twitchett knocked on the door of the kitchen. Mr. Glum's voice answered. We all marched in and took our seats.

No one was there except for Mr. Glum, and he had bags under his eyes and looked even more foul-tempered than usual. Sister Twitchett turned us over to him.

Our usual breakfast with china plates and centerpieces, folded napkins, and so on, was not there. There was nothing on the table except cold cereal. There was not even milk. Cook and Cook's assistant were not present.

Victor said, "What's going on? Where's our breakfast?"

Mr. Glum said sourly, "No talkin'. Rule o' silence and all that." He was seated at his usual place in the window box, not at the main table with us.

Colin said, "I need a proper breakfast with bacon and eggs. Otherwise I might have another fit of epilepsy."

"Shut up," said Glum.

"It's a medical condition! Dr. Fell said so! You can ask him, if you like. Where is he?"

Glum squinted angrily at him. "You shut up, or I'll give you a lip so fat 'twill stop up that hole in your face like a cork!"

I had seen Mrs. Wren at breakfast too often not to know the signs. Mr. Glum had a hangover.

It was Quentin who spoke up next. "If you please, Mr. Glum, can't we cook ourselves some breakfast? The cooking staff seems to be absent. The kitchen is only just through that door. You want something better than toasted wheat, don't you? I will make you a fine pot of hot coffee."

That Quentin was talking, and talking calmly, drove a cold fury over Mr. Glum.

"Will not be quiet, eh? Will defy me, eh?"

Mr. Glum stood up, a bald, wiry, stocky man. He was not muscular, but his body was toughened by many years of work in the gardens and grounds around this house. His tool belt was in a heap on the floor beside where he sat, and he stooped, took a hammer in his hand, and straightened up again. From the look in his eye, he was ready to do murder.

Vanity jumped up to her feet. "Grendel! I mean, Mr. Glum! There's no need for you to get up! I'll get the food! You want me to serve you, don't you?"

He squinted at her, dumbstruck. "Serve me?"

"Serve your breakfast, silly! I can cook, really I can. You can sit at my place, and I'll go make you coffee and eggs and stuff. Every man wants a woman to cook for him, doesn't he?"

"Oh," said Glum. "Oh, aye, that he does."

"Well, then!" she smiled brightly. She patted the seat cushion of her chair. "Just sit down here where I was sitting. I got the seat all warm for you. I'll go put the kettle on. No one will know."

Almost like a sleepwalker, Mr. Glum walked around the table. I could smell the soil and grease in his work clothes as he walked past my chair. He was not a tall man, but Vanity is rather short, and he loomed over her. He stepped very close indeed to her. From the way he bent his head I thought he was going to kiss her. Vanity, never flinching, kept her smile firmly fixed in place.

But Mr. Glum just sighed, and threw himself down in her seat, and put his hammer (clangk!) on the table next to his plate. He leaned back and put his boots up on the table. Tiny flakes of soil fell onto the polish.

"Aye," he said, tucking his hands behind his head. "Who is to know? Eh? Who is to know?"

We sat in silence, staring at Mr. Glum, while he whistled and stared at the ceiling. After a little bit, there came a noise or two of drawers rattling, a crash of crockery, and a sad little, "Oh no!" from the kitchen.

Then: "Um . . . ? Mr. Glum? I may need some help in here. Could you send in Quentin?"

Suspicion flickered in his eyes. "No, I think not. Quentin, is it? I will let Miss Amelia in there to help."

"But she doesn't know how to cook! She's a tomboy!"

Mr. Glum gave me the most unpleasant stare. "I am sure she will shape up into a woman, right enough, if'n she just had a man to train her to it. G'wan, Goldilocks. Go help in the kitchen."

Without arguing, I went to the kitchen.

"What are you doing?" I whispered to her.

"Quentin is up to something. He wants Mr. Glum to drink coffee. I'm making coffee."

"I know all that. I mean, what are you doing putting the coffee grounds into the coffeepot? This isn't instant coffee, you ninny!"

I found the filter and the brass percolator, spooned in the amount specified on the bag, and waited. The brass cylinder of the coffee percolator was very highly polished (Cook kept his kitchen as neat and bright as a Man-o-War) and I could see my reflection, distorted and thin, in it.

After a moment, I felt heat on my face and my nose felt heavy and there was a stinging in my eyes.

Vanity said in frightened wonder, "Why are you crying?"

"Quentin kissed me last night."

Vanity looked stone-faced. "What? Are you and he . . ."

"Don't be a ninny! He did it to shut me up! We were floating and the wind spirits were going to drop us. I slapped him. And he treated me horribly after that, ordering me around and everything!"

Her expression softened. "So what was the . . ."

"It was my first kiss. Dr. Fell erased his memory. And now, to Quentin, it never happened. Can you think of anything more horrible? Reaching into someone's skull and taking away their most precious memories? It's worse than death."

I wiped my eyes with my palm impatiently.

When the coffee was ready Vanity insisted on making us both put on the little lace caps the maids sometimes wore. She had found them in a cupboard.

Vanity also found some white aprons. She tied one so tightly around my waist that I could not breathe. I paid her back by tying hers even tighter.

She forced me to unbutton the top three buttons of my blouse and tuck my collar under, to make an impromptu décolletage. She did the same, and also stuffed some napkins into her brassiere, to push up her breasts like a showgirl's. (Not that she needed it to begin with.) She tried to do the same to me, but I put my foot down.

As a compromise, I hiked up my skirts till the waistband sat above my ribcage. With my blouse tails and the apron to cover it, it merely looked as if I were wearing a miniskirt. Vanity liked the look and copied me, and we spent another moment tying and untying the apron bows again, to see which one of us could force the other into the more wasp-waisted figure without fainting from lack of air.

We got a silver tray, a slim vase (but there was no flower to put in it), sugar bowl, creamer, and a pitcher of orange juice we found waiting in the refrigerator. Little china cups and some glasses, and we were ready. We arranged this all on the tray, and walked out into the breakfast room, swaying our hips.

Vanity threw her hand up in a gesture like a game show hostess, saying, "Ta-Da!"

I leaned over to put the tray down next to Quentin. Vanity curtsied toward Mr. Glum. Victor and Colin were staring.

To me, it looked like a contest to see whether Mr. Glum's eyes would pop out of his skull before Vanity's breasts popped out of her bra. Then I noticed, bent over as I was, I was just as much on display as she was, and they were all staring at my cleavage, too.

Quentin took the lid off the coffeepot, laid it carefully to one side, and said to Vanity, "Why don't you pour?"

She picked up a coffee cup and saucer, stepped over to Mr. Glum's chair—I noticed she stepped to the far side of the chair, so that Mr. Glum had to turn his head away from Quentin to keep his eyes on her—and curtsied again.

Quentin stood and passed her the coffeepot.

Mr. Glum darted a suspicious glance at Quentin. Quentin smiled, and sat, but picked up the sugar bowl and proffered it to me. "Perhaps Mr. Glum would like some sugar, Miss Windrose."

I took the sugar bowl and walked over to Mr. Glum. I curtsied again (Glum took the opportunity to make sure he hadn't forgotten what my breasts looked like) and said, "One lump or two?" I tried to impersonate the Lady Cyprian's tone, and make my voice coo.

It must have worked, or something did.

He was smiling at me. I cannot imagine how I could have been inspiring lust in any male creature at that moment. I had been crying; my eyes were red, as well as baggy from lack of sleep. I felt like a gym shoe. Messy, rumpled, and ill-used.

But Mr. Glum was looking at me like I was the Queen of Sheba. He was already drawing up filthy plans in his mind on how he would use me once he was done with Vanity. I was dessert.

And he hadn't looked at his coffee cup yet. There was a blue ice cube in it. The same little blue ice cube I had seen on the windowsill in the snow last night. It was melting, but it hadn't melted yet.

"I take my coffee bitter, black, and hot." Mr. Glum announced. He raised the cup, and started to take his eyes off me . . .

I snatched up a thin spoon from the tray. Glum looked up, puzzled. I kissed the spoon slowly. Glum stared at my lips.

I said in a husky whisper, "At least, let me stir it."

He held his cup toward me, his expression like a hypnotized man, but a smile beginning to tug at his lips.

I stirred the coffee, smiling down at him. Whatever he was. A sea creature of some sort. A mad thing. Maybe a killer.

But he looked so happy, just looking at me.

Vanity now moved around the table, putting down tumblers and filling them with orange juice for the boys. It amazed me how much leaning over was involved in pouring three cups of juice.

Colin held up his glass to me, "You there! Servant Girl! I need someone to stir my juice. Use that same spoon, will you?"

I blushed furiously. I am sure my ears turned red. I stomped over to him, wondering whether or not I should spit in the spoon. Mr. Glum had taken his feet off the table and let them drop loudly to the floor.

I decided that making a fuss might remind Mr. Glum of his duty to be watching us. So I merely curtsied to Colin and stirred his juice with the spoon I had kissed.

I touched his glass to steady it. The ice cubes were trembling in the glass. His hand was unsteady. Standing as close to him as I was, I could hear that his breathing was unsteady as well.

Because I wasn't actually stirring anything into his cup, I wasn't sure when to quit. Colin reached up and touched my hand with his, and said hoarsely, "Thank you."

It did not even sound like Colin, not the irredeemable, unflappable, mocking Colin I knew.

Boys are so odd. All I was doing was stirring juice.

Mr. Glum stood up suddenly, and threw his coffee cup across the room. It splashed and made a brown stain on the wall.

He turned to Quentin, "You done sommat to me, witch-boy. You witched me. Now I am going to break in your skull bones with this hammer." And he picked up the hammer.

Quentin stood up. "Mr. Glum, you underestimate me. Do you think I poisoned you? Look." He poured himself a cup of coffee from the coffeepot, and sipped it.

Glum stared at him, licking his lips.

Quentin said, "Come, sir. We drank from the same pot. What makes you think I have done anything? Are you sleepy? That is only because you had a late night last night. Don't you expect to be tired when you've had a long night?"

Glum said, "No. You're trying to trick me. It won't work if I don't listen."

"Do you believe in magic, Mr. Glum?"

"Course I do. Who don't?"

"Do you believe I am a magician? I have Power?"

Glum nodded. "Up until I break your skull bones."

"You think unseen spirits wait on my command. Creatures in the air, made of subtle essences?"

"I seen you feeding them blood from your arm. In the woods. You're a spawn of The Gray Sisters. I know your kind."

"Then you believe I can make your hammer too heavy to lift, don't you?" He pointed his finger at the hammer. "It is getting heavy. Too heavy. Iron and wood, things of the earth, long to return to the earth, their home, and they pull downward. Downward. You should not have raised it against me in anger."

Glum dropped the hammer.

Quentin pointed his finger at Mr. Glum's knees. "You put your feet on the table, where you know they should not go. That was impertinent. That was rude. Now your feet are going numb. Your legs will no longer support you. Sit."

Glum sat in the chair, flopping down like a puppet with its strings cut.

Quentin pointed at Glum's face. "You stared with covetous lust at a girl young enough to be your daughter. That was worse than rude. Worse than a crime. Your eyes are filled with low thoughts, low and heavy thoughts, and now they will shut. Close your eyes. Fall. Sleep."

Mr. Glum sagged down, and his head fell onto the table with a thunk.

We all sat staring in silence for a moment, awed.

Colin stood up and clapped his hands, like a man at a concert applauding a maestro. "Brilliant! Bravo! You magicking him! Sucked the energy right out of him!"

Quentin sat down, looking pale and weak. "Don't be an ass. There is no such thing as magic."

Colin pointed at the snoring bulk of Mr. Glum. "Then what's that?"

"Dr. Fell's medicine. I didn't drink it last night."

I laughed and clapped. "The blue ice cube!"

Victor said, "Ice cube?"

Quentin said, "I spit Dr. Fell's medicine into a little wax cup I keep hidden about my person for just such occasions. I thought it might be easier to carry up my sleeve if it were frozen—the potion, I mean—and left it on the windowsill last night. I had an idea for an experiment I wanted to try. I lowered myself by a rope, and started walking North . . ."

He spread his hands and looked up, woebegone. "And that's it. That's about all I recall. I don't remember what the experiment was or what my idea was. I don't remember Dr. Fell finding me. I woke up strapped to a table in his lab. Dr. Fell did something to me. Injected me with something, or did something to my brain. What did I do last night?"

Vanity pointed at me and said happily, "You tied up Amelia and made her kiss you!"

Everyone turned and looked at me.

Quentin's eyes slowly traveled up and down my body, examining my ankles and legs, lingering over my hips and my narrow waist, pausing at my cleavage, but coming to rest at my tear-stained eyes.

"Well. Damn Dr. Fell to Hell," he said softly. Brave words, but he looked like he wanted to cry, too.

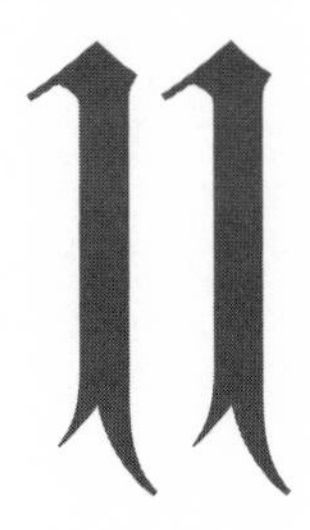

PARADIGMS AT BREAKFAST

1.

The first words out of my mouth were: "The Greek Gods run the school. We're hostages in a war. They're afraid to kill us, because our families will attack. Quentin can fly. They're going to send us to Hell for safekeeping. Except Vanity is being sent to Atlantis. Zeus is dead and Mars and Vulcan both want the throne. Mercury was in the Common Room last night, and he knew I was in the wall, and he said he'd give us anything we wanted. Taffy ap Cymru is actually a goddess. And a cross-dresser, I guess. Taffy works for Mercury. I fell into the Fourth Dimension, and Miss Daw, who is actually a fourth-dimensional siren shaped like a wheel, played music, which forced me back into normal time–space, except I landed in a pile of snow."

Everyone was just staring at me.

"Mercury made it destined for me to find a hypersphere that awakened my powers, which is locked in a safe in the Great Hall, where I was hiding because Dr. Fell caught him, because Boggin (whose real name is Boreus) was waiting for me, and he shined a blue beam of light on him and Quentin had this look on his face but I couldn't tell what he was looking at that looked so horrible and I wanted to ask him but now he can't remember. Someone in a dream told me how to break the spell. Vanity has to help. Her real name is Nausicaa."

Everyone continued to stare.

I said, "You believe me, don't you? Would I make up something like this?"

Colin said, "Did Quentin really tie you up? And make you kiss him?" Without waiting for an answer, he turned and pointed at Quentin, "Big Q!" then he gave him the thumbs-up, "You the man!"

I said in exasperation, "It wasn't like that! I was only blindfolded."

Vanity stamped her foot. "You said he kidnapped you and threw you out the window!"

I said, "No, I said he picked me up and carried me out the window. We were flying, or levitating, or something."

Quentin looked both pleased and sad. "It worked, then. It actually worked! I'm a genius!" Then he muttered: "The best night of my life, and I can't remember it."

Colin said to Quentin, "I am so jealous of you it is going to make me barf. How come you get the blonde? Dibs on the redhead."

Vanity stamped her foot again, "Shut up your horrible face, Colin, or I'll have Quentin turn you into a toad! Amelia is trying to tell us the most important thing we ever found out about what is going on here, and all you can do is jabber!"

Victor said, "Amelia, did you mean that the dream told you how to break the so-called spell on Quentin?"

"Yes. No. It was ambiguous."

"We should hear your story out, but also try to get Quentin repaired as soon as possible. Two witnesses see things one witness misses."

I said, "It's a long story. I am not sure how long we will have the house and grounds to ourselves. There was some sort of party last night after the Board meeting, and Venus was running it. I think everyone is sleeping it off."

Victor said, "Are you saying we should try to undo Quentin, first?"

"And maybe break into that safe I found. It's on the way. The table in the Great Hall is the thing the dream said could break the spell."

Quentin jumped to his feet. "Let's hurry. Actually, let's run."

"Good idea. Race you." Victor leaped to his feet and was out the dining room door, followed closely by Quentin. Their footfalls echoed in the corridor.

Vanity hesitated. "Are we just going to leave Mr. Glum laying here?"

Colin rose to his feet and was sauntering toward the door, in no great hurry. "You're right. Let's slit his throat now. Save us the trouble of doing it later."

"You're sick!" she said, and ran out the door.

Meanwhile, I was not relishing the prospect of an early morning run through the snow, so I was not moving any faster than Colin. I tried to tug my skirt back down into place, but the apron strings were tied so tightly behind my back that my skirt (which was hiked up high and trapped under it) was pinned in place. I was trying to undo the knot when Colin stepped up behind me.

"Allow me," he said.

"Thank you. It will be a relief to breathe again."

"Here, suck in. I need some slack."

I blew out my breath and then tried to make my waist even smaller, and Colin tucked and tugged at my back where I couldn't see. He hummed happily to himself.

I should have been more suspicious, more quickly. I tried to turn, but he yanked, and the apron sash cinched even more tightly.

"You bastard!" I clawed at the small of my back, but the knot seemed to have somehow grown into a super knot.

He grabbed both my hands by the wrist just a moment before I was about to swing on him. He watched me struggling a moment, smiling darkly.

"I'm stronger than you," I said, feeling foolish. "I can move huge iron doors you can't lift."

"Show me," he said.

Because he was standing behind me, he simply twisted both my arms up behind my back. My possible options at that point consisted of arching my shoulders back as far as possible and standing on tiptoe.

Somehow, somewhere, Colin had turned from a little annoying boy into a dangerous young animal. I could not even really struggle in his grip; he had grasped me too cunningly.

I noticed that he smelled nice. And tall. When did he get to be taller than me? I hadn't noticed. Had that happened this year?

And strong. And ruthless and confident.

I suddenly began to feel silly and out of breath. I told myself it was because Colin was holding me in an awkward position that I could not catch my breath. I tell myself a lot of things. I lie to myself a lot.

It was because Colin was holding me.

I had been trying to toy with Victor, and so I let Vanity, harebrained

Vanity, talk me into one of her flirtatious schemes. I had hiked up my skirt and pulled down my blouse, thinking a little nectar would attract the bee I wanted. I had gotten a wasp instead. There was something dangerous and reckless about Colin that Victor did not have.

I do not believe a man can hold a girl, squirming and helpless, and not know the effect it has on her. I wanted him to do something. I wanted him to kiss me. But he just stood there, his grip getting tighter, his eyes like two blue embers glinting like the eyes of a devil.

I was blushing with furious embarrassment by this point. I told myself I was blushing with fury. Like I said, I tell myself a lot of things.

"Let go of me." My voice came out in a husky whisper. That surprised me. He had only had his hands on me for a moment, no longer. I was in love with Victor. Wasn't I?

"Why?" Little mocking sparks seemed to glitter in those blue devil-embers of his eyes.

"Because, from this position, I cannot kick you in the crotch, break your nose on my knee when you double up, and step on your neck when you fall over."

Colin whispered in my ear, "Don't make me jealous of Quentin. He's my best friend." I felt his lips brush my earlobe.

Victor and Vanity all reappeared in the doorway at that moment, with Quentin looking downcast behind them.

Victor said, "What are you doing, Colin?"

There was a sharp snap in his voice I had never heard before. Jealousy . . . ?

Victor's eyes drank in the sight of me. I felt as if he were looking into my soul, reading my mind. He saw the rose blush to my skin. Unlike Colin, Victor knew what it meant. I could not hide the blush on my skin, the shortness of my breath, the dilation of my pupil, or the helpless quiver deep inside me. I could not even move my hands to cover my face because Colin was still holding me, helpless as some prize doe caught by a hunter, exposed to the penetrating gaze of Victor Triumph.

Victor looked in my eyes and he saw that I wanted Colin's strong hands on me. I wanted to be helpless in his arms. He saw how pleased, how flustered I was by the sensation. He saw everything.

But that wasn't the message I wanted him to see. It was your hands, Victor, I wanted; your strength I want to triumph over me.

Victor turned away, his face cold. My heart reached a nadir. If I could have died by a sheer critical mass of misery, I would have ignited into a ball of darkness, then and there, and taken most of the school with me.

Colin was oblivious to all this. He spoke in a tone of lilting mockery.

He said, "I was telling the serving wench what I wanted for breakfast."

Victor said, "Well, if you two are done with your mating ritual, we have serious business."

Colin let go of me and jumped back.

It felt strange, for a moment, to have my hands loose and free. The misery in my heart changed shape suddenly. It was as if it said in my ear: don't blow yourself up in a ball of darkness! Just get Colin!

Good idea.

I carefully stepped over and picked up Mr. Glum's hammer from the table.

"Tut! Tut!" said Colin, scampering back out of range. "Serious business to discuss!" To Victor he said, "She wants to hurt me!"

Victor threw himself down in his chair and put his feet on the table. "Probably serves you right. Amelia, make sure you get Mr. Glum's fingerprints on his hammer after you do the deed."

Colin backed up, pointing a finger at me. "You're not going to kill me on an empty stomach, are you? None of us has eaten yet. This may be the only day we will ever have the run of the kitchen!"

Quentin smiled, and then laughed. He said, "That is true, Victor. Food first. Death later."

Victor looked at Quentin, looked at his own feet on the table, frowned a little nervously, and sat up, putting his feet back on the floor. "True enough. Amelia, no skull bashing till later. Colin, stop acting like a jerk. Quentin, decide what you want us to make you for breaky. It's the least we can do since we can't undo your memory block yet."

Well, I was not going to disobey a direct order from Victor. Beside, their lightheartedness was contagious. I reluctantly put the hammer back down on the table.

2.

"What happened?" I asked. "You were gone for only a moment."

Victor said, "We could see from the front door that there were workingmen swarming all over the Great Hall. They're pulling the roof apart to lift the table out. The table you say we need. If they pull it out the way they put it in, it should be kept under a tarp in the Blacksmith's Shed until they can find a lorry big enough to haul it."

Vanity said, "The good news is, no one else is up yet, though."

Quentin said, "Maybe we should run, and run now. Just pick a direction and keep moving. Between Dr. Fell's drugs and Mr. Glum's hammer, and what little Amelia already said, we may be in a lot more danger than we know."

Victor said, "Amelia? How dangerous is it? More dangerous than heading out along the highway without money? So dangerous that we can't wait for you to tell us your story?"

I said, "The War God will kill anyone who kills us. And it would cause a war. And I don't want to run without at least breaking into that safe. I can't see into the new directions without the hyperlight it gives off. And I am not walking anywhere until someone helps me take this damn thing off!"

Colin said loudly, "I object! The serving girl is trying to get out of uniform!"

Colin was staring at my cleavage again. I made an angry noise and started to reach for my buttons to do them up.

Quentin said, "Wait a moment." He looked at Vanity, who was also beginning to tug at her skirt, and to reach for her buttons. Vanity and I stopped.

Quentin looked at Victor. "I think we should have a ruling on this, Victor."

Victor nodded, trying not to smile. "Quentin's right. He has been viciously attacked, I dare say, wounded, by Dr. Fell. We all need to do our part to keep Quentin in good spirits, don't you agree, girls?"

Vanity put her hands on her hips. "What are you saying? I only did this to distract Mr. Glum!"

Victor rose to his feet. "Very good. Commendable. Now stay like that until I say otherwise. You too, Amelia."

Vanity and I looked at each other. She squinted at me, a little impish smirk begging to appear on her lips. She was waiting to see what I would do. I was waiting to see what she would do.

Colin stepped up behind me and swatted me across the bottom. "Go to, wench! Go to! Your kitchen awaits!"

He did not duck quickly enough to avoid my counter swing.

Victor put his arms around Mr. Glum and unceremoniously dumped him on the carpet. He straightened and said, "You're going into the kitchen, too, Colin. Only Quentin is excused."

Colin was holding his mouth. "Of course. Wouldn't miss it. Kitchen is where the girls are."

Quentin stood and picked up his chair. "Since this seems to be sort of an impromptu birthday for me, I will come and watch. Whichever girl isn't involved in some part of the cooking process will dote on me. Agreed?"

Victor said, "Agreed."

Colin said, "And the other girl will be . . ."

". . . Kicking you in the balls, over and over again," I said. "Agreed?"

"Agreed!" said Vanity.

She took Quentin's arm and I took the other one. We both pressed up against him, wiggling our bottoms and batting our eyelashes, as we escorted him to the kitchen.

Colin muttered, "Fie. And he says he's not a magician."

3.

How long does it take for happiness to be complete? I do not know how long we were in the kitchen. I suppose, objectively, it might have been as little as an hour, or even less. But it seemed to last all day. Like an endless vacation.

The kitchen was huge. All the brightwork gleamed, all the pots and pans and kettles and knives were ranked and racked and arranged by size. There were two little refrigerators and a big walk-in, and a stovetop the size of Scotland and Wales combined.

And we could have anything we wanted. For the first time in our lives, we made what we fancied in whatever way suited us. An omelette of a dozen eggs; beef that we fried in grease instead of boiling; slabs of bacon as thick as your hand; cooking sherry poured into measuring cups and drunk as toasts. Mostly, we made a mess.

Colin drank coffee for the first time in his life, the grown-ups' drink. He made a face and pronounced it an abomination. But he drank a second cup, just because it had been forbidden him for so long.

Vanity had always wanted to taste a hamburger; she ground up several types of meat in the blender, and used toast for buns, and cucumber because we found no pickles. She put catsup mixed with horseradish on the resulting mass, calling it "secret sauce," and claimed she had made a Big Mac. It looked like ground meat on toast to me, but when she gave me a bite, it was delicious. No matter what it tasted like, it was delicious, because she had made it with her own hands.

Quentin was juggling eggs with one hand, six, seven, and eight, while ordering me hither and thither for the various things he wanted in his giant omelette.

And, to my astonishment, Victor could cook. He took one cookbook off the shelf of ninety or so that Cook had, and flipped the pages as fast as his thumb would move. Then he measured and chopped and set timers and mixed with the precision of a machine, or a mad scientist. He was good at it. We ended up eating almost all what he made, because what we started turned out somewhat burnt, or raw.

We sat on the spotless floor in a big circle, plates and bowls and saucers spread about us in Roman luxury, eating everything with our fingers.

We had dessert before, during, and after the meal. Colin had discovered where the dessert pantry was—that famous pantry we had never been able to find as kids. It was locked, but Victor ran his hand over the jamb, and the lock clicked open of its own accord.

They had gathered all sorts of treats, meatballs, and cheeses, and little snacks in folds of sugar-fried bread. There was tray after silver tray of it, all gathered for some after-the-meeting reception, which, because Venus had shut down the meeting, the Visitors and Governors never got to. There were éclairs and pastries and a cake of seven layers. The things I remember best were these cupcakes made of chocolate foam, topped with froth of a different kind of chocolate, where the cups were not paper, but yet a third kind of chocolate, hard and crunchy, yet melting like a snowflake on the tongue. I had never seen anything like it before. Edible dishes! Like something out of a Roald Dahl book!

And there was a bottle of champagne.

Things became quite merry after that. Part of the reason why the boys were merry, I am sure, was seeing Vanity and me in our absurd impromptu maid outfits, waiting on them. Part of the reason was that we were lightheaded from sipping champagne.

But we were drunk on information. I had unearthed a treasure trove of secrets, secrets which had been kept from us our whole lives.

And I was merry because I was the center of attention during the first half of the meal. I talked and talked and not even Colin interrupted me.

Quentin had found Cook's account books and was writing notes on what I was saying on the back of pink receipt slips.

What a funny feeling. No one had ever thought what I had to say was important enough to write down before.

4.

Then came questions.

Colin asked: "Her name is Nausicaa or Nausea or something. Your dream called you Phaethusa. Did you find out my name? You didn't, did you?" And he threw an olive at me, using his fork as a catapult.

Quentin asked: "Those creatures were Hecatonchire, the hundred-handed giants from Greek myth. They looked like humans, I am supposing, because something in the human world makes them. But they said the table gave them the ability to use their powers nonetheless. Notice this is the same table mentioned in Amelia's dream."

Victor asked: "Why did you fail to mention that the staff here thinks we will get sick and die if we get too far from the boundaries of the estate? That might be a good thing to test before we make our escape."

Vanity asked: "Why did you keep slapping Quentin? It's not like he *wanted* to kiss you!"

Colin asked: "Why was Mavors or Mars or whatever his name is carrying both a spear and a pistol? What the hell is the point of that? Are they magic items? Are there different laws of nature in different worlds?"

Quentin asked, "You said that when you were in the Fourth Dimension, you saw behind you both a wheel surrounded by a lesser wheel, and two cone-shaped things. What were those things—?"

Victor said, "I don't understand this whole idea that they are mythical gods and goddesses. I mean, how is it supposed to happen? Homer sits down to write the *Iliad*, and some real god becomes immediately aware of it, and sends telepathic particles into the poet's brain to make him write down what the facts are? If so, why didn't these gods just publish newspapers? Of course, I am making the assumption that there was a man named Homer, and he did write a book called the *Iliad.* They might have made up that whole poem, just before they opened the school, just to teach us. Greek could be a made-up language, which they forced us to study just to annoy us."

Vanity said, "Who eventually fell in love? At the ball?"

Colin: "And what the hell was Boggin actually trying to accomplish?"

Quentin: "The man whose head was off was Orpheus. Was there anyone else at the table who talked as if they were in his group? The Unseen One he is representing is Hades, the god of the Underworld. The Psychopomp is the guide and guardian of souls to the Land of the Dead. Hermes is supposed to be in that position."

Victor: "Are we members of the same race? Were we adults before they made us into the shape of children? You know we must all be shapechangers, don't you? Why else would they measure us every night?"

5.

There was one question in that mess I could answer: "It must have been the Hecatonchire. The cone-shaped things I saw behind me. I was looking through the wall at that point, and looking at the people around the table.

"You said it yourself, Colin, that they are giants in their own world. Why a cone? Imagine you saw a boy growing up into a man, but that you could see through time as a dimension. His three-dimensional cross sections would continually increase in the direction of future, continually decrease in the direction of past. A cone. Except in this case, I do not think the directions are past–future. I am calling them 'red' and 'blue' as one seems to Doppler shift light to higher energy states, and one to lower."

Vanity asked, "What did you look like?"

I said, "What?"

She said, "In the fourth dimension. I keep trying to picture it, but all I can picture is that you would see yourself as a flat person. Her skin is a line rather than a surface. Her internal organs are flat, like an ameba's. She only has one eye. Uck. Yuck. Just trying to picture it is gross."

"No, you're wrong," said Colin pulling up one of his eyelids. "It would only be *half an eye.*"

"Ugh! Ugh!" said Vanity, entirely discomforted.

Quentin said, "It is a bit unnerving. If you, Amelia, are like Vanity's flat person in a plane, let's say something like this floor, then by rotating in the third dimension—a dimension of which creatures living in the floor would have no conception—they would see you turn into a line. So what would happen in three dimensions? Would you become flat, like picture?"

"No," I said, "You'd see a cross section. The man from flatland, if tilted, would have only two points of his skin surface intersecting the world-plane. By analogy, three-D folk would see a tilted four-D person as a hoop of flesh surrounding a flat section of blood and internal . . ."

"Oh, please!" said Vanity. "Pul-ease, can't we talk about something else while we are eating!"

I said to her, "But I don't think I'm flat. I mean, I don't think I do not have other three-dimensional surfaces embracing my volume. My hyper-volume. What I saw of myself, I seemed to have streamlined-looking wings or fans reaching off in other directions. And branches, or lines of energy—bright things, made of sound, or thought, or music. Or something. I think what we call matter and energy are merely two different rotations of the same hyperparticle. I had other senses, too."

Colin said, "So you looked like a squid with wings, and you actually have a cluster of eyeballs and dripping ears on the end of stalks hidden in n-space where we cannot see them. I will still think you are lovely, Amelia."

Victor said, "You could poke your finger into someone's brain without touching his skull."

Vanity said, "Ugh! You people are as gross as toads! Can't we change the topic?!"

Colin said, "Yeah, but we are only toads that have been run over by a car, and flattened. Amelia is a real fat 4-D toad. We can't see what she really looks like because we flat folk only have . . . *half an eye!*"

"Ugh! Uck! Make him stop!"

Quentin said, "One last question, then we can ask more about the pagan gods. Amelia, what was the sense of weight you said you saw coming from the safe?"

"It was the sphere. The hypersphere. And it's mass, not weight."

"Why?"

"Mass is an intrinsic property. Weight is a behavior of matter under . . ."

"No, no. Why was the sphere massive?"

"Oh. Simple geometry. Picture the amount of area covered by a circle. The ratio of the area to the circumference is pi *r* squared. Rotate the circle on any axis, and the area swept out will be a sphere. The volume of the sphere will be four-thirds pi *r* cubed. You see?"

"No."

"Um. If I used a crayon to draw the circumference and another crayon to color in the area, the first crayon would lose a bit and the second a bit more. Use a third crayon to color the surface of a balloon, and a fourth crayon to somehow fill in the entire inner volume of the balloon. The first crayon uses a bit and the second crayon loses a whole lot. Rotate the balloon in the fourth dimension to create a hypervolume. The first crayon fills in the volumes of the six balloons that form its hypersurface, the second crayon has to fill in a hypervolume raised to the fourth power. You see the difference would be enormous."

Quentin blinked. "I don't get it."

Victor said, "Why six?"

I said to Victor, "Oh! You're right! There are only six points on the hypersurface where the axis intersects it that form 3-spheres. I guess I was confusing the number of right-angled intersections with the Kissing Number, which in the case of 4-D equals 24. I was fooled because I was thinking that if a sphere is all points equidistant from a given point, such that $x^2+y^2+z^2=r^2$, then a four-sphere would satisfy $w^2+x^2+y^2+z^2=r^2$. This implies that for any values where one axis, let's say *w,* falls to zero . . ."

Victor held up his hand. "Now is not the time." To Quentin, he said, "The four-dimensional sphere is more massive for its volume than a three-dimensional sphere for the same reason that a fishbowl of water is heavier than a pie plate of the same diameter filled shallowly. See?"

Quentin shook his head, "I cannot picture it. I am sorry I was not there to look into this so-called fourth dimension. I had always thought such a thing would be spiritual in nature. I wonder if Amelia—no offense—is merely interpreting things in a geometry metaphor because that is what she understands."

I laughed aloud. "We're all doing that."

Blank stares of incomprehension greeted me. Colin shrugged and passed the champagne bottle around again.

I said, "You've never noticed? All the understandable things we each see—tables, chairs, Vanity's bosom—we each see in the same way. When we see the unknown, however, our brains each interpret it differently. For example, Quentin sees the Hektor-sherrys . . ."

"Hecatonchire."

". . . as man impressing vital spirits onto an airy phantasm. I saw it as a multidimensional effect. Colin . . . ?"

"Well, I wasn't there, but it was obviously psychokinesis. They put their energy into moving the objects. They moved. We just saw Victor here use his TK on the lock to the pastry pantry, didn't we?"

Victor shook his head. "I moved the interior workings of the lock with magnetic particles. Some organ in my body produces them. You cannot move matter without using matter to push it. Newton's Laws, remember?"

Colin said, "How did you get such an organ?"

"Amelia's story makes it clear our captors—and I think that is the correct word to use—consider us to be shape-changers. All that means is that our peoples developed a technology for moving and manipulating cellular and perhaps atomic structures, maybe with molecule-sized tools woven throughout our bodies. So why couldn't they build organs which had other useful tool properties? Magnetic beams or limbs to manipulate things with? Amelia might have her brain programmed to tag such limbs with cartoon images in her eye, so she can see to manipulate them. What she sees seems not to be made of flesh and blood, she thinks they are in this so-called higher dimension."

Quentin asked, "But, if that were the case, how could you be manipulating them, these so-called tools, with your thoughts?"

Victor said, "Nothing moves for no reason. If my hand is made of matter and my brain moves my hand, then my brain is made of matter, too."

Quentin said, "Thoughts? Memories? Love?"

"Chemical reactions in the brain. Epiphenomena."

Quentin smiled and shook his head. "Matter is material and thought is spiritual. How can it be otherwise?"

Victor pointed at the champagne bottle. "How can drinking affect your thoughts if thoughts are not made of the same substance, not in the same dimension, as Amelia might say, as the champagne? This is just an alcohol. A chemical. Carbon and hydrogen and oxygen atoms in rows."

"It contains spirits. The blood releases more subtle spirits and humors into the blood. The blood carries it to the pituitary gland . . ."

Now it was Colin's turn to join in: "You are both wrong. This champagne bottle is an illusion. It is a belief. You believe it will make you drunk, and you give it your energy. You give it enough energy and it has the power to rob your energy. What happens when a man is drunk? He lacks energy. That's all. Matter is just an idea, and a bad idea at that. The fact that Victor here can turn locks without touching them and Amelia can walk through walls proves it. If such things are unreal, we only see them because our eyes lack power. Ladies and gentlemen, a toast! To the real world! The one where there are no locks, no walls."

"Hear, hear!" we all called, raising our glasses.

After the toasting was done, and we were passing around the tub of ice cream we had found, making root beer floats with champagne instead of root beer, Vanity stood up. She had not had as much as the rest of us, but it made her cheeks rosy and her eyes glitter. Her skirt seemed shorter than it had been a moment ago, her neckline lower, her waist thinner. Was that the champagne? Maybe we were shape-changers, and she was feeling prettier, the way I had done when I used to stare in mirrors to turn my mousy hair blond and my brown eyes hazel, then green.

Vanity said, "None of you boys heard a word Amelia said. Not a bloody word. There are different versions of the universe. Different paradigms. Different states of mind. Each paradigm, each model, has something it cannot explain. Something unknown, dark, incomprehensible, irrational. Something it fears. Each philosophy has one question it cannot answer. A different question for each one, but at least one. You see? Chaos. We are from the question mark."

Colin said, "What do you mean, 'we,' White Wench? They said you were one of them. A non-Chaos person. What would you call that? An orderist? An orderly? Neat Freak?"

Quentin said, "The opposite of Chaos is Cosmos. A citizen of the Cosmos is a Cosmopolitan."

"Oh, God!" said Colin, taking another swig of champagne. "Say it after me. 'Vanity Fair is a Cosmopolitan.' "

Vanity Fair struck a pose, her hands on her knees and her bottom stuck out, her elbows pushing her breasts even more dangerously further forward. "I'm two glamour magazines!"

Victor said, "What is her paradigm?"

I said, "Listen to the way she talks. She is actually a solipsist. She explains everything in terms of different states of mind of the observer."

Quentin said to me, "How does she explain magic?"

Vanity said, "Magic is what we call the unknown."

Quentin said to her, "And what do we call it once it is known?"

Vanity shrugged a bit. "The unknown is a blank spot on the map. How different people fill it in is different, I guess. Depends on their tastes, I suppose. Isn't that what we are all talking about here? Different tastes in the way we choose to see the universe?"

Colin guffawed. "Sort of like picking out a new hat . . . ? I do not like stars and planets; they are so very out of fashion this season! I want the lights in the sky to be little lamps carried by elves! All in favor say 'aye'! Come on."

Vanity looked outraged. "But you are the one who just said life is an illusion!"

"Yeah, but I said life actually, really, is an illusion, and that's a fact. I have proof! Would Victor be able to wish a lock on a door open, if all this were real?"

Quentin said, "I hate to gang up with Colin against you, Vanity, but you are being a bit of a solipsist. Let me take an example. Suppose you climb a hill or go into a valley no one has ever seen before. The moment your eyes light on it, do trees appear?"

She shrugged, saying, "Who knows? Why assume trees you never saw before were there before you saw them? You can make any assumption you want. That's what assumptions are. You fill them into the blank spots in your knowledge."

Quentin smiled, saying, "Who or what decides how many leaves each branch of each tree has, or how many veins on each leaf?"

Vanity waved her hands at him. "Now you are being silly. Nobody sees every leaf in the forest at once."

Quentin said, "Do you pick a number in your head before you look?"

Victor said, "The forests children see would have fewer leaves than the ones seen by, for example, professional astronomers, who can think in scientific notation. Hottentots could not see more than 'three' because they don't have a word for any number higher than that."

Vanity said, "You are both being ridiculous! We see dreams, don't we? But we do not sit down with typewriters and write out a script before we fall asleep. We just see them. They must come from somewhere. For all we know, the number of leaves on a tree could just be the same way. It comes from somewhere. Maybe from the same place as dreams. I mean, nothing comes from nowhere for no reason, right?"

Victor said, "I move we shelve the discussion of the nature of reality until after we decide what to do with what we've learned. Right now, they don't know we know. With Dr. Fell blanking out Quentin's memory, they think they've covered their tracks. There are at least two factions, maybe five. Mavors, Mulciber, Trismegistus we know; they spoke about Pelagaeus and the Unseen One at the meeting. The Satyr was representing the Vine God . . ."

"Dionysus," said Quentin, "And Pelagaeus is Poseidon."

". . . who may be in the same camp with Hermes, according to what Amelia overheard. Now then, they all think we can give victory to whatever side we help, and they are afraid to kill us because the threat to our lives as hostages is all that is holding back Chaos. For the moment, Cyprian has to talk to Mulciber to get his agreement to the plan to have us moved to the Unseen One's control. Or, they might instead just decide to take Vanity and give her to the Atlantians. Does that sum up the facts?"

Colin said, "Suppose Hermes is on the level. He got in trouble—you said—for making a deal with our folks, the Urine People."

"Uranians," said Quentin. "Sons of Uranus. Titans."

"Whatever. How do we contact him, if he's the one we decide to go for?" said Colin.

I said, "He must have thought it obvious, so he didn't say."

Victor said, "Taffy ap Cymru. Also a shape-changer, by the way. Works for him. Hermes knows you know that. He gave us Taffy. As a gift. Don't any of you see it? If Taffy doesn't do what we ask, we turn him over to Boggin."

Quentin said, "Boggin would have power over him. That is how one acquires authority over the soul of another. Get a man to break his word to you. Or break a law."

Colin muttered, "Have them put their boots on the table."

Quentin said, "Immorality is weakness. Virtue is strength. You can't hex an honest man. That's what Boggin wanted, Amelia. Permission to hex you." Quentin looked around the circle. "Did anyone else promise him anything, when he talked to you?"

Victor said, "I asked him to define his terms. I said that if I were a child, he could not make a contract with me in the eyes of the law, and that if I were not a child, he could not keep me imprisoned here. I asked him which it was."

Colin said, "I pretended that I had forgotten how to talk, except to say 'Go on.' Whenever he asked me a direct question, I said 'Go on.' I timed it, to see how long he could go on with me not saying anything. Forty minutes, ten seconds."

Vanity said, "He didn't talk to me."

I said, "The people at the meeting seemed to imply that the Phaeacians can somehow open or shut the boundaries between reality."

Colin said, "Meaning what?"

"When the boundaries are open, our various powers work. When they are shut, we're just kids."

Colin said, "How did you come by that notion, Bright Eyes?"

"Several things they said. Also, just seeing a sphere from my homeland enabled me to travel through other dimensions and walk through walls. I wonder if the other objects in that safe are similar reminders. Keys. To turn us on. They always meant to use us, right? The only question holding them back is not whether to use us, but who gets to use us, right? If reminders of our homes can do that to us, what happens when we find the boundaries between this dimension and our various homes? There are four boundaries to the estate, and four of us. Four Uranians, I mean. Vanity, or Nausicaa, rather, is from Phaeacia."

"Very interesting," said Colin, "But could you give me some milk?"

"The carton's right by you."

"No, no," He said, putting his glass right under my breasts, "I meant, could you *give* me some . . ."

Vanity gave a little shriek and leapt to her feet.

Colin said, "What? What? It wasn't that funny!"

"I'm Nausicaa! I'm *that* Nausicaa. The girl from Phaeacia who discovers Odysseus washed up half-dead on the shore! Don't you see . . . ?"

We looked at each other.

"I actually did those things. I had a mom and a dad and brothers and sisters and maybe even a dog and a palace and everything. I had favorite foods. I had people I had fights with. A faith. Things I thought. Things I wanted to do. Maybe artistic talents or a lover or . . . They've taken it all away. All I remember is this place. They've killed me."

And she started crying in earnest. Quentin went to put his arms around her, and said, "Shush, shush . . ."

Victor stood up. "I move we put memory restoration at the top of the agenda. We all add to our running-away caches, and we all steal money when we can, except you, Quentin. I don't think we need to flee just yet; they don't know we're on to them, and I also want a crack at that safe Amelia saw. As for the memory thing, let's try the thing in Amelia's dream. Let's do that right now."

"But we need the table," I said. "The great green table in the Great Hall."

Victor smiled. "There is also a table made of a similar green marble in the waiting room in front of Boggin's office. Is it the same? Let's go upstairs and find out."

12

THE MAGIC OF MERE MATTER

1.

Victor and Colin stayed behind in the kitchen to loot it systematically. Victor wanted a certain amount of imperishable foods, lightweight canned goods, and other things like knives, all packed away and hidden before the escape attempt. The outside weather was cold, so even perishable food would keep for a while, hidden in the woods or the Barrows.

When Vanity and I were finally released from doting duty, she had to cut me out of my apron strings with a paring knife. I looked in wonder at the knot Colin had made. It seemed to have no beginning and no end, and have no place for slack to form: a topological impossibility. Perhaps he had done magic to it, "put energy into it," as he would say. I stuck it in my skirt pocket for later study.

Buttons done up and skirts pulled down, Vanity and I, along with Quentin, made our way up to the Headmaster's office without incident.

There was the antechamber. Mr. Sprat was not at his desk; no one was around. Beyond the door was the waiting room. As quietly as mice, we crept in. A low table of green marble squatted on heavy crooked legs of wood before the red plush length of the couch. Tall wing-back chairs, red as Catholic cardinals, looming solemnly, crowded close. The two clocks, ticking half a step out of time with each other, stood like sentries to either side of the far door. Two strips of light from the archer-slit windows, one to either side of a book cabinet with dusty glass doors, threw angular lines across the rectilinear shadows.

"This place is a tomb," Quentin announced. "Someone is buried here."

Vanity stole over to the other door, which was coated with soundproof leather and a pattern of studs, and put her hand on it. She pushed it open a crack. She sniffed sadly, turned, and came back.

"What's wrong?" I asked.

"Boggin is not there."

"That makes you sad?"

"But Odysseus is in there!" She said. "The guy I rescued from the sea. What kind of people would do this to me? Make me read my own story about my own life as an assignment for Greek tutorial? I had to write those damn papers on the *Odyssey*! They were all laughing behind their hands at me." She looked up. There were tears in her eyes.

She said to me, "Please tell me this will work on me, too."

I said, "The dream did not say."

Quentin said, "I found Apsu, pardon me, I found my walking stick where you had left it in the snow on the windowsill. I must say, I was mightily confused, before I heard your story at breakfast, as to why I had left it there. When I picked it up, it was heavier than normal. That usually only happens when a True Dream, a dream from the Gate of Horn, had flown by on owl-wing. Do you remember your dream with particular clarity? If it came at dawn, it may be a *Phantasma Astra,* a dream of prophecy rather than a *Phantasma Natura,* which merely records images or eidolons passing from your passive intellect to your active intellect."

I repeated the words the egg had spoken to me in my dream. *" 'Nausicaa must stand upon the boundary stone, and grant passage to the power from Myriagon, your home. Recall that thoughts are all recalled by thought and thought alone; undo the magic of mere matter, and the night of no-memory shall break.' "*

Vanity said, "Why are we assuming he meant me to stand on a table?"

I said, "The Stone Table, the Boundary Stone Table, is what Boggin and his pals called the big green table in the Great Hall. Also, the Hundred-Hand Man said the table allowed his powers to work outside of his native land."

Quentin asked me about the first stanza of the dream, and I repeated the words of greeting.

Quentin said, "And he said your name was Phaethusa?"

I said, "Either that, or I was supposed to pass a message along to her. Do either of you recognize that name from myth or books?"

Quentin said, "We've all read the same books, Amelia."

"But we don't all get the same grades," I said, trying to preserve a look of dignity.

Vanity said, "Melly here would crib off me in Greek and Latin. And she did my math for me."

Quentin looked shocked. "You didn't do your lessons?" The idea seemed to astonish him. "I thought only, you know, kids on TV sitcoms acted that way. And Colin. But I thought he was a freak of nature, or something."

I said, "We're all freaks of nature."

Vanity said tartly, "No, only *I* am a freak of nature. I am from the universe. You guys are freaks of Outside of Nature."

Quentin said, "Amelia, turn your back."

I blinked. "What? Why?"

Quentin said, "Or don't, as you like."

Vanity was beginning to look both suspicious and flustered.

Quentin stepped up to her, took both her hands in his hands, stared into her eyes for a long moment.

He said. "Vanity, no matter what we discover, now or ever, what I feel for you shall be unchanged and unchanging."

"Quentin, I . . ."

"Hush. I am going to kiss you."

Vanity blushed and looked at her feet. "You've drunk too much champagne . . ."

"I said, 'Hush.' "

And he took her chin in his fingers, tilted her head up.

Vanity closed her eyes and pursed her lips. I have never seen a face look more sweet, before or since, than she looked at that moment. Or more trusting.

He kissed her.

I know I was really not supposed to stand there gawking, but wild horses could not have dragged me away at that moment. I had known, for months now, how Vanity felt about Quentin.

He stepped back, his eyes filled with emotion, but his face calm. The same way, earlier, I had seen an expression that made me think he was a five-year-old, now I saw what he would look like when he was twenty-five, when he was forty-five.

Quentin laughed for mere joy, and said, "Colin told me never to 'ask' a girl for a kiss, merely to inform her so she knows you're doing it deliberately. I have no idea why he thinks he knows anything about women, since he's never met any I haven't met. But maybe he knows the right thing about women."

Vanity's face, all freckled and round and flushed, lit up like the sun coming out, and her smile peeped up, grew larger, kept growing. She said, "It's not what you know about women. It's the women you know."

Quentin glanced at me. "You know why I did that, now?"

I said quietly, "I have a guess."

He nodded, turned away from me, and said, "Let's begin."

The hand by which he held her he now raised to help her mount up to the stone. The dream had said she must stand upon it.

Vanity stood there, her black patent leather shoes turned ever so slightly inward toward each other, her hands toying with the pleats in her plaid skirt, her shoulders half raised in a shrug, her head half lowered in a blush. Even though Quentin was now standing below her, she seemed to want to look up at him, through the tops of her lashes.

2.

My guess was this: He wanted this to be his first kiss. At the moment, it was. If the experiment worked, and he got his memory back, this memory would still contain, nevertheless, in all innocence and all solemnity, love's first kiss.

And then I had a bad thought. What if Nausicaa was already in love with someone else? Someone whom Vanity did not remember? Homer made her out to be pretty sweet on Odysseus, as I recall.

I had been assuming the spell, if it worked, was meant for Quentin. It had come in the middle of a dream about Quentin. But what if it worked on all of us?

And what about me? What if Phaethusa was, I don't know, a murderess or an adulteress or an environmentalist or something? Someone who couldn't do math, or who liked Tony Blair?

Did I want to be an adult, suddenly?

I did not think too highly of adults, not the ones I had met so far in my life. They seemed like the Upside-Down Folk to me, worrying about everything trivial and blithely ignoring everything great and fine and true in life.

I thought about what Victor would say about my doubts. First, he would look skeptical, and then his skepticism would deepen into a sarcastic grimace, and he would ask: "Is this the right thing to do?"

That is what he would have said. "Sorrow is merely an emotion. Pain is merely a stimulation of nerve ends. Neither one has any necessary relationship to what we have to do in order to survive. If our enemies"—and Victor always thought of them as enemies—"if our enemies make it more painful for us to do what we must do, that merely increases the wrong they do us. It doesn't decrease our obligations. It therefore is irrelevant to our decisions."

Thank you, Victor.

Aloud, I said, "I'm ready."

3.

Vanity said, "I'm ready, too. What do we do?"

I said, "What do your instincts tell you?"

"Hmm . . . Let me think . . . Avoid falling from heights, dark places, and loud noises. Have babies."

"I'm serious!" I said.

She looked at me with her wide, wide green eyes. "I am, too. What does 'listen to your instincts' mean?"

Quentin said, "The first thing to do in any ritual, is sanctify the area. Either the time, or the place, or the persons must be set aside, held pure, from other influences, chthonic or mundane . . ."

"What does that mean?"

"Put on a white robe, or something. That way the spirits know you are about to initiate a transformation."

"I don't have a white robe."

"Some witches go sky-clad . . ."

"What's that?"

"In the nude."

"You naughty, naughty boy!"

I said, "Enough banter! Banter fun, ha ha, very funny, you are both cute. Now stop. Quentin, I do not think your magic is her paradigm."

"What is her paradigm?"

I spread my hands and shrugged. "You heard my theory at breakfast."

"She interprets everything in terms of herself? Her own awareness? Hmm. I am not sure how one expands one's awareness. Vanity, maybe you have to sleep, or chew peyote, or something."

"I've drunk champagne. That's all we have time for," she said.

I said, "You could always just command the table to open a dimensional gateway to Myriagon. You know, say, 'Boundary, Open!' Or, 'Path to Myriagon, Appear!' Like that."

Vanity tried a number of variations on this phrase. She tried singing the command, she tied sounding solemn, she tried asking nicely. She tried at least a dozen different phrases and tones of voice.

We two were getting bored.

Vanity looked up. "I am talking to a rock. Whose idea was this?"

I said, "Maybe if you tried harder; if you really felt, deep down in your soul . . ."

Quentin said, "No. That is a Colin paradigm. He is the one who thinks everything is done by an inspired effort of will. I do not think any two of us have the same paradigm."

I spread my hands. "Suggest something."

He frowned and looked around the room.

I said, "If Colin were here, he would make a suggestion."

"Colin would suggest tantric magic," Quentin muttered.

"What's that?"

"Something sky-clad people do . . . Hang on."

Vanity said, "What part of you am I to hang on to, then? If you're nude?"

I said, "Enough banter! No more banter!"

Quentin was looking at the book cabinet. "What do we know about the Phaeacians? From Homer's *Odyssey*? What does he say about them?"

I looked at him blankly. The only thing I remembered about the *Odyssey* was that it was harder to translate from Greek than Socratic dialogues (which were filled with labyrinthine sentences of angular complexity) and much harder than the New Testament (which was written in baby-talk Greek). "I . . . um . . . Wasn't it the same island as Corcyra? The place where all that civil mayhem went on in Thucydides?"

Vanity looked embarrassed. "Gosh, I am supposed to be from there. I don't remember a thing. Is that the place were they landed in a harbor and sent the messenger, and the messenger got eaten, and all the ships but one were destroyed by these bronze chariots? Nice, peaceful villages filled the valleys, but those people were actually just cattle for the man-eating men, the super warriors, from the hills?"

I said, "There was a Cyclops who ate people, but . . ."

Quentin was looking back and forth at us. "Uh, no. Vanity is right that there were anthropophages who dressed from head to foot in bronze, and destroyed the ships. They were called the Lystragonians. The Phaeacians were very hospitable. In fact, I always thought one of the points the poet was trying to make was to show the nature of hospitality versus barbarism, and the abuse of hospitality. The suitors of Penelope, for example . . ."

I said, "Rule number one: No banter. Rule number two: No digressions."

"Fine. This is what I remember about the Phaeacians. I thought they were supposed to be fairies. Here's why I thought so: The fruit was always in season there; their island never suffered winter's cold or summer's heat as did the mortal world. Their doors were guarded by dogs of gold and silver, made by Hephaestos. And their ships were magical. They sailed anywhere from any port to any other in a single night of sailing, and they needed no hand at the tiller, no oar nor sail, because the ships knew what their captains desired without a word, and a living spirit moved them. They also left Odysseus on the beach of his country surrounded by gifts, asleep, and stole away without seeing anyone or waking him up. Don't you think that was strange? I mean, suppose the prince of, I don't know, Sweden, were stranded on Dover Beach, and Princess Diana found him naked, and brought him to court to get a ride home. Don't you think, instead of leaving him all alone and asleep, dropped off in a back alley of Oslo, Her Majesty's Government would at least communicate with the government of Sweden to . . ."

"Babbling! Babbling!" I said. "Don't make me make another rule!"

"Well, I am saying that's why I thought they were fairy folk. They were shy of being seen."

I said, "And the magic metal dogs didn't give it away?"

Vanity broke in with a question. "Hey! Was there a range limit?"

Quentin said, "On what?"

"You said their ships could read minds. Did you have to be aboard the ship for it to work?"

Quentin simply smiled at her, and looked proud.

That smile brought a chill to my heart. No, I did not disapprove of what they felt for each other, nothing like that. It was just that I had feelings for Victor. And Victor never looked at me that way. He never looked proud of me.

4.

Vanity spread her hands and shut her eyes. She said aloud, "Ship! Whatever ship princess Nausicaa once owned, I have forgotten you, but you must remember me, now! Or if any ship wishes the favor of the princess of the land which built you, listen to me! The boundary between . . ."

She opened one eye.

"Myriagon," I whispered.

She closed her eye ". . . between Myriagon, and this place, must be opened! Sail there, come here, bring my friend Amelia Windrose . . ."

Quentin said softly, "Phaethusa, daughter of Helion."

". . . Um, who is also known as Phaethusa, daughter of Helion, her powers. You knew my thought before I asked! Let it be that you set sail two nights ago, so that you already have been to Myriagon, and are even now approaching with your cargo! I conjure thee, I conjure thee, I conjure thee!"

She opened her eyes and looked at us. She smiled.

I said, "Did you feel anything happen?"

Her smile faded. "Was I supposed to feel something?"

Quentin said, "Maybe we should go to the harbor, I mean, if there is a magic ship coming . . . Ack! Yikes!"

He grabbed Vanity around the waist and picked her up off the table.

She giggled and looked pleased. Does love make people stupid? Meanwhile, I said, "What is wrong?"

"Don't you see it?" He was staring at the tabletop.

5.

The surface of the table turned translucent green, then leaf green, then clear as crystal. I was looking down a long tube or tunnel of crystal to something far, far below.

It was a head. A severed head, with its neck bones, torn throat-muscles and veins, all showing from beneath the matted tangle of the beard. The black hair was spread out in each direction from the skull, tangled and knotted around the green things growing to each side. It looked like someone had thrown a man's head into the center of the ring of bushes.

No. Not bushes. Oak trees. Oaks trees set, not in a ring, but in a widening spiral with this head at the center.

I tried to estimate the size of the giant head, if a fully grown oak tree only reached the distance from the back of its skull to its ear, or its cheek.

It opened its dead eyes.

Like brown water in a rusty pipe, a voice, deep, slow, coughing and creaking, rose from far below: "Who trespasses the bounds I watch?"

6.

Suddenly, it seemed to me as if the tunnel of crystal down which I looked was not "down," nor left nor right, fore nor back, nor any other direction that had a name. It was an opening into subspace, the low-energy direction I called "red."

Quentin opened his mouth to speak, and then checked himself, looking at Vanity.

Vanity looked at the both of us, spread her hands, and shrugged. Some of the glow from the champagne was leaving us at that moment, and she looked frightened and clouded in her wits, as if she was having trouble concentrating.

She said, "I am not a trespasser."

The dead mouth spoke again: "Burner of ships, daughter of virtue, I know you, though you do not. You stand with a fallen one born old before he was young, from lifeless seas beyond the seas of life; you stand with an unknown one born before the fall, from dark heavens above the heavens which hold stars. They are the foes of the Green Earth and the Blue Sea, of bright heaven above the world and dark underworld. At your word, I destroy them. Speak, and I let slip the Wild Hunt."

She said, "These are my friends and I love them. Don't hurt them."

The dead face kept its motionless eyes turned toward her, quiet as a statue in a graveyard.

She said, "My friend Amelia is closer than a sister to me. She needs her powers from her home to undo a great wrong. Let her powers pass through to her. If any ship of mine is coming on my errands, let it pass."

Vanity's face was shining with sweat. In a cold room in the middle of winter, she was sweating.

Eventually the creaking, slow voice spoke again. "Cromm Cruich the Worm of Mist rose against me, and my songs threw him down. The Sons of Nemed, the Men of the Bolg, the Parthalonians, and the Giants of Fomor attempted these shores, and were driven back to Eire, or driven underground.

"Rome's eagle stooped here for a time, clawing and tearing at this land, but Caesar lost his sword to Cymbaline, and Constantine called back the haughty legionnaires, departed never to return.

"I breathed a storm upon the Spanish King Philip, whose great Armada sank beneath the sorcery of the Virgin Queen; when the German Caesar sent his flying iron sky-things to hail fire and death upon this Kingdom, I spoke into the place where Arthur still recovers from his wound, and bleeding, he rose up, and drove the Huns away.

"This is my land. Her green hills and mountains, heaths and highlands, forests thick with red deer, rivers running blue into the channel or the iron-gray Northern Sea. The rain, the mist, the fogs are mine. The folk are mine, these proud, cold, silly, solemn folk, in whose bosom the first torch of liberty ever was found again, since the day the venial nobles in Rome allowed Caesar's bloodstained hands to quench it.

"Crude Chaucer, and Milton most august, alike are mine; angelic John Keats and devilish George Gordon, Lord Byron.

"The victories at Waterloo, Trafalgar and, yes, at Rourke's Drift are mine. Even the massacres done to the helpless aborigines of far Tazmania are mine.

"All this island is, I am. Do you understand me?"

Vanity said softly, "Yes."

"Then swear your most profoundest oath, swear by the blackest water of the River Styx, by the Cauldron of Arawn the Just, by the Grail of Christ the Merciful, by the Wounds of the Fisher-King and Spear that cured him, swear! Swear and bind those two you call your friends to the oath. You will never harm this island. No matter how this land offend you, nor what her crimes, nor even if all the Lordly Dead most beloved by you call with deepest tears, on knee, upon you, you shall do no hurt unto this island. Swear, and I shall let your ship pass by me."

She said, "I swear."

I said, "Um, so do I. God save the Queen."

Quentin stepped over to where Headmaster Boggin had set out a box of cigars for his guests. There was an ashtray here. With the penknife used to trim the cigars, Quentin cut a strand of hair from his head, set the lock of hair in the ashtray, and ignited it with the matching cigarette lighter standing next to the box. The hair burnt with a truly disgusting smell.

Quentin said quietly, "May my life be cut as quickly, may I be burned as terribly, as this frail hair I cast into the flame, should I break this vow. I love England and will do the land no harm; no matter what crimes I am done, nor who calls on me. Black water of the Styx, Cauldron of Annfwn, Grail of Christ, Red Wounds of Alan le Gros, and Spear of Joseph of Arimathia, I pray you witness and enforce this oath, and never release me from it. So Mote It Be."

The head said, "Done! For the span of time it takes to sing the Compline, the fetid stain of Myriagon shall be permitted to mar this place."

The crystal tabletop darkened, transparent, translucent, opaque; and the head was gone.

I said, "How long does it take to sing the Compline?"

Quentin said, "Thirteen seconds. 'Keep watch, dear Lord, with those who work, or watch, or weep this night . . . ' "

Even though the crystal tunnel was now opaque, I could still see it, like a green pillar issuing from the tabletop and reaching into the "red" direction. Looking at Quentin, I saw, stretching parallel to that, world-lines intersecting his nervous system, and distorting the natural flow paths of his thoughts.

". . . and give your angels charge over those who sleep . . ."

It was the same effect I use to distort the at-rest mass-path of a heavy door to make it lighter. Something was distorting the at-rest state of the white dot at the center of his brain.

Vanity, seeing my face, shrieked and put her fingers over her mouth.

". . . Tend the sick, Lord Christ . . ."

That dot was not, precisely speaking, "in" his brain. In the same way what we called a "song" was the terdimensional manifestation of a higher singularity, Quentin's brain activity was an ongoing representation in time and space of the rotation of the surface of a fourth-dimensional object–event.

". . . give rest to the weary . . ."

The dot was a monad. It was his noumenal self; the part of the self in which self-awareness resides.

". . . bless the dying . . ."

Vibrations radiating from the monad formed six different types of energy, depending on what three-dimensional axis intersected them. Three were space, one was time, one was para-time, and the final one . . .

". . . soothe the suffering . . ."

. . . It did not have a name. A new sense impression I had not hitherto been aware I possessed apprehended the nameless sixth vibration. The first five directions established relation and duration; this sixth gave self its self-ness. It was eternal, timeless, indestructible . . .

". . . pity the afflicted . . ."

And it was tilted off-axis. The shadows it cast into Quentin's nerve paths were deflected. I could see bright areas and dim areas in his cortex. Certain of his thoughts and memories were attempting to create a greater effect in the future. They had the potential for setting in motion chains of cause–effect which would influence his actions and change him. This was being blocked. I was looking, so to speak, at his happy memories.

". . . shield the joyous . . ."

Bits of dark matter were also floating in his nervous system. They were the source of the blocking. It was very complex, a web of energy-interactions it would have taken years, centuries to trace . . .

". . . and all for your love's sake . . ."

But I did not have to. No matter how complex the web of matter was inside Quentin's brain, whatever was not connected to the governing monad in which his noumenal self-resided was, by definition, non–self-correcting. Only living systems can love themselves, change themselves, grow, correct themselves, put out new stalks and branches on the tree of possible futures issuing from their actions.

The dark matter, on the other hand, was inert. "Inert" equals "actions determined" equals "low probability." All I had to do was . . .

I said, *"Thoughts are known by thought and thought alone."* And I reached out with . . . something . . . and twisted his monad back into its proper alignment, to bring the blight areas along the thought-axis parallel to the para-time axis of the dim areas inflicted by the dark matter in his brain. And . . .

". . . Amen."

The universe collapsed on me, crushing me back into three-dimensional space. I still had my . . . call it a hand . . . outside of its normal volume, reaching into Quentin. I did not have time to fold up properly.

And so I (my body compressed at the wrong angle) screamed; Vanity (looking at me) screamed; Quentin (clutching his head) screamed.

We all screamed. It was not a good moment.

7.

I fell over and struck the floor. Whatever it was (A limb? A song? A thought? A psychic extension? A manipulator made out of solidified time?) that I had inside Quentin, slipped out as I fell, in the spray of reddish sparks.

I had not even been aware that I had a telescoping 4-D form meant to fold smoothly back into 3-D geometry until I was stuck half-folded. That sense of heaviness, of massiveness, which surrounded my hand when I tried to reach through the safe walls the night before was now spread unevenly through my whole body. Some organs felt compressed, others, distended.

I tried to look at myself, but my eyes were not working. Everything was afflicted with a blue haze. Instead, sense organs meant for some other level of reality were giving me information. I was receiving a sense of the internal nature of things from one pair of organs, and another organ told me how useful or useless certain objects and events around me were to my will.

Vanity's internal nature was sweet and giving; Quentin was sad; the table was stern; the cigars were filled with malice; the doors to Boggin's chamber were watchful and careful; the two clocks were bitter, filled with hate, and watching me.

Neither Vanity nor Quentin were of any use to me at the moment, my other sense informed me. That is, none of the world-paths issuing from me had any greater potential when passing near them.

But there was something shining with use-light coming quickly from a parallel area. It was either nearby in time or in space.

I twisted my head to see if I could bring another sense organ to bear. Through the wall, I could see two nervous systems, surrounded by glowing lines of superpotential, great usefulness, jogging up the stairs.

Then the first was at the door to this room. I could not see the door, but

I heard it open, and the inner nature of watchfulness gave way to something masculine, selfish, disobedient, willful, lustful, and rough.

Behind the rough object was someone whose inner nature was logical, detached, dispassionate, stoic, skeptical about outer things, certain about inner ones.

I said, "Colin? Victor? Is that you?"

No words came out, but there was a rush of music radiation from me, flashes of wings of light.

Vanity screamed again.

Victor said, "Fascinating. Is that Amelia?"

Colin put his hand out. With a bump, the world snapped back into place. My new senses went blind. I was blinking.

I looked around. Everything was normal looking. No noises from subspace, no ripples of hyperlight thudding through skew planes. Just a room, and four friends staring down at me.

I looked down at myself. Honestly, I expected to see unimaginable horror, arms and legs twisted into Moebius strips, my body stretched into a Klein bottle, bones at right angles, lungs turned inside out, my head shaped like a question mark, with webs of flesh connecting me to older and younger versions of my body. Something like that.

But I was just normal. A girl in a plaid skirt, white shirt, black patent leather shoes, and a stupid string tie.

"What happened?" I asked.

Colin said, "You had too much energy in you. I sucked it away."

I said, "How?"

Colin leaned over and offered me his hand. "I wanted you back the way you were. My desire was stronger than the desire of the world to keep you looking weird. I won."

I put my hand in his hand. Instead of lifting me to my feet, he just caressed the back of my hand with little motions of his thumb.

"But—how did you know what to do?"

He smiled. "It's not something I do consciously. It's like lust. I mean, a man can't ejaculate just by a silent act of willpower. He needs a girl to lick his . . ."

I yanked my hand away and climbed to my feet without his help. He started to brush off my bottom, and I clipped him one on the ear.

"Ow!" he said, clutching his ear and stepping back. "And you're welcome for me saving your life."

Quentin said, "I wish I had his paradigm. No fuss. No knives. No candles. No lists of names."

Victor said, "Clap, and the dead Tinkerbell gets better, only if you really believe. Seems like a rather inflexible system to me. How can you perform experiments? If you can only do what you really believe in, you cannot be curious."

Quentin said, "But look at how well he does with women!"

Victor said, "Does what? Annoy them?"

I said to Colin, "Thank you for saving me. Do you want me to say I'm sorry about hitting your ear?"

Colin, still rubbing his ear, said, "No, thanks. I want to stay mad at you, I'll have an excuse later on for hiking up your skirts, turning you over my knee, and spanking you. Hit me again."

Vanity said, "How come everyone starts talking about spanking when Amelia is around?"

Colin said to her, "It had to do with the shape of her butt. Some girls, you can just tell from the shape of their butts, that what they really want is a nice, strong . . ."

"Ugh!" said Vanity. "Just shut up! You're the kind of fellow who thinks boogers are funny."

"Well," said Colin, looking a little puzzled, "Boogers *are* funny, most of the time. There is humor value both in the long, droopy kind and the hard, crumbly . . ."

"Speaking of gross things," I said, "What did I look like? Just now, I mean."

Colin said, "Big squid with eyestalks, just like you said."

Vanity said, "It was gross. You got all thin and stretched, and these blurry lights and colors and sounds were coming out of you. I think you had wings. And tentacles—fiery tentacles coming out of behind your shoulders. There was a white spike through your head."

Quentin said, "You had wings like an angel, and the horn of a unicorn. You looked like a centaur. From the waist down, your body was deerlike and very sleek. More like a dolphin, than a deer, actually. It was beautiful."

Victor said, "I saw four legs, also. You had a long tail or flukes trailing behind that, which seemed to be embedded in the bookcase behind you. Although that must have been an optical illusion, because I can see the bookcase is unharmed. From the waist up you looked fairly like your self, except that your neck was longer and your head was smaller, and surrounded by a reddish haze. You had wings, or some sort of fans or vanes hovering behind you. They did not seem to be connected to any particular place on your shoulders. Streamers of energy composed of groups of light-dots were issuing from your arms and shoulders, and reaching to various points around the room. I also noticed a group of bulbs or globes floating in the air near your head, thought some smaller globes were floating further away. You were also playing music, and filmy lights like aurora borealis were rapidly coming out from your wings in concentric ripples. There was an intense magnetic disturbance. I think the bulbs near your head were sensory apparatus. When Colin and I were still in the hall outside, we both saw a trio of bulbs appear in a splash of red light and move toward us. Colin told me you were looking at us."

Vanity said, "Oh my god! She has floating eyeballs! Yee-uk!"

Quentin said, "I think you are being too harsh, Vanity."

Vanity said, "You don't understand! Girls get freaked out if we have a mole or if one breast is slightly bigger than another. Little things. A crooked nose. A blackhead. You know. The only thing you boys actually judge us on. So how do you think we should feel if we grow another hand out of our forehead or something? Even a nice-looking hand with long nails? And now she's got energy and matter and music and god-knows-what coming off of her, and too many legs, and . . . Do you know a guy won't look at you on the beach if you have one toe missing? One toe!"

Colin said, "You were never on a beach."

Quentin said to me, "It really did not look that bad. There was something spiritual about the shape. It looked . . . hmm . . . more 'real' somehow and less frail, than the normal objects in the room here."

Colin said, "There were other shapes, beyond what we saw. Maybe one for every different angle she can turn in this so-called 'fourth dimension' of hers, or whatever dumb visualization she uses to focus. There's more. I sense the untapped energy."

Victor said, "Shape doesn't matter. Beauty is an arbitrary judgment."

Colin said to me, "Look here, Amelia, a flat picture of a girl can be as good looking as the 3-D real thing. Better looking, actually, of she takes off her shirt for the camera. So why can't a 4-D picture of a girl look good?"

I said to him, "(A) I never said I thought I looked bad, only Vanity said that, so you don't have to try to cheer me up, and (B) I thought you said I looked like a squid?"

He said, "A cute squid. What's the problem? We're all shape-changers. You just happened to be the first one to pop up a new shape."

Victor said, "You also can manifest limbs at a distance. There was also a mist or cloud connecting various disconnected bulbs and wing elements around you. Wherever an object—I assume part of your body—was appearing or disappearing, there was always a puff of cloud and a visible light distortion. Parts of your body seemed to be energy fields rather than flesh and bone."

Quentin said, "The misty clouds looked just like the ones we saw around the hands of the Hecatonchire last night."

I looked at him in amazement, dumbstruck.

Vanity said, "How do you know that, Quentin?"

"Because I remember, now," he said quietly.

And he smiled.

13

THE FOREST WHITE AND STILL

1.

Vanity was staring at the two oblong clocks which stood to either side of the door. She cocked her ear to one side, listening.

"What's wrong?" I asked.

"They sound funny. Weren't they ticking slower earlier . . . ?"

Meanwhile, Victor was saying to Quentin, "What do you remember?"

Quentin said, "Maybe things are more dangerous than we think. There was a woman in Dr. Fell's office. A vampiress. She tricked Fell into stepping outside, and she tried to kill me."

Colin said, "Why don't we just leave? Right now, right this second, money or no money? We walk to Abertwyi and steal a boat."

Victor said, "They'd send the police."

Colin said, "So? So we tell the police that there are ancient Greek gods kidnapping us, and they lock us up in a madhouse. At least we won't be here. And if our powers work on Earth, you point your little pinky finger at the locks and we walk out. We could hunt in the woods for food, or work, or live off the dole. They don't let children starve in England, despite what Maggie Thatcher wanted."

Quentin said, "Amelia, you're not going to leap to Prime Minister Thatcher's defense? You are her biggest fan."

I said, "Those clocks are in time with each other now."

Victor said, "What?"

I said, "They were out of synch before. Now they are in synch. When

I was in the Fourth Dimension, I sensed their internal nature was watchful, and trembling with hate. They're beings. Alive things. I think they may be listening to what we say."

Quentin turned to Victor. "They know we know. The head of Bran appeared out of the tabletop here and called us by name. They saw us do our magic. There is no chance of fooling Boggin any longer."

Colin said, "I'll go get the fire axe." And he ran out the door and down the corridor. We all knew which axe he meant; it hung by a fire extinguisher on the second floor landing.

Vanity said, "If we chop up his clocks, Boggin will know."

I said, "What if we chop up the clocks and take Colin's plan and just run away? Now, before they wake up or get back from wherever they went?"

Quentin said, "There is an amnesia drug Dr. Fell used on me. I could go down to his office, steal some, and bring it back."

Victor said, "Where would we inject the clocks? Do they have veins?" And he went over, stooped to examine the panel in the front of the clock. He ran his hand over the lock, it clicked, and the front little cabinet opened just a crack. Victor peered in.

"Oh, that's just lovely," said Victor in disgust.

"What?" we all said.

He pushed the door shut and the lock clicked. "It's nothing I want you girls to see. Quentin, do you know those large canvas sacks we found in the kitchen? Go down and get me two. If you pass Colin charging back up here, tell him to go steal a shovel from Mr. Glum's shed."

Quentin pointed. "There are corpses inside those clocks, aren't there? Dead bodies."

Victor said, "Yes."

Quentin blanched and Vanity said, "Yeeew!"

Victor said, "I was going to pop them in sacks and give them a proper burial once we're all in the woods somewhere. If I do that, and reset the clock mechanism, maybe whatever inside this clock Amelia says is watching us will be disabled. It's just a guess, mind you. But I thought it would give us more time before they noticed anything wrong. Amelia, bring me Mr. Glum's hammer. If we leave it in this room, maybe they'll think he did it."

Colin was at the door. "You mean I don't get to chop down the clock?" He had the fire axe in his hands.

Victor said, "We must be unanimous in this. Is everyone willing to leave? Now, this minute?"

I said, "What about the things in the safe?"

He said, "Tell Vanity what of your things from your room you want. Vanity, we'll give you ten minutes or so to pack. We boys will go bury the remains in the clock."

Colin said, "There are dead bodies in the clock? You were all looking at dead bodies and I missed it?"

Victor continued, "That will give you ten minutes, Amelia, if you think you can bluff or brass your way past the workmen and get to the safe."

Colin said, "Wiggle your nipples in their faces, Aim. It worked on your boyfriend, Glum."

Victor said, "If you want to take the risk. Otherwise, we can always try to sneak back on the grounds later on, and crack the safe then."

I said, "You should do that, not me. You can wave your hand and get it open. I don't think my powers will turn on unless the sphere is ringing, and the sphere only rang because Miss Daw's music was shocking it."

Vanity said, "I want to hear Quentin's story!"

Quentin, as if summoned by his name, came trotting back in, carrying empty canvas potato sacks. "Mr. Glum is still sleeping soundly. But out through the window, I thought I saw two people walking toward the Great Hall. Miss Daw and a man in a coat. I didn't recognize him, but he was too short to be Dr. Fell."

Victor said, "I hate doing things in haste, but we're short on time. We have an opportunity to escape while everyone is drunk or asleep or whatever happened to them. We have to be unanimous in this; we have to be of one mind. Who wants to escape now?"

I asked, "As opposed to what?"

"Waiting, preparing, getting a better chance later, getting some notion of where we are running to. Quentin, now or later?"

"Now. The woman I talked to last night is dangerous, and she is not afraid of Mavors. One of these factions—I don't know which one—wants to provoke a war between Chaos and Cosmos. Killing us is how to start the war."

"Colin? Now or later?"

"I think we should stay till Halloween, so we can dress up like goblins before we run away, and feed ourselves by going from house to house asking for trick-or-treats. Maybe if we stay till Christmas, they'll give us a present in a box with a ribbon, or we'll all get invited to the wedding of Vanity and Grendel Glum. I want to be a flower girl."

"Is that your vote? To stay?"

"No, you great git. I vote go now. It was my damn idea."

"Vanity? Now or later?"

Vanity said, "I think they are afraid of the human beings for some reason. Mortals think these guys are myths, right? So if we hide among the human beings, how are they going to find us? The only point in staying here is to see if we can find out more. But what if we contact our families? Or just write a threatening letter to Mr. ap Cymru? We get him to tell us what we want to know or we reveal him to Boggin."

Colin said "Yak, yak, yak. Can't you just vote?"

Vanity answered hotly, "I didn't go on as long as you, and I am saying smart things instead of smart-mouthed things! Anyway, my point is, before I was so rudely interrupted (geez!) the only advantage to stay is to learn more, but we might learn much more and at less risk if we were living in London, and had jobs as fashion models or film actresses or something."

Colin said, "Oh yes, we'll hide by having you appear in a swimsuit on a billboard. Great plan. Isn't there already an actress named Vanity, anyway? You'll have to pick a stage name. Something unusual. Like Jane."

Victor said, "Shut up, Colin. We have two votes for leaving immediately and one vote for going to London to be fashion models. Amelia? Now or later?"

I said, "I vote 'now.' I waited my whole damn life."

"Fine. I vote 'now' also. We have to see how far we can get away from the boundaries before we start getting sick. We may not all be equally affected; Vanity might not be affected at all. Even if we are captured again, it is crucial to know how far we can go and which of us can do it. So the vote is unanimous."

Colin said, "I demand a recount."

Victor took the sacks from Quentin and shoved them into Colin's hands. "For that, you get to carry the corpses in the clock."

2.

Less than ten minutes later, Victor and I were lying on our stomachs behind a little mound of snow, watching the Great Hall. There were two dozen workmen there, with block and tackle, lowering ropes into a wide hole they had opened in the shingles of the roof.

My plan had been just to walk by them, no matter what they said, unless they grabbed us and threw us to the ground to sit on us.

But not only was Miss Daw there, watching the workmen work, but there were three men in blue uniforms with batons, who looked like some sort of police or private guard.

Miss Daw was sitting on the front steps, wearing a slender, buff-colored coat with mink fur at the wrists and collar. She had a stole wrapped around her throat, and earmuffs in a matching hue. The fur was so fluffy and fine that she seemed half buried in it, with only her nose and eyes above. Little snowflakes rested on her lashes, and she was a picture of loveliness.

A man in a long blue coat and a snap-brim fedora was sitting at her feet, playing a ukulele, and singing silly songs, while Miss Daw laughed and applauded.

There is nothing worse than listening to someone play a uke to your music teacher, who has a voice like an angel, and who is mercilessly strict with you and your lessons, but who just smiles when this clumsy-fingered man misses a note or sings off key. Unless you are sitting in the snow, listening, cold and annoyed and wondering why they didn't pick another place to play. That makes it worse.

The man turned his head to offer her a drink from his hip flask. We could hear her clear voice over the distance, saying, "It is too early in the morning, Corus, darling."

He said, "It's got to be night time somewhere in the world. Isn't this one round?"

She laughed her silver laugh in return.

I whispered to Victor, "That is the flying man from last night. The one with bright blue wings."

Victor said, "What's he doing here?"

"Victor, sometimes you are such an idiot."

Victor looked at his watch. "Let's give it another five minutes. Maybe she'll get bored with his limericks or have to go to the bathroom, or something. Oh, damn. Look."

Through the snowcapped bushes in the middle distance, we could see Headmaster Boggin, walking toward the Great Hall, stepping across the snowy lawn.

I almost did not recognize him. He was not wearing his mortarboard, and his hair lay long and loose and red, falling across the shoulders of his black silk robes and trailing down his back past his shoulder blades.

In step with him was the man who, last night, had been dressed in blue, green, and white scale armor, the Atlantian with the gills behind his ears, now stepping across the snowy lawn.

The Atlantian was dressed in a heavy coat of seal fur with a tall Russian-style cap on his head, like a shako without the visor. He wore black leather gloves and black boots of sharkskin. The whole ensemble gave him a rather ominous appearance. He walked with his hands clasped behind his back, and his head nodded forward.

It was Boggin I stared at, though. I had a strange embarrassed feeling when I saw, where his flowing black robes parted in the front, Boggin was not wearing a shirt. Little red hairs, hard to see against his flesh, made curls across his chest. His pectorals were well developed, his stomach flat and ribbed with muscle. He was wearing, of all things, blue jeans beneath that. He was not wearing any socks or shoes. Boggin walked barefoot in the snow. That was more ominous than wearing a fur cap.

The corner of the library was between him and the workmen. He stopped, and would not come around the corner, but instead exchanged a few words with the Atlantian. We could hear Boggin's comments, but the Atlantian had his head turned away from us and, besides, his voice was quieter.

"The security arrangements are entirely in your hands, this time, Mestor. You simply cannot ask the school, on our budget, to defray the costs of guarding your table in a warehouse until the Oni-Kappa Maru arrives at Port Eynon."

Mestor asked him a question.

Boggin said back: "Possibly, but I know not everyone will be happy to have another shipload of mortal sailors disappear. I could give you some of Dr. Fell's excellent medicine. You could administer it to the crew of whatever human ship you hired and they would remember nothing the next day. What about that?"

Mestor pointed toward the Manor House, toward the upper stories.

"No, I don't want you to take Miss Fair as yet. We need to hear from Mulciber, for one thing. What would you do, keep her tied up in the warehouse under guard as well? And who would pay for that?"

Mestor dropped his voice, made a comment in a soft tone, speaking with quiet emphasis.

Boggin said, "Ah, well. You do make a good point. Hmm. You would have to give me your word and be in my debt. Agreed?"

Mestor said a single word.

Boggin said, "Have some of your men go wait in my office. I will write a note excusing Miss Fair from class, and asking her to report there. Your men are mortal and therefore the good Mrs. Wren will have no real ability to object if they manhandle Miss Fair a bit. Do you want Dr. Fell to provide you with chloroform or something?"

Mestor made a scoffing comment.

Boggin answered, "Oh, it's not that. I just would prefer to avoid any screaming or fuss, or anything that might disrupt the routine today more than it has been. In fact, by Thunder, I am not sure where the students are right now. That's annoying. Everything is at sixes and sevens. Mr. Glum was supposed to turn them over to Miss Daw for first period, yet there she sits, being serenaded by my little brother."

Mestor peeled back his glove, looked at his watch, said something.

Boggin answered: "If possible, we should have Miss Fair spirited out of here before her little playmates know anything is wrong. Who knows what they are capable of? I can have Miss Fair's things sent along after. What's that? Well, I am sure any hardware supply shop would carry sturdy rope and duct tape in whatever amount you require."

They exchanged pleasantries and good-byes.

Boggin said, "Oh, and, one last thing, my dear fellow. Remember that if she dies, Mavors will kill you and your family without speaking a word."

Mestor stopped for a moment, as if trying to think of some rejoinder. But then he merely walked on. Mestor stepped around the corner and approached one of the men in uniform. That man saluted him.

Victor whispered to me, "We have less time than I thought. Crawl back till we reach the corner of the Manor House, then run."

I am still faster on my feet than Victor, and I made it to Arthur's mound before him.

3.

Colin and Vanity and Quentin were waiting there. The fire axe was still in Colin's hands, and Quentin had his walking stick. Vanity was holding a shovel.

As they saw me running toward them in such haste, Colin pointed Vanity toward the outliers of the woods to the South, and slapped her on the bottom. She shouldered a laundry bag, slapped Colin, and began running.

I came up the mound. "Search has already started. Boggin is going to send Vanity off with the sea-people."

Colin handed me a duffel bag filled with clothes, canned food, blankets, and other gear. "This is all we could find for backpacks. Can you do your trick to make them light?" Quentin held a second duffel bag. A third was on the ground.

Two canvas potato sacks were also on the ground. From the way the folds fell, it looked as if two thin children were curled up in foetal positions inside.

Victor came up. "I thought you were burying those."

Colin replied, "You said ten minutes. Do you know how much of a hole I can dig in ten minutes in the ice-cold ground? Let me tell you—not deep enough to prevent Mr. Glum's dog from rooting them out."

I said, "Give me your duffels. Both of you. I can carry more."

Quentin said, "What do we do, Victor? I hate to leave . . . dead people . . . just lying here unburied. That would be horrible." He passed me his duffel.

Victor told Colin to take one corpse; he picked up the other. I shouldered three huge duffel bags filled with stuff.

Colin said dubiously, "Can you carry all that, Aim?"

I said, "I'll make it to the edge of the woods before you, slowpoke."

And I did.

4.

Because the trees had begun to lose their leaves, the woods were less cover than we hoped. We could still see the buildings and folly towers of the estate behind us for many minutes as we walked.

The trees got taller as we went deeper. At first, we were guiding our steps in the direction of the sun, but when the clouds grew thick, the sky turned into a dull, dirty gray the same color as the ground.

"If they haven't plowed the highway yet, we'll miss it," I said.

Victor said, "We can estimate distances by counting paces; if we come across a clearing between two parallel rows of trees, lined with telephone poles and metal guard rails, that will be the highway."

We jogged and walked, jogged and walked. A hour went by, maybe two. The snow became patchy in places, and cropping of rock and gray grass began giving the ground texture, like the dappling on a white whale.

The trees deeper in the forest were utterly leafless, as if the seasons here were not quite synchronized with those back on campus. Tall and skeletal, the trees spread icy branches against the sky. Each twig was coated and limed with transparent ice and, even in the gray light, they caught points of brightness in them, gemlike.

The air was still and utterly without wind. The nets and angles of branches and twigs overhead grew thicker. Whenever a flake of snow fell from an upper twig, it fell plumb straight.

It looked like fairyland. We were free, and getting freer every step. I have never known the air to taste more sweet.

Eventually we slowed, and stopped.

By the roots of a huge oak tree, Victor and Colin put down their burden.

The boys took turns digging a grave.

After a full minute of argument, I convinced them to give me a turn digging. Colin timed it with his watch, and I piled my dirt into a pile separate from the one the boys had been making. When, in the same amount of time digging, my pile was bigger than their combined piles, Victor put me in charge of the burial detail.

They wouldn't let me touch the canvas potato sacks the corpses were in, though. Digging a grave was woman's work, but only manly men can touch a sack with remains in it, I guess. Go figure.

Now it was Quentin who argued. He was much quieter in his voice than I was, but more insistent. He wanted to bury them right, and say a few words. For different reasons, Vanity and I both backed him up.

Colin scoffed at us, saying, "You three are being silly. If you close your eyes, the sun doesn't go out. Spirits can move from place to place, but they can't 'die.' Can a concept die? Can a god? It's all the same substance. There is no reason to make a ceremony out of it."

Victor's face showed less emotion but he scoffed, too: "These bodies are composed of the same amount of atoms before and after vital functions ceased. There is no quantitative difference, no reason to get sentimental about it. Quentin, say whatever words you want to say and make it quick."

At Quentin's polite request, Colin chopped down four branches, and we used a hank of twine from one of our bags to make two crude crosses to mark the graves. Colin drove the crosses into the frozen earth with blows from the back of his hammer. He must have been angry, or "putting energy" into the blows, for he drove the uprights nine inches or so into the ground with one blow each.

Quentin said a few words over the bodies, "In sure and certain hope of the resurrection to eternal life through our Lord, Jesus Christ, we commend to Almighty God those whom we have carried to this place, their names unknown to us; and we commit their bodies to the ground; earth to earth, ashes to ashes, dust to dust . . ." That sort of thing. Simple and moving. I did not know who these people were or how they got into Boggin's clock. I did not know if they were children or if they had just shrunk because they were mummies. I did not even know if they were human beings. But I felt sorry for them.

Then, after a praying like a proper church-going Christian, Quentin took one of the kitchen knives we had stolen, cut an unsightly hunk of hair from his head, and tossed some of it into either grave, as if he were suddenly a pagan again, and he threw in four tuppence from his pocket change, two into either grave. He took out one of the bottles of pop we had taken from the kitchen, shook it, and sprayed it against the roots of the tree, asking the Meliad Nymph of the tree to kindly guard the remains, in return for the libation he poured out.

I had only shoveled about four great spadefuls into the first grave, when there was a motion in the near distance, and Mr. Glum's dog, Lelaps, trotted into the clearing.

We all stood motionless, staring at the huge hound.

The dog sat on his haunches, tilted his head to one side, and let his tongue hang out.

Vanity pointed away South. "That way. We're going that way."

The dog barked once, and immediately trotted off the other direction.

"Nice doggy . . ." said Vanity softly. Then she said, "I am beginning to get a good feeling about our chances."

A few minutes later, and we were under way again. I shouldered one duffel bag, Victor carried one, and Colin and Quentin flipped a coin to see who would take the third.

Because Lelaps was likely to lead any pursuit astray, we shared Vanity's confidence, and did not set too hard a pace. We talked as we walked, and some of us, envious of Quentin's walking stick, had asked Colin to cut staves for us from the branches around. Colin used the axe handle as a cane, and leaned on the axe head, in a fashion I thought most unsafe. He had also been running with it in his hands. I thought it was only a matter of time before someone got cut with it.

I said to Quentin, "What was all that 'Lord make his face to shine upon you' stuff back there at the grave? You're not a Christian anymore. You told me so."

"I'm still English," he said mildly.

Vanity said, "Are you going to tell us what happened to you last night?"

Colin agreed, "Let's have the tale, Quentin. Do tell, do!"

We trudged along beneath gray skies as he spoke, in the crisp air beneath the woven white lace canopy of frost-touched trees, and in the highest spirits we had ever known.

14

I DO NOT LIKE THEE, DR. FELL

"I did not see him in the snow when I stepped out onto the roof, because he was buried in it. He was laying face up under about an inch of powder, and he sat up. All he was wearing was a white lab coat. How he got by without breathing, I don't know.

"His forehead opened in a vertical split, and behind the split was a third eye, blue as gunmetal, every part of it. He projected his spell from the eye, and it struck me, and I could feel my magic snuffed out in an instant. Do you ever think of your own body as a coffin? That is the way I felt. As if my soul got smaller when his spell struck.

"I walked with him back to his lab. I remember asking him along the way if he was a Cyclops. Amelia and I had seen another man with a third eye earlier that evening.

"He said that his real name was Telemus. 'You are thinking I am a triclops, aren't you? But this,' and he pointed at his own face, 'is merely an appliance, like the one your fellow inmate Victor Triumph wears . . . I can see you are curious,' he said.

"And he leaned down and drew his eyelid wide with his fingertip and asked me to touch his eye. Well, I thought it was my chance to escape, so I took it. I poked him in the eye as hard as I could with my finger, and turned and ran.

"His eye was as hard and as dry as a marble. I had run perhaps twenty yards—a fair distance—and turned to see why he wasn't following, and I saw him, with a hard little smile on his face, flicking a blood drop from the end of his finger at me. Even though he was too far away to hit me with a little finger-flick, he did.

"It had the shape of a red needle when it hit my pants leg, and it vibrated, like a dentist drill, and sank into my calf. A cold sensation seized my leg. I could feel it spreading through my veins. I fell down and could not get up.

"He walked up and told me the running was to get my heart rate high, so the effect would spread faster. He threw me over his shoulder as if I had no weight at all, and he walked back to his lab. He did not turn on any lights as he walked through the corridors: I think he has perfect night vision.

"He strapped me to a gurney, and—Victor, may I leave out certain details? Well, never mind. We are among friends here. I had dirtied myself when my legs went numb, and he yanked my pants off and wiped my bottom like I was a baby. I was a baby, I suppose, or as good as. He didn't seem disgusted or anything. I don't think he noticed I was a person at all. Anyway, that was not the most humiliating thing that happened that night.

"He never did turn on the lights in his office. The only light was a little moonlight coming in through his windows, and shadows of his instrument cases and files were black as pitch.

"He goes over to a cabinet, mixes some things together, and steps up to a table. There was a patch of moonlight there, and I saw what happened. Dr. Fell holds his hand over a beaker, and blood wells up out of his fingers like sweat. He did not cut himself. He stares at his hand and it starts dripping.

"He opens his third eye again and cooks the blood in the light that comes from this eye.

"He says to me, 'The science of cryptognosis is based on the insight that all structure in the nervous system is based upon previous, cruder structures. The nature of any hierarchy is that different functions are carried out at different levels; for a neural hierarchy, this means that structures in the thalamus and hypothalamus influence the content and priority of sense impressions before they reach the cortex, whereupon other structures in the midbrain organize, file, and recover past impressions according to the coded signals they receive from other areas of the brain. Whole areas of decision-reflexes are coded and carried out without sending any paths through the cortex. Once set in motion, the reflex cycle automatically completes itself. Anything that mimics or masks these signals can alter signal priorities and set the reflex in motion. This includes both muscular reflexes—' he squinted at me, sent a dot of blue light out from his third eye, and my whole body jumped '—glandular reflexes—' and he made me wet myself again '—and neural reflexes. One such set of neural reflexes controls what is passed on to long-term memory, and what is dumped.'

"He stabbed me with the hypodermic needle. 'I have programmed the molecular engines in the serum to seek out the control-ganglia for memory in your nervous system. The effect should take twenty minutes or so to complete. After that, I can induce narcolepsy by activating the sleep-center in your pons, and turn on your delta-wave function by stimulating your medulla oblongata. When you wake, the last twelve hours or so will be gone.'

"I should mention, he did not walk over and push the needle into me. He pointed, and the needle levitated by itself, flew across the room, and stabbed me. He curled his fingers and the empty hypo floated back to his hand.

"I tried to get him to talk. I said that since I wasn't going to remember anything of what he said, could he please tell me who I was or what was going on?

"He answered the first question, but then got bored with the game, and sat down and began writing notes or something. He sat there in nearly complete darkness reading from one book and making entries in a journal. I could hear the scratching of the pen on the page.

"I heard footsteps then, and the lights came on. They seemed so bright after the gloom. But Dr. Fell did not blink. His eyes are just painted marbles, after all. He just stood up at his desk.

"Here I am strapped to a table with no pants on, and a drunk Japanese woman comes into the room. Very pretty, like a china doll, if she had been sober. She is wearing a kimono of a blue floral pattern with a wide red sash—what are they called? An obi—with silver tracery running through it. But on her, it is all hanging loose and askew, and her cheeks are all bright pink with strong drink, and you can smell the alcohol on her breath. Her hair is done up in one of those elaborate folded masses, with pearl combs and bamboo chopsticks and little ornaments in it, but it is half-undone, and strands are everywhere. She lost her shoes somewhere too, and is walking around in these toe socks.

"Oh, and she had this thing that looks like a big celery stalk in her hand, a wand about two feet long, twined with ivy and with a pinecone at the top.

"Naturally, the first thing I say is 'Help me,' and she drifts over, giggling, and stares down at me. Me, strapped down to this rack, with no pants on.

"She says, 'This is one of them, isn't it? I've never seen one before. It looks like one of us, doesn't it? They can do that when they want to.'

"And now she turns and makes a tsk-tsk gesture at Dr. Fell, and she says—well, never mind what she says. She jokes about whether or not he has been molesting me sexually, which didn't seem very funny to me.

" 'You are allowed on the estate under a safe-conduct to attend the meeting, not to go frolicking about. You know the rules,' he says. She says back in sort of an unsteady giggly sing-song voice, 'Oh I don't go when Orpheus is there. You know how he feels about us.'

"It was actually funny, but he tells her off in that same dry monotone he uses on us when he tells us off in class. I mean, the same tone of voice he might use on Colin for getting an assignment wrong, the same condescending phrases. "I am very disappointed . . . perhaps had you been thinking, you might have considered . . ." like she was a schoolgirl. He was mad because she was supposed to act like a human around us, or where any witnesses might see, and she talks back, and he gets all cold and nasty, and she laughs and sways back and forth. He says to her, 'Our obligation while we are guests here on the Promethean world is not to interfere with the creatures of Prometheus. Besides, Mulciber has annexed this domain, and we do not want to run afoul of his machines. You know how he feels about killing men.'

"At this point she says Boggin wants to see him right away, something very important, another one of us has gotten away or something. It made me have a moment of hope, because, you know, I thought one of you was coming to save me. But the moment Fell is out of the room, she turned to me with this sly look on her face, and I realize it was just a trick to get him out of the room.

"I ask her again to let me up, and she says, 'Serve my master and be his man, and I will let you go.'

"I asked her if she could stop Dr. Fell's potion from erasing my memory. She looks a little puzzled, and then mad, once I explain what's going on. Her cheeks get even redder than the drink made them, and her eyes get even brighter, her hair more wild.

"She says, 'Swear, and if you don't remember tomorrow, all the better. The Master really doesn't want you to obey him, you know. If you disobey him, that is just as good.'

"At that point I knew that I had better die rather than swear.

"But I say, 'Tell me something about him, so I can decide. Does Dionysus have any other agents working here? What do you know about the situation at this school?'

"She actually looked a little nervous or flustered at that point. 'You things are dangerous, even all tied up. How did you know my Master's name?'

"I tell her I will trade her question for question.

"I am really proud that I had the nerve to say that, and calmly, too, since all I wanted to do was beg her for help and cry like a girl. I was so full of fear that my stomach hurt like someone had kicked it.

"So she says, 'Sure, why not? You're not going to remember anything tomorrow anyway.'

"So she tells me what she knows about the school. Lord Terminus sent an expedition to recover certain hostages from the Four Houses of Chaos. He was on the brink of a civil war with his own children at that time, but it hadn't broken out yet, and so, in order to placate them, four or five of his sons sent different agents along as part of the expedition.

"As it turned out, when Lord Terminus dies suddenly, the expedition has no place to go and no one to report to, and the various people from the various factions are suddenly terrified and suspicious of each other.

"But they find they have to work together, because each of the little orphans from Chaos has a different type of magic, a different version of the universe they draw upon for their power.

"Four types of magic, and each type has one other type it trumps, one it is trumped by, and one to which it is equal and opposite.

"The Athanatoi of Cosmos are descended from the Titans of Chaos. The lesser gods and goddesses, their powers also fall into the same four types. Except for the Phaeacians and the Olympians, who command two new powers created by Saturn and Rhea.

"I am a fallen spirit, a son of Phorcys. My power (Lamia tells me) is theurgy, the study and command of immaterial essences. A very potent power indeed and, in her opinion, the noblest and greatest of the four.

"Just by good fortune, Dr. Fell is here to stop me. He is a cyclopean, an atomist. One who commands matter. Whenever his power and the power of my house come into conflict, his will always prevail.

"I asked her who were the other houses and who stopped who, but she says, oh no, it is her turn now. How did I know she worked for Dionysus?

"I told her I read minds, and she says, 'You lie to me, little boy, and we had an agreement. You are now in debt to me, and my power can touch you now.'

"She takes one of the combs out of her hair and jabs me in the neck with it. The tines are so sharp I almost don't even feel anything. She puts her head down and starts licking at the blood dripping from my neck.

"There are bloodstains around her mouth at this point, a little trickle running down her neck. She throws back her head and moans, and strokes her own throat with her fingertips.

"She says, 'For my first charm, I call upon your blood to tell me the truth of how you knew the name of the Vine God, Anacreon, Lord Vintner. I look into your blood, and I see your soul. I taste it, and I know. You did not read my mind, you read a book. Why has Boggin been teaching you about us? What kind of fool is he?'

"I said, 'I call upon your oath to gag your spell. If my blood answers a second question without your answer to a second one of mine, then your promise to me is broken, and I am released.'

"She took out one of her hair needles and stabbed me in the arm with it. It was a pipette and she sucked at it like a straw. But the taste of my blood must have annoyed her now, for she spat it into my face. It stung my eyes.

" 'Ask your question, boy, little boy, clever little boy.'

"I repeated it. 'Who were the Houses in Chaos? Whose power stopped whom?'

"She said, *'The Dark rule the dreams and Nightmares of Old Night; Cimmeria their land, Morpheus their king; the Fallen rage in darkest Dis, weeping for lost Elysium, and the lost virtue, which, forsaken, lost them all and everything. The Lost fall through the Abyss, silent and serene as rain, Typhon is their eldest, but the Lost will suffer no one's reign; the Telchine are their serfs on Earth, Ialysus their golden isle, rich with treasures wonderful and fine. The Unknown live beyond all things, in a Fortress Incomprehensible of uncountable sides and unimaginable design, and, prelapsarian, still laws recall that Uranus knew before his fall.'*

"Now she climbed up atop me on the gurney, and began lapping at the wound in my neck like a dog.

" 'Oh, now I see,' she says, 'Boggin taught you all what you needed to know. He taught the Telchine boy physics and Newtonian mechanics, and taught you poems and myths and lore, taught music to wild prince of Night and Dreams, showed the Prelapsarian girl the strange secrets of strange Einstein, where math proves nothing is just where or what it seems. He has been forging you as a weapon for his own use, then. Right under everyone's nose, right in the light where they should be the least blind. So the old puff of cold wind just *gave* you the paradigms you needed. And maybe he thought no one would mind.'

"She smiled and said, 'Ask me another question.'

"I said, 'I have no more.'

" 'I do not mind telling you, I am going to kill you and all your friends in any case. I can make it gentle and slow, you feel more warm and heavy, and you fade away to night; or I can start by scooping one eyeball from your face.'

"At that moment, a black vulture, of which, yes, I know, there are none in England, and yes, I know, they do not fly at night, landed on the window behind her.

"I said, 'We are protected, me and mine. Mavors will avenge us. Look! His bird sits yonder, watching you!'

" 'I scoff at him,' she said. 'His mother killed my children, one and all. I cried until my eyes dried up like raisins and fell out. My hate keeps me alive. Are you a child? It is given to me to kill children. Under the law, I am allowed.'

"I said, 'You are not a Bacchant. You do not work for Dionysus. Who do you work for . . . ?' And I bit my tongue, because that was another question.

"She said, 'I serve one who will rejoice when Chaos sweeps the established Earth away, and pulls the broken arch of heaven down into the poisoned seas lit up with flame. My death will be small price to pay, if, by my acts, I make all things pass away. My last question is this: Are you a child, or a man? If man, I cannot kill you; but if child, I can.'

"She pressed my neck with her hand and drew a palmful of blood to her lips.

"I said, 'You did not answer my question perfectly.'

"She spat my blood out again. 'The answer I tasted was ambiguous. You yourself do not know. But a man can sleep with a woman. A child has not that power, though.'

"She parted her robes, and I saw she was not wearing any underwear.

" 'Pleasure me, young pup, young baby boy,' she said, smiling with her teeth all red, 'and you survive. But if your manhood remains flaccid, soft, and weak, I will know it is a boy, and not a man, to whom I speak.'

"Well, I am sure Colin would have found it perfectly acceptable to have a drunk, naked, grown-up woman kneeling on top of you, with your own blood dripping down her chin, with the smell of wine and urine and foul chemicals still hanging in the air. He would have performed. God, he would have found it a turn-on.

"But I can't even imagine anything worse. Being killed is bad enough, Being killed in a disgusting way, by a disgusting person, and just being humiliated and embarrassed, and . . . ugh. I wanted to cry. I wanted my mommy. I sure did not feel like a man in any sense of the word.

"Well, I didn't cry. She sort of rubbed up and down against my body for a long time, while I lay there, waiting for it to be over, and hoping she would kill me rather than continue.

"I tried to think of something to do or say.

"She climbed off me and, well, she laughed at my dick. She pointed and laughed. I mean, what way is that to treat a child? I would be embarrassed even to talk about it, I would not be talking about it now, even to you, except I think my capacity to be embarrassed is completely burned out of me, and gone forever.

"She said, 'You are a child, then, aren't you?' And she took another hair ornament out of her hair, and it opened into a scalpel.

"It was the last moment, the last second of my life.

"And I had an odd thought.

"How am I going to act, this second? How should I behave . . . ?

"Normally, we do things, we are polite, or we obey laws, because we want to get something out of the situation. We want to win applause and esteem, or escape punishment, or better ourselves, or something. All that went blank in my head. At this point, there was no such thing as better off or worse off. There was no advantage or disadvantage to anything I did.

"So I did what I wanted to do. What I wanted to do was scare her. I mean, I could not hurt her in any other way, so I said, 'Lamia, I know you. I call you by your true name. I deliver now to you my curse. Hear me! Unlawfully you have drunk my blood and taken it inside you. That blood I call upon now to curse and unmake you. It has the poisons placed in it by Doctor Fell, the poison that will erase your mind. He told me the minute and second that his poisons would begin to act. You told me that my powers and spells are helpless before his powers. But your powers are the same as mine, Lamia, and are bound by the same rules. You believe that Dr.

Fell's little molecular engines are beginning to dissolve your brain, don't you? You are helpless.'

"She screamed and raised the scalpel, 'Weep and shriek! Weep and shriek! It is what children do when they are about to die!'

"I laughed in her face. 'Then part this shell of flesh that encumbers me, Mother of Vampires! The mortal part of me I always knew would die! Strike!'

"The knife came down toward my face, and it . . . jumped . . . out of her fingers, hung in the air before her face, unsupported, hovering.

"Then it moved and stabbed her in her eye.

"She flung herself backward, with blood and vitreous humor gushing from her ruined face.

"She screamed again, this time in anger, and started running toward the door, pulling hair ornaments out of her hair with both hands, and flipping them open into little throwing knives and hooks. She was running to the attack.

"I turned my head and saw what she was running at.

"Headmaster Boggin stood in the doorway, with Dr. Fell half a step behind him.

"Boggin had his hands clutching the doorframe, and his face was dark with wrath. His black robes started to billow around him, and his hair flew up out of its ponytail, came entirely unraveled, and started whipping around his face. His mortarboard went flying off. He braced his legs, and his chest swelled up to twice its size. Then (as his shirt was ripped into shreds) three times its size. Then he trembled and swelled up to four times his size.

"Dr. Fell, looking slightly bored, opens his third eye, and the little knives and sharp hair ornaments halt in midair, hang there a moment, and jump up to embed themselves in the ceiling boards, out of reach.

"And the Headmaster blows. Don't imagine the puff-cheeks and pursed-up lips of a man whistling. Imagine a man opening his mouth as wide as possible, in a scream of utmost rage which is tearing out his lungs and guts and bowels. Now imagine a wind tunnel, one of those big ones that they use to test supersonic jets, with all its air compressed down and forced through an opening the size of the man's mouth. Also imagine the temperature dropping to below zero in one second.

"That's what happened. A hurricane exploded out of Boggin's mouth, one of those tornado things that can pick up a piece of straw and impale it through a solid wood fence. The Lamia was picked up and thrown through the bank of windows on the far side of Dr. Fell's office, knocking out concrete bricks as she went. Everything else in the room went flying up, too, including the table I was strapped onto, except Fell pointed his finger at the table and the metal bars bent out and grabbed onto the ceiling, and hung there while the hurricane blasted past.

"There's not that much more to tell. Fell says, 'Headmaster, that blow won't kill her, not if that was Lamia.'

"Boggin says, 'It was Lamia. Our Mr. Nemo would not be mistaken about such a thing. Get him down from there and untie him at once. We will have to organize a search for her. I don't care if it takes all night; we must find her.'

" 'Are you worried that she knows what we are teaching our charges, here?'

" 'I take it you did not hear Mr. Nemo's brilliant analysis of the situation. She's not going to remember.'

" 'Then why worry?"

" 'Never mind what I am worried about, my dear Ananias. Just do as I say, there's a good lad.'

" 'Do you think to keep this hidden? Everyone heard the sonic boom.'

" 'Not if they are using ears that hear sounds carried by the air. Only my brother, Corus, would hear it. Go! And use your molecular engines to rebuild this wall, while you are at it. As soon as Grendel's hound finds a scent, I'll come out and help look. I can see this is going to be a late night.'

"Here's the epilogue to my story. Headmaster Boggin got me off of that damn gurney, and brought me to the kitchen, and woke up the Cook. He sent Cook out with the search parties, and stood there at the stove in his ripped clothes (even his pants were ripped; he had to borrow some jeans from Cook), and made me some chicken soup himself.

"I started crying in earnest then. And he put his arm around me, and told me what a good boy I was. He said not to worry about what she had done, because trying to humiliate a man's pride is simply another form of attack, as much as stabbing someone.

"And he said he was proud of me, proud of how bravely I had stood up to Lamia, and he only regretted that I would forget all this in the morning. He sat there and comforted me while I cried on his shoulder and ate soup."

THE SILVERY SHIP

1.

As we continued to hike, my duffel bag got heavier and heavier with every step. The little white clouds of breath hanging before my lips began to turn into puffs. I asked for a break.

Victor called a halt for lunch. We sat in a circle on a patch of dry ground beneath an overhanging rock erected by some ancient peoples. We rummaged through our bags, trying to find the most perishable things to eat first. Unfortunately, the things every housewife knows, none of us knew, so we just sort of guessed that maybe the peaches should be eaten first, as well as some of the hors d'oeuvres, fish paté and caviar, and little spicy hot dog things.

"The most elegant escape ever," commented Colin, passing me a cracker with caviar on it.

I bit into it. "Bleh. This might have gone bad already."

"No, it's supposed to taste that way," Colin asserted.

Vanity said to Quentin, "So is Headmaster Boggin an enemy, or is he trying to help us, or what?"

Victor answered her: "He's an enemy. An enemy who is nice and polite is a nice, polite enemy, not a friend. We have a tool to blackmail him, though: we can tell the other factions that Boggin intended to use us in the war against them."

I said to Quentin: "What is your name?"

He smiled back at me. "Quentin Nemo."

"No, I mean, you said Dr. Fell told you what your real name is."

"If you promise not to tell anyone my real name, I'll tell you. You all must promise."

Four voice spoke at once: "Sure, I promise." "I'll do whatever you say, Quentin." "I'll never talk, Big Q. Bring on the naked torture girls!" "Not knowing what information is useful to the enemy, it is only logical to tell them nothing."

Quentin said, "My name is Eidotheia, son of Proteus."

Four faces stared at him blankly. Colin shrugged, "Are we supposed to recognize that name? Is it one of the women Zeus ravished or something? I lost track in class after the bull, the swan, and the shower of gold."

"Proteus is a man. The Old Man of the Sea. The greatest of seers and magicians who ever lived. He could take any shape as pleased him, and his wisdom is as deep as the ocean."

Vanity said. "Who is your mother?"

"Dr. Fell said I had three mothers. Do not ask me the biological arrangements, Dr. Fell did not go into details. Their names are Enyo, Deino, and Pemphredo."

Colin said, "You are not honestly expecting us to recognize those names, are you?"

I said, "Isn't Enyo a singer? I love her music."

Colin said, "Yeah, and Dino is the dog on the *Flintstones.*"

Quentin looked a little miffed. We were talking about his mothers, after all. "We read about them in Hesiod's *Shield of Hercules* and in the Pythian *Odes of Pindar.* You did those assignments, right? They were the Graeae, the three women, gray-haired from birth, the sisters to the Gorgons. Don't you remember the Perseus myth? The three Gray Sisters had but one eye and one tooth to share between them, and they passed it back and forth between them to see and to chew. Perseus stole the eye until they told him the secret way to the cave of the Medusa, whom he slew." He looked back and forth between us.

We returned blank stares.

"Well," he muttered, "There *is* a constellation named after him, and one for Andromeda. We're not exactly talking about the most obscure of Greek myths here. It's in Hyginus, the *Poetica Astronomica.*"

I said, "We didn't have to do the Hyginus. Mrs. Wren let us translate Sappho instead."

"Well, I did that one on my own."

Colin said, "And what myth is Proton from? I thought that was the name of a molecule or something."

"Proteus is mentioned in the *Odyssey* of Homer. Menelaus tells Telemachos how he found his way home from the Trojan Wars. Menelaus hid under a seal skin, and when Proteus came by, Manelaus leapt from hiding. Proteus turned into a lion, a bull, running water, raging flame, but Menelaus kept hold of him, and he had to answer his questions. It was said Proteus knew the past and future, and all things."

Colin asked in a lofty tone, "All things except the fact that there was this guy sitting under this seal skin waiting to jump out on him. I don't remember that part of Homer at all. Was it before the Cyclops thing?"

Said Quentin, "The first part of the story where Telemachos is looking for his father, Odysseus. I think you skipped that part and went on to the sea adventure stuff in the middle. You paid me in honey bread to do your first four books of translation for you, remember? It was the thing we did right after the *Iliad.*"

"My first and worst don rag. I still have nightmares," reported Colin. "What was I doing while you did my homework?"

"You were writing love letters to actresses in—Hey! Did I tell you? Those Hollywood girls wrote back. Virginia Madsen and whoever else you wrote to. Boggin intercepted them."

"Well, well!" said Colin, looking as pleased as I ever have seen him, folding his arms behind his head with a look of infinite satisfaction. "I really do have psychic powers after all."

Vanity said, "And a photographic memory like Victor! Hey, dodo, you don't have to worry about grades ever again. It doesn't matter what is on our permanent records. We're all princesses and sons of kings from other dimensions or beyond the edge of space and time. No more lessons! No more books! No more Grendel's dirty looks!"

We all sat in our circle on the ground, looking smug and well pleased.

I said, "You know, there is one thing that worries me."

Colin said, "Oh, don't spoil it. Britney! Tiffany! Natalie! Did they all write me back?"

I said, "However our home dimensions are run, they cannot be Democracies. There's no point in holding the daughter of a Prime Minister hostage."

Colin said, "Look, who cares how they run things? If our families have psychic powers, they'd end up running things. And now it's clear we all have powers."

Victor stood up. "I am not sure we do. Watch this."

He stood up and dropped a fork on the snow.

Then he stooped, picked up the fork again, and dropped it again.

Colin said, "This is supposed to mean something to us, for what reason, again?"

"It didn't float," said Victor.

Colin said, "Forks don't."

Quentin put his hand out to where his walking stick lay on the ground, frowning. He didn't touch the stick; he just frowned at it.

Victor said, "Powers off. We must be too far from the school boundaries. Amelia, did you say your bag was getting heavier?"

2.

Quentin was looking more and more pensive as we walked on, staring left and right across the snowy tree scape, as if searching for something. Colin trudged along, scowling and answering any comments with curt sarcasm. Vanity was happily depicting her future life in London as a model or actress. I was daydreaming about the new Age of Discovery that would follow once I told the men on Earth that there were other dimensions to be found and named and mapped, and other worlds in them. Victor marched without pause and without fatigue, slightly ahead of us, expressionless.

Vanity commented to Colin, "There's no need to be so bleak! Everyone else on Earth gets by without magic powers. We can live our whole lives as normal people, free, doing whatever we want!"

"Great," Colin muttered back, "There's a zenith for you. I can climb the adverse cliffs and after fateful struggle find what's shining at the utmost peak: the triumph of being 'normal.' Write that down in the history books. They'll name cars after me."

Vanity said, "Well, for you, getting to the level of 'normal' will involve a climb."

"Sure. And your dream for your new life is what again? To be a clerk in a shop, or wait tables, and haunt bars after hours to find a lonely butcher or an investment broker to marry?"

Vanity snapped back: "It will be better than your new life as an inmate in the psychiatric hospital for the criminally stupid."

I said, "Actually, we do not know if we are interfertile with human beings. Or, for that matter, with each other. We're not the same species."

Colin said, "If we must test it, we must. I'll make the sacrifice for Science. Do you girls want me to do you both at once, or one after another, or . . ."

Quentin said suddenly: "It doesn't make sense."

Colin said, "I'll say it doesn't. What does 'species' mean to shape-changers? We should be able to alter our sperm and sexual organs to be able to . . ."

Quentin said quietly, "Why didn't they build the school here?"

Colin said, "What? In the woods?"

"In a spot where our powers didn't work. Why raise us on the estate grounds, if our powers worked there? Why not raise us five miles East or West? Or in Timbuktu?"

I said, "I can think of several reasons. One: We might have needed our powers to keep us healthy when we were babies; Boggin said something to that effect. Two: Our powers might have arisen back so slowly, that they don't even know we have them yet, and the original estate was wide enough to keep the boundaries out of range. Three: Boggin actually wanted us to develop our powers, because he wants to use us on his side of the war. Four: Our powers only work when there are Greek gods around, and, no matter where we were raised, Boggin had no choice but to be nearby himself to . . ."

Quentin interrupted me, which was unusual. "Or we are under a curse. Remember how you said Mrs. Wren stopped Dr. Fell. We crossed a ward of some sort, or violated a prohibition. It was just after lunch."

Vanity said, "Dr. Fell. He could have put something in the food."

Victor stopped. We all stopped.

He was a score of yards ahead of us, climbing a gentle slope where broken rocks protruded through the snow. Ahead of him, we could see, the tops of the trees growing on the far slope. The far slope must have fallen sharply away before Victor's feet, because the crowns of these trees were no higher than he was.

He turned his head, and shouted (for he was many yards ahead), "We missed the highway entirely. I see the bay."

I shouted up, "Which bay? Rhossili Bay, Port Eynon Bay, or Oxwich Bay?"

He shouted back, "It's not labeled in a prominent place!"

I shouted up again, "If you see Cornwall across the Channel, you're looking South. If you see Worm's Head, you're looking West!"

I paused to look upward as I said it, but the sky was still as gray as old cotton, and the clouds were no brighter in one direction than the other. I said aloud, "How could we reach the water without going through Penrice, or the campgrounds? Even if we were headed due East instead of South, we should have crossed the B-4247 between Rhossili and Scurlage."

Colin stomped up the slope past me, kicking snow from his boots at every step. He gave me a dark, sinister smile, saying, "Anyone can make a dot on a piece of paper, write a name by it, and pretend there is a town there."

I stepped into motion again, toiling up the slope next to him. "But we've all been to Abertwyi. Where is Abertwyi?"

Colin said, "We were *led* there. We didn't go there under our own power."

"Why would that make a difference?"

"They changed the paths there. If there is a there."

"How?"

"The girl who believes in the Fourth Dimension is asking me to explain it?"

"Look, there has to be a world somewhere. What about France?"

"What about Slumberland, Narnia, and Oz? France is obviously a made-up place. Those places only exist if we believe in them."

"You're more skeptical than Victor is."

Colin just snorted at that. "Hmph! Vic? Well, I should jolly well hope so."

And in a tone of voice that made it clear he thought Victor was both (1) the most naïve and (2) the most dogmatically pigheaded boy in our group or, maybe, in the world.

At that point, Vanity and Quentin (who had forged ahead of Colin and me while we slowed to talk) achieved the brink of the slope where Victor stood.

Vanity let out a shriek of pure joy. "She came! She really came! All my life I've been waiting, and I didn't even know it . . . and, and . . . Victor! You idiot! Why didn't you tell me she was here!"

Colin and I raced up the last few steps of the slope.

A silver ship, a trireme sleek as a spear, lay shining atop the waves below. By the prow a painted eye gravely gazed toward shore, wise and watchful. I think it was painted.

"Oh, she came!" Vanity breathed in breathless joy, and her whole soul was in her eyes.

3.

The land fell very sharply down. A few trees clung to the far slope, and then, in a sudden brink, a cliff fell to the sea. White and gray water surged among the rocks; white and gray seagulls hopped from stone to stone, or shivered in the chill wind. One or two birds skimmed the waters on crooked wings, silent.

About a quarter of a mile out in the water was a ship. Perhaps I should call her a boat, she was so small.

She was silvery-white, with a prow like a Greek trireme, sloping like a sleek nose into a bronze-jacketed ram at the waterline. Two eyes had been painted on the prow, one to port and one to starboard. A mast like a white finger rose from blocks amidships. Aft, a small deck rose into a shape like a peacock's tail.

She was slender and sleek, built for speed like a racing scull, but the rail and the fantail were set with hammered silver, and the bench at the stern was carved and polished and set with white cushions held by silver nails, and all so finely crafted as to make the whole vessel shine like a lady's jewel. The mast held nothing but a second lamp, intricate with silver wire and nacre. There were no oars; there was no steering board or rudder.

The whole vessel was perhaps forty yards long, four yards broad at the waterline, with planks forming outriggers perhaps six yards wide above. She lay as lightly on the waters as a swan, as slim and finely crafted as a Japanese sword.

4.

Vanity exclaimed happily, "She can take us anywhere in the world in a day and a night!"

She started down the steep slope, moving quickly, almost running. The snow began to slide and curl around her legs, so that little growing snowballs were trickling down the slope with her.

Colin said, "Hoi! Careful!" And, ignoring his own advice, with that axe still in his hand, went pelting and sliding down the slope after her.

Victor said mildly, "We should approach with care, if that ship was seen by the enemy."

Quentin said in a hushed voice, "There is something ill afoot here. Vee and Coll usually aren't so rash." Then, shouting: "Come back! You two! Come back!" And he started down the slope, slipped, and fell, sliding at least two dozen yards before he spread his arms and legs and caught himself in a little wash of snow. His duffel bag went rolling and bounding and gliding down past where Vanity was skipping gaily down-slope, past where Colin was half-skating, half-stumbling. As it tumbled past, the bag began to spill canned goods from its unraveling mouth.

I saw Quentin's walking stick, his precious walking stick, go shooting over a hump in the snow like a little toboggan, and vanish into the trees.

Victor said, "My wits, at least, are not clouded. Amelia, follow me. We are going to go left and circle this slope, and go down along the gentler slope over there, where those pine trees are. You see where I mean?" And he picked up Colin's bag, which Colin had left behind. Vanity's duffel was about forty yards down-slope from us. She had abandoned it, and it had rolled to catch up against a leafless tree, bringing down a little shower of ice particles.

In a moment, Victor and I were among the spruces, jogging quickly down a somewhat more level slope. We could still hear Vanity squealing and Colin cursing. Even quiet Quentin was bellowing to them to shut up. I felt an impulse to shout at them, and call out, and the impulse grew stronger until I had to put my glove in my mouth and bite down on it to prevent myself from yelling at them.

Victor looked at me oddly.

I said, "Something—a hypnotic influence—is trying to get me to call out. Quentin's right. There is a spell here."

Victor did not seem affected. All he said was, "Let's hurry. We can cut across this slope as soon as it levels out, and rejoin them."

Unlike the leafless trees we had been walking through all morning, the spruce pines blocked our view with their thick needles.

Fear gripped my throat when the voices of Colin and Quentin fell silent, and Vanity let out a long scream.

Victor said, "Maybe we should run. Let's drop the bags. We can come back for them."

We ran. Victor simply put his hands in front of his face and pushed through the snow-laden needles of the spruce, letting branches whip him. I followed in his wake, ducking whipping branches, letting him trample a path clear for me.

We broke into the clear. Now I began to pull ahead of Victor. Even with my powers turned off, I was still a swifter runner than he was.

Then I slowed, looking up. Victor came up behind me.

We could see Colin and Quentin on the brink of a little cliff, but we had passed them, somehow. A little empty round glade filled with snow lay between us and the foot of the cliff. The cliff was up-slope and above us, a wall of icicle-dripping rock, atop which Colin and Quentin stood.

There was a cleft which cut the cliff into two cliffs, as if a giant with an axe had chopped it neatly in half. On the far side of the cleft was Vanity, alone on a little island-cliff of her own, with snow in her hair, and her garments mussed. She was standing, gazing back at the slope down which she had just toppled, as if trying to see a way back up the slope, across, over, and down to where Colin and Quentin were.

In the seaward direction, behind us, away from Quentin and Colin, was another sharp drop, this one not as tall, leading down to a rocky beach. The ship, gleaming silver-white, was clearly visible behind us, delicate as a cloud, pale as starlight. It seemed closer than the quarter-mile she had been before. The eyes on the prow seemed to be watching us.

Vanity shouted, "I can see a path down from here; there is set of rock shelves, almost like steps, leading to the beach."

Colin shouted, "We're stuck here. Up-slope is too slippery, and I don't see any way down left or right. Is the rope in your duffel bag? We could tie it off to the rock here and rappel down. Heck, we could practically jump it."

Victor made a little trumpet out of his fingers and bellowed up at them, "Amelia and I will go back and get the rope, and throw it up to you. Vanity, you stay right where you are. Do not leave each other's sight." I could hear his voice making flat, metallic-ringing echoes from the cliff we faced.

Victor turned. I said, "I could go around the foot of the cliff to see if I can find the bottom step of Vanity's staircase."

"Let's not split up," he said. Again, I felt a strong urge, almost dreamlike, telling me to leave Victor and go off to find where Vanity would be going. I closed my eyes and tried to imagine or visualize the little dot of light in my own head, my own monad, snapping back into place the way I had done for Quentin, when his memory had been influenced. It did not seem to work. The tugging impulse would not go away.

I said, "Victor, something is trying to stop me. You'll have to drag me."

At this same time, I heard Quentin yelling something across to Vanity. I did not hear what it was, because I was distracted by the sensation of Victor putting his hand around my upper arm, pulling me after him. Victor is much stronger than the other two boys, much more swift, definite, and precise in his motions. Much stronger than me. I wondered what it would be like to have him pin me down, as Colin once had done.

I heard Vanity call out in a solemn voice: "Bran! I call upon our agreement! Let open the boundaries which hem us in! Let the Four Powers of the Four Worlds of Chaos come forth from their homes to this place!"

At once, I could see my monad, my noumenal self, hovering in the fourth dimension above and inside my nervous system. I could sense the pattern of energies rippling through them, and detect a disturbing force. I tilted the rotation of my monad, to bring the identity/meaning axis back into alignment. The disturbing forces blocking my proper nerve-path flows flickered and went down, but I could sense them changing, gathering forces, moving into another position to attempt to set up another nerve block. It was not the system Dr. Fell had used; this was not an infection of dark matter; it was different. It was self-correcting in nature, organic, perhaps self-aware.

I turned my head. From somewhere, Quentin had found his walking stick. He had not had it a moment ago. Now he did.

Colin was staring down at the snow below. He said something to Quentin. It was too far for me to hear the words, but it was something about the snow being deep enough to break his fall if he merely believed hard enough that it was. Quentin knelt, looking left and right nervously, and put his hand on Colin's arm, and was urging him to crouch down and hide.

Victor looked up. I looked up, too, and saw nothing but heavy, gray clouds. He said, "Boggin. I recognize his magnetic signature."

"He's here?"

"I think the masquerade is over. They are going to reveal their powers."

"What do we do?"

"Go get the rope for Colin and Quentin. If you make us both lighter will that let us go faster? I get the feeling we are not going to have much time."

We made it back up through the pines in record time. Of the cluster of world-lines leading from our bodies and snaking through the trees, certain ones had higher potential, and occupied a smaller time-depth. These were the faster paths. I selected one for myself and Victor. For some reason, even though I did not tell him which trees to dodge around, or where the path I'd picked was, his feet found the path swiftly and without error.

There were little metal aglets holding the bag laces shut. Victor squinted at them, even while we were several paces away. The bag's mouth opened of its own accord. I could see the dark-matter particles like little specks flying out of his forehead and applying magnetic force to the bag.

I got to the bag first. He turned around while I was grabbing the coil of brightly colored mountaineer's rope from the mouth, and he was ahead of me as we raced back.

We pushed through the trees, and were once again in the little bowl of snow beneath the feet of the two cliffs. Atop one cliff was Quentin and Colin. The other cliff was bare.

Vanity was gone.

GOOSEY, GOOSEY, GANDER

1.

Victor shouted up, in a voice of cold anger: "Where did she go?"

Colin gave a pantomime one-handed shrug (the axe was in his other hand), and shouted, "Since when can I control her?"

Quentin said, "She's gone down the rock stairs to the White Ship. She said it was calling her."

"Idiot!" Victor almost never lost his temper, but now he looked worried, angry.

"The curse is still fuddling her," Quentin shouted.

"You're a warlock! Can you stop the curse?" Victor called up

"No such things as warlocks! But I can challenge the curse," Quentin called down.

Meanwhile, during this exchange, I had taken the coil of rope and thrown it up toward Colin. It was an easy throw, and there was no way I could have missed it. I missed it. The coil spun through the air, clattered against the rocks some six feet below him, and fell lightly to the snow a dozen yards to my left.

Colin, helpful as always, called down to me: "Nice throw. Aim next time, Aim."

I ran, picked up the coil, wound up, and threw again. Again, the rope coil fell short, bounced off the cliff side, fell back down to my level, and went spinning and bouncing another thirty or forty feet across the snow of the little glade. I ran after it again.

I was now about forty feet across the glade from the foot of the cliff where Colin and Quentin stood. I was at the top of the seaward cliff, the shorter one leading down to the rocky beach.

Around a shoulder in the rocks down below, I saw Vanity come into view. She was picking her way from boulder top to boulder top, while foam and spray from the waves fell around her feet. A larger wave sent spray reaching up past her head, and it fell like a shower around her. The water must have been cold, because she shrieked.

I shouted and motioned for her to go back, but she did not look up.

Looking back toward the cliff side, I saw Colin gesture toward me impatiently. Quentin was holding up his walking stick, and had his eyes closed. Victor was standing with his back to me, his arms akimbo.

I looked at the rope suspiciously. How could I miss two throws in a row? I have a good pitching arm. I closed my eyes and traced out the world-paths leading from the rope up to the cliff. The umbrella of possible paths spread out before me. Many of them were smooth parabolas leading up to the dark blotch representing Colin's position.

And the parabolas were being warped. Like flower stalks bending in the wind, fewer and fewer possible world-paths led to the cliff, as they were pushed left and right, like a curtain parting.

I opened my eyes. Mrs. Wren stood on the cliff with Colin and Quentin.

2.

Mrs. Wren was about twenty yards away from the boys, standing on a tall rock she could not possibly have climbed. And she was in costume.

In her hand she held a broom. It was an old-fashioned besom, just a bundle of twigs and straw tied to a staff, obviously handmade, and by hands that were none too steady.

She wore a green cloak that bore a tall, pointed hood. Around the point of this hood, like a horseshoe around a spike, was a crown of holly leaves with bright red berries. Her face was a smiling mass of wrinkles, surrounding eyes of tired sorrow, eyes that gleamed like black pebbles washed smooth and bright in a stream.

She laughed and smiled, saying, " 'Goosey, goosey, gander, whither dost thou wander? Upstairs and downstairs and in my lady's chamber?' "

If anyone had ever told me I would be frightened to see Mrs. Wren in a dunce cap and wearing a Christmas wreath for a hat brim, I would have laughed. But I was not laughing.

Victor (always the logical one) shouted up, "If she got up, you two can get down. Push past her and find the path she used. Amelia and I are going to try to get to the beach where Vanity is."

Quentin said, his voice trembling, "Her power comes from deep roots, from the core of the Earth. We can't just push past her."

Victor said, "Then kill her."

A silence seemed to fill the area. Even the sea waves, for a moment, paused.

One seagull, below me, let out a mournful, high-pitched wail.

I said in a voice grown thick with horror, "You can't mean that, Victor. What's wrong with you?"

Victor said curtly, "This is not a game. Colin? Quentin?"

Colin, without taking his eyes from the old witch, nodded and hefted his fire axe. Quentin looked sickly pale and did not answer.

Mrs. Wren called out in a bitter voice of mingled mockery and sorrow, "Oho, kill old granny Wren, is it, my goslings? Not enough to leave her alone, and go scampering off, my little ungrateful ducks, no. Is this how you pay her back, the woman who raised you, fed you, and nursed your fevers, kissed your scraped knees and wiped your tears away, changed your shitty diapers, and taught you right from wrong? You pay me back in a false brass coin, my pups, my poppets, my young wolf-cubs. And now you think to wring old granny's scrawny neck, it is, or chop her frail bones with a terrible sharp axe? Surely, surely, it is the greatest commandment, and the most ancient law, that thou shalt honor the woman who mothered you, that thy years shall be long upon the Earth."

3.

Victor was walking quickly across the snow toward me. "Can you see a path down?" he shouted.

I said, "The cliff is lower both to the left and right. We can make it down by going either . . ."

I heard music to my right, beautiful, beautiful violin music.

About thirty yards away, at the point where the cliffs to my right dipped down to a slope leading to the beach, looking as pretty as a china doll in her white fur and earmuffs, Miss Daw was standing in the snow, one fur-lined glove on her bow, one fingering the slender neck, of the violin she had pressed up to her red cheek. She wore a slender buff-colored coat, cute little black boots, and she had a hat of silver fox fur shaped like a dandelion puff on her head.

Victor turned and looked at her. He had come forward toward me, and so was about twenty feet closer to her than I was.

I could see wheels of ivory, as solemn as floating angels, as quiet as U-boats, approaching from the fourth dimension, the high-energy "blue" direction. The nearest had already dipped an arc into three-space, and was sending out concentric waves of energy, whose cross-section manifested themselves in our continuum, as music.

I ran a few steps toward the left-hand slope, not even bothering to wait for Victor.

Scrambling on all fours up the icy granite rocks was Mr. Glum. He was nude, except for a loincloth, and he had what looked like a bearskin rug draped over his head and back. The jawless skull of the bear was on his scalp like a hat; the claws had been tied to his forearms, he had painted his face with a wide brown stripe above the eyes, like a Red Indian. He was watching the placement of his hands and feet, and hadn't seen me yet.

Over my shoulder, I said to Victor, "Victor, you have to stop Miss Daw! Her power is the one that cancels mine out! I'll meet you down on the beach with Vanity."

He said, "Glum is somewhere that way. I can see his emission trail. Can you make it past him?"

I twisted my hips into the fourth dimension to bring another aspect of my legs into this continuum. Centaurish, I now looked like a sleek silver doe from the waist down. I shifted the aspect of my back, so that my wings, made of white light and surrounded by little echoes of music, dipped into this dimensional plane, also. A cluster of misty fireflies and silver bubbles appeared in the air around my head, like a halo, when I "opened" my higher sense-impressions. I could feel my flesh growing denser and hard, hard enough to stop a bullet, as more mass was pulled into this cross-section. This increase in mass-energy made a bluish light shimmer from my flesh.

I reared up on my hind hooves and lashed my unicorn tail. "He'll have to be pretty quick to stop me!" I said in a voice like a silver bell.

4.

I spread the possible paths down to the beach in front of me like a fan, selected the briefest one, and charged down the slope, with little sparks of energy from higher dimensions flickering and shining around my deer hooves.

With my manifold senses, posted many fathoms in each direction on the shifting foam of curved space, I could now see, not merely in 360 degrees, but globally, overhead, underfoot, in all directions. Surfaces did not impede my sight.

Other senses came into play. I could sense the internal nature and utility of objects; I could see the flow and ripple of time and probability; sense nervous system energies and distortions; I could see moral order (and disorder) like webs (and snarls) interconnecting all the free-willed beings in the area.

Strands went up to two places above the clouds. From the interrelationship of moral duties between the two points, I knew they were brothers. One I did not recognize; the other had an internal nature that was jolly, cold-hearted, kindly, sinister, and calculating. Boggin. The other point must be his brother, Corus, the blue-winged man.

Elsewhere, I could see another strand of moral order reaching to a point beneath the sea, and saw the world-paths caused by the rapid approach of the Atlantean, Mestor.

I focused a distance-negating sense on him, and saw. He had his arms back in a swan dive, legs pointed, and was simply being propelled forward through the deep, his black hair streaming.

The propulsion was a space-effect. The scales on the armor amplified it. I could sense the aura of a similar effect around the white ship, and also deep in the cells of Vanity's body. The Phaeacian power?

Mestor reached out into time and . . . did . . . something.

In the time-images I saw around Vanity, I saw first one, then nine, then eighty-one, and then all of the images changed, as one probability suddenly shifted to a certainty.

One image, a certain one, remained: Mestor, all shimmering with sea spray, was about to rise up out of the waves, his blue-and-green-and-white scale jacket ringing, and grab Vanity. One hand would go over her mouth and nose, another around her waist, and he would fall back into the ice-cold ocean, dragging her along. He would wrap his cloak of mermaid hair around her, so that the cold would not kill her, and he would pinch her nose and breathe bubbles into her mouth, while she struggled in panic . . .

I charged down the slope toward Vanity, gathering my legs beneath me to carry me "past" the volume of space occupied by Mr. Glum. He had seen me now, and he stood up on his legs and spread his arms, as if ready to catch me.

It looked so foolish. As if a flat cartoon man in a two-dimensional world were trying to reach out of his cell to stop a bird from flying past.

I laughed and leaped, spreading my wings, shedding silver notes of light and motes of music from them. The world turned red, flattened, and receded.

5.

In hyperspace, the world is merely a flattened disk, surrounded on either side (red and blue) with energy-structures that inform its laws of nature and the shape of surrounding space–time.

There is no visible sun here. Gravity works in an inverse-cube rather than inverse-square law, and radiant energy likewise. There is no way to form stable orbits, stable atomic arrangements, or to see the reddened, reddened light from even a nearby star.

But there was something here, a thick more-than-matter that filled the ambient hypervolume.

The medium absorbed and flattened the ripples in time and space issuing from our continuum, like a heavy blanket. The gravity well of the Earth also forced the time–space into a curve. Unfortunately, the curve was negative; "away" from me in all directions. Rather than being the shortcut I had hoped, I encountered more time-intervals per second than in three-space. The moments here were longer.

Distances were, in effect, greater between two points here than in three-space. It would take me, not just one, but several seconds to pass "over" Mr. Glum's position.

6.

I had the time to spare a glance at the cluster of energy-lines I had oriented to watch Quentin and Colin.

I space-folded a light-receptor away from the scene faster than the speed of light, so that I could see what had happened. Slightly to my past (during the same moment when I had first seen Miss Daw, and exchanged a brief word with Victor) Quentin raised his walking stick as if to ward off a blow, and said loudly back to her, "Wise One! You misquote the scripture! The Commandment is to honor the mother, not the nurse! What is the penalty for twisting the words of God? Does that not take His name in vain . . . ?"

Before he could finish, she said back, "Your mouth is stuffed with stolen food. Thief! I steal your voice!"

Quentin choked.

Colin started running at Mrs. Wren, brandishing the axe. My sense impressions around him went black as he negated reality itself in some way, and leapt up the rock she stood upon, in a leap no legs could make. He was carried by nothing but his desire.

Mrs. Wren ignored him as he closed in on her, and instead pointed her twiggy broom at Quentin. "You turn my teachings against me; my birthday gifts to wound me; Ingrate! Reprobate! The Spirits of the Great Mother recoil at your crimes! Your staff is broken!"

Quentin's walking stick shattered in his hand. He fell to his knees and clutched his head.

Even Colin could not bring himself to chop down an old woman. Colin struck her with the flat of his hand, knocking her crooked body backward onto the stone, and stood over her, flourishing the axe.

"Cut it out, old witch! Stop it! Stop it or I'll kill you! I swear I will!"

She smiled up at him, " 'There I met a brash young man, who wouldn't say his prayers; I took him by the left leg, and threw him down the stairs.' Have you not said your prayers, little dragonet? Say them now."

He struck with the axe.

It missed her.

Colin chopped himself in the leg. Red arterial blood sprayed out. I heard the distinct noise of a bone cracking.

Anyone else watching would have seen Colin stumble back, drop the axe, and fall . . .

But I saw the strands and lines of moral order snarl into a twisted fist, reach down, and slap the axe from his hand, and then lash back to pick him up bodily and throw him headlong from the top of the cliff.

Over the brink he went, screaming . . .

7.

With another group of lines, I was watching Victor. He closed in on Miss Daw, running down the slope, his legs like pistons, his eyes watchful, his face without expression. Since her power was the one that stopped mine, it was logical to assume that she could not stop him. How hard could it be for a strong young man to take a delicate violin out of the hands of a slender woman a foot shorter and one hundred pounds lighter than him?

I saw the energy-chord carrying her music reach into his nervous system from four-space and twist his monad out of alignment. Sections of his nervous system went dark. Energy-bundles carrying control signals reached down at the same time and seized his motor centers.

Victor was not like the other two boys. In many ways, he was flatter in the direction of four-space. Once the matter in his brain had been affected, there was no other part of him to fight back.

The Victor-puppet stopped, and sat down on the ground, looking calm as ever.

At least she was being somewhat of a good sport about it. She could have made him dance a jig.

8.

I felt a disturbance in my own nerve patterns. Two thoughts came to me, more or less at once.

First, why had Victor and I split up? It had been my idea, but where had that idea come from?

I realized that the curse, the influence which had been trying to get us to split up, to make noise, to act rashly, had not been driven out of my brain; while I had been distracted, it had altered itself and grown again. It had wanted me to go this way, and alone.

The point of splitting us up was to get us into the hands of the person who could trump our powers. They wanted to come at us in ones and twos. That is why they were closing in on us from different directions.

Second, I realized that if Miss Daw's power was the one that negated Victor, then she was merely my equal. We shared one paradigm.

Whose power negated mine?

Dr. Fell's power trumped Quentin; that seemed clear. Quentin and

Mrs. Wren operated out of the same paradigm: both were magicians. Dr. Fell and Victor were both in the same paradigm: materialists. That left . . .

As I passed through Mr. Glum, reality shut off for a moment. Mr. Glum put his hand out. With a bump, the world snapped back into place. My new senses went blind.

I was a girl again, not a centaur. I was toppling through the air, falling onto Mr. Glum.

For a moment, as I hung there, I saw his face, his terrible face, all red with cold, and lust, and hate, and desire. I saw his eyes, surrounded by war paint; I saw the sick little gape-grin of his mouth.

Somehow, I knew that his desire to capture me, to force me back into the shapely body I had been so proud of, was greater than my desire to get away. I had flinched at the idea of killing an old lady in order to get away; I saw he would not have flinched.

No wonder his world was filled with lust and hate. His desires, his burning, frustrated desires, gave him strength.

Mr. Glum drove his elbow into my midriff as he caught me. Little black metallic lights danced before my eyes as I dropped to the snow, dazed, with no strength in my limbs.

9.

"Well, well, the proud blond princess going to run me down, eh? Ah, what's this? You brought me some rope. What to do with it, I wonder?"

I felt his arms go around my waist, pin my elbows to my sides, while I was still struggling to get a breath. I felt his desire somehow enter the rope, and it writhed like a snake, twisting tightly around my elbows and waist, forming knots he could not possibly have tied that quickly.

During this horrible moment, I kicked at him with strengthless legs and made a hoarse noise, not yet quite a scream.

He yanked my wrists together, crossed them. My hands were tied together, pinned in place behind my buttocks. Again, the rope of its own accord lashed itself tight more quickly than it should have been able to.

A second hank of rope ran from my wrists to several quick turns around the ankles of my boots. The hank was short enough to prevent me from standing up.

I wondered if the knots were like the one Colin had playfully made in my apron string; a topologically impossible knot, impossible to untie.

He pulled the scarf off from around my neck, the same one Quentin had used to blindfold me last night. I clenched my teeth, knowing it was nearly impossible, without hurting someone, to get something in past clenched teeth.

He put his fingers on my jaw and my muscles lost all strength, and he pushed a wad into my mouth and wound the slack around my head to gag me.

I could not make a noise. That was also, by the way, impossible. Merely having a wad of cloth between your teeth, you can still make noise with your nose, and scream, and carry on, and even make a few words. It is only in the movies that gags block all sound.

He was doing it. Mr. Glum was making me silent. His willpower. The cloth in my mouth was just a symbol.

Looking up at him in his silly bear skull and furry skin outfit, his skin beneath turning blue in the cold, I had the terrible intuition that he was able to do this so quickly and easily because, as Colin might say, he had put his "energy" into it. He had daydreamed about it by day, imagined it at night. Perhaps it was Vanity who had appeared in his visions more often than me, but I could not believe I had been absent.

Night after night, for years. How much "energy" was that?

"She wants to run away from Boggin, my pale gold princess, does she? Aye, well, who doesn't? A right fine idea, in fact! Let's see how far we can get."

And he threw me over his shoulder, like Tarzan carrying Jane, clamped a meaty hand on my buttocks, and went leaping from rock to rock in awkward, giant thrusts of his legs, around the shoulder of the cliffs, out of sight of the others, and away.

LORD OF THE NORTH WIND

1.

Grendel's desire to run must have been very great at that moment, for he ran like a man inspired. In a few minutes, he was swarming up the rocks, and I kicked my legs (as far as the rope would allow me), hoping to throw us both off balance and have us plunge to our deaths on the sea-swept rocks beneath.

He mounted the cliff, but at a point far around the shoulder of the slope, out of sight of the others. He paused just a moment to tug at the rope running between my wrists and ankles, tying it off to allow for no slack at all. My legs were now bent double, pushed up against my thighs, motionless.

Once again, I noticed the unreality of the situation. Why weren't the bindings at my wrist cutting off my circulation, if the ropes were so tight? Why wasn't my bruised solar plexus (where he had struck me hard enough to knock me half-unconscious) making me vomit into my gag, since that same spot was now bouncing up and down on his shoulder?

Because Grendel did not want me to be uncomfortable. He did not imagine that I would be.

He ran through the woods. Soon, pine trees were thick about us.

We came to a spot at the foot of a mound, where two slabs of stone, leaning on each other, formed a mouth to a cave. Pine needles carpeted the area beneath the shadow of the stone. From deep, deep back in the cave came the sound of water dripping slowly into a deep well.

At the mouth of the cave he put me down in the pine needles, and smoothed my hair with his hand. His look, at the moment, was not one of lust, or not merely lust, but one of pride.

"Who'd have thought old Grendel would have such a prize as you, eh? You're like a fine work of art, you are, like sunshine."

He smiled and touched my cheek, "I helped make you, you know. I bent my will on you when Boggin and the others weren't looking. I made you so you were the kind of girl who likes it rough. The sort who don't mind being carried off by force, if'n the right feller does the carrying-off, see?"

I made a little mumbling moan in my gag. I assumed he liked moans; otherwise, I assume I could have made no noise at all. I was actually trying to ask him a question, though, because a large black vulture had just landed on the ground across the clearing behind him.

"I have the corpse of the preacher down in my lair; he'll have us wed within the hour. I'll have to strangle you if'n I ever get Vanity, for she was promised to me, and I cannot have two wives, for that would be against the law."

Well, that was evidently the wrong thing to say. The vulture opened its beak and screamed. A loud, harsh, terrible scream.

The temperature dropped. One second it was merely cold; the next it was numbing.

Headmaster Boggin dropped lightly out of the sky.

Twenty-foot-long pinions swept the air to either side of him. His long red hair was floating as if it were underwater. He was bare-chested and bare-foot, wearing baggy purple pantaloons, tied off above the knee. He wore a ring on his big toe, set with a green marble stone. It made him look like a pirate, or the King of Siam.

His wings were the same color as his hair, a bright red with brown and gold highlights. Unlike Corus, he used his wings, and was flapping them energetically.

He landed on a rock above the cave, at a spot where I could not see him. All I could see was Grendel's face, slack with fear and hate.

"Hi ho! Well, now Grendel, I must say I am . . . very . . . disappointed. It seems to me that we had an agreement. Back when all this started, you swore fealty to me."

Grendel squinted up at him. The hate was fighting with the fear on his face.

"My will is stronger than yours is, my dear Grendel. Do you know how I know that? Because once you swore to me that you would not do this thing you are doing now. That means your desire is imperfect. Funny things, oaths. Why, do you remember that oath, my dear Grendel? Certainly you do? Of course you do. I see that you do."

The hate melted away, and the fear grew. Grendel's lip started trembling. His eyes blinked tears.

Boggins voice came smoothly: "We are all one big happy family, committed . . . may I say devoted? . . . devoted to the same goal. But from time to time we are tempted, and, yes, I see how one might be tempted, to pursue some private pleasure of our own at the expense of the group. We cannot have that, Grendel, can we? Do you think we can have that?"

Grendel fell to his knees. "Don't kill me. Don't kill me. Don't kill me. I have a mother, she's got no one but me. Please—oh please—"

I smelled urine on him. He had wet himself.

"Oh dear, now stop all this blubbering. It looks bad in front of the children. I will tell you what. I will let you off with a reminder. At some point during the next week or ten days—and you will not know when it is about to happen—you shall have an accident, Grendel. A bad one. You will chop you foot with a firewood axe, perhaps, or crush all your bones in your hand with a hammer. Or fall off a ladder and break your legs in three places. Or maybe you will slip while pouring the tea, and scald your crotch with a terrible, terrible third-degree burn. Something like that.

"Now, the thing is, Grendel, oh, and you will love this part . . . if you do something terrible, simply terrible, to yourself first, the accident won't happen. You see? If you can get up the nerve to poke an eye out with an awl or stick your hand into the blades of a rotary fan, then you will get to pick where the damage will land. I mean, you would rather have your left hand maimed than your right hand, wouldn't you? You'd rather have an eye splashed with acid than a testicle, I am sure.

"Well, think about your options, Grendel, and think about what you've done. We do not need to say anything more about this little incident, do we? You are sorry, very sorry, aren't you? Yes, I thought you were. Now, run along. I will see to our Miss Windrose."

Grendel turned, gave me one last sad, hopeless look, and ran away.

Immediately I began making a nasal yelling noise through the gag. My legs were suddenly tense with pain; certain sections of the rope now bit into my flesh uncomfortably; others had grown strangely slack. I started wiggling and wriggling to see if I could get out of them.

Boggin dropped down in front of the cave mouth. He looked down at me with a strange expression.

"Why Miss Windrose, you look quite, ah . . . fetching . . . at the moment. But I suppose it cannot be comfortable. I hope you will permit me to unlace you?"

2.

"Fetching" he called it. With my ankles and wrists two inches apart, my back was as arched as it could be. My elbows were pinned behind my back, practically touching. This combined to thrust by breasts out so far, that I finally knew, in that moment, how Vanity must feel at all times.

Maybe he thought the gag cutting into my lips was cute. Men must like it when girls can't talk back.

I am sure that being mussed, and scared to death, and angry, somehow also added to my sex appeal. My hair had come unbound and loose during my adventures; I assume Mr. Glum did not like me wearing it braided up.

With Mr. Glum absent, I was able to crane my neck partway into the "other" direction, and push the gag with my tongue in that direction until it turned red and got less dense. Once it was an inch or two into four-space, the scarf (or, more specifically, the shadow cast by the scarf) lost the ability to interact with matter, became permeable, passed "through" my head without sensation, and landed with a soft noise on the pine needles beneath my cheek.

Well, I was glad the thing did not fall straight to the center of the Earth, though I was at a loss as to why it didn't. It was my favorite scarf.

"Thank you, but no thank you, Headmaster," I said in an irked tone of voice. "I think I can manage better without you!"

I turned my body a little sideways into the "blue" direction, so I was occupying a small 3-D cross-section, and the ropes seemed to turn red and recede from me in all directions. With a shimmer and a jerk I jumped to my feet, as the world flickered dark and then bright again as I passed briefly into and out of hyperspace. The world's normal colors returned as I tilted back into full cross-section.

The ropes slid "through" my body in a spray of red sparks and landed in a heap on the pine needles.

With a soft thud, my boots and socks and pants and coat and blouse and bra and undies and everything else landed atop them. Suddenly, it felt very cold.

"Oh, you're right, Miss Windrose," said Boggin, an unreadable expression on his face, "That *is* much better."

He cleared his throat and ostentatiously turned his back on me. He spoke without turning his head. "While you are getting dressed, please allow me to ask a question or two. I must confess to being mildly surprised at your own lack of surprise. Did someone tell you, Miss Windrose, that I had wings?"

I have to admit that I had been relieved when Boggin, angellike, splendid and handsome, had swept down from heaven to rescue me from Grendel Glum. Had I not been in the midst of trying to escape from his school, I would have felt more gratitude, I suppose. Boggin did not want me to be carried off and married to a man-sea monster; he did not even want me to be embarrassed.

I was grateful; he was my white knight; my rescuer. Except . . .

Except the others had all been caught by now. I was the only one left. I was the only one at liberty. If we all got caught, our chance of escape again was nearly zero. If one of us was still at large, able to move freely, learn to use her powers, to get help, to contact our parents in Chaos, then she would be able to sneak back and get the others out. Right?

Even if she didn't want to. Even if all she wanted to do was be a good sport, admit she had lost this round, and go slinking back to her cold bed in her locked room at night, safe and sound, in the same room she had always slept in as a child. Cold and safe. Safe in Boggin's keeping.

Because Victor would not want her to be a good sport about it. This was serious. This was not a cricket match. We were Indians and they were Cowboys. We were Jews and they were Nazi prison guards.

Dr. Fell was going to do something horrible to us if we did not get away, like erase our brains. He had already done it to Quentin once.

Even if Amelia's body was going to stay alive, for all practical purposes, they were going to kill me. Part of me.

I was thinking of Victor. I was thinking of what Victor would have thought, a look of polite disbelief on his face, deepening to a never-to-be-erased disgust, when he asked, "An enemy in time of battle turns his back on you, offering you a perfect target, and you did what, again, exactly? Picked up a rock and then . . . what? Apologized for running away?"

Duty. Do what you have to do.

Think of Victor. Get angry.

Come to think of it, what business did Boggin have anyway, turning his back on me? It was so very polite, so Victorian, so proper.

So condescending. There are women in the military in Israel. Tough women, who do whatever they have to do to survive. No one turns their backs on them, I bet.

I picked up a heavy rock from the cave, one about the size of a softball, used my little trick to make it heavier instead of lighter, stepped up softly behind him, and brought it swift and hard into the back of his skull. Clunk.

There. That will show him how to treat a modern girl!

"Ow!" he said, and he fell forward on to his knees. I suppose if I had really been trying to kill him, I would have simply inserted the rock through the fourth dimension "past" his skull and directly into the delicate tissue of his brain. Maybe I didn't think of that at the time. Maybe I did and could not make myself do it. Maybe I wasn't really trying to kill the angel who just saved me from Grendel.

I ran past him. All I can say about running stark naked and barefoot through the pines in the wintertime is that it is very, very cold. Actually, I will also say that it is a very good argument for the invention of clothing. It is amazing how many sensitive places on your skin a sticky pine needle can stab you when you are running quickly between two trees.

The world turned dreamlike for a moment, and twisted like taffy. My thoughts were confused and sleepy.

Then everything snapped back into focus. I woke up, and the cave was directly in front of me again. Boggin was climbing to his feet, looking very annoyed. He had done a some sort of space-manipulation effect, similar to what I had seen Mestor do earlier to propel himself through the water. It was the same type of energy-substance I had seen clinging to the planks of the White Ship.

I turned to run another direction. He pursed his lips and made a sucking noise.

A tube of vacuum, with the power of a gale-force wind, like the spout of a tornado, picked me up and yanked me toward him.

He caught my naked body in midair with one arm, with his lips forming a little circle of painful suction on my back between my shoulder blades. His other hand was still clutching his head.

He puffed (his breath was like the air from an open freezer) and dropped me at his feet.

Boggin looked at his foot, and said, "Bran! Hear me! I hereby close the boundaries between this place and Myriagon." To me he said, "Now let's have no more nonsense, Miss Windrose, or I shall take that rope and truss you up again like a Christmas goose. Ow. Ouch."

He took his hand away from his head and stared, aghast, at the blood on his fingers. "That was really quite savage of you, Miss Windrose! I see I am going to have to be quite severe."

I stood there, hugging myself and shivering.

He snapped, "Please get dressed at once. I should not like you to escape your punishment because you catch pneumonia."

"Turn your back," I said, pouting, wondering how stupid he was.

He must have been wondering the same thing, for he just crossed his arms and said, "Do not annoy me, child. I gave you an order. Be quick about it."

I put my back to him while I put on my bra and blouse. I glanced back to see him glaring down at me, while I tugged my panties into place, picked up my jeans and pointed my toe to step gingerly into them.

He must have thought I was trying to show off my bottom to him, and glancing back to be coy. (Nothing could have been further from my mind; when you are cold and scratched enough, you think about how cold and scratched you are, and that is all you think about.) He said in a cross tone of voice: "I would be more in a mood to appreciate your considerable charms had I not such an acute headache at the moment, Miss Windrose."

I put my coat, boots, mittens, and scarf back on, and retrieved my aviatrix cap, which I began tucking my hair under.

He stepped forward and pulled the cap off my head. "No," he said. "You look better with your hair down. You apparently think you are old enough to wear it that way."

I looked at him with something akin to hate in my eyes. "Do you get to say how I wear my hair, now?"

He threw the cap back at me. "Touché. I concede the point. You are the mistress of your hair, Miss Windrose. You may wear it in any fashion which is appropriate for school."

I let the cap bounce off my folded arms and fall to the ground, untouched. Because I was angry, and because I did not care, I said, "You pick my uniform and shoes and everything else I wear. Do you want me to look prettier for you? Why don't you just dress me up like a Barbie doll, and order me to report to your bed at night. That's what you really want, isn't it?"

"Speaking for the males on the staff, I am sure that is what we all want, Miss Windrose. It may even be said to be my prerogative as your rescuer. You are, however, too young."

He stooped and picked up the cap. He winced when he did it; the act of stooping brought pain to his head wound. "I am sorry I made an inappropriate comment about your hair, Miss Windrose. Do you want your cap?"

"Well . . . yes. I mean, it is rather cold."

"Of course. Everyone gets cold around me, sooner or later." He watched while I donned the aviator's cap and tucked up my hair.

3.

He said, "I am now going to give you a choice, Miss Windrose. I fear I cannot trust you to walk beside me back to the estate, without getting into mischief. I cannot ask you for your word of honor, because you have given and broken that to me, and I find I can no longer trust it."

He bent over and picked up the rope, and began drawing it into coils. I noticed he once again winced when he stooped over.

I said softly, "What's the choice?"

"If we walk, I am going to tie your hands, and lead you on a string like a cow to market. This will not stop the nonsense, I am sure, but it might minimize it."

"What's the other choice?"

"I carry you. I am reluctant to offer this, because I see you have been given reason this day not to believe that all members of our establishment are above reproach, and you may feel this is an unwanted intimacy."

"Carry me in your arms? All the way back to school?"

He spoke with slow and condescending tones: "Well, yes. I cannot very well carry you with my legs, now can I? And the school, I must point out, is our destination. I will not be under any need to restrain you, since you will hardly be in a position to do anything too athletic, all things considered."

I looked at the rope in his hand, looked at his face. "Um, Headmaster, is there something I am missing here? I don't think I understand what . . ."

"Through the air, Miss Windrose! Carry you through the air."

"You mean . . . fly?"

My face must have lit up, because he actually smiled back at me.

I stepped up close and put my arms around his neck. He tilted me back like a man about to deliver a kiss, or a dancer in some sensuous Spanish dance, and put one arm around my thighs, one around my waist, and swept me off my feet.

He did it better than Quentin did it.

He hefted me once or twice, as if trying to guess my weight. Maybe he liked the feel of me in his arms. He looked up as if scanning for something, some signal in the wind or cloud.

Whatever it was, he seemed to find it. Boreus smiled down at me.

"Are you ready? Snuggle close. If I pass out during the flight, all your troubles will be over, Miss Windrose."

He kicked the ground away.

4.

What is joy, except to feel, in thought, the soaring wonder which we really feel in truth in flight?

The snow-clad pines and leafless trees of fairy frost now fell below, as we soared up a long smooth slope of transparent air, like a glissade rising from note to note to ecstasy and triumph.

The ground became a textured tapestry, hills were stones and trees were carpet weave. I saw the crawling table of the sea, streaked white with tiny caterpillars of foam. Low clouds appeared to rest upon the surface, illusionary islands made substantial by distance.

I saw a glint of silver-white, a toothpick in a bathtub, a toy boat.

There seemed to be other toy boats, blacker, blockier, and larger around it, hemming it in, like the little metal square counters in a war game played on a board.

The sight suddenly stung tears from my eyes, even amidst my joy of flight, because I realized I was not flying, not me, not really.

Then fog sent a streaming arm down past us, and a fine mist fell. The fog grew thick and I donned my goggles as small waterdrops began to collect on my face.

Then we came up from the fog bank like a dolphin leaping from the waves, but a leap that went on, up and up, and did not end. I laughed! I laughed because I had not realized (how stupid of me not to!) clouds and fogs were one and the same. Oh, I knew it intellectually, of course, but still I had somehow felt that clouds would feel strange when I passed though one. But no; they were made of the same water molecules that the ninety percent of my body was. They were not so different from me, these sky-dwellers.

And what dwellers they were. The landscape down below had had no sun; this one did. Here were hills of alabaster, towers of white marble, high arches and cupolas of fine ivory, and rippling fields of snow. Slowly, slow as whales, these towers and vales and nodding hills of weightless white were changing to new shapes, or pacing solemnly against an aquamarine blue, icebergs of mist in a sea of atmosphere.

And where the red sun glanced his rays against them, the architect of heaven had used rosy-tinted marble, or ruddy gold of lambent hue, to decorate his coliseums and cathedral domes.

But, by heaven, it was cold.

I turned in Boggin's grip, and he clasped me at my armpits from above, so I could lay facedown in the streaming air, my legs trailing back, my arms stretched out to either side as if I, too, had wings.

The continent of cloud we passed across suddenly broke into a shoreline of peninsulas and archipelagoes of lesser cloud. In the bay, beneath these islands, sunk Atlantis-like beneath the crystal wave, I saw the estate grounds, and the school, little dollhouse buildings of well-crafted make, shingles of gray or slate, chimneys of red brick or white, windows winking like miniature gems.

We fell, and there was no plunge below the waves as we passed beneath the clouds again, there was no sensation of drowning. The make-believe school grew larger underfoot, the buildings swelled and rose up against us like monsters, growing. Growing, I should say, larger, but not any more real.

As we fell further, the gray and white buildings, the blank brick walls, seemed more and ever more like the square pillboxes of a fortress, or a prison camp, growing to full size, no longer toys in some game.

We landed on the balcony of the clock tower, high above the Chapel roof. Boggin dropped me lightly on the balcony next to the huge hanging cylinder of the bell, and he made one great circle around the tower. I saw his hair like a red battle-pennant streaming back from his harsh profile, and the sunlight glanced off the sculpted muscles of his shoulders, chest, and the iron-hard ridges of his stomach. With a swoop and a whirling flutter of red wings, he pushed in between the pillars of the balcony, and landed. One tiny red feather, shaken loose, hung in the air, rocking back and forth, ever so slowly descending.

"Welcome home," he said.

18

ATOP THE BELL TOWER

"It's not my home," I said dully.

"Perhaps not, Miss Windrose, but none of us seems to have much choice in the matter, eh?"

He reached up into the mouth of the bell, and took out a long coat, shirt, and his black academic robes, which had apparently been hanging on a hook or a hanger on the bell clapper.

Now he sat down on the balcony rail, his back against one pillar, his foot against the other. He did not put on his coat or robe, but instead laid the fabric across his knee. Out of a large pocket he took a vial of oil and a shiny brass tool shaped something like a cross between a dagger and a comb.

With one hand he drew his wing around before him. With the toothy dagger or sharp comb, or whatever it was, he began prying and primping at his feathers, one after another, row after row. Every now and again, he would pause, pour some oil from his vial onto a channel in the comb made for that purpose, and then continue preening.

I watched him for a while. He worked with a slight, absentminded frown, but his movements were deft and careful. A pleasant odor came from the wings, and the feathers seemed to take on new color under his hands.

"How old am I, Headmaster? Really?"

"Miss Windrose, you are fourteen and three months."

"Oh, come on! You're lying."

"You should not speak that way to your elders, even when they are lying. You are not a Yankee, after all. You should say, 'I find that hard to believe.' "

"I find that hard to believe."

"Unfortunately, when Miss Fair, who is somewhat older than you, began to develop her ah . . . rather generous signs of puberty, you also wanted to be older, and quickly, like most girls. Most girls, however, are not shape-changers. Despite our efforts, your powers are still influenced by your subconscious desires. In a few months, you had the body and the glandular reactions of a fully mature woman of twenty or so; and, like all girls your age, you wanted to look like a fashion model. Very few real women—I am tempted to say no women—actually have the perfect wasp-waisted hourglass figure you have wished on yourself."

"But I am older than Vanity!"

"Actually, no. She is four years your elder. You obviously wanted to be older, bigger, stronger when you were still a very young child. Many young children have this wish. Most do not have the power to make their wishes come true. You had the body of a five- or six-year-old when you were three. It was quite trying for all of us, I am sure."

After a while, when he had done all his feathers but the ones on the shoulders of his wings, he sat up straighter, and took out a mirror, craned his head back and bent his arm over his shoulder, and began doing the wings along his upper back.

"Can I do that?"

He looked at me sidelong. "I beg your pardon, Miss Windrose?"

"I mean, I could help with the spots you cannot reach."

"Do I want you standing with an object as sharp as a knife right at the small of my back, Miss Windrose?"

"I could promise . . ."

"No, Miss Windrose, I am afraid you can not. I mean, you could say the words, any words that you liked, but it would not be a promise, would it? Not really."

He folded his wings up on his back, and took out a long ribbon of black satin, which he tucked around his wings with both hands, and pulled shut. This forced the feathers into a compact package. He drew on his jacket, which was constructed with one huge pocket all along in the inner lining, into which he carefully tucked his folded wings. His shirt was a pretend shirt, the kind a quick-change artist at a sideshow might wear. It attached around the neck and at the belt, and it had sleeves, but no back.

Now he took out a rather more ordinary comb and brush, and he brushed his hair out. As deftly as a girl (more deftly than I do it, really; usually Vanity French-braids my hair) he twined his red locks in a maypole dance to form a short braid.

He kept wincing as he combed his hair, and he sucked in air through his clenched teeth while be braided it. I saw spots of blood on his comb.

"Shouldn't you put some iodine on that?" I said.

"Oh good God, no! Iodine stings like the devil."

"What about an ice pack?"

He gave me a dark, sardonic look, half-amused. It is the look Victor sometimes gives me when he thinks I am slow on the uptake.

"What? What?"

"Nothing, Miss Windrose. Thank you for your solicitation about my health."

He looked halfway transformed back into Headmaster Boggin. But his purple pants and bare calves—and that odd green ring winking on his toe—reminded me that he was Boreus.

I said, "I didn't break the agreement."

"No . . . ?"

"I agreed that I should not do anything to make you ashamed of me."

He said only, "Is that so?"

I said, "You think I did the right thing, admit it! It's the duty of prisoners of war to try to escape."

He turned away and drew on his trousers, tucking the folds of those purple short-pants inside the legs.

I said, "You would have done the same thing, in my place, admit it! If Vanity was your friend, and you knew she was going to be taken away, what would you have done?"

He kept his eyes on his feet as he sat on the balcony rail once more, to don his socks and shoes. I noticed he did not take that big green ring from off his big toe, and I wondered if the shoe was specially cobbled to have a little socket or pocket for it.

I said, my voice growing more desperate, "In fact, if I had just stayed here, and done nothing, then you would really have cause to be ashamed of me."

He spoke absently, without looking up, "Miss Fair is a fine young woman. Surely you don't think I would act against her best interests . . ." His voice was so calm, so patronizing, so condescending.

"You were going to have Mestor kidnap her and take her to Atlantis, while you didn't even wait to see what Mulciber had to say about it!" I exclaimed. "And with a Lamia running around loose, looking to kill us . . ."

He jerked the last lace shut on his shoe with an angry tug of his fingers, and looked up. I saw now why he had kept his face turned away while I was speaking. His eyes were gleaming and glittering with emotion, despite that he was trying to keep his face still. Fear, anger, and pride were among some of the emotions there. There were others.

I stepped back, putting my gloved fingers up to my mouth. My stomach turned cold and sank away.

He stood. He said in a tone that was calm on the surface, "Are we sure we have our facts straight, Miss Windrose? What war are you a prisoner of? Where did you hear such interesting names; Mestor, Mulciber, Lamia?"

I shook my head and stepped backward. Victor's first rule was: never tell them what you know. Even if they guess, do not confirm their guesses.

If they know what you know, they can also find out how you found out, and one channel of information will be cut. Let them guess.

Boggin stepped forward, towering over me. His chest seemed as broad as a wall. "A little slip of the tongue, was it, then, Miss Windrose?"

I backed up again.

His hand shot out and grabbed my arm above the elbow. "Have a care, Miss Windrose. I should not be able to catch you if you stumble, not with this coat in the way."

My feet were on the brink of the square hole in the floor above which the bell hung. I could see the bell cords swaying below me, going down, down, into the gloom.

He put out his other hand and took my other arm, also above the elbow. He did not draw me any closer. I stood trembling on the edge of the drop.

"Something seems to have made you nervous, Miss Windrose. Surely you do not doubt my strength, at this point?"

He flexed his arms and picked me up. My toes were about an inch off the floorboards, and I had to fight to keep my legs from kicking. He did not bend his elbows. With his arms straight, using just the muscles in his shoulder, he held my weight off the floor.

He said, "I do not suppose you will tell me where the leak is in my organization, or where I should shore up my information control? Hmm, no, I thought not. One of your Victor's rules, I suppose. You see, you do take me . . . by surprise. Yes, that is the word, surprise. I am not used to being flummoxed. Usually, in these types of things, I am the flummox*or* rather than the flummox*ee,* if you will permit the expression."

In fencing class once, on a bet, Colin and I held rapiers across the back of our fingertips, at arm's length. Just held them there to see who would tire first. Those little puny practice blades hardly weigh anything. But even after two minutes, I was sweating, and my arms ached, and ached, and . . .

I don't remember who won that bet. I think it was me.

There was no strain in Boggin's voice as he continued to hold me in midair, and talk.

"You have settled a matter of my curiosity. I had wondered why, of all times, you and your fellow students chose this day to take your little frolicking holiday into the woods of Arcadia.

"Well, let me return the favor, and settle a matter of your curiosity, Miss Windrose. Or should I call you, Phaethusa the Radiant, daughter of Helius Hyperias the Terrible High One, and of Neaera of the Dark Moon? We captured Lamia climbing out of the window of a children's hospital in Bristol. The details are too horrible even for someone from your race to hear easily. Our good Dr. Fell—one of the few people on my staff who takes our responsibilities seriously—used his science, which he calls cryptognosis, to blank out her memory. We sent her back among the Bacchants, with some of our agents instructed to keep an eye on her. A very close eye. She does not know that we have penetrated her disguise, and goes about her business. We are curious to see from whom her instructions come, to whom her reports go.

"Mestor, son of Atlas, assayed a crude blackmail against me; but he is, if you will pardon the expression, a fool. By the time he attempted to force my hand, I had already informed the creatures of Mulciber, who are without pity, where and when Miss Fair would be taken. In fact, I am going down to have a meeting with Arges, their chief smith, before lunch today. Mestor is presently in a jail cell buried, it just so happens, under this very building. He will find that his only way out is to have me prevail upon Talos and not to press charges, so to speak.

"Naturally, I will do this if and only if he swears unconditional fealty to me. Our own Erichtho, whom you know as Mrs. Wren, will oversee the application of the oath, and the terrible Gorgons will fix it in place, and the Hour known as Eunomia—who owes me a favor—will speak to the Fates about what punishments will befall a violation of that oath.

"Once Mestor is—how shall I say?—a player on my team, this will put me in a better position to keep an eye on, so to speak, and have a hand in the doings of the Sea God and his faction, which, till now, has been the biggest unknown factor in the scheme of things. I will also be able to disarm Mestor's blackmail threat without further damage to myself, my reputation, or the school.

"I had also hoped, perhaps, this might demonstrate to our fair Miss Fair, that I have a sincere interest in her well-being.

"Oh, and, of course I get to keep Mestor's table. It will make a nice addition to the Great Hall.

"Do you have any questions, Miss Windrose?"

The posture he held me in was beginning to make my arms ache, and my shoulders were hunched up in an ongoing shrug. Against my will, little tremors were running through my body, and my fingers were twitching (with nothing to grab on to but my pant legs) and my legs kicked involuntarily, seeking some purchase in midair.

"Why are you holding me?" I said.

"Well, I wish I could make it sound romantic, but we are like bank robbers clutching a teller before us, so the bank guards do not shoot. In this case, the bank guards are monstrosities from outside of the ordered part of the universe, and their guns are very large indeed."

"No, I mean . . ."

"Oh, you mean right now? I was hoping you would try to move into the spirit world, as you so thoughtfully showed me you were capable of doing when you turned insubstantial and floated out of Mr. Grim's macramé project."

I shook my head.

"Oh, do be a sport, Miss Windrose. I have not had a chance to say, 'Resistance is futile!' and 'Escape is impossible!' and all that sort of stuff."

I shook my head again.

He said, "Well, if you simply take my word for it, fine. Facts, though silent, are louder than words."

He relaxed his arms so that my feet found the floor. Not that it did me much good; my knees were now wobbly, and I was having trouble supporting myself. Not that he let go of his grip. If anything, his hands got tighter.

In fact, now that I was on the floorboards, I was forced to stand slightly closer to him, to avoid the brink behind me.

Too close. Closer than a schoolgirl should be standing to a teacher. I could smell the oil he had rubbed into his wings. It was scented, like an aftershave.

His eyes filled my sight, and my heart was hammering so in my breast that, for a moment, my breath was gone. This close to him, it was as if he and I formed our own little world, a world meant for us and us alone.

His hands were so very strong, that I was overcome with an awareness of my own fragility. It made me feel almost faint; me, the big, strong, athletic one, a little china doll in his hands.

I wondered what he was feeling, what he was thinking. He was staring down at me, an expression of perfect arrogance in his eyes. I saw how the light caressed the cheek, bringing out the contour of the muscles around his mouth, the strength in his cheekbones. There was a ghost of reddish hair to the skin of his jaw, and it created the illusion he was blushing with pleasure. Maybe it was not an illusion. His lips were ruddy, finely sculpted. I could not help but stare at them.

I realized with a fearful thrill that I had somehow come to be in the same posture girls assumed in novels when they are about to be kissed.

His voice was a warm rumble, as if an earthquake spoke. I could feel the trembling in the air.

"What am I to do with you, Phaethusa? On the one hand, you are a monstrosity from beyond the edge of space and time, a member of a race and clan bent on the destruction of this world and every other. You have powers growing beyond our control, and the danger you pose to us is real."

"Let me go."

"I cannot do that. Your race would see that as a signal to launch the final war, the Rangnarok."

"No, I mean right now. I mean, let go of my arms."

To my surprise, he did.

I stood uncertainly on the brink of the hole, rubbing my arms, and looking up at him. He still was blocking my way, huge and tall, though I suppose I could have tried to sidle past him to the left or right.

I was not sure I wanted to. I enjoyed having him have a hold of me, even if cruelly.

"We're going to have to put you in a cell, you know, Phaethusa, at least till we can figure out what to do with you. Since you can walk through walls the only thing I can do to keep you there is threaten your friends with harm, if you attempt to escape. This is a dreadful and unseemly thing to resort to, and I fear it is turning me into a monster worse than your people are."

"You're not really going to put me in a cell, are you, Headmaster?"

"I fear I am. Chains, manacles, leg irons, bars on the window, whatever may be required." His face had a hollow look to it.

"Required? Required for what?"

He barked an angry sort of laugh. "Required to undo your damage. If the factions (who never agree on anything) agreed that I was too weak or too foolish to keep you four from wandering around on your own . . ."

"You mean 'escaping.' "

"It is quite rude to interrupt, Miss Windrose. But, yes. If the Olympians agreed that I was unable to keep you from escaping, you would be taken from me. Most likely the four of you would be split up; with Mavors, Mulciber, Lord Dis, and the Sea-Prince Pelagaeus each getting one. Or two, in the case of Lord Palegaeus, since he might end up with Miss Fair, also. That way they could maintain the balance of the threats they pose to each other. Oh, none of you might cooperate with any of them in their wars but, then again, none of them could be certain of that, and even the prospect of your involuntary help might be somewhat alarming. A second civil war would soon start. While your people would no doubt rejoice to see us cutting each other up, you yourself might be sad to be without your playmates."

I said, "Pelagaeus is Poseidon?"

He nodded. "We take different names in different worlds and situations. Speaking of situations, have I explained the present conundrum in sufficient detail for you to see the gravity of the matter? Certain members of the Board of Visitors and Governors were present during our recovery of you children. They saw you become a centaur; they heard Mr. Nemo cast back part of Mrs. Wren's curse, they saw Mr. mac FirBolg's rather prodigious leap. And no one could mistake the meaning of the vessel waiting for Miss Fair. You see, had it just been kept among us here at the school, I might have been able to hush up the matter quietly. As it is, some show of severity is required. It has to be severe enough that even people like Lord Dis will think I am too strict. I trust you comprehend what I am saying."

"You are asking me to cooperate?" I said, astonished.

"No. I am telling you, Phaethusa, that if you deduce how to escape from the cell into which you are about to be dragged, you should fear to do it. If you deduce how to escape, don't escape. I will harm you and my other children if you do. We are gods; we control the sidereal universe. The only result of a second attempt will be that the Olympians will take you away from me and press you into a slavery which will be far worse than study hall and being required to wear school uniforms."

"You said 'my children.' "

"Ah. Did I?"

"We're not your children. We have real parents."

"My students. I meant to say 'my students.' "

Apparently I had not been grabbed enough that day, because now he put out his hand and took me by the upper arm again. "Come along!"

I dug in my feet, and made him drag me a few steps. I really, really did not like the idea of going into a cell.

I was leaning far back, digging my reluctant boots into the floorboards, being yanked, and stumbling, leaning back again. He was pulling me toward the door that hid the bell tower stairs.

I said, "What's the other hand?"

"I beg your pardon?"

"You said, on the one hand I am a monster. What's on the other hand?"

"Ah. On the other hand you are a confused little girl who has gotten too big for her britches, and perhaps the only thing you need is some stern correction. In fact—!"

Now he smiled, and stepped towards me. Since I was pulling against him, the sudden relaxation made me stumble a step or two and I caught myself against the balcony railing.

Headmaster Boggin stepped around me and seated himself on the rail. My elbow was still in his fist, I was pulled half-turned around, not quite facing him.

"In fact, to throw a monster who tries to escape into a dungeon is a good policy, but it is clearly not the right thing to do to a girl who breaks her word and tries to break open a teacher's head with a rock."

"What are you going to do?" I said. There was a gleam in his eye. Call it a Grendel gleam, but I have seen it in Colin's eye, too.

I knew from that gleam what he was going to do. But there are some things that just come out of your mouth, no matter how dumb they sound, whether you want them to or not. The only thing possibly stupider to say in a situation like this is something like, "You wouldn't dare!"

Boggin looked deeply into my eyes, as if pleased at the uncertainty he saw growing there.

"Miss Windrose, our agreement was not that you would not make me ashamed of you. Our agreement was that you would do nothing to make me regret my decision. I have a terrible headache because someone hit me in the head with a rock. Surely, I am right to regret that?"

I would have had as much chance resisting the force of a wild stallion as I did resisting the strength of his arm.

He pulled me facedown across his knees. The railing he sat on was high, and I could not reach the floorboards with my feet. My hands flailed in midair a moment, and then I grabbed the poles of the railing, which were to my left.

"I must see to it that you regret it, too, and in a fashion which will bring home to you quite forcefully that you are not as old as you think you are."

I was breathless; a shy feeling was actually sending tremors through me. All my skin trembled with goose pimples as all my little hairs stood up. This made my skin more sensitive; I could feel every nuance of the texture and fabric of my skirt, which suddenly seemed quite flimsy and thin on my bottom. I could feel the air on my exposed upper legs. I could feel the muscles in his legs beneath my stomach.

I said the dumb thing again, "What are you going to do—?!" It did not sound any better the second time around. Higher-pitched. More girlish.

He did not bother answering that, but he held one hand on the small of my back, and waited while I kicked my legs in midair. There was nothing within the range of my feet to get a purchase on.

What was he going to do? I knew what he was going to do.

I cannot say that I did not deserve what was about to happen. That little dark knot of guilt in my stomach I had felt ever since I realized that I had a duty, a duty to Victor, to bonk Boggin with a rock, that knot began to relax into a warm and pleasant fear.

Why pleasant? I cannot explain my emotions. I am not sure where they come from. But, at that moment, I felt a strange combination of fear and gratitude.

Why gratitude? Because I did feel bad about what I had done. Clonking my red-haired savior angel with a rock. This man has raised me from a child my whole life. That has to count for something. Being saved from Grendel Glum counts for something.

This will sound like a paradox, but: if a man too big and too strong for me to resist punished me, I would be relieved of the responsibility of feeling any guilt. There is no guilt after you've been punished for it, right? And he is too strong to fight, so even Victor could not expect me to get out of this, right?

When you feel bad, you want to apologize. It's natural. But you cannot apologize to an enemy in time of war, can you? That is not the way people who are serious about winning a war act.

But what if you were forced to apologize? Even the little imaginary image of Victor I carry around in my head in the spot where other people keep a conscience, even he could not complain that I was not "serious," because I could always tell him I had been forced. See?

And there was an even darker, naughtier pleasure trembling beneath the fear and confusion in my body. Because I knew this wasn't a teacher punishing a schoolgirl. This was a man spanking a woman. He certainly would not have done this to any man. And he might not even have done it to Vanity. It was something for me. A bad thing, maybe even a terrible and humiliating thing, but it was mine.

So I said, "You wouldn't dare!"

"Miss Windrose, I want you to count." There was a smile in his voice.

I could see the upside-down floor of the bell tower, and through the square gateway formed by his legs, my own legs hanging down into my view. I kicked again, but now he merely reached out and took both my ankles in his grasp. His one hand was large enough that he could close his fingers around both my ankles.

"I don't want to count." My voice was clearly trembling now.

His chuckling voice floated down from somewhere above and behind me. "I will, of course, go to a number twice as high, if I must do the work of counting myself, Miss Windrose."

OK. Maybe I did not feel that guilty after all. I looked over my two options; defiance plus twice the ouch, or nondefiance . . . ?

"Would it help if I said I was sorry?"

"If you actually were sorry, yes, it might. It might help a great deal. I suspect, however, that you are not sorry at all. Nevertheless, despite that, I would like you to *say* you are sorry before every number you count. I will do twenty full strokes less than I would have done otherwise."

I was beginning to feel lightheaded. Clearly he intended a number much higher than twenty if knocking off twenty was such a light matter.

"How high am I counting?" My voice, even to my own ears, sounded small, and frail, and faint.

"It is five more than it was before you asked that question."

After a moment, he said, "Well, Miss Windrose?"

I could not seem to catch my breath or gather my wits. My heart would not stop pounding. Had you ever been upside down on the knee of a man who you looked up to when you were a girl? Not an ugly man, not a weak one. He had that quality Victor called serious. Serious about winning. Serious about overcoming me. Serious about forcing surrender. He was going to win.

I said, quietly, "I'm sorry."

He put his hand on my bottom. He waited.

I said, quietly, "One . . ."

SOLITUDE

1.

No, he wasn't kidding. Yes, they put me in a jail.

He was not even kidding about the chains. There was an iron collar around my neck, with a heavy lock on one side, a crude iron hinge on the other, and a ring just above my collarbone. A chain led from the neck ring to a staple in the middle of the ceiling, next to the light fixture. The slack of the chain described the radius of my freedom.

Directly below was a cot, fixed to the floor. To one side was the barred window, as promised. To the other, the barred door. Next to the door was a shelf for a food tray. A water bucket rested on the floor beneath. There was a tall, three-legged stool of wood.

The room was a cube of gray blocks. There was a drain in the floor. Oh yes, there was a chamber pot. Let us not forget the chamber pot.

There I lay on my stomach, both hands on my red, red bottom, tears making a little puddle in my gray-green blankets, which stank of starch.

I didn't hate him. I could not think of him as an enemy. Mean, yes; foe, no.

I do not pretend to understand myself. I don't know why I think certain things. But the mere fact that he had spanked me made it impossible for me to hate him. Imagine, for example, that Wellington, having routed Napoleon at Waterloo, has the Emperor of France pulled from the saddle of his white horse, dragged before the drumhead court . . . and told to stand in the corner and go to bed without any supper. Or imagine that

Adolph Hitler, instead of committing suicide in his bunker, is hauled in chains before the international war crimes tribunal in Nuremberg . . . and Prime Minister Churchill tans the hide of his backside with a belt strap, and washes out the mouth of Minister Goebbels with a bar of lye soap.

So I just cried. After that, I lay there, thinking about how there was nothing to think about. I cried some more.

It was the counting, the saying I was sorry, over and over, that had been so humiliating. I could not pretend I was some proud, disdainful heroine of the French Resistance, silent and unflinching as she faces her sadistic Nazi captors; or a patrician of Rome, captured by marauding Huns or Vikings, willing to perish to preserve her family's centuries-old tradition of stoic military virtue, but not willing to cower.

It is not the way I had imagined I would behave when captured by the enemy. We were not even talking about the rack, the thumbscrews, the Iron Maiden, the boot. It was just a man slapping my bottom. Picture Joan of Arc, taken by the perfidious English, before her trial even starts, "Oh, sure I'm a witch! Let me sign the confession! Just don't swat my behind! I'm too frail!"

Or maybe I felt so bad because I thought, deep down, that I deserved it. I should not have tried to brain the Headmaster with a rock. I hadn't even really wanted to do it.

It was the kind of thing a heroine in a story was supposed to do. Wasn't it? If it had worked, if I had hit him slightly harder, I would not be here now. I could have been on the outside, with my powers still active, working to free the others.

Instead of here. Chained by the neck.

It had been Victor, hadn't it? I had been trying to impress him. I had been trying to do the kind of cold-blooded, tough-as-nails, tough-guy kind of thing people are supposed to do when they are serious.

It was hard to be serious with Boggin. It was hard to think of him as the enemy.

And Victor, I am sure, would not have been impressed with that light little love-tap I gave him. On the other hand, the idea of a rock all covered with blood and brain-stuff . . . Bleh. I hadn't been able to bring myself to do it, had I? I hadn't tried hard enough.

I hadn't been able to bring myself to do what I had to do to keep myself out of this place.

I twisted to look up at the gray stone ceiling. What kind of prison was this, anyway? The Germans would have had something modern; white, spotless, with sterilized dental instruments standing by the specially designed torture chairs, and technicians in crisp uniforms. The French would have had something cunning; an ordinary-looking room, covered by one-way mirrors, microwave beams, foods containing subtle doses of sodium pentathol. The Russians would have plied insidious psychological tricks; setting clocks to wrong hours and speeds, playing tapes of distant birdsong at midnight, bringing meals at irregular times, having false messages tapped on the walls in Morse code, as if from other prisoners. But this?

This looked like a cellar dating back to the time of Bloody Mary. It probably was. A typically British jail, then; inefficient and traditional.

The damn chain looked like an antique, too. Not some modern lightweight thing made of titanium alloy or stainless steel; it look like the links were hand cast or cold hammered out of iron.

And the collar was the same way; heavy, dull metal, also an antique. I doubt many tool-and-die shops these days are turning out slave collars too small for anyone but girls. But England has a long and glorious tradition of torture, oppression, slavery, and cruelty. If you don't believe me, ask the Irish. (Or the Welsh, or the Scotch, or, for that matter, the Tazmanians, the Chinese, the Indians, the Africans. Heck, ask anyone.) So I am sure that in Surrey or Whitehead or York there were stockpiles of witch-collars and stocks and leg-irons, eye-gougers, tongue-slicers, bone bores, dunking stools, and disemboweling spindles dating from the time of Cromwell, or Elizabeth, or William the Conqueror.

Boggin probably called up one of his friends in the special "Pain Through the Ages" office of the British Royal Museum. "Hallo, Harry (or whoever)! By the by, old chap, could you ship me a gross of those old iron collars we used back in the good old days? Not the heavy big ones, no, and not the grown-woman collars, either. We need something smaller. You know those specially designed sixteen-year-old-virgin collars, used for controlling Irish maidens caught stealing potato crusts to live on, or falsely accused when they refused to sleep with their manor lords, when the young beauties were chained up in gangs to be transported to Australia as mail-order brides? Hey, and send over a chastity belt or two. You see, I have this fellow named Glum . . . What? No, we won't need any whips or hanging cages or branding irons to control this one! She already was apologizing at every slap while I spanked her, and crying like a girl! Well, of course, Harry (or whoever)! Of course she is a girl! Damned if I know why she ever thought she was anything else!"

Well, the fun of thinking about how I wasn't actually being tortured or burned as a witch wore off after a while.

Why had he made me count, damn him?

For a while, I fortified myself with the knowledge that someone trying to humiliate you, to wound your pride, is no different than someone trying to wound you with a knife. Except that, unlike a knife wound, this one can't cut unless you let it.

That made me feel better, for a time.

Then I remembered where I had heard that idea. Quentin had been told that, when he was being comforted after his ordeal. Quiet, gentle Quentin, who, despite his fear, had spit defiance into the face of his tormentress at the time when he seemed sure to die. Comforted by Boggin. It was Boggin's idea I was repeating to myself.

That made me cry all over again. I am not sure why. But it did.

After I went through all these thoughts and recriminations, I stared up at the ceiling some more. And then, like a phonograph record, I went through all these thoughts and recriminations again.

When that was done, I did it again.

And again and again.

You see, it helped prevent me from thinking about the unthinkable nightmare thoughts, wondering helplessly what was happening, what was being done to Victor, Vanity, Colin, and Quentin.

2.

You are wondering why I did not simply duck into hyperspace and slide out from there, or at least slide out from the collar?

After Boggin had reestablished the boundaries which Vanity had opened for me, while I could see a little way into hyperspace, I could not move that direction, not at all.

I could "see" that the collar was only "around" my neck in the way a flat circle of inch-high bricks on a floor in a plane might go "around" someone sitting on that floor. But if that someone cannot get up that inch, that flat line is just as good as a tall wall.

And there was nothing to look at in hyperspace. It's dark and murky, and filled (at least, near the surface of the Earth-disk) with a heavy fluid medium. Whatever sunshine there might be falls off too rapidly to reach the Earth.

And my new senses did not give me much to look at, either. My utility detector was deaf; there was nothing useful to me in the room. The internal nature of the cold iron collar was that it was heavy, merciless, and powerfully antimagical. There were no lines or strands of moral obligation reaching out from me; iron was inert, unthinking, dull. Only creatures who are free to act, can do good or do bad.

And time seemed to go slower when I stared into the dimness of the four-space. No, I did not have much to look at. And the endless distances, the volume upon hypervolume of wide, curving voids out there, an inch out of reach, just mocked me. Staring into hyperspace made me feel like a crippled angel at the bottom of the well, able to see the distant stars of the infinitely high night sky.

Believe it or not, staring at the ceiling stones was more fun.

3.

At the end of the first day, there came a noise at the door. It was the beautiful Miss Daw. Behind her was Sister Twitchett, the school nurse.

"Am I to be released?" was the first thing I asked them. To me, it seemed as if I had already been in the cell for as long as would serve any purpose, as long as could be imagined.

Miss Daw took out a tiny tape recorder of a type I had not seen before; it played a crystal disk that shimmered with rainbows instead of a cassette. When she pushed the button, the sound of her own violin music filled the cell. It was one of these intricate things by Bach, all grace notes and mathematically symmetrical themes and counterpoints. Even though my powers were off at the moment, and my higher senses were dim, I could still tell it was flattening space in the area around me.

"I didn't know you could do that with a recording," I said. Again, no answer from either of them.

Without speaking, the Sister took out a hypodermic, rubbed alcohol on my elbow, found the vein with her needle, and gave me an injection.

The first of several.

They no longer trusted us to drink our medicine, and I am sure the doses were larger. I grew faint from the medicine, and they dressed me and put me to sleep in the cot.

I wish the drug had knocked me out. After they went away, I spent most of the night unsleeping, feeling sorry for myself, and fearing that I would roll off the cot in the night and choke to death.

4.

Two days went by, then three. The only person I saw was Miss Daw. She would appear at the door, holding a bowl of food and a beaker of water, dressed in some smart outfit of plum or burgundy or palest rose to bring out the color in her peaches-and-cream complexion. On the third day, there was a fresh roll of toilet paper on the tray.

She would pick up the bowl from the previous meal, which I was supposed to have washed with my limited supply of washing water, and carry away the chamber pot.

In the evening, she would come by with a bucket of warm water, led me over to the drain, undress me, and give me a sponge bath. I wore the same nightgown I had before, and the same school uniform by day, plaid skirt and white shirt. They did not have any prison tunics, I suppose.

5.

The only fun thing I did on the third day was trying to use my trick to decrease the mass of the collar. I waited till just before Sister Twitchett and her nightly hypo were due, figuring that Dr. Fell's foul drug would be weakest at that time.

I found I could move a few of the plumb-straight world-lines, which ran from the collar toward the core of the Earth, to the left or right. This did make the collar lighter, but it now wobbled unexpectedly on my neck, shifting weight oddly, as if it were on the deck of a pitching ship, even though my body was firmly on shore. That hurt more.

A forth day went by. A fifth.

Miss Daw was always dressed nicely, as if for a social call. I do not know which was more ill-suited to a dungeon; her high-heeled pumps and sleek semiformal dresses, topped by tiny Continental hats pinned to her hair, or my schoolgirl's uniform, knee socks and jacket and with a bow in my hair. And heavy iron collar and chain. Let's not forget that. At least I did not have to wear that dumb string tie.

I complained about the collar to her. She was clearly under orders not to talk to me but, when I talked about chafing and bruises and raw spots around my neck, she nodded. "I'll see what I can do, dear."

That was the only human voice I heard for days. That one comment. "I'll see what I can do, dear."

And that was my life.

No, he wasn't kidding. Yes, they put me in a jail.

And jail was boring. Bee, owe, are, eye, an, gee. Boring.

6.

I began to find other things to think about. I wondered how old I really was.

You would think I could have at least established a minimum age, right? I mean, count how many winters since you started having your period. Find something you know happened the summer before that, and the Christmas before that.

One problem was, I did not know, when I was young, that I was supposed to start counting. I did not even know people had ages, till I came across the idea in a book I read when I was young. I started keeping track then, but how old was I when I started reading? There were no younger kids around to measure myself against, except for Colin and Quentin and Vanity. They started reading younger than I did.

A person who had met a hundred five-year-olds, and had them clearly identified, knows what a five-year-old looks like. At what age do boys grow beards? A normal person knows the answer, or at least can give a range of dates. All I had to go by was Shakespeare's speech about the ages of man given in *As You Like It.* When I was young, I thought I would know when Victor had reached the age of being a soldier because he would start having strange oaths on his lips.

What age is a girl when she develops breasts? Nine? Twelve? Twenty? All I knew is that Vanity had them before I did, and I thought they would get in the way of swimming and wrestling.

I did not know years had numbers until we came across them in a more modern history book. Herodotus and Thucydides didn't have dates in them, aside from so-many-years since so-and-so. No dates are given for anything in the Bible, except, "Augustus ordered all the world to be taxed . . ." Or "When Herod was governor of Syria . . ."

We had lessons, but we did not have grades. I could not say to myself, "I must have been in grammar school when I read Euclid and college when I read Lobechevski . . ." because I did not know when other students read things.

Once or twice, we were let out to play with some of the children in nearby Abertwyi. Mrs. Wren organized a game, or something. If, during our chatter, some topic came up from schooling, the village children simply seemed like bumpkins to us. Even children much older than us seemed not to know grammar, or languages, or geometry, or logic, or rhetoric, or astronomy, or electronics, or the sciences. I met a boy I was sure was older than me, once, who told me that the Earth has weight because of the spin on its axis. I asked him if things were weightless at the North Pole, and he was stumped. Other boys we sometimes played ball with talked about people they wanted to be like when they grew up. I had never heard of any of them. Were they sports figures, perhaps? Rock-and-roll stars? But they did not know who Admiral Byrd or Sir Edmund Hillary or Yuri Gagarin were. They never heard of Sir Ernest Shackleton. They thought Captain Cook was a character from *Peter Pan.*

They seemed to know a lot about how to cheat on tests, they knew all about their computers and electronic games, and they knew about the characters on television. We were only allowed to watch the television in the Common Room once a week. Headmaster said it would rot our brains if we saw too much.

I just could not believe that everything the Headmaster said was a lie. So much seemed to be true. I believe what he said about television, for example.

But when I added up memories, and counted events, I knew I was older than the fourteen years he gave me. Unless my puberty was very late, I doubt that I was actually twenty-one.

But, thinking back, I realize that Headmaster Boggin certainly must have lied. I did not envy Vanity when she started having her period, and frankly I was not that much enamored of growing up to be a pale sissy like Miss Daw. And if I could control my body so much as that, why hadn't I always stayed stronger and faster than Colin and Quentin? It was absurd to think that I secretly desired to be defeated, overpowered, and outmuscled by men.

That thought cheered me for a while. Then a haunting memory rose up in my brain. I remember Grendel Glum saying he had done something to me, influenced me with his willpower, to make my secret desires exactly so.

7.

On the fourth day, despite the drugs, I was able to get my fingers under the collar and push my neck slightly into the fourth dimension. Not enough to get it off my head, mind you, but it made the collar seem slightly larger. The iron had the faintest blue sheen to it when I did that, and the faintest red sparks glinted like fireflies around my fingertips. (I could place a point of view a few inches to my left, half an inch into the "red" direction, to glimpse this.)

It must have set off some alarm, because Miss Daw came to the door almost immediately. She set up her music player, and had it play Beethoven's Ninth Symphony.

On the fourth and fifth day I had music. That was nice, I suppose.

Whenever the disc got to the same track, and played the Schiller poem from the middle of the Ninth, however, and I heard the German voices singing about the Joy of Man, light, free notes rising and rising to unimpeded glory, I cried again.

8.

On the sixth day I begged Miss Daw to speak to me, but she shook her head and looked pensive. I asked her if I was to be allowed to go to Chapel tomorrow; I needed to pray for my soul.

That got a reaction out of her, a little smile with her head tilted to one side. "I had not heard that you were especially devout. In fact, I have heard rumors to quite the opposite effect, if such rumors can be countenanced."

Two dozen words, or more! An oasis after the endless sand dunes of silence.

"Everyone gets religion when they are in prison, Miss Daw."

That answer perhaps was too flippant, for she smiled a gracious but cold smile, and began to turn away.

"Oh, please!" I said, "For the love of God, please! Even if you don't believe me, even if you think it's just a trick to get me out of this horrid room, please Miss Daw, please, isn't it simple decency, simple plain English decency, to let a girl who thinks she is about to die go pray?"

"Who has told you such a falsehood, Miss Windrose? No one is going to kill you."

"Who told me otherwise? You won't talk to me!"

She looked around the cell; a soft, sad look came into her eyes for a moment. She was thinking that I had been waiting for days for some execution, tormenting myself with a fear that was utterly false, a fear she could have alleviated with a word.

"Well," she said, "I will see if you can be taken up to the Chapel tomorrow. You do not have the energy relationship in the moral direction a person devoted to his God normally manifests. Your relational structures are extensional rather than intentional, and form nodes going into two time-directions, but not toward eternity. This type of atrophy is typical of atheists and agnostics. But—take heart, my dear, do not be so downcast. The forms must be observed. That is why we have forms to begin with."

"Then I can go to Chapel?"

"I'll see what I can do, dear."

My lip trembled. "That is what you said about this collar . . ."

"That will be looked into."

20

COMPANY, OF A SORT

1.

That Saturday was the worst, and also the oddest. After long hours of watching the square of sunlight from the barred window crawl west-to-east across the floorstones, Miss Daw and Sister Twitchett come to the barred door, unlocked it, and let themselves in. Miss Daw was carrying a dress on a hanger, protected by a plastic sheet and smelling of lavender.

Miss Daw gestured to me, indicating that I was to put on the dress she had brought. Because I was tired of silence, I pretended not to understand her gestures, "What? I beg your pardon? Is something wrong with your voice?"

"You must don this, please," she said. Miss Daw has a voice like silver crystal, soft and pure.

Anyone speaking after Miss Daw speaks sounds like a crow. Sister Twitchett spoke after Miss Daw, "Put it on and no back-talk, or we dope you up and dress you ourselves. Save us work, if you heed."

After being spanked by Boggin, merely disrobing in front of two school staff did not embarrass me. My shirt and jacket unbuttoned along the front; I wasn't wearing a sweater or anything else that had to be drawn over my head. Soon I was standing there, just in the iron collar, a swaying 'U' of slack chain leading away from it.

"Socks and shoes, too," said Twitchett.

"Where are the others?" I said. "Are they dead? Are they back at school? Is Vanity safe?"

When neither one answered, I tore the clothes she held from Miss Daw's hands and threw them on the ground. "I am not getting dressed or doing anything till you tell me!"

Twitchett looked frightened. No one has ever looked frightened of me before. She thought I was the monster from beyond space and time that Boggin said I was. I saw it in her eyes.

She said to Miss Daw, "Let's open the window and leave. She'll want to get dressed in the morning, after the snow blows in."

Miss Daw said to me in a gentle voice, "The other students are quite safe, but they are confined in cells like this one. I would not allow anything to happen to you."

(That was interesting. Not "*We* would not allow," but "*I* would not allow.")

Sister Twitchett looked at Miss Daw, "We were told, Ma'am, not to jaw with her . . ."

Miss Daw inclined her head to Twitchett with a tiny smile. "I would be in your debt, if you only told the Headmaster how cooperative Miss Windrose was. Need I say more?"

Twitchett frowned, but said nothing. Miss Daw put her little gloved hand on the other woman's elbow, thanked her, and turned back to me.

I said: "Tell me what happened to them! Where's Vanity?"

Miss Daw said in a voice as soft as ripples on a pond, "Once you are dressed, I will tell you."

The dress was a peach silk affair, almost too sheer to be an evening dress. The bodice laced up the back, and spaghetti string ties ran over the shoulders. The bosom cups were made of stiff, reinforced fabric and decorated with black and white lace. The skirt was unpleated silk, with tiny darts at the waist, and a handkerchief bottom. The underwear, bra and panties both, were built into the inner lining of the dress, so that it clung very tightly, but with no sign of lines.

Black nylon hose came next, which were suspended from a hidden garter belt, also woven into the inner lining of the lower part of the bodice. Miss Daw knelt to fasten on slender stiletto heels.

"I can't walk in heels that high," I said.

"You won't be needing to walk," said Sister Twitchett.

The sister brought over the stool and had me sit. Out from her medical bag, she drew several lengths of chain.

"Oh, you've got to be kidding," I said. "What are those for?"

Miss Daw said, "This is not as bad as it seems. It is all part of the process."

"What process? I don't want to be part of any process!"

Miss Daw said, "I won't let anyone harm you, child."

Sister Twitchett rolled her eyes. I could almost see what she was thinking. The shape-changing monster looks like a girl, but it is not a girl.

Twitchett crossed my wrists in my lap and chained them together with a pair of handcuffs. A steel chain wound around my waist, so that I had to keep my wrists close to my navel. A second steel chain, about three feet long, dropped down between my legs. This attached to a pair of ankle cuffs that hobbled me.

Neither one had the heavy, cast-iron links of the collar's chain. These looked machine-tooled, modern.

I had seen such a get-up before. On some documentary on one of the rare days when we could see television in the Common Room, our program had been interrupted by pictures of some famous criminal (I forget who) being led from a police van in handcuffs, with a belly-chain and leg irons. I think it was an American, because he wore an orange jumpsuit instead of a normal prison uniform.

This increased my hope and my fear. Were they about to transport me somewhere? If my friends were being transported too, I might be able at least to see Victor and the others. If we were all put in the same van, I could talk to them.

Maybe this was a party dress. I began to imagine that I was to be hauled before some ballroom full of guests, Mavors in a tuxedo and Lady Cyprian in a ball gown, with other gods and monsters present, so that Boggin could show them how roughly he was treating me.

Or maybe they were about to transport me more permanently. Boggin may have already failed, and the four of us were being sent to four destinations. Perhaps they had thrown lots for us. Maybe the Satyr or his faction had won me, and insisted I be dressed up before being sent along.

2.

While Sister Twitchett was kneeling down, stringing chains and locking locks, Miss Daw brought out a makeup kit of truly absurd size. It unfolded and unfolded again. There were more brushes than an artist would use, and lipstick, eye pencils, crayons, blushes, and creams. There were little tools and implements I had never seen before. There was a thing that had handles like a pair of scissors, but which led to a curved rubber pair of jaws, meant for clamping onto eyelashes.

Miss Daw's hands were soft on my face, and I could feel cool touches where she applied various layers of base and blush. I had never worn lipstick before, but it tasted terrible. I also had thought lipstick was just gunk in a tube, but Miss Daw used three or four tubes, and a little pencil. There was something that tasted like spearmint, which she rubbed onto my teeth with her finger.

I was nervous when she painted my eyes, and worried when she kept putting her fingers too close, but I obeyed her instructions when she told me to look left and right, up or down. She brushed my lashes with a little comb the size of a toothpick.

She took out a powder puff and dusted my shoulders and the tops of my breasts where the bodice pushed them up.

Sister Twitchett was done with her chaining up long before the makeup was done. She packed her bag and I was left alone with Miss Daw.

There I sat, chained up on a stool in a very nice, very sheer dress, with Miss Daw standing behind me, combing and brushing out my hair.

3.

In my heart, at that moment, I was convinced that maybe Boggin had told the truth, and that I was only fourteen, not the eighteen or twenty Victor said I was.

"Miss Daw, I'm scared," I said in a trembling voice.

"Hush. Don't be scared, child."

"What's going to happen to me?" I could not get the tremble out of my voice.

"Nothing ill will befall."

"Why are you dressing me up this way?"

I could only think of one reason, and it was a very terrible one.

Miss Daw leaned over, and brought out a velvet box one inch on a side. She opened it. Within were drops of diamond no bigger than teardrops.

She lifted them out of sight behind my head. I felt little metal clamps pinch my earlobes.

"Ow!" I said.

"Sorry," she said. "Most of mine are for pierced ears. This is what I had."

I would have lifted up my hands to take them off, but I only had about an inch or two of play, up or down, due to the belly-chain.

She held up a large hand mirror from her bag. I saw my face in the glass.

"There," she said. "How do we look?"

I thought I looked pretty much the same as I always looked, except now I was painted. There was blue eye shadow above my eyes and black pencil around them, and my lips were too red.

But I could feel a lot more stuff on my face than I could see. She had taken my flesh-colored flesh and put flesh-colored hue on top of it. Take a girl's face and paint a girl's face on top of it. What was the point?

I did like the earrings, though.

"Are you done? You said you would say . . ."

At that moment, there came voices from the corridor. I heard Mrs. Wren's cracked, wavering voice, and Mr. Glum's breathy growl answering her.

There was a strange noise as footsteps approached. Thump-clack, thump-clack.

Miss Daw leaned and whispered in my ear, "Your friends are safe. The boys are in cells like this one; Miss Fair is in your room, under guard. They are in low spirits, naturally, except for Mr. Triumph, who is not easily perturbed . . ."

Mr. Glum came to the open cell door, looking more grizzled than usual. His bald spot was sunburned and his jawline had a five o'clock shadow. He was dressed in a long brown jacket, and he had what seemed a broomstick in his hand: a hoe, actually, with a scarf wrapped around the blade of the hoe.

Beneath the hem of his coat, on the left, I saw his brown pants, tucked into the top of his boot. On the right, was a peg. His right leg was gone below the knee.

He put his elbows, one to either side of the metal doorframe, and let the hoe, his makeshift crutch, dangle in his hand. He lowered his head and stared at me.

I should say that his eyes widened, but that is not quite right. He actually squinted. But his pupils dilated.

I became very conscious of how I was sitting, bolt upright on the stool, hands folded in my lap, with cold metal circling my wrists and ankles, and cold air touching my bare shoulders, naked arms, almost-naked legs in their stockings, almost-bare bosom pushed up in its bodice. I have never felt smaller and more fragile than at that moment.

He seemed so . . . hungry . . . when he looked at me. Like a starving man. But sad. Hungry and sad.

Glum spoke without taking his eyes off me, "So that's it, eh? Boggin is to have her. All tarted up and fine. He's had his filthy hands on her, has he? And Vanity, too! Why should he have both? And him not married! 'Tis clean against the law, that is."

Mrs. Wren, from the corridor where I could not see her, said something sharp to Mr. Glum. He apparently wasn't supposed to talk to me. He did not answer her, but twisted his lips and spat on the floor.

Miss Daw put her small hand on my elbow. "Stand up, dear, and let's have a look at you."

I stood up, wobbling slightly on the high heels. The heavy chain running from my neck to the ceiling rattled and wobbled, too. Standing pulled tight the chain running from my ankles to my wrists, and I had to push my hands downward, pulling the chain around my waist tightly down against my hips, in order to ease the pressure on my ankles.

Mr. Glum stumped forward, wobbling himself a bit, wincing and half-hopping, half-propping himself on his hoe.

He put his rough, callused fingers, fingers with his dirty nails, on my cheek, and tilted up my head to look at him. I had glanced down to look at my shoes (because I was afraid of toppling) but the moment he touched me (as if the past had somehow changed shape) I had been keeping my eyes down because I was shy.

Or maybe I was afraid.

I heard Mrs. Wren's voice from the door, "You're not to touch her, old tree stump, old iron lump, old clod!"

Glum ignored her. He was staring into my eyes.

He said to me, "It were only for a small time, I know. But I had you, me. And you were mine and no one else's for that time. All made of gold. I were nearly afraid to touch you, like I'd leave a dirty fingerprint, like on a wineglass, or a white china plate."

I said, "I'm sorry." And I did feel sorry for him.

He said in a low voice, "I never seen a girl like you before. Girls like you have boys of their own, whole strings of 'em, young men with straight backs and straight teeth and thick black hair. You think me wrong to've carried you off? Course I were wrong. But you'd not of talked to me. Were I s'posed to woo you? Bring you posies? Nawr! If you'd watches on both your two wrists and us standing in the middle of a clock maker's shop, you'd not of told me the time of day."

"I might have done," I said in a quiet little voice. "You didn't ask."

I have already mentioned that I do not understand myself, or why I say some things I say. Here I was, apologizing to my would-be rapist, for being too stuck up and high-class.

I think I read somewhere that they call it the "Stockholm syndrome" when girls feel sorry for their own kidnappers.

But I did feel sorry for him. I mean, for goodness sake, Boggin made him chop off his own foot with an axe! How mad was I suppose to stay at him? And for how long? Forever?

"Oi? I didn't ask, did I? Is that it?" He stepped slightly closer, and still kept my chin between his fingers, tilting my head up. It was not as if I were able to raise my hands to push him away. I was scared, and taking faster-than-normal breaths in through my nose. I could feel the stiff silky fabric of the bodice cupping my breasts tightly as my chest rose and fell.

"Miss Windrose—or mightn't I call you Amelia, seeing as how we been close—?" He said, tilting his head slightly down.

Miss Daw, whom I had almost forgotten was there, said in her silver voice, "That would not be appropriate."

Well, thanks a bunch, Daw. Here she was supposed to be protecting me. How come she was letting my ex-kidnapper stand there toying with my chin?

I could not nod much of a nod, but I twitched my head back a little bit, and sort of dropped my eyelashes. He was staring at my lips, but he must have seen that tiny motion, and he took that as a nod.

"Amelia—" (he pronounced it with a burr, so it sounded like "Ah, Melia") "—Ah, Melia, what were I suppose to ask you, eh? What were I suppose to be able to give you, a man like me, what has nothing?"

"Freedom," I said. "Help free me. Help my friends."

He stared for a moment, stepping back. His eyes wandered over me, caressing my hair, my eyes, lips, chin, shoulders. His gaze lingered for a time on my breasts, then came to rest on my hands, which seemed so small and white compared to his, folded (as if demurely) in front of me. A moment more he spent drinking in the sight of my legs, ankles, my feet.

I finally understood the purpose of high-heeled shoes. They are not just meant to retroflex your knees, extend your legs, and make you callipygous. They also make you look like you're standing on tiptoes, like a little girl reaching for a jar of sweets on a too-high shelf.

A delicate little girl. One who can't run away.

He said, "Free you? Would you sell your body to your jailor to buy the jailhouse key, Ah, Melia? That would make you a right whore, then, wouldn't it? Nar. You'd ne'er come to me of your free will, Ah, Melia, for you'd have to hold your nose to of done it. To lower yourself. And I'll not have you lower yourself. You wouldn't be worth the taking, then."

I said, "Hold it. That doesn't make any sense. If . . ."

He put his hand on the loose hanging 'U' of chain depending between the ceiling and my neck, and tugged it. I wobbled unsteadily, started to fall, and sat back down on the stool somewhat more forcefully than I would have liked, even though Miss Daw put her hands on my arms to guide me back down.

I sat down hard enough to make my bottom sting, and it reminded me rather too much of Boggin's thorough spanking. The sensation of humiliation, of being pushed around, was too much the same. Tears came to my eyes.

Glum was looking down at me with something like awe on his face, as if I were a goddess. I think he thought I was crying for him.

He said, "I'd never let you go. I'd never free you. You're too fine. You're gold, you are. If I could carry the sunlight in my poke, I would not let it up, either, but I'd hale it back down to my house below the waves, where all is but murk and filth and gloom, and my house would be the one bright one, and you the one bright thing in it."

Mrs. Wren, from the door, called out, "Time to walk or hop away, old crab, old five-toe, old Ahab. There is no more for you to see here! Come! Or must granny get her doll and fishhook out?"

Mr. Glum did not argue, but put his hoe under his armpit like a crutch, and hopped and stumped backward and out of the cell, never taking his eyes from me.

4.

I sat on the stool, shaking.

Miss Daw brought out a key ring, and began unlocking the cuffs and leg-irons and belly-chain. She had to pause and puzzle over the locks every now and again; she did not seem as adept at prison matron work as Twitchett. Perhaps it was because Twitchett was Catholic.

The huge, heavy collar stayed on.

Miss Daw took out a cotton ball and some cream in a bottle to wipe my face clear of makeup.

I said to her, "Is that it? You brought him by to look at me. Just him? Just to look? Is that it?"

Miss Daw started daubing my cheeks clean of blush.

I said, "Two hours of making up for two minutes of being looked at by a man?"

Miss Daw said, half to herself, "Now you have had your first lesson in what it is like to be a real grown-up woman in a man's world, my dear. We are judged by our looks, and men are not."

"Why? Why was Glum brought here? Why all the chains? Am I some sort of prize to be given to Mr. Glum for his good behavior?"

No answer.

I said, "Am I supposed to seduce him? Were you doing this to mock him, or to make me feel bad, or as part of some spell or some scheme, or . . . what the hell was the point of that?"

"Please be careful with your language, Miss Windrose." And she wiped my mouth to carry away the lipstick. It was almost as effective as Mr. Glum's gag in silencing me.

But when she started daubing the powder off with a small sponge, I spoke again: "Why? Why, Miss Daw? Why should I be careful? Or else you might chain me up and paint me up and put me in a nightie and have Glum come by to ogle me?"

"It is not a nightie."

"What kind of dress has underthings sewn in?"

"I am given to understand that it is used by ladies of the theater."

"You mean ladies of the evening, don't you?"

I have never seen her blush before. The perfect Miss Daw, always so polite, so distant and restrained, had red crawl into her cheeks, and she could not raise her eyes.

I said, "You were just taunting him, weren't you? Using me to taunt him."

Miss Daw did not answer that, but said instead, "Swear words, when used in vain, sometimes create echoes in overspace. The thought-energy creates a space-distortion effect, and decreases the distance between this plane of space–time and those achronic entities whom we call Furies, whose business it is to harass and torment the wicked."

"Define 'wicked.' What do you call people who dress up girls and tie them up, in order to sexually arouse men old enough to be their grandfathers?"

She did not answer but curtly told me to close my eyes while she wiped mascara from my eyelids.

With my eyes closed, I tried to look in the direction she mentioned, toward hyperspace. I could see nothing, sense nothing. I could not remember what the other directions looked like, or where they were.

She washed my face with warm, soapy water, and a towel. While she did, my eyes still closed, I tried and tried to look.

But trying hard was not my paradigm. For Colin, for Grendel, wishing made it so. Not for me.

"Stand up, please. I do not think you want to sleep in that dress."

I opened my eyes. "You did it to blind me."

"Stand up, please."

I stood up. Even normally, I was taller than she was. In heels, I was practically Boggin.

I said down to her: "You were so mean to him. Didn't you see how bad this made him feel? I know you think I am an evil monster. But isn't he on your side?"

She could not raise her eyes. "He and I are kin. He is a male member of my species."

"A male Siren? He sings?"

"He does not sing. He dances on the waves, and the waves turn to fury and swamp ships and pull down houses near the shore. He is one of the brood of Echidna, who cannot die, but lives forever to work harm to mortal men. The business of his kind is to slay mariners lost at sea, so that their widows back ashore will never know the hour or fashion of their death. Grendel is not a kindly person."

"So I am only supposed to feel sorry for kindly people? Who exactly does that leave? Besides Jesus Christ and babies who die at birth?"

That was the wrong thing to say, because it stiffened her backbone and drove away whatever shame she felt. "Your comments are inappropriate, and impertinent. They may even be blasphemy. Nor need you be overly concerned with Mr. Glum. He does his duty, as do we all, whether he will or no. Some duties are pleasant; some are unpleasant. We who serve are given the ability, if we kick against the goad, to make the pleasant ones less pleasant. We cannot make the unpleasant ones more pleasant. You are a dangerous and super-human being, child, and we must take what steps we can."

Then she said: "Turn, please, so I may undo you. We must have that dress off."

"If you answer my questions. Otherwise I'll rip the dress in half!"

"Oh, come now, Miss Windrose. What earthly good will it do you to rip a fine dress?"

"You come now! What earthly harm will it do you to answer me? I'm curious, it's not hurting you, and you'll get me to cooperate."

"Very well. Turn around and suck in. Let me get these laces. Let's hope Grendel's power has not made them fast."

I tried to hold my breath while speaking, and my words came out all squeaky. I said, "What is the range of his power? In his paradigm, how far away can he be and still affect me?"

"Breathe. If you know enough to ask that question, you have nearly deduced the answer."

The dress fell down around my legs. The silk caressed me on the way down, like a ghost.

I said, "This was a fantasy of his, wasn't it? To see me all chained up like a white woman kidnapped by Moors, for their sultan's harem. To see me in all my girlish, female glamour. Why?"

Miss Daw looked away, her eyes becoming distant, as if staring at an unseen horizon. The ashamed Miss Daw was gone, and the remote, dispassionate, polite Miss Daw was back. "Please step. I am really not supposed to be talking to you at all, Miss Windrose. It is possible I will fall under some penalty for it."

"His power works by desire. You had to enflame his desire."

She did not look up, but began to blush again. Dispassionate Daw was losing ground. "Your shoes please?"

Suddenly I was short again. But still taller than her.

"But why make it so sick? So weird? Handcuffs and high heels . . . ?"

The ashamed Miss Daw carried the day. She knelt to roll down my stockings. She spoke toward the floor stones in a haunted voice, as if reciting an old lesson, "Desires which are constantly frustrated are stronger. Men who desire wives, children, a hearth and home, all the wholesome things I shall never know, they can know contentment. But men who have unnatural desires, or who dream sad, unfulfilled and unfulfillable dreams, their impossible desires bloat up beyond all bounds, huger than kragen from beneath the sea. See sadistic Grendel, who desires a wife, but only if she is forced with whips and chains to love him; and he dreams only of having a woman he knows he is never worthy of, and to beat her gives him the pleasure other men have from caressing her. Like a man at a feast table, who gnaws the wood and leaves the food to rot, a pervert starves, for what he thinks will sate his hunger never does, but leaves him hungry still. He has lost all taste for wholesome food."

"I don't think he wants to beat me. I think he just likes rope."

"You have a very generous heart, Miss Windrose, which is a credit to your innocence." The distant, detached Miss Daw was coming back. "Your stockings?"

They were down around my ankles. I had to sit to get them off my feet. I sat on the cot, as the stool was too high. I had to tease them off my heels and toes; they were as sheer as smoke.

I said, "You didn't really answer my question."

She straightened up, stockings in hand. "I thought I had done. Grendel's power, if his desire is strong enough, works both by day and by night, whether he sleeps, or whether he wakes. The distances mean nothing to him, if and when he believes they mean nothing. His greatest desire is to see you as he saw you now: beautiful and enchained, a fair prisoner, unable to escape. His belief will make it so that you are unable to escape."

I put on my nightgown. Supine once more, I could see the snake of the iron links reaching up to the staple in the ceiling. There was something odd about it.

Miss Daw swung the grate shut and locked it.

I said, "Can you douse the light?"

She did.

It went dark. Into the dark, I called, "What about my friends?"

Miss Daw knew exactly what I meant by the question, for she said, "None of them has been treated as badly as you. Mrs. Wren put the handle of the axe Mr. mac FirBolg used to attack her under his bed, and that stole the power from his limbs. Dr. Fell gave Mr. Nemo an injection. I introduced a disjunction into the nervous system of Mr. Triumph, so that he cannot activate the sections of his brain that control his matter-manipulation abilities. Mrs. Wren and I cooperated, to set up blocks to prevent Miss Fair from activating her attention-energy gathering faculty, from which her tesseract-creation power springs."

I said, "Vanity can tell when people are looking at her. When she finds an area of space-time where no one is looking, such as inside a wall, she can fold space, and negate the distance, create a shortcut. Space is merely the interval measuring the energy needed to cross it: when the energy level is unknown or undetermined, the space-interval is not fixed. Isn't it?"

"That is basically correct, Miss Windrose."

"But some intelligence must act to fill in the details, to make walls and floors that preserve visual continuity, that fit in to the general picture of the surrounding space—something like Descartes' demiurge: a spirit. That is why you need the help of a witch to stop the Phaeacian power. You don't really understand what Vanity does, and can't understand, because it is not your paradigm. Am I right?"

"You were always a very clever student, Miss Windrose. Perhaps too clever. I can see why the Headmaster had Mr. Glum come by to enforce your security."

Her footsteps receded in the dark.

5.

Then I noticed what was different. The strangling weight that had kept me half-awake with fear and coughing was now gone.

The collar. It didn't hurt any more.

I touched the collar with my fingers, but I could not see it, even had there been a light, without a mirror. But it felt lighter and stronger in my hand. It did not chafe, and my sores were gone.

Glum's fantasies about harem girls did not admit of the slave collars hurting them.

It put me in the first good mood I had known since imprisonment.

At about the time when the moon came up, my mood rose even higher. I realized what it was Miss Daw had told me. She had given me the secrets of all the powers that kept us here. She had told me who stopped whom.

Well, that thought was pleasant enough to allow me to fall asleep. I had not slept a full night in a long time.

THE SEVENTH DAY

1.

Miss Daw did get permission to take me to Chapel in the morning. She brought my Sunday uniform on a hanger. Dr. Fell came by, once I was dressed, to help escort me.

Miss Daw unlocked the chain from the ring at my neck and then toyed with the key and lock under my ear (where I could not see) for several moments.

She said to Fell, "Grendel altered reality. I cannot get the collar off. Can you dissolve it?"

His third eye opened in his forehead, glistening and metal-blue. I saw it only inches away.

It seemed to consist of nested concentric spheres of semitransparent substance, hard and shining. There was something like a pupil, or at least an aperture, one in each sphere. By lining up the different pupils in the different spheres he seemed to get a stronger or weaker ray. When enough apertures opened, I could see down a tiny well of clear holes, to a hidden spark of incandescence at the center, a starlike pinpoint of fuel in the tiniest, innermost chamber. Perhaps the different spheres had differing filters or augmentations for different effects. It did not look organic at all. It was clearly a machine thing; hard, finely-tooled, insensitive.

He said, "It has clearly shrunk somewhat, and seems to be made of a lighter, more bluish-white metal. The atomic latticework has been replaced with continuous substance. It is the Aristotelian paradigm, and outside of my competence. It is no longer made of iron, but of a ratio of earth essences with fire essences. I can remove it, but it might hurt the girl."

The center of his eye turned red and an aiming beam came out. The various apertures began to slide together. I smelled ozone . . .

"Um!" I said, "It's OK! It doesn't hurt! Really!"

With a dizzying, chameleon eye–like optic motion, Dr. Fell rotated certain middle spheres to thicken the number of layers blocking the inner chamber. The metal eye dimmed, as if idling on standby. "Move your hands out of the way, girl."

Miss Daw said, "Where is Mrs. Wren?"

Dr. Fell frowned slightly. By some intuition, I knew that he did not like to hear her saying, in front of me, any hint of whose power stopped whose. He said curtly, "She is unavailable at this time."

That was what Dr. Fell usually said when Mrs. Wren was drunk.

Fell said, "Should I continue? You have primary responsibility for this subject."

Miss Daw said, "It is unforgivable that a girl should be forced to wear such a cruel thing in the House of the Lord."

I admired her for saying that.

". . . What would people think?"

My admiration dimmed.

Fell said, "Is that permission to proceed . . . ?" His eye lit up again.

I screamed and jumped back (hey, it was really, really nice not to have that big chain hanging there). "Get a hacksaw! Don't let him blow my head off!"

Miss Daw said, "Let us not alarm the child, Ananias." She looked pensive, and said, half to herself, "It does seem much smaller than before. Perhaps people will think it is jewelry."

2.

No one else was there. Not Victor, not Colin, not Quentin, not Vanity. This one week I had gone longer without seeing them than I had my whole life previously.

Even the other members of the staff and administration were not there. I was hoping to see Taffy ap Cymru, and blackmail him into letting me go, or getting a message to his boss, Hermes. But the Chapel was deserted except for the vicar, the altar boy, and us.

Miss Daw sat on my right side, her beautiful face glowing as if with an inner light. Dr. Fell on my left. Fell had an indifference to religion that went beyond contempt. During the service he sat with a checkbook and a pocket calculator, doing sums.

Our services were given by a vicar named Dr. Foster, a tall, dim-eyed, white-haired man, thin as a rail, who muttered and murmured mildly for his sermons, and who managed to make even the most interesting Bible stories into boring digressions into abstract theology or Trinitarian speculations. He was the only person I knew who used the word "consubstantiality." At others times, instead of Bible lessons, his sermons somehow led down twisting paths to end up as descriptions of the metaphysical disputes he had against his friend, the Rev. James Spensley, from Mumbles, who was a Wesleyian; or the Rev. Price, from the Dissenter's Church at Llangennith, who dared to be, of all things, a Calvinist.

I owe much of my agnosticism to Dr. Foster and his somnolent, sonorous sermons.

As horrible as this sounds, it was not until that day that I ever thought to wonder what denomination we were. I had always assumed we were High Church because our ceremonies were elaborate and beautiful. But were we? We said our Sunday prayers in English, from the Common Book, so I knew that we were not Roman Catholics (or "Reprobate Papists" as Dr. Foster liked to call them). Although Vanity and I had, when we were young, said our prayers at night in Latin.

Or, at least, we had been saying *something* in Latin. Maybe Mrs. Wren (who was, after all—let's face it—a witch) was not telling us true prayers.

Our Chapel had both icons and stained glass windows, so I knew we weren't Lutherans, and we had saints, but we were instructed to revere them without prayer to them per se. And Miss Daw and I went to the altar rail to kneel and accept the Host, which Dr. Foster blessed, and an altar boy, whose name was Jack Jingle, held the salver beneath my lips as I knelt and took the wafer.

Dr. Foster, as sometimes happened, stood at the lectern, blinking, having forgotten what part of the ceremony he was in. Miss Daw and I continued to kneel at the rail, and she took the opportunity to lower her eyes in silent prayer.

I wondered what would happen if I ran up to Dr. Foster or Jack the altar boy and begged for sanctuary, like Esmeralda in *Notre Dame de Paris*.

I looked over at Jack speculatively. He looked younger than me, and he always had, a boy who had not yet grown hair. I am no judge of ages. Eight? Ten? Six? He was young. In his hands he held the silver plate that carried the Host, and he was looking at Dr. Foster with some worry, and polishing the salver with his long, flowing robe sleeve.

I was reminded of something Quentin once told me. He said that the purpose of holding a mirrored surface beneath the mouth of someone taking Communion was to discover whether any vampires had infiltrated into the body of the Holy Church. The altar boys were supposed to pour the Holy Wine over their head, should that happen, whereupon it would instantly turn into the blood of Christ, and burn the vampire to a crisp. That was Quentin's theory.

Once, long ago, after services, I had asked Dr. Foster about the question of vampires. He blinked at me and told me the essence of the wine was transfigured, but not transubstantiated, while remaining substantially the same, and that it was done by the grace of Christ, rather than by the authority of the priest.

I could not imagine Foster being able to understand that I was a prisoner.

I could imagine, very clearly, if Foster did get the idea that I was in trouble, demanding an explanation from Dr. Fell, or calling for him to bring a telephone (at once!) so that he could summon the police. I could also imagine Dr. Fell, a bored look in his thin, gray face, opening his third eye and burning Foster to a crisp. Or—why be so crude?—stunning him with a jolt and injecting him with something to erase short-term memory.

And the little altar boy? Because he did not seem to age, I wondered if he, like Lelaps the dog, or Sister Twitchett, was one of their creatures, disguised as a human boy and here as part of the stage scenery. After all, I never saw Jack except on Sundays, and he did not seem to live in Abertwyi. The local children didn't know him. Maybe he was a homonculus, and was kept in a box during the week in Dr. Fell's lab.

I did not tell them I was a prisoner. Instead, I knelt and prayed.

Yes, I prayed. Why not? The advantage of being an agnostic over being an atheist is that I always had the possibility of being wrong, and could still entertain the hope that the universe was better organized than it appeared to be.

But I did not know to whom to pray.

What if Henry Tudor had been wrong and God was Catholic and not

Anglican at all? What if Paul had been wrong, and God was Jewish just like He had been in the Old Testament, and hadn't repealed any of the Old Covenant Law after all? People always said that God did not care about denominations. Everything in His Holy Book said that He cared about denominations very much. What were the Pharisees, so earnestly and bitterly criticized by Christ himself, if not a denomination? Why spend page after boring page describing the vestments, dietary restrictions, and sacrificial animals sacred to the Chosen People, if these things were trivial? Why kill the guy—I forget his name—who was trying to straighten out the Ark of the Covenant when it fell over?

Well, I wanted to pray, and I did not think it right to pray to Archangel Gabriel, not this time. It was time to pick a God.

For a while, I thought I really ought to pray to the God of the Koran, and become Mohammedan. For one thing, the Koran was written after the New Testament, the same way the New Testament was written after the Bible, so it might be a more developed form. Also, the Mohammedans seemed to be more devoted to a simple and severe form of worship, and did not clutter up their monotheism with saints or trinities.

Two things stopped me. First, I had no idea which direction Mecca was in from Wales. South and East, I assumed. Second, I did not know if women were allowed to pray.

Even as I was kneeling and thinking all these flippant thoughts, a prayer rose up in me as if of its own accord. I whispered very softly what was in my heart.

"God of Abraham, who led the Israelites out of bondage, and freed the slaves from the cruelty of the Pharaoh, free me. Free my friends. Lead us from this Lion's Den, and let us find our home, our families, our friends. Lead us from this alien land to a place where we belong. I beg you. You saved Moses and his people. Save me. Amen."

It was not as if I can take credit for making up what I said. It came out more or less without any effort on my part. Nonetheless, afterwards, I actually thought it had been a pretty clever thing to say. I mean, the God of the Christians and the Jews and the Mohammedans, whichever one He is, all of them are the God who saved the Israelites from Egypt. Right?

Miss Daw was watching me. I saw her eyes focused in a direction I could not see, and saw the slight frown crease the perfect whiteness of her alabaster brow.

3.

Dr. Foster, as it turned out, simply raised his hands and began the closing benedictions. "May the Lord make His face to shine upon you, and give you peace . . ."

We had skipped one or two hymns that were posted on the notice board, the recitation of the Nicene Creed, and the part of the service where we call responses to the prayer. I do not know what that part is called, but it was my favorite part when I was much younger.

Anyway, what Colin used to call the "crapshoot of the Foster Amnesia" sometimes led us to go through two services in a row, if Foster lost his place late on, and started again from the top. At other times, the "crapshoot" cut the service time in half, as it had done today.

Fell and Daw ordered me to walk ahead of them down the path, around the corner, and to the door beneath the bell tower. The entrance to the cell was less than a dozen steps from the main Chapel door. The cell was part of the same building, which may have been one reason why I had been allowed out.

There was still snow on the ground, but it was patchy. Apparently the weather for the week I had missed had turned mild. It was chill, but it was a crisp, refreshing chill. A week ago the early winter had seemed late winter, and December days were getting February weather. Now, early winter seemed like late autumn, and December air had an October feel to it. Like the realization that I had never missed my friends for so long a time, I realized that I had never gone for so long without seeing the weather in my life, either.

The trees had no leaves on them but, after my long confinement underground, they seemed as bright as any trees in spring. The clouds were few, and very white, and the sky was high and cool and blue.

I walked slowly, thinking that my prayer had not only not been answered, but that the service, by being cut short, had sped my trip back into the gray brick cube of my cell.

I tried to look in the fourth dimension. My visions and senses were still utterly blocked, as they had been from the moment yesterday when Glum had come to drool on me. I could not even remember what hyperspace looked like. I was a girl, an entirely ordinary girl, wearing an iron collar I could not take off, because that was the way Glum wanted it, and his desires could change reality in a way I could not sense or resist.

A tall black man, either a Negro or a Pakistani (I had never seen either in real life, and was not sure which was which) came suddenly around the corner. His hair was loose and lay along his shoulders like a girl's, instead of being wiry, so perhaps he was a Pakistani. His face was more handsome than the face of a statue. He wore a long powder-blue coat, with blue trousers and black boots beneath it, and he walked with his head hunched down, as if he (in this fine weather) were cold, and his hands made deep fists in his pockets.

We bumped directly into each other, and he brought up both his hands to catch me by the shoulders before I fell off the path.

"A thousand pardons, Miss," he started.

If he had just had his hands in an oven, they could not have been warmer. It felt good on my arms.

I grabbed the metal collar around my neck with both my hands and tugged on it, trying to show him it wouldn't come off. I said, "Help me! Please! Call the police!"

He looked a little startled. Without letting go of my shoulders, he looked up and said, "Telemus, is this one of yours? This is Phaethusa?"

Dr. Fell said, "This is Miss Windrose. She is not my responsibility. I did not take her out of her cell. And that is not the name I use here, thank you."

My heart started sinking.

The black man looked at Miss Daw, "You, then, Thelxiepia?"

Miss Daw stepped forward, her gloved hands folded at her waist, clutching the tiniest possible pocketbook, her high-heeled pumps clacking on the pathway. "I will thank you to unhand the young woman. Proprieties must be observed."

He said, "You keep her in the cell? That cell? The one Corus and I are cleaning?"

Miss Daw did not answer, but gave him a stiff look, as he still had not released me.

I said, "I don't know who you are, but I didn't do anything wrong. I am not whatever they told you I was. I'm just a girl. I'm really nice, once you get to know me. I'm not a monster and I don't like being locked up, and won't you please help me? I've never done anything to you. If you ever got caught by *our* side, and I could get you out of a cell, I'd do it! What's your name? I'm Amelia! I really am a person, just like you!"

"Notus. We are called Notus." To Miss Daw, he said, "My brother is being unduly cruel. What a wonder of cruelty! That cell is clearly cursed with a cur . . ." (or maybe he said "ker") ". . . and it cannot be healthy for a woman of this most tender age. The Great Lady Cyprian, I am thinking her happiness will not be a great thing, hearing of this."

Dr. Fell said drily, "They are organisms from Chaos. Prefrontal lobotomies would have been the best way to keep them restrained."

"To you, I will not speak!" exclaimed the black man. "You are a thing of gears and levers, you. I do not call you a man! Bah! You, Thelxiepia, you are a gracious woman. You know the secrets which cause men to die when they hear them. Can you not prevail upon Boreus? Tell him we will take these children away if they are not well cared for! We have an agreement with the Uranians!"

Dr. Fell said sardonically, "Why ask her, Notus? Boreus is your brother."

"Bah! Since I am not talking to you, I am not listening to you!"

I suddenly had the fear that the scheme Boggin had told me, about how sternly we were supposed to be treated in order to convince the others that we were secure, was about to backfire.

I said, "They really don't treat me that badly! Boreus is really nice!"

The black man had a look of slow horror come onto his face. Nothing I could have said would have convinced him more completely that I was being lashed and tortured.

He let go of me, which made my arms suddenly feel quite cold. "It does not matter. You may not take her back to the cell yet. We need Dr. Fell to bring his instruments to take some readings, to localize the breach. Come, Telemus!"

"I am not under your authority," Dr. Fell said coldly.

"You will come, or I will whirl you from here into the sea!" And the black man's long shining hair began to flow and sway as if in the breeze, except there was no breeze. A warmth came from him as if an invisible oven had suddenly opened its door.

Dr. Fell raised his hands, and said sardonically, "Well, your argument has some merit. It is what we call Argumentum ad Baculum, of course, but I am not prepared at this time to enter into the finer points of such a dispute. I will communicate with Mulciber about this."

"Bah! Again, I say my Bah! I am with the Lady Cyprian. I do not care for your Mulciber, Round-eye!"

Dr. Fell put his hands in his pockets and shrugged. "Neither, by all accounts, does the Lady Cyprian."

Then Dr. Fell wiggled his finger at me, and to Miss Daw he said, "Watch her. Guard her. She is the dangerous one."

The two men walked away, Dr. Fell marching with his stiff step (almost like a goose) and Notus, with many a glance back at me across his shoulder.

4.

"Can we walk around the estate? Just up and down a few paths, or see the Library? I'd like to get a book. I'm so bored! Please?"

Miss Daw just sat down on the bench that was there, a marble slab with feet carved into little cherubs blowing trumpets. Two dry rosebushes showed their thorns to either side. She patted the seat next to her.

Slowly, I sat. Then I threw back my head, and laughed.

Miss Daw looked at the horizon, and was preparing to take no more notice of me.

I said, "You are not going to ask me why I laughed, are you? It's because of what Doctor Fell said. He called me the dangerous one. Not Victor, not Colin, not Vanity, who can call a magical mind-reading ship from beyond the world's edge. Me! Why am I the dangerous one?"

I started kicking my legs back and forth under the bench. Maybe I should make a break for it? Pick up a rock and brain the frail Miss Daw over the head? She would probably go down harder than the unexpectedly brawny Headmaster Boggin.

I decided to give talking one more chance: "Why did Boreus tell you not to talk to me? He cannot be afraid of me. I am not the dangerous one. You cannot be afraid of me, Miss Daw; you've known me my whole life. You know me. I am not a monster. Really, I'm not. No more than any other girl my age, I suppose."

Miss Daw smiled, a sad smile, a very far away smile.

I looked around on the ground. Here were patches of winter grass, mounds of snow lining the edges of the path, a little strip of leafless and barren garden to our left and right. No rocks.

I could see the buildings of the estate all around me. Beyond the Great Hall was the main Manor House, with the Library to the North and the Stables and yards to the South.

No one was around. I was hoping Victor might come along the path. But there was no one.

"What are they doing in my cell?"

Miss Daw's lips twitched, but she did not answer.

I said, "Miss Daw . . . ?"

No answer.

". . . how long am I going to have to stay there . . . ?"

She thought about whether or not to answer. Then she said, "Be at peace, child. Matters will soon resolve themselves. One way or the other."

I said slowly, "But they aren't, are they? They are not going to go back the way they were. We're too old. Everything's changed."

Miss Daw said, softly, "Nothing is stable. Nothing is certain."

She hugged herself a bit. She murmured, half to herself, "Changes will come, but other changes will come after, wiping out each layer of change like waves on a beach, erasing the ripples in sand cast up by the previous wave. Everything is sand. There is only one rock to which we can cling."

I thought I knew what she meant. I said, "You saw me praying. What did you see?"

Miss Daw spoke in her silver voice, her eyes still on the far horizon. "Your prayers flew up. There was an echo in return. The relational energy went somewhere. Where, I do not know. Someone heard you."

Well, here was a topic I could get her to rise to. I said, "What denomination are we?"

She drew her eyes down from the horizon and glanced at me, a small quirk to her lips. " 'We'? Miss Windrose, that is an excellent question. What indeed are we?"

"Well, then, what are you? High Church? Dissenters? What?"

She smiled a half-smile, filled both with melancholy and with an aloof amusement. "I am of the body of the one true Church, and I am the last of that body. We called ourselves the Pure Ones. Others called us Donatists."

"And where was your Church?"

Her face showed that she had flown in thought, far away, far down the corridors of memory. At last she said in a soft, distant voice: "Our Archbishopric was centered in Alexandria, at a time when North Africa was the most civilized and cultured spot in the Empire. The European and Asian provinces had been wasted in the wars between the Four Caesars.

"We cast out from us the unfit, who delivered their scriptures and sacred vessels up to our persecutors under Diocletian; once the persecution was relaxed these *traditors,* these deserters from the duty of martyrdom, attempted to carry on as if their actions had not put them out of communion with the faithful. Bribed electors raised, and men outside grace ordained, a certain false bishop, Caecilian, above us; but we refused him, electing Donatus the Great from among the pure and faithful.

"How the Bishop of the Chaff hated the Bishop of the Wheat! The impure said that their bishops had authority to choose our bishop, and that we were their cattle. The archbishop of Antioch turned Constantine against us. Constantine was one who hated our religion, but sought to harness the power of the faith of Christ and use it against his political enemies.

"In time, Constantine declared himself Pontifex, and said his word ruled the Church as a matter of law. Him! Pontifex! As if the outcome of bloody battles made his the voice of God! The election of pagan and corrupt Praetorians could vest Constantine with temporal power, yes; but spiritual authority, we held, came from other sources.

"They called us heretics and schismatics, but they were the ones who strayed from the true path. A splinter group which rebelled against the Greek Church grew to power amidst the decayed and corrupted remnants of the Western Empire. These are the ones you call the Catholics, who were rebels against the Metropolitan authority of the Greek Church. Those of us in North Africa who remained pure in our faith were persecuted again and again. Then a time came when the Paynims from Arabia swept over the land.

"And that was the end of us."

She was silent for a while, lost in sad thought.

She said: "Nothing of the true teachings now remains. Our books are lost. The Gospels of Thomas and Simon are gone, the Letters of Instruction, the writings of Symmeticus, Antonius Thaumaturgos the Elder, Antonius Pius, and the Epistles of Peter, the Gospel of Judas, and the Book of Tubalcaine from before the Flood, are all lost.

"When a council was called by our enemies, to gather together the many sacred writings and the books which preserved the memory of Christ and His apostles, we were banned. Our gospels and epistles were not included in their books; and those gospels that they did include were voted upon to include or exclude by a show of hands. The Greeks drove away dissenters from the council, and so their hands were the ones most numerous.

"And what did they vote into their Bible? Fables and nonsense. To this were added letters and boasts by Paul, who never met Christ, but had a dream of Him, and who invented, out of the speculations of the Greeks, a washed-down version of Platonic and Neoplatonic theogeny.

"And forgeries not by Paul, but bearing his name, were added; as were letters written by several Greeks later said to be the writings of John and Luke, who were illiterate fishermen."

I said, "Are you talking about the Bible? I mean, our Bible?"

She looked at me sidelong, "You yourself delivered a four-page paper on the Pauline and Pseudo-Pauline epistles, including an analysis of First Timothy, when we were discussing the Markian Hypothesis and the possibility of the Q document in seminar last year."

"Um . . . sure."

"You did not write that paper, did you?"

"I wrote . . . part of it . . ."

"You wrote your name at the top."

"Vanity sort of helped out with some of the wording. And Quentin, uh, checked my spelling, and . . . Well, what does it matter if I cheated on one little tiny paper! I am just going to be killed, or sold into slavery!"

"You will not be killed, child. And an education is always important."

"It's not doing me much good right now. You people have me locked up in a cell buried underground!"

"Since you slept through our study of the Bible, you still have the pagan authors to comfort you. You have the solace of having read Epictetus and Marcus Aurelius. You have read the Crito, and you know from Gibbon the dignity with which Julian the Apostate met his fate. Epictetus was a slave, and he knew how to bear his lot with dignity . . ." And now she looked quite sad again, and her eyes turned back to the horizon.

I said, "What's it like, being the last Donatist?"

"Being the only one who knows the truth in the world full of lies? Every teenager knows something of the feeling."

"Miss Daw . . . ? I've been wondering. How can you be a Christian if you are a pagan goddess?"

"I am not a goddess. That word is reserved properly for the Olympians, who can influence the motions of the Fates, which I cannot."

"But how can you have faith in Christ? Is he one of you folk?"

She looked uncomfortable. "The matter is complex. There are those among us who claim that some upstart merely wished to steal the worship due to Jove; and that Baphomet, a child of Phorcys and Ceto, was the man crucified at Calvary; or else Simon the Magician, one of the Gray Sisters' sons. Still others say it was merely a man who died on Golgotha; still others say no one died, and that Christ is an invention of priestcraft. There are many of us who could make ourselves seem to die, and rise again from the grave; for that matter, there are humans who could perform some slight-of-hand, or swap a living body for a dead; and anyone can forge a document, or tell a lie. But none of us could raise a human being from the dead, or promise truly to raise all men; and none of us can forgive sins, or wipe the stain of wrong away."

"Why would one of you want to steal another person's worship? Do you eat it?"

She smiled. "Something like that. The Olympians receive their power from the moral order of the universe, but also from the laws of men, and the guilt of those who break those laws."

"Then how can you be a Christian, if you suspect Christ was one of you?"

She shook her head. "I suspect no such thing; I merely report what some among the immortals say. But even their opinion betrays the deeper truth. If the Redeemer was a fraud, Miss Windrose, my question is this: Who was he impersonating? Whose worship, as you put it, was he trying to eat? If Baphomet was a thief, there must have been real gold he was trying to steal.

"I am above humanity in the chain of being. The mere fact that there is a chain of being proves that there must be a top, a first link or Uncaused Cause from which all else emanates. Everyone fears and worships the thing that sets the circumstances and limits of his fate, as a hound might worship the master who owns him. Only something that is entirely without restricting circumstances, unlimited, infinite can be called Divine. Unhindered, it would be motionless. With no wants and no lacks, it would be entirely serene."

I said, "That could be any god of any religion. What makes you a Christian?"

She said, "In my youth I swam along the coasts of Carthage, and lured mortal sailors to their wretched deaths, promising them sweet kisses, and I laughed gaily as they drowned. A time came when the dying men called upon a strange and nameless God to save them, who was, at once, himself and his own son, and one of these forgave me as he died, though I was his murderess. Angered by the conceit, I determined to slay the next holy man of this new faith I came upon.

"I spied one who walked along the cliff overlooking the sea. He was dressed as a beggar, and leaned upon a staff as he walked, and he praised his God with every weary step of his long road. I swam ahead of him and scaled the rock, so that he found me combing my hair with a comb of shell, dressed only in my beauty. I tempted him with kisses, and he rebuked me sternly, and had no fear of me.

"It is our custom not to kill men until they fail to answer one of our riddles, because that failure shows their mortality and imperfection. So I asked the Holy Man if I had a soul, and if I could know salvation: this was a riddle to which I knew he knew no answer, since I did not know the answer myself.

"He raised his staff, and said it was no more likely that the dead wood in his hand could put forth bloom again, than that a mermaid could have a soul.

"No sooner did the words leave his lips, than the dry stick in his hand turn green, and flowers of unearthly beauty budded and bloomed all along the staff. I knew then that I was in the presence of a superior power: I dove from the cliff to flee from the saint.

"Like you, I can see the many dimensions of the world, and so I knew what it was that reached down through higher space to touch that old man's walking stick. It was a power above Saturn, older than Time, able to restore the dead and recover the innocence I had once and lost. Many a day I huddled in the darkness far below the wave, wondering and grieving.

"And now I know that Eternity is beyond even the gods of Olympus. There is a shadow, a hint, of what Eternity is like within this world of time and death and decay: for if there were not, we would have no notion of perfection, no idea of beauty, no love, no hope. We would all be Dr. Fell."

"Do you believe in souls? Do you think everything has a soul?"

"Only a creature with a soul could frame such a question."

I said, "Do you think I have a soul?"

"Of course, dear child, and it is a bright one, despite your anger and confusion."

"If I have a soul, I cannot be a monster. Boreus cannot be afraid of me."

"I do not actually think he is afraid of you, child."

"Then why did he order you not to talk to me? This conversation is the first one I've had in seven days. If you don't count the little scene with Grendel. I am so bored. Bored and tired and scared. Tired of being scared. Bored of being scared. Scared of being bored. I will do whatever you say. I will do what Boreus wants me to do. Just don't put me back in that cell!"

"We have little choice in the matter. Even Boreus has little choice."

"At least give me something to read or something to do. What about my lessons? I had a test this week that I missed because I was in jail. One of your tests: the Hawking formulations on Black Hole Theory."

"Naturally, I did not hold the test this week, Miss Windrose."

"Give me the materials so I can study! How often do you have a student begging you for work?"

It seemed she was not listening. She said absentmindedly: "It would be a waste of time, child. No matter what you learned, you would have to learn it again when you come out."

"At least come talk to me during the day. You must be bored, too, if there are no classes being held this week!"

She shook her head. Apparently she was not bored.

I said in an angry voice: "Answer me! Boreus cannot be afraid of me talking to you."

"No, child. He is afraid I might take heart from your example."

"Take heart?"

She turned and looked at me. Her eyes had been staring into the fourth dimension, and were still surrounded with a faint cloud of distance-negating energy, which, in the sunlight, made her eyes seem all silvery.

Solemn and sad, she said in the soft music of her voice: "I am a slave. These people are my captors, too. I am not from here."

"Where are you from?"

"From home."

"What home?"

"Home. Your home. My home. Our home. Myriagon."

22

TALES OF THE DEMIURGE

1.

She said, "Like you, I was once collared and penned up. Upon my parole, I am allowed certain privileges, to walk abroad in the sunlight, to take upon myself a fair-seeming shape, to drink wine and eat savory food. And to play my music. That is the kindest thing I am allowed, and also the most cruel."

Her perfect, ivory-pale face was calm; but old, old sorrow haunted her eyes.

"Sometimes, I look for it, you know. I look to see some shadow of Myriagon in the far distance, a shadow or reflection of her musical cross-section in the fifth or seventh dimension. Or something comes to me like a scent of apple blossoms, or the tremor of an energy path or thought-reflection issuing from the time-tress in those gardens.

"Once I saw what I thought was a golden dot, and senses I never had before and have never had since, opened up in me. I saw it only for a moment, but I was able to superimpose multiple shadow-pictures in my memory until an image built up.

"That dot was a globe of finite surface area but infinite volume, with towers and formulations extending in each direction. Each tower and each window opened up into a new direction, a new domain, and I could see gravity and time-flow folded like origami, engineered as part of that great structure.

"Time, space, and gravity were not there (as they are here) simply imposed from above. The gravity was manmade there, its moment and constants and characteristics. The time, and the space, and all were designed to serve the pleasure and convenience of those who dwelled in those towers, or in the private vest-pocket dimensions hanging like silver bubbles on the beyond-sides of those windows.

"The city with its towers and its gardens and its private timespace continua, occupied more than four dimensions, more than five or ten or a hundred. There were a thousand surfaces, a thousand volumes and hypervolumes, a thousand dimensions, or ten thousand.

"And there was reflected light shining from it, not merely the flat, thin light of this three-dimensional place we are in, but a solid, full, massive light, filling up volumes and hypervolumes of increasingly higher dimensions. Myriagon was orbiting something, something which shed that light, some singularity of even higher and ever smaller dimension I could not see."

Miss Daw was silent for a time, and then said softly, "In a way, that one moment of seeing my home was and is more solid in my memory, more meaningful, more real, than all my other life besides."

2.

I asked, "Are there more than four dimensions?"

"Many more, but they do not exist here, in the created world. When Saturn rebelled against Uranus and created the world of time, of entropy and decay, he knew he would be attacked both by those he had trapped within the orbit of his creation, and by rescuers from outside—other sons of Uranus."

"In other words, us," I said. "The Uranians."

"To limit the Prelapsarians—your people—he made this world to collapse the higher dimensions into infinitesimal volumes. He needed only a fourth dimension, in order to erect a superstructure of time, space, order, and to establish universal laws of nature."

"What is it like out there? In Myriagon?"

"I know only the old tales and stories repeated by my sister, Parthenope, and she had them from our grandfather.

"There is a singularity, called the Unknown, which retains the condition of time–space as it was before the lapse of reality into the Big Bang. Myriagon orbits this singularity. From the depths of its event horizon there arise, from time to time, lapses or folds in the substance of reality, which can be collapsed to form various areas and conditions of time, space, matter, and dimension. Most of these vest-pocket universes are small, no more than ten light-years across or ten years old, and containing trivial mass-energy.

"Larger universes can be created, she told me, if a diver is willing to go closer and ever closer into the event horizon. There are methods to create a disturbance within the deeper layers, which will cause the ejection of larger areas of time–space, more mass-energy ylem.

"No matter how swiftly or slowly your personal time is running, however, the deeper you go, the longer your journey seems to take from the point of view of outside observers.

"Saturn is a creature from the very earliest times of Myriagon, back when it was called Polygon, and only occupied two or three dimensions. He fell far more deeply toward the event horizon than any other of the Early Ones. Millions, billions, countless ages of time went by; albeit, to Saturn, it was but a single journey of a single day.

"When he emerged he controlled an area of time–space so great, and containing a mass-energy so large, that it created its own event horizon embracing the other universes. All the tiny realms of all the innocent people of Myriagon were unfolded and collapsed into his. This collapse of all life into his macrocosmic universe created time and entropy. Countless people died. Cosmos was created—the established world.

"Parthenope told me that no one knew why he did it. Whatever events had prompted him, whatever insults he was seeking to avenge, or ills he was trying to cure, had been forgotten in the billions of years since his departure. Only those few spirits ranging far afield, beyond all the established structures and private universes of the Prelapsarians, were spared. They returned to the wreckage of their great home, and slowly, despite that they were so few, rebuilt Myriagon.

"From time to time, certain of the Prelapsarians, driven by grief or compassion, attempt the long journey to enter into the established world, to rescue their trapped comrades, or to free other victims of Saturn's deed. Those who escape reach a world where there is no entropy, and nature's laws are subscribed to voluntarily, rather than imposed.

"Parthenope told me that the Prelapsarians have neither law nor crime. Scientific examination of their mental systems has achieved a state of perfection; and the moral order is obvious to their senses; they know neither mental disorder nor moral corruption."

I said, "Then they are not monsters."

"Far from it."

I said, "What about me?"

"What about you, Phaethusa?"

"I am not morally perfect."

"You do not know the secrets of their mind-science; and the eyes you use to sense the moral order, in this world of matter and decay, are shut."

"Why? Why make a world where people cannot see right and wrong?"

"This world, the material world, is a false and shallow copy, inside the realm of time, of something perfect which Saturn stole from Eternity. I do not know his reasons; no one does. The Olympians overthrew Saturn, but they saw no cause to change his system. They derive their power from having others break the rules of law and of morality."

"Where is Saturn now?"

"Confined in Tartarus, black realm of the Unseen One, and guarded by Tisiphone and by the huge hundred-handed Hecatonchire, whom Saturn had once imprisoned there; jailers where they once were jailed."

"You don't remember living there? Myriagon?"

She shook her head. "My father is Achelous, the son of Oceanus, eldest son of Uranus. Oceanus is one of those who, for the sake of pity, entered this world to battle the grim Demiurge. He was deceived by the nature of time, and did not know what it was he was entering. It took him fifteen billion years to cross the Pontic Ocean of 'false vacuum' surrounding this reality; by the time he reached here, Saturn was overcome, replaced by children, the Olympians, who were far worse than Saturn ever had been."

"Worse?"

She nodded. "If Milton's Satan in *Paradise Lost* at least remembers what bright virtue he once had, and regrets its loss, imagine how much worse sons of Satan would be, raised from birth in the inferno. They would be devils softened by no living memory of Heaven."

"And what happened to you? I mean, how did you come to be here?"

3.

"Once, long ago, there seemed to be the possibility of peace between Lord Terminus and Oceanus. Lord Pelagaeus the Earthshaker was given lordship over the inner ocean, where life is, and Oceanus the outer. Saturn was gone; Oceanus knew of no more reason to fight.

"As his granddaughters, we were treated with royal privilege. The Morae, the Fates, taught us how to sing, and showed us much regarding the future, and we studied the energies and forces that make up the nature of time. We became the companions of the Maiden, who was the daughter of Demeter. When the Maiden vanished, carried off by an unknown power from the fields of Enna, we were granted leave by Lord Terminus to use our powers within this world, and to fly from place to place, seeking her.

"Our powers, however, began to show us something of the nature of time and morality. You have the same senses I do. You know what we began to see. The internal nature and moral darkness of the Olympians became more and more evident.

"The Maiden had been abducted by the Unseen One, and raped. When the crime of the Unseen One finally came to light, instead of punishing his brother, Lord Terminus (who feared him) gave him the Maiden as his wife.

"We have never forgiven Lord Terminus his crime, this cynical and smirking act of corruption. What kind of punishment is it to a rapist, to have the victim of his outrages be given to him in bounds of matrimony, his victim to be his, forever after? Lord Terminus decreed that when a husband takes a wife by violence, it is not rape, but holy matrimony; honor is satisfied once the wedding is performed.

"Honor was satisfied, but we were not satisfied. The Sirens began to work against the Olympians. Secretly at first, and then more openly, we began to undermine their power.

"The power of the gods is augmented by the belief of men, in much the same way that Grendel's power comes from his own beliefs. We became famous for telling the truth to men, both the truth about the gods and the truth about the future, and the jealous gods killed them when we told them too much.

"Despite this, truth began to leak out. Your poets tell more about the Greek gods than others, don't they? Their tales portray them as more human and fallible than the gods of other peoples, who, after all, committed crimes equally as foul as those of the Olympians. The Greeks were a rational people, less in awe of their gods than other folk. That was our doing.

"Eventually, we were stopped. The Muses, to whom we had taught our songs, now challenged us. Oaths were exchanged. Our songs were sent against their songs in over-space, and the spirit world raged with the clash and clamor of the music of the spheres gone wild.

"The Morae, who had once been our friends, betrayed us and fated our downfall. The music of the Nine conquered us. We were given the choice between slavery and death. Some of my sisters chose death, and they dwell in the Dark House, with our old companion, the Maiden, who is Queen there. Those of us not bold enough to make so hard a choice, we had our wings plucked from us, and our feathers now adorn the crowns of the Nine Muses.

"Do not pity me. Slavery is a mercy if you live, as I did then, in a time when no conqueror could afford to let any member of any family whom he defeated left alive. The institution benefits the conquerors, and this spares the conquered from an otherwise certain death.

"And my first Mistress, the High Queen Acraea, also called Hera, is the kindest and most upright of all the immortals of Olympus. Only she had some concern for morality, courtesy, propriety. Yes, I know how Homer and the other poets depict the Lady Hera. But they were inspired by the Muses, who are bastard daughters of Lord Terminus, and who hate her. My servitude in the house of my Mistress Hera was not hard."

4.

I said, "If they have no government in Myriagon, what makes me a hostage? I can't be a princess if I am from a land of anarchists."

"Your father is the Titan Helion. He is famous and influential, and enjoys the esteem of his peers, which is how the Prelapsarians count wealth. Because of his wisdom, he is the strategist whom the other Prelapsarians consult to coordinate the war effort. It is merely out of pity and sympathy for him that they forebear, despite that he has not asked them to."

I said softly, "Help me to escape, all of us."

She smiled sweetly and sadly, "Your wish is unrealistic. Put it from you."

Desperation edged my tone: "We won't hurt anyone. You can send a message or something to the people in Chaos telling them we're safe, and they won't have any reason to attack."

"Matters are not that simple. I cannot break my word to my captors, lest the next defeated in war with the Olympians is killed, instead of taken. My sister, Aglaope, has already paid her mistress and been manumitted."

"At least, you should agree not to help recapture me, if I should get away. Can you do that? Or drag your heels, or do it badly. I know you don't obey every order they give you, or else you would not be talking to me now."

She patted my hand with her glove. "Everyone is in service to something or someone. Your service, no matter with whom you end up, will probably be relatively light. Whoever ends up using your talents will, no doubt, want you to . . ."

"You mean using me! You mean owning me!" I said hotly.

She said, "Hush," because, at that moment, Dr. Fell came marching around the corner of the building, with his stiff-kneed gait, his hands folded behind his back. The black man was not with him.

Fell said thinly, "Matters are prepared. Miss Daw, if you could bring your patient . . . ?"

I said, "I don't want to go back into that cell. It's horrible."

Fell turned his narrow face toward me. At that moment, even if Quentin had never told me, I would have known his eyes were nothing but hard marbles, painted to look like eyes.

"Do not make a fuss. You will be released by tomorrow afternoon. All conditions will be reset to the *status quo ante,* and we will continue as before."

5.

The cell did not look any different, except that the heavy black iron chain had been replaced by a modern chain of machine-forged steel links. Miss Daw's compact disc player was atop the little shelf near the door where it normally rested, out of my reach, playing beautiful clear music.

I spent the afternoon with selections of concertos by Brahms floating past me. I had noticed that the music did not repeat in the same order, as a phonograph record might have done. I wondered if this kind of music box was common in the outside world, if every child owned one, or only the rich.

I tried to turn on my other senses, but Grendel's curse was still on me. I wondered idly if I looked prettier to other people now, if Grendel's lust had made me look more like his daydream image of me.

That evening I was given a freshly pressed school uniform to wear, and a hurried and cross-looking Sister Twitchett told me to don it quickly.

While I was getting dressed, she frowned at the compact disc player, and shut it off. "Mustn't let them think we are mollycoddlers . . ." she said to herself.

When footsteps sounded in the corridor, she looked around worriedly, and hid the disc player beneath one of my two buckets.

"Look smart!" she snapped at me.

And she curtsied toward the barred door of the cell. She had closed it behind her when she had entered, which was unusual.

I could hear Boggin's voice. ". . . Your Lordship will forgive us if we have nothing prepared. The unexpected nature, one is tempted to say, surprise nature, of Your Lordship's visit, left us with no time to . . ."

A voice of gravel answered him, a voice as harsh as a clash of gears in a broken gearbox. "Heh. If your spies didn't warn you I was coming, cut their pay. You're not getting value for value."

"I am not certain I . . . ah . . . can permit myself to comprehend, yes, that is the word, comprehend, every nuance of Your Lordship's, ah, implication."

"Then think."

A grotesque man stomped up to the door. He was dressed in a perfectly tailored blue pinstripe suit with a fashionable overcoat atop that.

He was hunchbacked, and his hump made him look as if he were carrying a bag or a small child piggyback. His shoulders and chest slanted from left to right, but the slabs of muscle there would have made even the chest of a bull seem puny. It looked like he was wearing football pads. His arms were larger around than other men's thighs. His legs, on the other hand, were thinner than other men's arms, and one was crooked, like a monkey's leg, while the other was long and straight. He stood on them at an angle, with his knees pointed different directions, and his feet splayed out, so that his walk was a rolling sidelong shuffle, like the walk of a crab.

The crooked leg was clamped in a complex brace of shining steel, with gears and motors at the kneecap and ankle. In his hand he held a short steel bar. I assume it was a cane, but he never leaned on it.

His face was round and slablike, his mouth ringed with muscle, his brows jutted like an ape's. His skull was covered with short stubble. His eyes were narrow slits, and his wrinkles seemed to be scowling, squinting, and grinning, all at once.

I should mention that the suit was perfectly cut, but it did nothing to detract from his twisted hugeness. He had diamond cufflinks in white cuffs, but his hands were still hairy and heavy, and his sausage-fingers were brown with calluses.

He squinted (and scowled and grinned) at me.

"So this is the little bottom you've been spanking, eh?"

Boggin was behind, looming tall. The squat man's head was on a level with his navel, although the man's shoulders and hump were more nearly level with Boggin's chest.

"Your Lordship's meaning, ah, escapes me." Behind the squat man, Boggin waved his hand at me, and rolled his eyes toward Sister Twitchett. He wiggled his brows suggestively. It took me a moment to realize that he wanted me to curtsey, too.

The squat man said, "Well, you did on a bell tower in plain view of any-one within a mile. And my spies do give me value for value."

I took my plaid skirt in hand and curtsied. The steel chain running between my neck and the ceiling rattled.

"Let's see her close," said the squat man.

Boggin said, "Sister Twitchett, the key, if you please? Open the door for Lord Mulciber."

The Sister straightened up from her curtsey (which she had been holding for at least a minute) and made a great show of patting her pockets and frowning, as if she had forgotten where the key was.

The squat man said, "Never mind. Do it myself." Then, louder: "Iron! Cold Iron! Hot-forged Steel! Obey the Smith of Iron's Will!"

The door rattled in its frame, and the chain on my neck shivered and chimed, but nothing else happened. The door did not open.

The squat man crooked his head sideways and grinned (and squinted and scowled) at him. "Clever, clever, North Wind! Point taken. The girly here is not getting away."

Sister Twitchett suddenly found the key. "Here it is!"

"Heh. Right in the same pocket you groped three times. Funny, that," the squat man grunted.

"If Your Lordship will permit me . . . ?" Sister Twitchett simpered.

"Don't bother. I don't go into cells I can't get out of. Not with the North Wind breathing down my neck. I can shout from here." (He was not shouting; he was only two yards away from me.) "You, there, girl. What do you call yourself?"

Boggin said, "Her name is . . ."

"Shut it. Talking to the girl."

"Of course, Your Lordship," said Boggin smoothly. "If Your Lordship intends a private conversation with our, ah, guest here, I can step away . . . ."

"You might as well hear it live as on tape. Girl . . . ?"

I curtsied again. "Yes, Your Lordship."

"Your name?"

"They called me Secunda, Lordship, till they let me pick my name. I picked Amelia Armstrong Windrose. I think my real name is Phaethusa, daughter of Helion. But that could be a lie. I've been lied to a very great deal, Your Lordship."

Boggin cleared his throat and said, "Now see here, Miss Windrose . . ."

"Shut it. I won't ask again," said the squat man, his voice suddenly terrible.

Boggin blenched and stepped back.

The squat man shifted gears in his voicebox back to a more gentle growl, and said to me, "No more of that 'Lordship' stuff. You're not under me, and I don't deserve it nohow."

"What shall I call you, Your L . . . sir?"

"Oi, we are polite, aren't we? You can call me Stumpy. Everyone does behind my back. My back is so large, they figure I won't hear. Nothing wrong with my ears, though, except my ears got the same problem yours do."

I looked at him a moment. He grinned (and squinted and scowled) back at me.

"What problem is that, Lord Mulciber?"

"I hear a lot of lies. I hear a lot of flattery."

I didn't know how to respond to that, so I picked up my skirt and curtsied again. My neck chain rattled when I did that.

He growled, "You didn't call me what I asked."

"I am not going to call you by a cruel name, sir."

"Heh? Even if I tell you to?"

"You said yourself I wasn't under you."

"Heh. Heh. Aheh. North Wind said you were a clever one. Quite a looker, too, aren't you?"

"Only in three dimensions, sir. Otherwise, I look like a squid with wings. I have it on good authority."

"OK, Squid Girl. How'd you like to come work for me?"

"Wha—what? I mean, I beg your pardon?"

"You heard me."

I really enjoyed seeing the look on Boggin's face. He really wanted to talk and he was afraid to.

I said, "Doing what?"

"Scaring people. If they don't scare off, killing them."

"I . . . I do not think I can do that."

"Ah, come on! I'd only want you to kill bad people. War is bad for business. I'm trying to stop it. One way to stop it is to scare the other guy so he don't start nothing."

"I . . . I don't think it would be right . . ."

"Give you as much gold as you can carry, dental plan, medical benefits, weekends and evenings off. Give you a house. Palace, actually. Staff of servants if you want 'em—I got some just off the assembly line. Get you a gun. Anyone rude to you, tries to grope you or something, you shoot him dead, and I throw the corpse in the furnace. What do you say?"

"What about my friends?"

"Just you. Remember what I said about scaring folks so they don't start a war? You can't scare 'em too much, or they start one anyhow. It's a balancing act."

I said, "I don't want to leave my friends."

"I'll throw in an airplane. Have Daedalus build you one to your own specs. You tootle around up in the wild blue yonder, much as you like."

I said slowly, "Your spies do give you value for value."

"Yeah, well, I know your bra cup size, too. Never hurts to know stuff."

"It's Dr. Fell isn't it? Telemus feeds you information."

"North Wind is right. You are smarter than the others."

I just snorted to smother a laugh at that. "Sorry, Stumpy, that problem you mentioned with my ears just acted up again."

"Heh. And funny. Spies didn't mention that. OK, Squid Girl, last offer. I talk to the little woman, and she makes sure you meet your True Love; he's single, he's not a priest; no problems, no complications, no ill-starred fate. True Love. Can't do better."

"Little woman?"

"Aphrodite. The Love Goddess. My wife."

He actually got to me with that comment. My mouth went dry.

Victor. I wanted it to be Victor. I wanted him to marry me.

No problems, no complications.

"And you get all that other stuff I mentioned. If you don't like it, you quit. Give me two weeks' notice. Shake hands, no hard feelings."

I could not say anything. My mouth was still dry. I licked my lips and it was still dry.

Victor . . .

"Come on. True Love. Better than anything old Stumpy will ever get."

Finally I put my hand on the collar around my neck, and I rattled the chain. "Contracts made under duress are not binding. First I get out of here, get this thing off my neck, then we talk. And another thing. My friends. I don't want to make a decision without talking to my friends. I want to talk to them with no one else listening."

"Heh. Yes on one, no on two." He turned his massive shoulders and crooked his head around to look at Boggin. "North Wind! How soon can you finish up your special arrangements and get the girl out of this damn hole?"

"By tomorrow morning, Lordship."

"No more playing spanky-spanky with her. No more thinking with your Johnson. You treat her like a princess, like she's fine china, or else we'll have the Uranians up in arms and up around our ears. If I found out, they can find out."

He swung the massive shoulders back and squinted (grinned and scowled) up at me. "We'll talk later, Squid Girl."

And he clomped away, dragging Boggin with him.

As Mulciber turned away, Boggin looked coldly pleased with himself, as if the interview had gone as he intended.

6.

Twitchett apparently did not want to be left too far behind, for she unlocked the door and trotted quickly after them.

I blinked in surprise. A mistake. They had made a mistake in the security procedures.

I had to move slowly (so as not to rattle my chain too much) and I had to move quickly (because I did not have much time). Not easy to do both at once.

I took the disc player out from under the bucket, and pushed and twisted till I got it open. Instead of a tape cassette, or a record, there was a little disc of rainbow-chased crystal. It looked like a jewel rather than a piece of equipment, and I wondered if this was a man-made thing, or something the Olympians made with magic.

Then came the hard part. What I did next doesn't sound possible, but I am rather an athletic girl, and I had just spent a week in a cell with nothing to do but do calisthenics. I had even been able to do handsprings and tumbling without strangling myself. (In fact, I had done them more to overcome my fear of strangling myself than anything else.)

So I kicked off my shoes, put the little crystal disc between my left toes, stood on the cot, and wrapped a little bit of the slack chain around my shoulder, so that there was no weight on my neck.

Then I clutched the chain tight in both hands, and swung. Up, not far enough, back down, kick the cot, up the wrong way, back down, kick the cot again, and up again . . .

This time I was high enough to put my pointed foot through the bars of the cell window, and turn my foot sidewise. Ow ow, clang clang. My whole weight jerked back against my ankle; I was holding myself rather high off the floor, just on the bar I had hooked my little foot around. It hurt my ankle.

There was a tiny crack in the window were the fresh (cold) air came in, and I could see the little gray branches of a leafless bush beyond. This was a basement window, at ground floor, and I knew that this side of the Chapel had bushes all along its length.

I lifted my other foot. That was harder than it sounds, since I was holding the chain with both hands (so it would stay slack against my neck) and had to keep my other foot tense and hooked around the bar.

Try putting a little crystal disc through a mail slot with your toe sometimes. It is not easy.

But it is not impossible.

Then, point my toe, swing back, step onto the cot, unwind the chain, sit down . . .

Sister Twitchett was back at the door, which had, by the way, been left standing wide open this whole time. I rubbed my feet with my hands, as if I had just slipped off my shoes because they were pinching on something.

I smiled at her. "Forget something . . . ?"

She scowled, went over to the bucket, and pulled the (now empty) disc player out from under it. I had, of course, splashed water all over it, and bent the little pin that held its door shut, so that she could not open it to see that it was empty.

She put it on the shelf and clicked the button. I had doused the thing in water so that she might think the thing was shorted out. But she did not even pause to notice that no music was coming out. She just locked the door and scampered away.

7.

It was later. I did not have any clock except for the sundial of how far across the room my little square of window-light has traveled. After sunset, however, it is just a guess until it was time for Twitchett, and my evening injection.

There I was, laying on my back, idly swinging the chain from my collar like a vertical jump rope, sweeping out a football-shaped lozenge in mid-air.

I admit I was feeling rather relaxed and pleased with myself. I was getting out of here tomorrow, right? I had squirreled away a disc of Miss Daw's music, in a spot under the bushes around the Chapel. By tomorrow, if we held classes as normal, there would be some free time after Dr. Fell's tutorial. What was Monday? Molecular biology. Of course, I hadn't read the assignment, not since two Mondays ago. If only Miss Daw had let me get some books from the library . . .

I lay watching the chain spinning, spinning.

Back to the status quo, Dr. Fell had said. Special arrangements, Mulciber had said. Anything I learned I would have to learn over again, Miss Daw had said . . .

As certainly as if a soft, cold voice had whispered it in my ear, I knew. They are going to erase your memory.

8.

Everything you now know will be gone.

How far back? Ten days, at least, maybe more. What we overheard at the meeting, Vanity's secret passages, Quentin's discovery that he could fly, all of it would be gone.

The you who existed as once you were ten days ago will still be alive. But the you who is here now, will be dead, dead, dead. And none of these thoughts you are thinking now will survive. These thoughts now in your head, this chain of thought and memory, will come to an end, and stop.

Phaethusa will be gone, and only Amelia will remain. Her memory will be amputated, and she will be bewildered if she notices a missing week, but she will never even know what was taken from her.

This thought shall perish with the others.

9.

The morning when we made such a mess in the kitchen, making our own breakfasts for ourselves; that hour which, out of all the hours of all my life I could remember, was the brightest, that would be gone, too.

10.

I watched the chain swinging out its smaller and smaller circles, describing a spindle, then a cone, then a swaying line. It swept out a decreasing volume, then nothing.

I thought of people who might help, like ap Cymru or Lelaps the dog. But I had no way to get out of the cell to find them.

My thoughts skittered in circles like mice, smaller and smaller, looking for some way out of the trap I was in. Some way out of the trap. Some way out. Some way.

But there was nothing more to think. The more I thought, the more I would have to lose.

23

DREAMS AND DESIRES

1.

That night I had a dream. A man stood by the head of my cot.

He wore a breastplate of bronze, set with figures of men and swine. His helmet was made of large square oblongs of white, as if the teeth of some animal had been sewn atop a cap of bronze. In his hand was a spear but, instead of a spearhead, the shaft was tipped with a thin spine, like the stinger of a stingray.

Beneath his helmet, he had neither eyes nor mouth. Dried blood ran down his cheeks and chin. His armor was streaked over with running brown stains, and the gore had rusted the metal in places.

He said, "In life, I was Telegonus, son of Odysseus and Circe. You are my aunt, for Circe is the daughter of Helio. I slew Odysseus and knew not whom I slew. In penance, Queen Arete sent me to guard Nausicaa, her daughter. Poseidon's men overcame me, and at that task I failed. Erichtho trapped me in a box, as a toy for Boreus, and my spirit was tormented and would not rest; but I walked the world to and from my box, searching for the Lady Nausicaa again. My hate kept me awake, and I would not sleep. I watched and sought, watched and sought. I knew not then that the North Wind had other watchers watching me, unclean spirits as restless as myself, and when I scented some trace of the Lady Nausicaa, they fled to inform Boreus. Against my knowledge and against my will, my own loyalty to the Lady Nausicaa was used to snare her. I knew it not, but I was one of the watchmen of Boreus, and I kept the Lady imprisoned."

In the dream, I could move and speak. I said, "What do you want with me?" And my fingers trembled and my limbs shook, because of a terrible cold which came from the man, and a smell of dried blood, spoiled meat, and putrefaction.

"Eidotheia, child of the Graeae, buried my bones, and paid the toll for the ferry man, Chiron. Your prayer reached me in Hell, where I walk in the bloody forest hanging with corpses, set aside for kin-slayers, and gave me wings. I sped by the fifty heads of Cerberus, his teeth like daggers and his slobber more venomous than any serpent's and, though he howls and seeks me now, I am here. Once the cock crows, I am done for, and I return to double and triple punishments."

Out from the stained and tattered cloak, now he spread white wings, like the wings of a dove. The wingtips to either side almost touched the opposite walls of the cell. The starlight from the window caught the edges of each feather, and traced them in silver.

"Can you help me?" I said.

"I am a shadow. I can touch nothing."

"Why did you come to me?"

"Erichtho set wards around Eidotheia and Phobetor; the Telchine boy, Damnameneus, has no soul. But the music which walled you in is silent now, and that silence allows my approach."

"What can you do?"

"I can bring you in dream to one who dreams of you."

"Will that help me?"

"No. But you will come, because you will hope that it will."

He touched me with his spear, and I sat up. The collar and the chain melted away.

He pointed to the far wall. In the moonless dark, it receded from us, forming a long, dark corridor.

Down it I went, hugging myself in my white flannel nightgown, and the floorstones were cold on my bare feet.

2.

In dream, time and distance were without meaning. It might have been minutes I walked that dark and unreal corridor, or hours, or years.

Or, I might have been in that corridor since the beginnings of forever and would always be there, a lonely girl in a white nightgown, stepping on silent, bare feet down a black corridor that led away from imprisonment and toward some uncertain goal; while behind me walks, and will always walk, a dead man who died in the line of duty, but who still seeks, somehow, without hope, without fear, without life, to carry it out.

3.

At the end of the corridor was a square of reddish light. It hurried toward me like the light of an oncoming train in a tunnel, approaching far more quickly than my hesitant steps could account for, as if the corridor were collapsing like a folding telescope.

Then, with a motionless jolt, like the shock of waking instantly from a dream, I was there. Behind me there was no sign of the corridor through which I had come. I was backed up against the edge of a short desk or workbench. My hands were gripping the rough edge of the workbench to either side, and I could feel the wood pushed up again my bottom, through the flannel fabric of my nightie.

The fire in the stove was burning low, but its black iron door was open, and the dying embers still cast red shadows into the small interior of the hut or shed where I found myself. Wood was piled next to the stove, dingy with rodent droppings. There were holes gnawed in the baseboards, made by rats or mice.

There was a cot, smaller than my cot in my jail cell, on which a bundle of rags had been heaped. Beyond that was a refrigerator, two feet high. Half-empty cartons of take-away Chinese food lay on the floor before the refrigerator door. There was other litter here and there on the floor.

There was a cracked mirror above the stove to my left. In it, it looked as if I were half-sitting in the edge of the bench, about to rise.

Anyone who has had a normal life would not have understood what I felt then. I was entirely fascinated and entirely repelled. I had never seen mess before. I had lived in a manor house my whole life; servants kept the place clean, and I kept my things shipshape and tidy, or else was slapped on the knuckles by Mrs. Wren's dread meter stick. (That meter stick and the welts it raised is one reason why I will always prefer the English system to the metric.) The grounds and gardens were orderly and trimmed; everything was put away at nights.

But this . . . I had not imagined that people could live this way. It looked like the den of some animal rather than a place for people.

I wondered where in the world I was.

In the mirror, I saw the rags on the cot move, and a brown bear poked its snout out of the fabric and rolled off the cot with a squeaking of rusty hinges and old wood.

I gasped and turned my head. Mr. Glum was sitting on the cot, blinking stupidly. He wore a long night-shirt of dull red, patched and holed in places, and clumps of his chest hair peeked through the holes. One leg was on the floor. I saw his stump, and saw how the flesh had been folded over below his knee and stitched into a rough seam.

"Ah, Melia," he said. "You've come."

I tried to shrink back, but this only pressed the edge of the workbench more rudely into my bottom.

"Come over here," he said. "I'm in no mood to chase you. I am not to marry you, if Boggin has his way, but there is much to do which will not touch your maidenhead. Take off your shirt and get down on your knees, here."

The narrow door to the shed was on the far side of the cot from where I was. I started to edge toward my right, my hands still white-knuckled on the workbench, around the foot of the cot.

He gave a hollow laugh. "Stick, I truly want you now!" He put his hand out and his crude cane, made out of a hoe staff, flipped up from the mess on the floor and into his grip. He painfully levered himself upright.

Tottering on one leg, he thrust the cane against the boards of the narrow door behind him. "Door! Never have I wanted more that you should be locked fast, and let no fair maiden as fine as this escape my grasp."

I heard a heavy lock click shut, even though I could see plainly that there was no lock on the door.

Between the edge of the wall and the foot of the workbench was a corner. I pushed myself into it as far as I could go.

Here I was, a big and sturdy girl, tall and athletic, and there was him, short, old, and crippled. No doubt I could have pushed past him, clubbed him in the face with something, jumped over him, gotten away. If he had been a one-legged man in truth.

But I did not think he was a one-legged man. At that moment, I was convinced he was a three-legged bear.

Grendel cocked his head to one side, squinting. "You're out of the collar

I put you in. You look better in it. It shows the world that you're mine. I want it, I want it, I want it back on!"

He raised his hand and made a crook-fingered gesture toward my throat.

In the mirror, I could see my frightened face, and I could see a little shadow beginning to circle my neck, getting harder and more substantial . . .

"Ow!" shouted Grendel, doubling over, clutching one hand in the other. His cane fell to the floorboards with a loud clatter. There was a spot of blood welling up on one hand.

At that same moment, I saw in the mirror (but not in the room) a bloodstained shadow who had stepped out from behind me, and reached across my shoulder with a spear tipped with a stingray spine, striking Grendel's hand.

Grendel raised his head, his eyes grown white and terrible with fear. "Either your balls or your brains must be made of hard stone, girl. What were you thinking, bringing a ghost here? A ghost!"

He wobbled a bit on his one leg, and looked like he was about to fall.

He must have seen the confusion on my face, for he said, "You don't know, do you? Arthur's Table lies not half a mile off. It marks the spot where the backstairs go down into the Dark Land. This place, this damn school, it were put here because it were so close to the spot where the path to the House of Woe comes out. Ghosts don't walk here."

"Why not?" I said.

He shook his head. "It brings the Dog."

Even as he said that, the wind outside the hut began to moan and howl. Two more howls joined it.

The flames playing around the embers in the stove trembled and began to go out, one by one.

I looked over my shoulder. There was nothing behind me but the boards of the wall, badly caulked and water-stained. To the nothing, I said, "Telegonus, run away."

Grendel smirked, and said, "He ain't going to run away, that one. I seen him fighting Neptune's men when they killt him. Fought even after he'd lost. Even after he'd died. He don't give up. And he knows me. He knows how I got no power over you while he's here."

I said, half to myself, "Ghosts are from Erichtho's paradigm. The concept of a disembodied spirit is a dualistic concept."

One by one, little embers died. It grew darker in the small room.

"He's coming," said Grendel. "The Dog's boss. The Unseen One. I feel my bone marrow turning cold."

Grendel stooped and fell onto his cot, hugging himself with both hands. His face was slack and pale with fear. "Get out, both of you! Before He comes . . ."

More light died. More gloom grew. I could only see the silhouette of Grendel's face now, the texture of his scruffy cheek, the stubble of his bald head, the glitter of his eyes.

"Go! He might be here now. In the room. You, I'll see you in the morning, little golden princess."

I said, "You're the one. They need you to erase my memory. None of the other paradigms will work on me."

The shadowy head nodded. "That's right. All I need do is have the spirit in me move me to it. What I want bad enough, I get."

The howling grew louder. Now it did not sound like wind at all, but like a hound indeed, one as large as the sky, approaching as fast as the wind.

The last embers in the stove flared up and died. The coals glowed cherry-red a moment, then went black. The light was gone.

The door rattled in the frame. The little hut seemed to shake.

Then, suddenly, it all fell silent. The world seemed to hold its breath.

In the darkness, it seemed to me as if the shed walls had shrunk to the size of a coffin. I could hear Grendel breathing; I could almost hear his heartbeat; the sounds seemed louder in the lightlessness, as if Grendel were pressed up against me.

I only had a moment. I had to think of something to say.

I whispered, "Grendel, darling. Poor, handsome Grendel. You cut off your foot for me . . . because you wanted me . . . let me keep the memory of how much you wanted me . . ."

"Don't try to trick me, little bint," he growled back. I imagined I could almost feel his breath on my cheek.

"No trick. I am not in love with you and I never will be. I feel sorry for you, really. But . . . I am flattered. You almost had me, didn't you? I was tied up hand and foot, and gagged, and it was your hands that tied me up. I was hoisted on your shoulder with my hip pushed up against your cheek. We were alone. No one else saw it. No one else knew you had me, no one but you and me."

He didn't answer. His breathing sounded loud in the gloom.

I said, "Once I forget that day, the day you took me, who will know that it ever happened? Oh, yes, you will remember. But only you. How will you know that you didn't just imagine it?"

He spat, " 'Tis a trick. You want to make my desire weak."

I pushed myself away from the wall, took a step toward where I thought the cot was, and reached out with my hands.

I touched his cheek, and felt his razor stubble, and his shoulder, and the rough fabric of his patched nightshirt.

He jumped, startled, and grabbed my wrists with both his hands. His grip was tight, vicelike, and I could feel the leathery calluses of his hands dig into my flesh. His hands were so hard, so large, and so ill-smelling. I wondered how soft and small and fragrant my hands felt and smelled to him.

Oh well. Might as well go for broke. It was just words. Noises in a row. I could make myself say them.

"I want to forget it," I said in a low, soft voice. "I want to be able to look in your eyes tomorrow, and only see the stupid, low-class hired man I used to think you were. I don't want you to look in my eyes and see the submission, the desire to surrender, you put there . . ."

As well get hung for a ram as hung for an ewe. Time to pull out all the stops. I promised myself I would wash my mouth out with soap, later.

If I remembered.

I leaned closer and whispered teasingly:

". . . You told me you wanted me to be this way. A girl who likes it rough. A helpless little slave-girl in a collar. Your collar. But I'll have forgotten that all tomorrow. I'll have forgotten Grendel the Bear. You'll just be Glum, the groundskeeper. Dumb Glum. Not my master anymore. Not anything. You'll be calling me 'Miss' tomorrow, and I'll be looking down my nose at you . . ."

There was a polite knock at the door. Rap, tap.

Grendel let go of me. There was a rustle and a thump. A whimper. From the direction of the noise, it sounded as if Grendel was trying to hide under his cot.

A voice as cold as death said quietly. *"By that Final Justice, gone on Earth but known below; by Avernus and by Asphodel; by the eternal Law of the Abode of Woe; I charge thee and compel: Open, open, in the name of Hell."*

I had the very distinct and strange impression that no voice was actually speaking; that something like a cold energy was entering the room, and that it had an intention, dark, remorseless, severe, and pitiless. Something in the room was . . . changing . . . that cold force into words, into a little rhyme, to make it understood to me; but also to protect me from what would have happened to me if the naked radiations of that energy had gone, unfiltered, into my brain.

It was Telegonus. He was standing between me and the door, although I could not see him. The force from behind the door was passing through him. He was letting his body act like the leaded glass that blocks dangerous and invisible wavelengths of radiation.

The door creaked and opened. I could see the snow-patched grass, colorless beneath the starlight.

There came a blur, and a shadow darkened. I saw the silhouette of a cloaked figure in the doorframe. His elbows were up, and he was removing a plumed helmet from his head.

There was starlight on the snow behind him; I could see nothing of his armor or features.

He put the helmet in the crook of one elbow, and reached out into the room toward me with his fist.

Slowly, he rotated his fist so that it was palm upward. He opened his fingers.

There was a glimmering light there, as if he held a star in the palm of his hand. From the miniscule flake of light, I could see that that hand was covered with a black gauntlet.

Telegonus became opaque in front of me, and stumbled, and fell prone, like a puppet with its strings cut.

A three-headed dog now stepped out of the shadows of the black figure's cloak, growling and slavering.

With one head, it bit into the flesh of Telegonus, and began to drag the corpse backward, back into the shadows of the cloak.

The other two heads turned. One toward me, one toward the shivering cot.

A cold voice spoke. "Not these two, my pet. Very soon, my brute, but not yet. Grendel has a place prepared him in my domain, where he shall discover how weak and temporary is the pain his crimes inflict on others, when compared to perfect and eternal pain. As for the girl, it seems she comes to me in slices. This Phaethusa, on the morrow may be gone, and only Amelia, amputated in her memory, bewildered, will remain."

Once again, I had the intuition or impression that Telegonus was blocking the force radiating from this being, turning unseen thoughts into words. But now I could see the little light in the palm of the gauntlet flickering, as if in pain, as the cold force passed through it. It was Telegonus. That little light was him, the real him.

The gauntlet closed; the light was quenched.

At that moment, I woke in my cot, back in my cell.

4.

That morning, with no ceremony or ado, Dr. Fell and Mestor the Atlantian, Miss Daw and Nurse Twitchett, and Headmaster Boggin came down the corridor. Behind them, I could hear the stumping tap of Grendel's wooden leg.

Mestor was dressed in a dark suit and buff overcoat. He had bags under his eyes and did not look well.

I sat up in my cot with a rattle of chain. Miss Daw unlocked the bars and opened the door. She then turned and blocked the door. She said, "Headmaster, it is not proper for a girl to receive visitors clad only in her nightthings. Please take these men out of eyeshot while Sister Twitchett and I clothe Miss Windrose."

Boggin said jovially, "Ananias is a doctor; I am certain we can trust in his discretion. Dr. Fell, if you please? And as Miss Windrose may soon be asleep again in a few moments, there is no need to change her. Mestor and I will stay here, and check the environment for any other clues of the disturbance we had last night."

Mestor said, "The Wild Hunt was called by Bran; and the damned souls rode the storms, looking for one of their own."

Boggin touched him on the arm, and squinted, making the smallest possible shake of his head. "Let us not disturb our young guest here with news that does not concern her."

"Why not?" said Mestor. "The girl isn't going to remember anything in an hour anyway."

I clutched the starchy blanket in front of me. "What are you going to do to me?!" I shouted. "Why am I not going to remember anything in an hour?"

Boggin, ignoring me, said in a kind voice to Mestor, "Ah, my dear friend, not only have your frightened one of my girls here, you have evidently forgotten how much you owe me, and how much you still have to owe. I see that the full, ah, import, I am tempted to say, the full 'pressure' of the facts governing our new relationship together have not been made . . . ah . . . pellucid to you."

Saying that, without a single change of expression, he took Mestor's hand in both his hands. Before Mestor could blink or think to turn his hand away, Boggin put both his thumbs on the other man's pinky finger and flexed his hands, like a man snapping a wishbone to make a wish. There was a crack as Mestor's little finger broke. Mestor screamed and fell to his knees, astonished by the sudden pain and shock.

Miss Daw and Sister Twitchett turned away, shocked. Dr. Fell had not bothered to look up at the commotion.

I was the only one who saw Boggin bend down to Mestor, who was sobbing, clutching his hand to his belly.

I saw Boggin's lips move and I caught the smallest whisper of what he said in Mestor's ear. I was able to piece together what he was whispering.

"And I am not sure, dear friend, I have made it clear how upset, yes, I might even say, angry, your attempt to take our dear Miss Fair to your dreary, dank city of slaves made me. The thought of that young innocent with your fingers touching her . . . well, it was not a pleasant image to me."

Boggin straightened up. He cleared his throat and said in a normal voice, "Ananias . . . ? Could you see to this after you are done with Miss Windrose . . . ?"

Dr. Fell said, "Of course, Headmaster. The infirmary never runs short on business when you are around."

"What was that, Ananias . . . ?"

"Nothing, Headmaster."

I had jumped out of the cot at this time, and had backed up in the cell as far as the chain would allow. Dr. Fell and Sister Twitchett rather matter-of-factly closed in on either side of me, and grabbed my arms. The Sister was strong, but I could feel her grip getting unsteady as I tugged against her; Dr. Fell's hands were like the vice grip of a machine.

I screamed.

"Less noise, please," said Dr. Fell.

I screamed to Miss Daw, "Don't let them do this to me, Miss Daw! Please!"

She said in a voice emotionless and remote: "The choice is not mine to make, child." She turned and handed a small key to Grendel, who was limping in short half-hops past where she stood. He had not been maimed long enough to learn how to walk one-legged with any grace.

She said to him, "You will have to unlock her, Grendel. None of us can work the lock."

He scowled at the key and snatched it gracelessly from her hand.

I tossed my body with all my strength back and forth in the grip of Twitchett and Fell. Twitchett snorted when my flying hair slapped her in the face. I screamed and panted and arched my back and kicked with my legs.

I saw Grendel, staring at my writhing, struggling body in fascination. His expression slipped for a moment. Instead of the normal lust he might have felt seeing a helpless and nubile girl writhing around in a torn nightshirt, something like pity flickered in his eyes. He didn't like seeing me hurt. Maybe, in his perverted mind, he wanted me to be afraid, but he only wanted me to be afraid of *him.* He didn't like seeing other people make me scream. He didn't like seeing me imprisoned, not just then.

Reality slipped a bit, too. One of my higher senses flickered on, like a bruised eye prying its lids open for a moment.

I could see Dr. Fell. He looked . . . more flat . . . than the other people in the room. As if he were just made of matter, a random clockwork made of atoms, nothing else. I saw the drugs and potions he was carrying in a little case clipped to his belt. Atomic structures glistened in rows and long chains, suspended in the fluid of several hypodermics.

Time to do something. I was not sure what. Something.

I saw time-images overlapping the light-picture. In these images, one of the needles was destined go into my arm; one of the drugs was going to affect my nervous system.

I bent that world-line into a knot. The controlling monad for that group of chemicals was inert, and the final causes of the atoms were deterministic, controlled entirely by Newtonian cause-and-effect. The monad tilted in the fourth dimension and came awake, bringing its meaning-axis to bear. Quantum uncertainty increased in the atomic mixture. No different than what I had done to restore Quentin's memory to him. New branches and stalks erupted on the monad's tree of possible futures. It was no longer determined and inert.

It was done. The chemical in the hypo now had free will.

I found an energy wave passing between me and the controlling monad for that atom group. I impressed a communication force into the wave, and it passed on to the monad. I asked it not to hurt me.

The echo was an emotional wave, not words. But it was a feeling of puppyish friendliness, a sort of, "OK! Whatever you say!" enthusiasm.

Miss Daw saw it. She opened her mouth to speak.

I bent a world-line between me and Boggin, as if I were about to imprint a communication-wave running to him. Miss Daw saw the strands of moral order snarl around the both of us. If she betrayed my secret, I would tell Boggin that she had told me about Myriagon. Maybe Boggin would not care. Maybe he would.

Miss Daw glanced over at where Mestor lay on the floor. She closed her lips again, and assumed the mask she always wore; all prim and proper, distant and remote.

Headmaster Boggin said, "I just felt something bend destiny." He stepped over to the disc player which was on the shelf. He measured the distance between it and my cot, frowning.

He tried to get it open, but I had jammed it shut.

Dr. Fell was no more thrown off balance or moved by my violent struggles than a statue might have been. He said in a bored voice, "Permit me, Headmaster."

I did not see whatever magnetic force Fell reached across the cell with, but the disc player went *sprong,* and the little door snapped open.

Boggin said, "It seems the little dangerous one got the disc out somehow."

I didn't say anything. I didn't even change expression. All I did was pause in my struggles a little, and look at Sister Twitchett in surprise.

Boggin, Fell, and Miss Daw noticed it. They all turned and looked at her, too.

Sister Twitchett said in fear, "I had it on last night! I swear I hit that little switch!"

Boggin said smoothly, "We will discuss the matter of your dereliction . . . ah, of your gross dereliction, once we are done here. With the example of Mestor so, shall I say, evident? Yes, evident, before the eyes of everyone, nothing . . . overt . . . needs to be done to you. You and I will come to some understanding, I am sure. Meanwhile, check your purse and your locker to see where you left Miss Daw's delightful little digital recording of her music.

"Also, you and Doctor Fell will have to examine the girl quite closely to see that she did not write herself some note, or scratch any signs or marks into her flesh with her fingernails, or swallow anything which might . . . ah . . . come out later, and give her some clue as to what she is about to forget. The more thorough you are at that little bit of cleanup, the more lenient I will be when discussing this . . . unfortunate . . . oversight of yours. The music was not playing last night, and her powers are already beginning to stir. Grendel, if you will do the honors . . . ?"

Grendel hopped over to me, propped his crutch under his armpit, and took my head between his hands. His palms were rough on my cheeks.

My higher senses went dead. I was just the powerless girl he wanted me to be.

His eyes stared into mine. My vision started to fade around the edges, as if a tunnel of smoke were forming, with Grendel's eyes, Grendel's hungry, angry eyes, at the axis of the tunnel. My head felt light, like a balloon about to float away . . .

I licked my dry lips. "Master . . . ," I whispered. Or maybe I only formed the words with my lips.

The tunnel wobbled. His eyes lost strength. I could see the willpower leaking out of his gaze, the certainty evaporating.

In his paradigm, he could have anything he desired. If he desired it truly, and with all his heart. If he desired it, deep down, right to the core of his being, without any hesitation or doubt.

Such an easy paradigm to work with. But it had a flaw. Wanting to desire something is not the same as desiring it to the core of your being. You can't really order yourself to be obsessed with something.

That was my theory, at least. That was my hope.

And my theory, and my hope, seemed pretty flimsy when Grendel just smirked and squinted, and the darkness from the edges of my vision filled my eyes. This time, my head was a balloon with its string cut, and my thoughts and memories, just like that, just as quick as that, went up and away and were scattered.

Dimly, as from a great distance, I felt Grendel lower me gently (ever so gently!) to the floor stones. I wondered how he managed that with just one leg. Maybe it was something he really, really desired to do.

His voice: "I've made her body be just made of atoms, like you wanted, Doctor."

I felt a dab of cold cotton on my arm, and then a needle slid in. "She'll wake in the infirmary, and we'll tell her what we told the others; that she was gravely ill with pneumonia."

I kept thinking: *We failed: It is over, all over, ended, all ended.* Our little children's crusade, our rebellion against the gods and monsters pretending to be our elders, had failed. Once my memory was wiped out all five of us would be back where we had been at the beginning: merely dumb children again, weak, powerless, unaware of our heritage, our strange abilities. *Gone, all gone, all of it is gone.*

There was nothing to hold on to, no way to keep my thoughts my own. Have you ever woken up suddenly, eager to remember some perfect dream lingering in your thoughts, only to have it vanish, like fog, at daybreak? So it was for me. The prison doors were shut again: I was lost to myself.

But, deep in my veins, I felt a happy, puppyish sense of warmth. It stayed in one spot, and did not spread throughout my circulatory system.

Then it was night.

End of Part One
To Be Continued in Part Two

FUGITIVES *of*